I0670283

The Day:

THE EARTH SHAKES

GRACE FINLEY

Copyright © 2023 by Finley Books
All rights reserved. This book or any portion thereof
may not be reproduced or used in any manner whatsoever
without the express written permission of the publisher
except for the use of brief quotations in a book review.

Printed in the United States of America
ISBN (Kindle) 978-1-953781-15-4
ISBN (Paperback) 978-1-953781-16-1
ISBN (Hardcover) 978-1-953781-17-8

Finley Books | Phoenix, AZ
www.FinleyBooks.com

This is a work of fiction. Names, characters, businesses, events and incidents are the products of the author's imagination. Any resemblance to actual persons, living or dead, or actual events is purely coincidental.

FINLEY BOOKS

PHOENIX, ARIZONA

"The light shines in the darkness,
and **the darkness**
has not overcome it."
–JOHN 1:5

1
red line

"You look like you're in a good mood."

Samuel Gowon tightened his narrow lips into a curt smile as he passed the Press Secretary. She had just opened her crimson mouth to speak, to ask him for clarification on the questions she'd been peppered with at the press conferences over the past few days no doubt, but he shifted his eyes and turned into the Situation Room, leaving her standing there, lips pursed, eyes wide, like a dim-witted goldfish.

Everyone seated inside immediately fell silent. Except for Kit-bloody-McGregor, his Chief of Staff.

"Sir, we need to tell the press *something*," Kit complained, running his palm over his perspiring forehead. Kit was a former Olympic speed skater and had certainly remained physically fit, but he was infamous for sweating excessively when he was hyped up about something. He raked his fingers through his brown spiral curls. "We can't send Babbles Monroe out there again. I think everyone in this room had agreed she was a token choice in the first place. She was mediocre, at best, when she was fielding questions she knew ahead of time. Now that the press is giving her unscripted questions–"

"Her name is Babs."

"Excuse me?"

"Babbles is what the bigoted, racist low-lifes who hate our country call her because they can't stand the idea of an educated, successful, strong-minded racially and gender diverse woman stepping up to the podium and demanding respect."

Samuel felt bile collect in the back of his throat. Even after decades of the gender ideology and identity politics nonsense, he still found it difficult to stomach, however, it was still the easiest way to gain control over a conference room, a press conference, a debate stage. Everyone had a weakness, usually rooted in their various belief systems that compelled them to have an aversion to being thought of as being an asshole. Many misinterpreted the scripture and compromised their own belief systems, going out of their way to bend the knee to those who didn't give in nearly so easily.

The Cabinet members seated around the conference table exchanged looks. Kit McGregor had lost some color pigmentation in his face, knowing there would be only one reason Samuel would have the appearance of defending a moron like the infamous Babbles Monroe, who earned her nickname for her tendency to stumble with answers and give long, run-on sentence responses that made very little sense. One example was when she was asked about a treaty being discussed within the United Nations. The short answer was: "The President is in discussion with our country's closest allies, but as always, is only going to commit to agreements that strengthen our great nation." The key to give a non-answer answer to a question like this was to feign patriotism enough without using phrases that would draw a comparison to nationalist ideals.

Instead of providing this brief response and moving on, Babs had gone on about the history of the United Nations (using incorrect information), referred to Naples as a country, and swapped the word "treachery" for "treaty" twice.

"Her name is Barbara Lintz-Monroe. 28. Single, but beloved by her friends and colleagues. *Babs* has been a dedicated member of the People's House staff since she served as an intern during the previous Administration."

She just started last year.

No one refuted his statement, correctly assuming her employment file was being modified and social media posts were being retroactively posted that supported the claim.

"She was an intern in the previous Administration. She came from humble beginnings."

Her father runs an international pharmaceutical company.

"Do any of you know who receives the highest number of credible death threats after me?"

"Ms. Monroe?"

"Lintz-Monroe," he corrected. "And no. That would be my wife. Not very well-liked, my wife." He lifted his eyes to meet Annette's gaze, the corner of his mouth pinching upward briefly. "Lucky for her, I care little about public opinion polls, or what a neanderthal with a gun or a bomb has to say about my wife and what he would do to her given the opportunity."

Annette's close-lipped smile didn't falter, but there was a flicker of her eye.

"The Bureau has uncovered communication from a man named Declan Jefferson Wallace, a 30-year-old man who Ms. Lintz-Monroe dated briefly last year. In these communications, he declared his unrequited affections for Ms. Lintz-Monroe, but in such a way the Bureau finds threatening. Additionally, on a number of occasions, as documented by security footage, he's sent obscene messages to her phone, he's followed her to work, he's waited outside her apartment. When I saw Ms. Lintz-Monroe outside these doors moments ago, she appeared *unsettled*, like she sensed that Declan Jefferson Wallace might be planning to do something drastic." He lifted his brow, unable to prevent the corner of his mouth from curling upward, amused by how irrefutable the evidence would be. He imagined that peacock newscaster Garrison Chase discussing the grotesque details of the death of Babbles Monroe, eulogizing her briefly but dramatically before moving along to read through the talking points calling for increased psychological screenings as a prerequisite for employment and health benefits.

"It's reasonable to think that Ms. Lintz-Monroe has been distracted, *unnerved* after finding out that Declan Jefferson Wallace supports the neo-Nazi terrorists who would see our country burn to the ground over socially responsible and respectful policy changes that seek equity, inclusion, and justice for all Americans, that he considers himself a *vigilante* for the elitist nationalists. It's reasonable to think that knowing this has kept Ms. Lintz-Monroe from being as *effective* as she could be in her role. It's reasonable to think that she's been getting her facts crossed, that her unrefined, bungling, and downright *derisible* responses have been the result of personal struggles, possibly even untreated psychosocial conditions. It would be unprofessional and improper to speculate, and/or to flog her publicly for these mistakes when if we're honest with ourselves, we could do no better in her situation."

The cabinet members were doing very little to hide their shock, staring stupidly at him. Like this was the first time they'd disposed of a liability.

For Kit's benefit and his own amusement, Samuel added: "The theatrics are a bit much, I'll admit. I much prefer to keep things clean, in the most literal sense. It's heinous. But that is the nature of our enemy. May everyone in this room avoid a fate such as this."

*   *   *

Sometime later, after covering the other agenda items of discussion, Samuel Gowon took a sip of his coffee, beady dark eyes panning over the cabinet members making their way to the exit.

"Sir, what is our current plan of action for the Arks?" Kit asked with a sigh.

Samuel inclined his chin. "Who called them that?"

"I'm sorry?"

"Who called them that? 'The Arks'? Who came up with that name?"

"They did."

"They did," he repeated calmly, pursing his lips as though hearing it for the first time. "Is it an acronym?"

"No. Not to my knowledge."

"It's clever," he said, compressing his lips.

"Sir?"

"In business, you learn quickly that branding can make or break a product. 'The Arks' sets a tone, it's recognizable, it brings to mind powerful imagery, it's tied to a primary values system. Granted the primary values system is a fairy tale." He lifted his eyebrows. "Tell me, Kit, if my enemy calls himself King, do I bend to call him that as well?"

"King? No. Of course not."

"Then do not make the mistake of uttering the phrase 'The Arks' again. In or out of my presence."

"Yes, Sir." He cleared his throat, hesitating to continue. "With all due respect, we are rapidly approaching the deadline to meet their demands. I anticipated that it would have been an agenda item today."

Samuel allowed silence to fill the room long enough that Kit started to visibly recoil.

"Whose demands?" he finally said with precision.

Kit frowned. "The–*terrorists*?"

Samuel wavered his hand. "It's been over-used."

"Rebels?"

"People like rebels."

"Radicals."

"Overused. It can be used sparingly as an adjective."

"'Insurgents: Subverting government or authority'," Kit read from his phone screen.

Samuel shrugged.

"We should call them 'Insurgents'?"

"Yes."

"Is that the message we want to be sending? Citizens cling to the rebellious spirit of the country's founders. They'll cite the Declaration of Independence, the Bill of Rights, Amendments..."

"I will have no gray area, no question if this behavior, if these acts will be tolerated."

"I'm sorry, Sir. I was under the impression that discussions had started with the leaders of The Ar—the Insurgents—about reconciliation."

The corners of Samuel Gowon's thin mouth stretched. For anyone else, this might signify emotions associated with a smile–happiness or even vague amusement. For some, it could be construed as passive aggression. It would be a mistake to assume either of these things about Samuel Gowon. It was something a person only did once. Kit McGregor straightened himself, tightened his jaw.

"You are correctly informed that we have had communication with the Insurgency leaders. They are very enthusiastic about a diplomatic resolution to their—*predicament*."

"Sir, they have control over key resources, military, nuclear weapons, water sources, power. If they decide to act—"

Annette lifted her eyes to the map Samuel had abruptly pulled up on the large-scale monitor, taking a deep breath.

Kit took notice, regretful he had once again spoken out of turn, and yet he continued: "Our dependence on electric vehicles, vehicles with computer-based engines and components means that they can throw a switch at any moment and shut us down, throw the entire infrastructure, the entire population currently reliant on these vehicles, transportation, spiraled into chaos. We would have anarchy, riots. We would be sitting ducks for countries who would seek to invade our borders."

Samuel Gowon had gone silent, his face neutral.

Still Kit just couldn't shut his mouth.

"We have confirmation of Russian, Chinese advancement toward our shorelines, we've had spy aircraft in our airspace. It seems rational to think they are fully aware of the situation with the Insurgents and are looking to capitalize."

Gowon cleared his throat, picked his phone out of his pocket, scrolling with casual precision.

"What I'm saying is that as much as we don't want to admit it, the Insurgents have the upper hand. They've been able to secure control over these resources and maintain control utilizing security and technology that far surpasses our own. We can't fool ourselves into thinking we have the upper hand. These aren't unreasonable people." Kit's eyes floated over to Annette, who briefly made eye contact with him.

"You know, Kit. It's really inspiring to hear the conviction in your voice."

Annette turned her chin back to the map of the Arks just before Kit McGregor suddenly grasped at his chest, his eyes blistering with blood vessels.

"What do you think?" Gowon asked, turning to Annette. "Do you agree with our soon-departed colleague?"

Annette blinked slowly, taking a steadying breath. "I do think the– we're calling them Insurgents?"

"If you approve, my dear." Even his terms of endearment felt like a threat. She could practically feel the blade of a dagger against her throat, waiting for her to say the wrong thing.

"The Insurgents have a tactical advantage. They have clear paths to victory, while we face threats on other fronts, which make us vulnerable."

He nodded.

"But they're foolish. They're floundering. They don't have the killer instinct to strike while the iron is hot. Their faith makes them meek." She pursed her lips. "Allowing reconciliation after something like this sends the wrong message," she murmured steadily.

"Agreed."

Her gaze panned over to him.

"This was too close," he said, nodding toward the Ark boundaries, the color-coding of vital resources indicating they were currently controlled by the Arks. "The orchestration that this required happened right under our noses."

"We may not be able to identify everyone, but we have teams working on it."

"We'll find them eventually. Many are within the Ark boundaries, but clearly some are not." He pulled up the grid of photos of the Ark Councilmembers:

- Senator Mark Geoffreys of Texas
- Congresswoman Sadie Parker of Montana
- Governor of Texas Kyle McNeary
- Justice Declan Grainger
- State Representative Jonas Miller of Ohio
- Congressman Abraham Brink of Nebraska
- Senator Sylvia Shaw of Florida
- Congressman Chip Elwes of Arizona
- Congresswoman Gayle Mays of Alabama
- Pastor Nicholas Summers
- Doctor Theodore Crane

"There are those on this list who could be bought with the promise of power or money for themselves. Or vague threats against their loved ones. Others, less," Gowon reflected, taking in their faces. "Much less. It's amazing they've gotten this far if these are their leaders."

Annette agreed. "There's not a leader among them. The names I know are all show boaters."

Gowon peered over the edge of the conference table to where Kit still writhed on the floor, a trickle of blood emerging from the man's nostril, a thick foam appearing in his mouth. Gowon released a bored sigh. "Disloyalty irritates me, the inelegance of it, the desperation. Same for a lack of conviction. Stand for *something*."

"Do you see them following through on any threats they've issued?"

He chuckled. "No."

She nodded.

"I think of it like a child getting ahold of a parent's handgun. They've already turned the gun on themselves. We just have to wait for them to pull the trigger."

2

great and small

Bree quickened his pace over the rocky terrain. Esther squeezed her legs around the large gray Percheron's back and leaned forward, hoping to ease his load on the challenging incline. Though Percherons were known for brute strength, typically used as work or draft horses, they lacked the nimbleness of smaller breeds typically used for pleasure riding. Essie clicked her tongue encouragingly, running her hand over the coarse coat of the horse's neck, a clump of winter coat fuzz fluttering into the breeze from beneath her palm.

"I just brushed you last night, Narnian. You know, you're kind of becoming high maintenance," she teased, noticing the loose horse hair coating her pant legs. She patted his shoulder and the horse tossed his head up, causing a fluttering of his mane. "Yeah, you're handsome. I've never met a horse quite so handsome."

Bree snorted back with the affectionate breathiness he reserved only for her.

They were just reaching the Glacier overlook, Esther's favorite place in the Northern Ark. While the trek required some laboring over squared rocks, the rest of the ride was tame and leisurely, requiring only a moderate change in elevation. The area contained vast grasslands that faded away in winter, but filled in with brilliant, lush evergreen shades beginning in the spring, framed by layers of mountain range and dense forests. The centerpiece of the view was a vivid blue lake wrapping the base of a pyramid shaped mountain that bordered the Glacier National Forest. When the weather and sunlight were just right, she could see all the way to the bottom of the lake.

Bree stopped at the top ridge, awaiting further direction from his rider. In the meantime, he stretched his neck low to the ground and chomped down on an indulgent patch of grass.

Esther loosened the reins from her fingers and took in a deep breath of crisp, morning air. The sun was just rising to her right. During mid-day, the lake tended to mirror the sky, but in the early hours of the day, it was shadowed by the nearby mountains and had a mystical, foreboding presence. The dusting of snow that still remained a week prior was now melted, making way for warmer weather.

She rotated her hip and swung down out of the saddle. Her landing was complicated by the uneven ground and the fact that, no matter how many times she'd done it, the saddle on Bree's back was always a lot higher than she expected.

Bree nudged her backside, encouraging her to hold onto him to catch her balance.

"Yeah, I know you would have bowed for me, but you were busy."

The horse nibbled at her jeans.

"Stop that," she scolded with a chuckle. "I'm fine." She undid the saddle belts, slid the saddle and pad from his back, and balanced it on a nearby tree log. "There you go. Does that feel better?"

Bree shook off like a dog, fuzzy winter coat bursting into the air. He rotated two steps to his left to chew on another thicket of grass.

Essie removed a small paperback book from the saddle's satchel, stepped toward the sloped grasslands that led down to the lake, folded her legs, and sat. She took a deep breath and closed her eyes, silently said her morning prayers.

She typically began with thanking God for her many blessings, focusing on what stood out to her the most, asking for guidance, for strength. She then moved on to ask for blessings for her loved ones.

When she opened her eyes, Bree was circling the ground behind her. "That's it for your snack? Are you watching your figure for your girlfriend, buddy?"

The horse lowered his large body to the grass with a snort and rested his muzzle on Essie's knee. She stroked his forehead delicately, smiling as Bree closed his eyes, his breaths turning to indulgent grunts of enjoyment.

An hour later, Bree was huffing his way back to the ranch, needing no navigational assistance. Essie stretched her back, sitting more upright in the saddle and gazing toward the wildlife sanctuary on the other side of the valley. She could see the long necks of a tower of giraffes making their way to the feeding structures, a herd of elephants playing in a stream. The roars of two competing male lions, housed in separate enclosures, had been a particularly surreal noise to get used to in the early morning hours.

Despite a brilliant, warm sun on her left, an ominous sky lurked to the south of the ranch. She'd need to get the animals into the barn soon. Hopefully, if the weather cleared, she'd let them slosh around in the mud later.

When they first moved to the Northern Ark, she had opted to take a housing assignment in a condominium complex near the center of town. There had been a couple reasons for this, the primary reason being that if she stayed with her dad at the ranch, he would have known what work she was doing with Luther to create the antidotes. He would have been witness to her recovery. Since the discontinuation of these sessions, there was no longer a reason she needed to continue to live in the housing complex; it was far too confining for her tastes. There was much more breathing room at the ranch and the environment suited her, as did the proximity to her dad. The West's property was also "a stone's throw away," even though only Sara and Luke were occupying the house. From where they traveled along the trail leading back to the ranch, she could see their property to her right, a sea of cornfields spanning out from the house on three sides. The front yard was filled with apple trees, along with the entire stretch of road between the West's property and the ranch, a particularly beautiful sight when they blossomed.

While she wasn't entirely clear on his role in the Arks, she was fairly certain Luther had a hand in securing the idyllic living arrangements. It was her assessment that this had been the very least of his capabilities within the Ark. Based upon what she had observed, Luther had held a diplomatic role at some point, a role that included closed-door meetings with high-ranking leaders in different branches and sectors of the U.S. Government. His relationships spanned to foreign governments, as well, based upon meetings he'd taken during her recoveries in his cabin's den. It wasn't uncommon for her to drift in and out of consciousness hearing him speaking in a different language each time. She'd heard him speaking at least eight languages, including Spanish, Greek, Japanese, Portuguese, Hebrew, Italian and Farsi.

It was surreal to think of his significance within the Ark behind the scenes in stark contrast to seeing him push through the screen door to the ranch sheepishly carrying his contribution to a potluck meal, receiving only casual acknowledgement.

Luther's level of prominence in the Ark had most certainly shifted, however. She just wasn't sure why or how. For one thing, a structure had been established that included a council, which made all decisions regarding the Arks, and he wasn't a part of it.

Essie enjoyed sharing a roof with her dad again, and she frequently took advantage of being so close to the West house to drop in to visit, but it made her reminiscent of childhood, wishing they'd had this close proximity when she, Josh, and Gabe were kids.

Gabe was living in a vintage-looking motel that had been converted into apartment units. The interiors were actually quite nice and modern. Gunner lived in the same complex so that had naturally supported the two of them becoming friends.

Miles was incredibly jealous of their living accommodations, particularly the central pool area, which featured lawn games and fire pits, and frequent "block parties" with the complex's decidedly youthful occupants. The Ark certainly didn't seem to be the social hub Miles had been hoping for.

Josh's living situation was far more rustic, but had better views. He had moved into one of the cabins at a former Scouts camp a few miles northeast of the ranch. It was a single-room A-frame structure, but due to a grouping of pine trees that the developer hadn't been keen to tear down, the cabin had been constructed with some separation from the main group of cabins and had direct creek access.

Miles had eagerly accepted Essie's apartment assignment when she offered it soon after making it back to the Ark, having already decided she'd be moving to the ranch. A few days later, the motel renovation was complete and Gabe and Gunner received their assignments. Neither had been interested in trading with Miles and the complex was quickly at capacity.

Miles liked to complain about the apartment complex being dull, something she had a difficult time arguing with. She had previously referred to it as a socialist "utopia," as to her, the buildings were sprawling, fairly nondescript, the interiors functional and basic. After seeing the Government Housing Complex where Gabe had been living in Denver, which had been converted from a parking garage structure and despite having extra aesthetic enhancements, having been the first of its kind, lacked any sort of figurative or literal warmth, her opinion of the apartment complex had improved slightly, but not much. This had initially been a reason she invited him out to the ranch so frequently, because she knew what it felt like to be alone in that apartment, in that building, confined from nature or anything life-affirming.

The first few times he had come out to the ranch, he had looked painfully uncomfortable and out of place, eating stiffly, saying very little, keeping a pressure-sealed lid on his usual antics. It wasn't until she issued him another invitation, which he'd immediately accepted, that she questioned him about his behavior. Miles had smiled and for the first time in the years she'd known him, gave a sincere, straightforward answer. First, he told her how much he loved seeing the way she and her dad interacted, the extra boisterousness of when Sara and Luke came over to participate in game nights. Then he added: "But your dad's a pastor, Essie. If I'm myself, he's going to fast-track me to hell."

She had chuckled a bit, resting her arms across the open driver side window, since he had been getting ready to leave. "Well, *first* of all, fast tracking a person to hell is not a special power awarded to pastors."

"I just figure he has God's ear more than most people."

"No more than anyone else."

Miles lifted his eyes. "So, you're saying *I* could talk to God?"

"Of course you can."

He nodded. "How?"

"Just like you would anyone else. Well, *actually–*"

"Edit?"

She frowned. "No. You know what? Be yourself."

"I don't know about that. Have you met me?"

"God already knows who you are."

"So I'm doomed."

She lifted her eyebrows. "I'm not sure who you think you're fooling with the front you put up. I know you're fooling *some* people, but you're not fooling me and you certainly aren't fooling God."

He twisted his expression.

"The key part of talking to God, of praying, is to listen."

"Therein lies the rub."

She smiled.

"Maybe you can teach me? Or like, show me?"

There was a tickle on the back of her neck. "If you'd like me to, I'd be happy to show you how *I* pray, but it's different for everyone."

"It'll give me a starting point though."

Ever since, several days a week, Miles found his way to the ranch with and without an invitation. He'd simply settle into whatever the current activity happened to be. If she was brushing horses, he'd pick up a brush and join in, if she was mucking stalls, he'd pick up a rake, if she was lungeing one of the horses, he'd stand along the fence line and watch. She

15

didn't bring up his request, waiting for him to approach her with it again. When he finally did, he was exasperated that she wouldn't have brought it up herself.

"What did you ask me to do?"

"Show me how you pray."

She smiled. "And I have. Every time you've come over here."

Hwin whinnied, excitedly paced the paddock fence as she saw Bree approach from the overlook. Spotting Matteo emerging from the barn, the Belgian horse pranced toward him, then swung her head pointedly toward the mountains, blonde mane sweeping about elegantly.

"Yes, I see, Hwin," Matteo remarked, hanging up some tack lines on the inside barn wall. He ran his fingers through his wavy dark hair, which was speckled with more gray each time he saw his reflection in the mirror, and smiled at his daughter, who had lost the last bit of youthful roundness in her jawline and was looking undeniably her age. "How was the ride?"

"Lovely, as always."

Bree paused at the normal place in the fence, allowing Essie to slide off. He waited for her to undo the buckles, then stretched out his left leg so the saddle slid off easier.

"Does he shake hooves, too?"

Essie smiled, managing the saddle one-handed so she could give him an appreciative pat on the side. "So I finally finished *Wuthering Heights*," she said, lugging the saddle toward the barn.

"How was it?"

"Well-written but incredibly, *incredibly* depressing."

"It's a love story, isn't it?" Matteo asked, taking the blanket pad from her, folding it and placing it on the shelves just inside the barn. He turned and chuckled when he saw Bree shuffling along at Essie's side.

"Yeah, it's a love story, but not a healthy one. They're both crazy, codependent hotheads. Was this *really* required reading in schools at one point?"

Matteo picked up his coffee mug from the shelf, took a sip. "I believe so."

"Not exactly encouraging healthy relationships in the former education system, huh?"

"I'm not sure they were encouraging healthy anything in the former education system."

"There's not one virtuous character, which I guess is realistic, we're all capable of good and evil, *but–*" Essie removed Bree's bridle, pointing toward his stall. "You go tuck in, Narnian. I'll get Hwin. She'll want to snuggle during the storm." She patted his side and turned to the paddock fence where Hwin danced in place. "Speaking of codependent characters," she teased, opening the gate. The horse rushed after Bree, who snorted back at her. "Go on inside. I'll get some snacks for you."

Her dad was already on his way to the stall with a bucket of oats. "So, *not* your favorite read."

"Nope, definitely not my favorite read. I think I need a comedy after that. Holy moly. Hey, did *you* bring everybody else in already?"

"I did. I wasn't sure how soon the storm would get here. The mustang momma might be going into labor, too. I called Josh over to see if he could have a look at her."

Essie moved quickly to the first stall on the right where the white Mustang stood rigidly in the front corner, scraping her hoof against the ground. "Lilliandil, is that baby coming today? Oh, sweet girl, you're looking *really* uncomfortable–can I—" She let out a yelp.

"*What happened?*"

Essie jumped back from the stall, shaking out her hand. "She *bit* me."

Josh stepped into the entrance of the barn, carrying a canvas rucksack over his shoulder, shaking off the light mist that had coated his overgrown hair. He furrowed his brow, smiling lightly. "My dad will tell you–when it comes to pregnant beasts, keep the status quo."

Essie narrowed her eyes as he moved toward her. "You realize you just referred to your mom as a 'pregnant *beast.*'"

He grinned. "Let me see your hand."

She presented her palm.

"Right here?" he asked, delicately running his finger over the fleshy lower portion of her thumb.

She nodded, frowning.

"*Oh*, yeah that's already swelled up. Can you move your thumb at all?"

She tried. "It feels tight."

Josh winced. "Well, it doesn't *seem* broken, but it's probably going to continue to swell and bruise." He swung his bag around to the side and retrieved an individually packaged antiseptic wipe from an outer pocket then dropped the bag to the ground. He braced her hand in his and gently but firmly wiped her thumb, examining the skin closely around the imprint of teeth. "It doesn't look like she broke the skin."

"I'll be fine," she sighed.

"I know you will," he said softly, lifting her hand and gently kissing her thumb. The stubble on his chin tickled her skin. "Just keep an eye on it anyway."

Her cheeks tightened as she blinked slowly up at him. "Good morning."

"Good morning," he echoed, raising an eyebrow. His pin straight dark hair was a unique trait in his family that had developed in the time since Mandatory. Its overgrown state that curtained over his ears made his hair look even darker, and made him appear older than his 22 years, particularly with the usual accompaniment of facial stubble.

Essie tousled his hair with her opposite hand. "You need a haircut, Josh West."

He shook the hair out of his eyes. "Are you offering?"

She wrinkled her forehead, fidgeting with the cross pendant on her necklace. "Not sure you'd want *me* to cut it. I have zero qualifications." Realization caused her to stomp her foot. "Don't you dare buzz that hair again."

He grinned. "I don't have the right head shape for it, do I? Too pointy? I feel like it's flat on the left side."

"Your head shape isn't the problem I have with a buzzcut." Her chest tightened. She was surprised she actually said it out loud. He was joking with her; she knew she shouldn't take it too seriously, but she couldn't help it. She had shaved his head for Mandatory twice. Both times, she felt like she was being complacent, abiding by "mandates" set by government overlords who had no intent to have enlistees return home safely. It had been worse the second time he left for Mandatory. After the attack on the Children's Ministry when she'd learned about the first three years of her life being spent in a government research lab, helping Josh comply with Mandatory requirements was even more debilitating. It tormented her that the government had dictated her life as a child, and now, they still had the ability to steal away those she loved. They could still destroy her world. She remembered holding the hair trimmer to his head, trying to will her hand to stop shaking, terrified she'd never see him again.

She didn't appreciate having the memory return to the forefront of her mind, joking or not, but to tell him even the thought of a specific haircut caused her severe, debilitating anxiety sounded insane.

Or rather, *feeling* severe, debilitating anxiety at the memory of a feeling because the person the feeling was about means so much to her, while still not feeling ready to be with him or at least tell him how she feels...sounded insane. And also? Didn't make a whole lot of sense.

She considered her most recent read, which featured a narcissistic, depressed, bipolar, otherwise unstable woman who mistreated the love of her life. She didn't like the parallels her mind was drawing, whether they were built upon sound reasoning or not.

"I won't buzz it again," he conceded quietly, placing his hand over hers. He smiled lightly when her shoulders eased.

"Thanks for coming over," Matteo said, offering Josh a coffee cup, suddenly just behind her. He smirked when Essie appeared startled by his presence, by the fact he'd witnessed their interaction. She reset herself.

Josh accepted the cup with a gracious dip or his chin and stepped toward the mare's stall. "So she's restless–and sweaty, I see–and clearly irritable."

"Well, she bit the horse whisperer so I'd say so," Matteo said with a wink to his daughter.

"I'm only *Bree's* favorite. The rest probably tolerate me at best."

It was then that Fenway came sprinting into the barn.

Essie stepped around the men, clearing a path. "Were you sniffing *outside*? So many smells! Say, what are all those smells?" Essie said in a higher octave as the German Shepherd barreled into her shins whimpering and insistently nudging her head under Essie's palms.

The Mustang whinnied sharply.

"Oh, let's keep Fenway away from–Ess, what on earth did you name this horse? *Lilliandil*?"

"Yes," Essie said, "though she is *not* living up to her namesake's gentle nature." She patted her legs, encouraging Fenway to follow her back out of the barn. There she crouched and gave the Shepherd an enthusiastic and indulgent scratch around her head using both hands, squinting up at the clouds that were starting to spit rain. In the back of her ears, Essie could hear her dad's explanation of Lil's progression. When she looked up, Josh was standing on the second bar of the stall gate taking a closer look, while keeping a respectful distance from the horse, who must have laid back down, given the way he was having to contort his neck.

"Something like 80 percent of foals are born in the middle of the night so if she can help it, I'll bet she'll keep that baby in until we give her some privacy."

"Is that right? I guess I never realized that."

"Yeah, she's in early-stage labor so she's obviously uncomfortable, but this could go on for at least a few hours."

"I just wanted to be sure we were doing what we're supposed to be doing."

"Just let her do her thing. She knows what to do."

Matteo nodded. "That's reassuring."

"I'm not on-call for the clinic so I can stick around today, just in case any issues come up."

"Josh West," Essie called out in a deep announcer voice. "*DVM.*"

"Not quite," he said, though his cheeks tightened.

It was only once they got back to the Ark that Essie learned Josh had been able to earn concurrent associate degrees before leaving for Mandatory. She'd known he was working on the coursework and he'd mentioned something about it from time to time, but it just wasn't something he went on about. Josh wasn't the type of person to talk about the work to be done; he just did it.

Having been homeschooled all his life, his schedule had been fairly flexible. Early mornings were spent tending to the animals. During the late morning and early afternoon, he'd have homeschool classes mainly centered on math and sciences with lunch somewhere in there, then he'd head off to town to spend a few hours at the library, headphones clamped over his ears, attending virtual and online-based courses that had evidently earned him concurrent biology and veterinary science degrees before he'd left for Mandatory.

During the eighteen months or so that he'd served with MET, he'd acquired substantial veterinary experience, both on missions and when he had "respite." He'd spent the five months since they'd been full-time at the Ark gaining as much experience as possible. His supervising veterinarian had been encouraging him to take the qualifying exam to grant him credentials, which the vet shrugged off as merely a formality.

Like most institutions in the country, veterinary colleges were a bit less structured, less formalized. There weren't ceremonies or rigid schedules, just a lot of on the job training. It wasn't clear if credentials issued would be honored under a more critical review if the country returned to its prior state, but his knowledge was recognized throughout the Ark.

Matteo took another sip of coffee. "You're sure you can stay?"

"Yeah, I've got some studying to do. I'll just set up shop out here in the barn if that's okay?"

21

Essie stood upright. "I'm going to run into town real quick before the storm."

"Did you want me to go?" her dad asked, lifting his eyebrows toward Josh.

"I'll be like twenty minutes. I need to pick up a couple boards to fix that fence, a new water bucket for Eustace since he decided to chew his. Oh and Margie from church insisted on making some sort of baked good for you, Daddy. I told her I'd swing by her house. Unless *you'd* like to," she said suggestively.

Josh perked his eyebrows. "She's the one who used to have the pie shop?"

"Josh, the pie is for my dad from his not-so-secret-admirer. Maybe he doesn't *want* to share." Her smile widened.

Matteo shook his head. "Don't be a turd. She's like 90 years old." He rolled his eyes then leaned into the stall, taking another look at the mare, and avoiding further razzing.

"Need anything from town?"

Both men shook their heads and Essie started for the pickup truck. At the barn opening, she chuckled. "Hey, Josh, your girl seems to think she's coming with me."

Josh followed her to the entrance and peered out, shaking his head when he saw Fenway sitting at full attention in the bed of the pickup facing straight forward at the back window. "Yeah, I'm not sure she's been *my* dog since the day she met you."

"Do you have a leash in your truck? I know she doesn't need it."

"Yeah, some people get a little antsy when she's roaming around. It's in the center console."

"I've got the radio if you think of anything you need. You're sure we have a few hours on that Mustang baby though?"

"Yep."

She grinned, running her fingers across his jawline.

"Do I need to shave, too?"

"Well, now it's grown past the stubble stage. It feels kind of nice. Exfoliating, but nice."

Josh tilted his head to the side, suppressing a smile as he watched her cross to the driveway. She retrieved the leash, invited Fenway to jump into the cab of the rusted orchard truck, then climbed behind the wheel. There she searched around the dash and center console. Finally, she slid on a pair of mirrored blue sunglasses that were much too large for her face.

"It's raining, but it's bright," she explained.

He lifted his brow in agreement.

She leaned out of the open window as she backed out of the drive. "These belong to Miles."

"They look better on you."

She perked her eyebrows suggestively and patted Fenway on the head before pulling away.

3

virtue

The moment Essie pulled up the driveway an hour and a half later, the rain had started to pour down in sheets. She pulled as close as possible to the barn door so she wouldn't need to trek as far. The side door closest to Lil had been closed, probably to minimize noise and splash from the rain. She and Fenway, who had happily ridden shotgun, made a run for it once she got the driver's side door open.

The barn was far darker and quieter than when they'd left; it was hard to believe that there were so many farm animals housed inside. Eustace was the exception, bleating in a constant rhythm in his really angry pitch.

Josh was leaning against a stack of hay in front of the second stall on the right, which sat vacant since Hwin was in with Bree, two large textbooks lying open before him on the floor. He smiled as they came in.

"Hey, you two," he said quietly, patting Fenway's back as the dog slinked to the ground beside him.

Essie furrowed her brow, hearing the register of Eustace's bleating becoming higher and more alarmed.

"That really is the angriest little goat I've ever met," Josh remarked, nodding toward the far end of the barn, where a single goat leg poked out. "He has food, water, I even put in one of those salt licks in there thinking it would quiet him down, you know, like a baby pacifier?"

"Oh he's a big drama king. When I took out his water pail, which he'd chewed to bits, he chomped a hole in my jeans and then he was mad because I didn't then give him attention."

"Not the Goat Whisperer either then?" He grinned.

"I told you, Bree and Fenway are the exceptions, not the rule. I think the other animals can tell I'm winging it, but they tolerate me because I feed them. My dad also says I'm a pushover with treats."

"Based upon observation, I'm pretty sure you do a lot better than just 'winging it.'"

Essie stopped to peek in on the mare, who was lying down in the front corner of the stall. "Where did my dad go? His truck's gone."

"Yeah, he said he was meeting someone at the church."

"Luther probably."

Josh nodded. "I still don't understand how Luther's not one of the Ark leaders."

"He says he never wanted to be a leader; he just wanted to help people." She carefully maneuvered around his bag and collection of textbooks.

Josh pressed his lips together, patted the ground beside him. "That's the best kind of person to have as a leader."
Essie winced as she accidentally put weight on her thumb lowering herself to the floor.   "He still has a role, I'm just not sure what that role is."

Once she was seated, Josh lifted her hand to re-examine it. A bruise covered most of the thumb and palm.

"I'm fine, Dr. West," Essie chided, pulling her hand away. She immediately leaned against him, dropping her head to his shoulder.

"Tired?"

"I didn't really sleep last night."

He lightly rested his cheek against the top of her head. "Nightmares?"

She nodded.

"Do you want to talk about it?"

"I don't think I could describe them very well. Lots of flashes of images, things happening. There usually isn't, like, a *plot line*, which doesn't *sound* very scary, but–" She let her voice trail off.

"It depends on what you're seeing."

"It's like snippets of horror movies all spliced together."

He took a deep breath.

"I'd complain to the dreams programming director," she said facetiously, "but you know, that's my subconscious and hippocampus or whatever the memory center is?"

"Hippocampus. You got it."

She did a mini celebratory fist pump. "Nice. Hey, you're a scientific sort—isn't there a maximum storage capacity for the brain? Like, if I continue to read new things, learn new things--"

"Like the functions of the hippocampus?"

"Like the functions of the hippocampus," she repeated, "eventually my brain will have to off-load some of the bad memories, right? But I suppose I don't get to pick and choose."

He briefly considered the Sim technology. Danny had reverse-engineered a tech that would theoretically retrieve memories for those who had undergone Mandatory and other Sim training, but he wondered about some of its original functionality: erasing memories. All it took was the image of Essie in one of the Sim theaters with the censors, electrodes attached to her head, having to not only endure the memories to properly map the location of the memories in her brain, but to then have the Sim cause literal brain damage, for him to immediately rule it out as a feasible option.

"I suppose there's a purpose, right? To the brain holding onto memories you'd rather forget? Something with survival?"

"What do you mean?"

"Well, say all my memories from when I was a lab baby disappeared. I mean, most are hidden away anyway, it's not like I'm thinking about them any other time, but say they disappeared. My mind would have no starting point for dealing with, say, if a situation like that came up again. Like, going through that helped my mind when I did the antidote runs. I don't know, I'm probably not explaining it very well.

"You know the phrase 'It's like riding a bike'? It's like that—it might be years since you last did it, but the idea is that your brain remembers so it comes naturally."

"That makes sense. But I hope the memories you're talking about? I hope they never have another opportunity to prove themselves helpful."

"I know. It's just how I tell myself there's a purpose to them. I just don't understand why my brain feels like I need to re-live the memories so often."

"Do you only have those kinds of dreams at night?"

"I tend to sleep harder when I nap during the day. I've had bad dreams during the day, but it's not very often," she said with a lethargic shrug. "I get more anxious at night, I always have."

He took a deep breath, internalizing his frustration for the seemingly endless impact of what she endured as a child. It wasn't an experience she was expected to have to live with, at least not for very long. Not that the researchers cared.

Once they'd returned to the Ark, Josh had made himself re-watch the videos Luther had, years earlier, circulated on social media, as well as many he hadn't. As it turned out, Luther had the entire video library of every testing session in the STRONG experiments. Most children had one or two videos maximum. Essie had seven hundred and twelve videos spanning over 13,000 hours of experiment and recovery time footage.

The social media campaign had focused on specific sessions, mainly her earliest experiment at just a few hours old and her final experiment. The aim of the campaign had been to try and find a common ground with the ruling party, establish boundaries for what was acceptable and what was simply not moral. The videos sparked *some* controversy, *some* conversations, but by the time the videos made the rounds, a quarter of the population was on some sort of government support/social program so most people were focused on their own suffering, didn't have access to social media, or had chosen to turn away from social media, as

Josh's parents and Teo had. For those who were still paying attention, the media reprised their role to "discredit" the videos, dismissing them as disinformation. They questioned the authenticity of the images. When that didn't work out, they had several digital and media production experts on to confirm that the images were not computer-generated. The angle then became that there were groups creating these videos to destabilize the country. They questioned the mental state of those who would create a video of its nature, who would torture a child in order to so viciously attack the government?

Those who were able to publicly accuse the government of running such research labs were labeled as conspiracy theorists and extremists. With the exception of Christopher Loop, who was still releasing new episodes of his news commentary program, there were fewer and fewer dissenting voices, either due to accusations being made about them, personal tragedies that forced them from the spotlight, or they simply disappeared. If suspicions about certain events grew to a level that even "politically neutral" reporters started to question something, there were always distractions: wars, extraterrestrial discoveries, deaths of beloved, though expendable celebrities.

It was excruciating for Josh to watch the videos. Many could cope with the video content if they dismissed it as a hoax, if they had some separation from it. It was different for him; he recognized her eyes, her small rounded nose, the purse of her lips; she still interlocked her toes when she was nervous.

He rotated his chin toward Essie and kissed the top of her head. "A sleep aid isn't going to work for you, is it?" he asked rhetorically, knowing her body metabolism made medications, alcohol ineffective.

"Not unless the sleep aid is a frying pan."

He sighed. "My mom is really into meditation and prenatal yoga these days. Maybe she can help with some visualization stuff?"

"She doesn't need to be stressing about me."

"She loves you, Ess. She'd want to help."

"But if it didn't work, I'd feel compelled to lie to her so she doesn't feel bad."

The unspoken portion was that his parents hadn't made the connection, to his knowledge, between the videos and Essie, despite it not taking much stretch of the imagination to see the resemblance of Essie when they first met her to the little girl being called a Nazi and being forced to inhale poison gas.

If she told Sara she was having trouble sleeping, there'd be a line of questioning. She'd go into full mom problem-solving mode, not wanting to leave any stone unturned.

Essie continued to lean more heavily into him, tucking her cheek more securely against his shoulder.

He sighed. "In a purely supportive capacity, I *could* stay over, if you think that might help."

Her cheeks tightened. "Are you going to ask Pastor Teo about that one, Cowboy?"

He grinned.

"Are emotional support humans a thing? I could probably get a doctor's note from Luther."

"I think Earthlings call those friends, Essie."

"Well I've got the best one of those." She was nuzzled in so close he could feel her smile.

"You and Miles have really gotten close, huh?" He hated himself for the remark. He'd meant it to sound funny or somehow self-deprecating, but it sounded jealous instead.

Essie lifted her chin, her eyes swollen, her eyelids heavy. "Actually, we *have* gotten close. It's sort of bizarre, isn't it?"

"A bit."

"He's a good guy."

"As much as he tries to deny it or prove otherwise."

"And he certainly does try."

Josh smiled. "You've had a decidedly positive impact on him. I suppose you're going to tell me you're 'winging' that, too?"

Her mouth stretched upward. "I've been trying to get him to come to church."

"Oh yeah?"

"We've been talking about things: Jesus, the Bible, faith. He brought it up all on his own." She had a sleepy smile on her face.

Josh pulled his arm back and wrapped it around her shoulder. "You're a good influence on him."

She rotated onto her left hip, nestling herself into the nook of his arm. "I meant you. Before? The best emotional support human thing? I meant you. That was clear, right?"

"Yeah," he said, giving her shoulder a gentle squeeze, briefly leaning his head to rest on hers. In the months they'd been in the Ark, he'd become well-versed in being patient, waiting for things to move forward between the two of them. It felt like a constant imminence. He'd frequently visualize himself spontaneously kissing her.

As often as he imagined it, as close as it felt like they'd come to that sort of moment, they hadn't done so once in the time they'd been there. He'd committed himself to the promise he'd made to her in the truck cab on the drive to the Ark, to be there for her no matter what role she needed him to play in her life. Of course that was the night before she'd been, for lack of a better word, kidnapped due to a "misunderstanding," then returned the following day. Whatever the true story was there, the night she was gone, despite Luther assuring him she was safe, a part of him thought he'd never see her again. When they were reunited, every part of him wanted to throw all the things he'd promised to the wayside, take her in his arms and never let go.

But he didn't because he'd made a promise to her. He had misread the situation between them for basically the entire eighteen months he was involved with MET. He hadn't supported her the way she needed all that time she was working with Luther; he was committed to setting things right. She deserved that.

Truth be told, he never anticipated it would take so long for the situation between them to reach a resolution. He thought returning to the

Ark would help, having Gabe safe would allow her to finally release all the anxiety she'd carried since the Calvary attack. She seemed more capable of relaxing, or at least giving the appearance of relaxing, caring for the animals, managing the ranch, working at the church. His parents were certainly under the impression that she was back to "normal," hence why they kept a very close watch on their interactions for signs that things had progressed.

The truth was, he could feel the weight of her thoughts, fears, worries, and they'd only become heavier since they'd gotten back. He knew she needed to come around to verbalize things on her own, but he had recognized a shift since they'd been back of her reliance on him for quiet support.

Even so, there continued to be an intimate dynamic between them well beyond friendship that was only growing stronger. It just wasn't something they talked about. They spent several hours a day together, but the topic was never broached.

It felt like it would be breaking his word to bring it up, like it would be rushing her into something she wasn't ready for. If it all fell apart because he'd rushed her, it would be his fault. He knew what she'd been through. He knew she needed time to process things, to experience being "normal" again after subjecting herself to 120 antidote runs that wreaked havoc on her physically and psychologically, still coming to terms with what she faced as a child, but he struggled with the anticipation of getting to call her his, as well as the fear that when the dust settled, he might not be what she wanted or needed after all.

In the absence of any new definitions to their relationship, they'd eased back into their old habits of interaction, of teasing, of gentle physical horseplay, of platonic physical affection.

He was grateful for the familiarity of it, he was grateful to have her, but he maintained a low level of anxiety, waiting for an answer that didn't seem any closer to arriving.

She stirred suddenly and lifted her chin to look at him. He suspected she'd briefly nodded off. Her brow flinched, picking up on something in his expression. Her eyes drifted to the textbooks before him and she sat up, stretching her neck. "I don't want to keep you from studying. I can do some chores in here while it's raining."

"Or you could sit and read with me." His objective was to get her to relax and maybe nap, but he didn't want to say so.

She winced. "I finished the book I was working on this morning. I don't know if I have any others stashed out here."

He reached for his rucksack and removed a hardcover book in laminated library binding. "I brought this for you."

Essie smiled. "*The Hobbit*."

"I remember reading *Lord of the Rings* a few years ago and thinking you might like the series, but I never got around to giving my set to you. I think they may have gotten left behind at the farm. I'll have to do a better job at finding another copy of the rest of the series. I'm guessing you'll be through this by the afternoon."

She flipped through the pages affectionately, her smile widening. "Thank you, Josh."

"The hobbits remind me a bit of you when it comes to food."

"They have ravenous appetites?"

"Yes. They have such a thing as second breakfast."

Her jaw fell open. "Am *I* secretly a hobbit?"

"Doubtful. Your feet aren't hairy enough."

"Hairy *enough*? What hair do I have on my feet?" She moved to tug off her boot. "Actually, no. As keen as I am to prove I have no hair on my feet, I'm not going to inflict stinky boot feet upon a mother in active labor."

"Never mind me?" He grinned.

She perked her eyebrow. "You're *used* to the smell of farm animals. I'm pretty sure you can handle it, but I'll spare you just the same." She leaned in and hugged him. "Thank you for my book."

He fought the strong urge to kiss her head again, settling for taking a slow inhalation of her hair. There was the subtle scent of her shampoo, but as had been the case since he'd known her, she smelled like open fields, fresh mountain air, and rain.

When he lived in a Mandatory dormitory set in an industrial harbor along the California coast, his nasal cavities were constantly assaulted with unpleasant stenches of unwashed humans, rotting fish, and polluted seawater. He would lie in his bunk and visualize being at home. He'd picture the grassy pastures, the fresh stream, the snowy mountains, the dirt kicked up by the horses—all the aromas that accompanied a single breath of her hair. He shifted his eyes toward the sheet of rain pouring down over the ranch outside the open barn door.

She resituated herself out of his hold, easing back into the haystack so their shoulders were side by side. She casually crossed her ankles, opened her new book, and looked pointedly toward his books.

Josh pressed his lips together, stretched his legs straight out in front of him alongside hers, and pulled a textbook closer to him.

*   *   *

Josh stirred awake some time later to find the rain had stopped and the sun was trying to make a bold appearance, the sky oppressively bright outside the barn. It was considerably warmer than it had been earlier, the humidity a bit stifling with the limited circulation.

Essie had been reading when she'd fallen asleep, the book still braced in her hand, her thumb holding her page about twenty pages in. Her head rested on his shoulder.

Through the single open barn door, he could see an additional vehicle parked at the house. He was just sorting out that the burgundy SUV belonged to Luther when he heard another set of tires trudging across the wet dirt.

Fenway growled defensively from her position by their feet. She had her muzzle resting on Essie's ankle.

The squeak of the brakes startled Essie awake and she abruptly moved to sit upright, head swiveling around to look over his shoulder to the stall.

"Did Lil have the baby?"

Josh peered back at the mare, still tucked in by the wall. "She seems to have settled for now."

"She can just decide to *stop* labor?"

He shrugged. "They do it in the wild if they sense a threat." He glanced at her hand resting on his chest. "Your hand's not even bruised anymore. Is that part of your healing superpower?"

She released a sudden yawn, then propped herself up on his chest,. "How long was I asleep?"

"A couple hours? I nodded off, too, I guess."

Her tired eyes watched his lips as he spoke, her mouth turning upward in a nondescript smile. It wasn't the first time she'd done something like that, but the intimacy of the moment, her body tucked beside him, heightened the tension and anticipation that it could be the turning point.

The engine of the newly arrived vehicle shut off.

Her attention snapped toward the barn door and she reeled back her hand from his chest, sitting fully upright. "Who's here?"

"Luther, I think. Someone else just pulled in though."

Essie frowned, listening to the footsteps, the displacement of dirt and gravel as the new arrival walked across the drive. "It's Gabe."

"How can you tell?"

"He's the only one around here who wears *boat* shoes." She rose to her feet, walking quickly toward the door, carrying her new book with her. She unlatched the closed left door, slow-walked it open, then turned to embrace Gabe.

Fenway rushed toward them to assess the situation.

Gabe's body had filled back out to some degree, but he still had a gangly appearance he'd never had growing up, his shoulders curved forward, his joints a bit loose. His time at Mandatory had appeared to prematurely age him, his eyes lined with crow's feet that were certainly not the result of smiling.

Their parents were fearful of the impact Sim training had on him; they'd heard the stories about enlistees who'd come home and become violent, acting out of character. There were rumors that talked about enlistees actually murdering their families and neighbors. Perhaps their families were identified as disposable in the population reduction efforts and weren't partaking in the government's vaccine programs, which would have fixed the pesky issue of their existence.

Danny acknowledged the possibility of this, but also considered that these were rumors circulated to cause distrust and fractures in families, in social circles. "Fear is a really powerful weapon," he had said with a shrug.

Despite Gabe being given what Josh had observed as a pretty positive reception, Gabe had been struggling to acclimate. It had started from the night he'd arrived. After Christmas Eve service, when their mom had been beside herself with emotion and burst forward to embrace him, Gabe had flinched away, his movements rigid. He'd been slightly uncomfortable in his interactions with Josh as well, but this hadn't been unusual for them. Any peculiarities in his behavior, Josh had attributed to detoxing from the Sim training, but the edginess he'd had with their parents was concerning since it appeared involuntary and *wasn't* typical for him.

Things were different, as they had always been, with Essie. Gabe had always been serious and task-driven, not overly comfortable with hugs or other signs of physical affection even as a child, but he'd always shown an ease with these things when it came to Essie. While Gabe had become even more standoffish with everyone else since his arrival at the Ark, Josh had observed his brother becoming increasingly affectionate with her. When they were younger, he'd observed Gabe interacting with her in a purely platonic manner. Protective. Gabe liked to assert himself as an older brother to both she and Josh, always presenting himself as the most knowledgeable, the most mature, the one to emulate.

At the entrance to the barn, Gabe continued to embrace her, tightening his arms around her with an intensity that one might have holding a life preserver.

As they finally parted, Essie's expression turned serious. She reached for his hand, but her rushed words were too low for Josh to hear.

Josh silently pushed himself off the ground, busied himself with looking in on the pregnant mare, who had stood and was beginning to feed. In his peripheral vision, he could see Essie framing his brother's face in her hands.

They hugged again.

The mare nudged at his hand, searching for treats, which provided a welcomed distraction.

"Hey, Josh?" Essie said quietly what seemed like moments later, suddenly a few steps away.

His hand jolted and Lilliandil snorted angrily at him.

"Are you okay?" Essie asked. "I said your name a couple times."

"Yeah, fine. Sorry." He looked up toward the barn entrance. Gabe was out of view, but he could see his brother's elongated shadow on the ground.

"Oh, so you'll let *him* near you?" Essie said in a teasing tone.

It took Josh a moment to realize she was speaking to the pregnant mare and not echoing his bitter internal dialogue. He reset his footing. "Not really. She's been taking treats though. Maybe she just thought your hand looked tasty."

Essie twisted her expression. "Doubtful, but I was probably being too much of a helicopter barn mom. I'm used to Bree's codependency." She started to reach her hand toward the horse out of automation, but quickly thought better of it.

Josh smiled, retracted his own hand from the stall.

"Are you staying for a while?"

"I'll probably go check on a couple cows down the way, head back this direction later."

She glanced across at him. "I'm gonna go for a drive with Gabe," she said carefully.

He nodded without turning his head.

"You *are* coming back though, right?"

He lifted his eyes to meet her gaze, the upward slope of her eyebrows reminiscent of her as a little girl. "You bet."

She flashed him a quick smile and turned on her heel.

*   *   *

Essie was sitting on the front porch, knees folded up to her chest, gnawing on her right thumb nail when Josh returned a couple of hours later. She paused her conversation with her dad to watch him drop out of his pickup and trudge up the porch steps.

"He comes bearing gifts," she remarked, smiling lightly.

"My mom's in a nesting phase. She said she made too many quiche? I'm not sure I've had whatever that is."

Matteo paused the rocking of his chair. "She doesn't seem to get the concept that people should be sending her food, not the other way around."

"Oh, she'd appreciate the gesture, but she doesn't trust anybody else's cooking. I was afraid to ask, but what *is* a quiche?" Josh placed the pie pan on the table between the rocking chairs.

"It's an egg pie basically."

Essie leaned forward to look at the dish, pulling a face. She quickly neutralized her expression.

Matteo grinned at her. "Yeah, I've never been a fan myself, but if Sara made it, it must be pretty good."

"Still no baby?" Josh asked, raising his eyes to the barn.

Essie shook her head, motioning toward a radio receiver on the table next to the quiche. "No, but I set up a radio in the stall so we'll be able to hear if something happens."

"'Clever girl,'" Josh said with a hint of a British accent.

Matteo cleared his throat to disguise an involuntary chuckle. "Wow, would you *look* at that sunset," he observed, looking up at the horizon as he rose from his chair. It was perhaps the least impressive sunset they'd had in weeks. "I'm going to take a little walk before dark. You can take my seat, Josh."

Esther stared at her dad's back as he made his way down the steps, shaking her head, cheeks tight.

Josh furrowed his brow as he obliged, taking the chair across from her, watching Teo continue toward the overlook.

"*So*, how are the cows?" Essie asked, tilting her chin toward him.

"Cranky."

"Even with you?"

"Especially with me."

"Oh I'm sure you have an excellent stallside manner. Very calming."

"Not as calming as I'd like." He realized she probably didn't know what he was seeing said cows for, but he was grateful she hadn't asked. It would be difficult to segue conversation away from '*Both dairy cows have bacterial infections in their udders so in addition to treating them with antibiotics, I'm having to manually extract pus that has filled the milk ducts to try to give them some pain relief.*'

They were going on day four of antibiotics, so he was optimistic it was the last, or second to last time he'd have to perform the procedure.

"Where's Fenway?"

"At my parents'. I figured she'd just make Lilliandil nervous."

"Probably true." Essie rocked back and forth in the chair, suppressing a smile. "You're staying over then?"

"I'll just bunk out in the barn."

She frowned. "My dad won't have that. He's much too fond of you."

"You used to sleep in our barn."

"Yeah, well, we don't have much of a summer season here." She scrunched her nose. "Never mind what my dad says, *I* won't let you."

"'Never mind what my dad says'?" Matteo echoed in disbelief, suddenly ten yards away from the porch.

"Is that what people your age call a 'walk'?"

"I spotted a bachelor bear. I'm going to call over to let Luke know, but figured we'd need to lock things down."

Essie stood, started immediately for the steps. "Gotta watch out for those *bachelors*," she said, peering over at Josh, who was following her lead toward the barn.

"Well, *this* bachelor is helping secure the barn so we can't *all* be bad."

4

afloat

The stream that ran through the West's farm was approximately fifteen feet wide. Not exceptionally wide, but not small either. Unlike many waterways on other farming properties in the area, which were essentially dug out ditches filled with mucky, questionable groundwater, the stream was lined with rocks and was natural to the environment, a side passage of the Jameson River, which flowed directly from the Rockies. During storms and inclement weather, the streams could develop a moderate current, but on a typical day, it offered a calm, gentle flow of freshwater.

Sara and Luke had chosen to homeschool Josh and Gabe. With this autonomy, they were able to adjust schooling schedules to coincide with farm work, fair weather, poor weather, and pretty much anything else that happened to come up.

If the boys found themselves occupied by schoolwork or farm tasks, the property offered plenty of sights and activities to keep Essie occupied if she happened to be staying with them. One of her favorite places was the stream, particularly on warm days. Her latest read, Pride and Prejudice, *sat under a tree by the grassy shoreline. She had been keeping the cover hidden from Luke, as a complicated love story would be just the thing he'd poke fun at, albeit in an affectionate way.*

Bree quietly grazed near the tree, swishing his luscious white tail to shoo away any lurking flies.

Esther had decided against wearing all of her clothes in the water, fearing the chill of the wind on the long walk back and had undressed down to her underwear and a sports bra. The heat of the sunshine on her back was warm, but the mountain-sourced stream was still quite chilly and it took her breath away as she submerged her body up to her shoulders. She waded a few strides across into the sunlight, released her feet from the basin and began to float.

Her long, unruly waves soaked up the cool water and billowed out around her head. She could feel the tension in her body still trying to maintain some sense of control. She took a deep breath and focused on relaxing her body, muscle group by muscle group. She slowed her breathing, listening to the individual breaths seeming to echo in the water, the gentle sound of the water lapping against the river stones.

The sun began to warm the skin of her arms, her stomach, her cheeks.

She felt no muscle aches from the earlier exertion mucking stalls. She didn't feel her body at all.

And then she heard the murmur of a voice in her ears:

It's better not to feel.
It's better not to think.

Essie squinted her eyes open to find the sun still shining brightly overhead. Her chest constricted with tightening breaths. She tried to relax again, tried to slow her breathing, feel the sun, feel the water.

It was too quiet. She could no longer hear her breathing echoing in the water. She could no longer hear the gentle echo of the current flowing over the river rocks, splashing against the shore. There was no sound at all.
Her eyes flew open at the same moment she felt a hand clasp over her mouth and then her body was being pulled underwater.

5

chapter one

Annette stared at the cover of the new biography, featuring a photo of Gowon standing out on the balcony of the People's House, gazing out over the South Lawn and fountains.

Samuel Gowon:
Entrepreneur, Philanthropist, Father of the Next Great Era in American History

Chapter 1: Childhood Beginnings

In the heart of Boston, Massachusetts, on a chilly autumn day, Samuel Harris Gowon III was born into a loving and ambitious family. It was October 28, 1996, a date that would mark the beginning of a remarkable journey for the young boy who would eventually become the single most important leader in American history.

Samuel Gowon grew up in a warm and close-knit household with his older sister, Sadie. Their parents, Samuel H. Rawling Sr. and Amelia Clouser, were both exceptional individuals who met at Harvard. Samuel Sr. was a soft-spoken and promising Neuropsychology student with a deep fascination for the complexities of the human mind. He had an innate ability to connect with people and a profound desire to contribute to the medical field. Amelia was an athletic and outgoing Law student, actively involved in student leadership and passionate about advocating for justice and equality. Her determination and strong sense of empathy made her a force to be reckoned with, both in the classroom and beyond.

The Gowon children grew up in an atmosphere that encouraged competitiveness and a drive for excellence. Their parents firmly believed in nurturing their individual strengths while instilling in them the values of compassion and empathy. They were raised to be not just successful individuals, but also responsible and caring members of society. Samuel's sister, Sadie, excelled at swimming and soccer, in addition to being awarded with countless academic honors throughout her prestigious schooling, while Samuel favored the mysteries of science and technology, the emerging field of artificial intelligence, demonstrating an aptitude for complex principles at a very early age.

Samuel shared a special bond with his mother, Amelia. He admired her ambition and her tenacity, evident in the brief tenure she served in a prestigious Boston law firm. However, everything changed for her and the entire Gowon family when Seth Atticus Tate came into their lives.

Despite an otherwise healthy pregnancy, the youngest of the Gowon household was born with Down Syndrome, a condition that presented significant physical and cognitive challenges. Amelia was forced to give up her promising career to become a full-time caregiver. As Samuel grew older, having witnessed his mother's countless sacrifices, he knew he had a responsibility to use his abilities to help others who faced similar challenges, so they would not be constricted by the same burdens she had faced, forced to make the same sacrifices."

Annette knew better than to verbalize her opinion, even if she was alone. When they first began a "romantic" relationship, Samuel had warned her that there were "ears" everywhere, meaning listening devices.

Since the revelation of the Arks, the orchestration of resources, all happening under Samuel's nose, he was taking no risks. There were overt cameras everywhere. Every microphone fed into an AI system, developed by one of his companies, that sought out particular words, phrases in any variation, any accent, in any language. She knew he had specific search strings he had programmed to alert him directly.

She took a steadying breath, turning the page, though her eyes were not focusing on the words.

She was thinking of her daughter.

Such a strange concept, that she had a daughter.

Esther Evin.

Her name was not one she would have selected for her. Before the incident at the Capitol Building, her baby literally being ripped from her body, Annette had been torn between the names Florence, where she was born, and Marion, where she spent summers every year. Whichever she chose, Esther would have had her grandmother's name as her middle name: Leah.

Annette startled, realizing she'd been turned to the same page for far too long. She cleared her throat, scribbled something illegible on her notepad. She could make up something to remark about to Samuel when he inevitably asked.

No, she needed something concrete to say or he'd be suspicious. She turned to the next page in her notebook and jotted down:

Amelia – what an inspiration. Ask Samuel if he'd like to display a photo of her. Perhaps commission a painting?

She turned to the next page, quickly let her mind wander to the day at the Capitol Building again, the day Esther was born. She hadn't planned to go in at all, she wasn't going to play along with the theatrics. She had confided in Torrance Dixon the night before that she planned to issue her resignation via email, travel home to the cabin in the small Oregon town she'd inherited from her grandparents; it seemed idyllic for raising a child. And that would be it. Whatever the repercussions were in the District, she didn't care. She had stopped watching the news long before or reading any online publications. She'd simply ignore what was going on for as many news cycles as it took for speculation about her to fade away. She'd move on with her life with her daughter. If she felt so inclined to reenter the political arena at some point, it would be in local races. She could run for mayor. Her family was well-established in the small town; she'd have no trouble securing enough votes.

She shouldn't have picked up the call. She should have simply gotten in her car and started the drive.

It had been subtle, the strategy used to keep her in the District, which was why she hadn't suspected anything. Ellis Broderick called to confirm he could count on her vote on the Capitol. The Republicans were playing dirty he said; they were forcing an in-person vote. No proxy voting. She needed to be there to ensure the spending package would pass or there could be a government shutdown.

Annette had justified that she could still be on the road by lunch. She could be several states away by dinner time when she'd pull off for the night. She'd be breathing much easier knowing she'd done the right thing for herself and for her daughter.

The vote had happened as planned and as Ellis had indicated. She should have immediately left. But then there was the press conference where she was invited to be the one to address the press, essentially securing credit for the accomplishment.

One last press conference. A swan song.

She could still be on the road by 2pm. She'd send her resignation as she left the District.

The book chapter was now going into detail about Samuel's childhood, science fair competitions, scholarships he applied for, won, but didn't need. It was really chump change given the wealth he was born into, but the book attempted to depict his taking the time to apply for the scholarships, knowing he would win, then donating the funds to marginalized minority students as "his first act of philanthropy."

Blah, blah, blah.

She should have left that morning. To hell with the spending package, which didn't, in fact, need her vote after all.

If she had just left, everything would have been different.

They would have still come for her, she justified silently. *They probably would have taken her and killed me.*

Esther had her natural hair color and her freckles, but that seemed to be where their similarities ended.

After Demetri had left with Esther, Annette had spent some time looking through old family photos at the cabin. The pictures from her childhood and early adulthood had an artificial look to them that she'd never noticed before, highlighted when she examined them side by side with photos from her parents' childhood albums, which were not as composed or put-together as hers, but seemed to capture more authentic views of their lives.

Even with the softened filters on the photos from her high school years, Annette found her face had a sharp, haughty look. She looked older than her years, which had been her intent at the time. She doubted her mother had any photos that Annette hadn't personally approved, anything she deemed unflattering deleted.

At the time she thought she was so put together, she was doing as everyone else did, she had proper validation from her peers. She was fitting in. She had a respectable number of followers on social media.

Looking back, she was surprised at how insecure she looked. How miserable. The constant need for approval, to wear the right thing, to say the right thing, to look just so, to project an image of herself, her life that people would envy.

She remembered how her frequent check-ins on social media could make or break her entire day, depending on how many likes, how many validating comments she received from strangers.

It was almost laughable how artificial it all was, the trickery of it, the facade.

It was a contrast to the life Esther had lived, something she was grateful for. This was perhaps most evident in the video Luther had forwarded of Esther singing in church. She was a few years younger, her face still with the roundness of childhood, but she had a natural beauty. It took no special effects, no trick lighting, no filters, no makeup. Esther simply stood at the front of the church strumming on an acoustic guitar singing *It Is Well*, never overdoing the vocals or trying to add any distracting variances or enhancements, just effortlessly confident.

Annette felt chills throughout the performance; she could only imagine being in that church. It was astounding how this young girl sang with so much passion, stirring so many to raise their voices and their hands in worship. Cheers started as she sang about God throwing the mountain that stood before her into the sea.

Several voices from the congregation joined in for the chorus, which brought a smile to Essie's face, a small dimple dipping into her cheek.

... So let go my soul and trust in Him
The waves and wind still know His name
So let go my soul and trust in Him
The waves and wind still know His name

As the song closed and the music faded, Esther slowly opened her eyes, the spotlights illuminating her youthful face, her big silver eyes. She gave a courteous tilt of her chin and stepped back into the shadows of the altar, removing her decal-covered guitar, and set it tenderly on its stand. The pastor had stepped up to the front by that point, placed his bottle of water, Bible and notes on the small table, and glanced affectionately over his shoulder at her. Esther smiled nervously, moving quickly toward the steps at the edge of the elevated stage. Her eyes lit up as she made brief eye contact with the man who raised her. Her dad. The only parent she ever knew until their brief meeting at Annette's cabin.

Luther had no doubt sent the video as a goodwill gesture, to give Annette some insight into Esther's life, and she had been grateful for it, but it was bittersweet. This was the child she had carried, who she felt like she had gotten to know in that time before she was born, who she had mourned–and she was certainly alive, but she was no longer her daughter. Nothing she had become would have happened if Annette had raised her. She would have never set foot in a church, for one thing. For another, if she had shown a scrap of her talent for singing, Annette would have had her in vocal lessons, in singing competitions, starting an Instagram account, a Spotify artist account, Annette would be using her connections to get her doing talk show circuits, opening for popular singers.

The relief Annette had felt to know her child had not died had slowly been replaced with a resentment that Esther had no resemblance to the person she would have become as her daughter. She hadn't died, but she had still been stolen from her.

It was difficult to know who she thought did the stealing–was it the bureaucrats–and Samuel Gowon, running the STRONG program? Or did she blame Esther's adoptive father for being such an influence on her, stealing away the daughter she would have otherwise become?

She couldn't deny that seeing Esther in such a light, singing in front of a congregation with such confidence, such security in her identity, made her feel proud. When she got down to the bottom of things, wasn't that what she wanted for her? To not face the same insecurities that she had at that age? To not feel like she had to prove herself? To not have it cross her mind that she wasn't good enough? That was what was most important, right? That her daughter knew who she was–even if it was someone very different from the daughter Annette expected to raise? That was ultimately Annette's problem with her parents, wasn't it? They didn't allow enough freedom to be who she wanted to be? To branch away from the core beliefs they'd instilled in her and have her own mind?

Of course, the Esther she met was changed from the girl in the video. Her confidence had faltered under the extreme pressure she'd been facing–and yet, there was still a purity to her, an innocence, a hope–in the slant of her lips, in the sparkle of her radiant silver eyes when she spoke about her dad, her friends. Despite everything she'd faced, she'd managed to not lose herself along the way.

Annette knew she couldn't honestly say the same about herself.

The hallway door clicked open and Annette straightened her posture, but found it was only the culinary staff setting up dinner.

She gave a light lift of her eyebrows in greeting–nothing too welcoming that Samuel would disapprove of. Taking a deep breath, she closed the book, placed it aside on the end table on top of her notebook.

Samuel had asked her to read the proof of his biography, give some notes before final revisions were made.

"Asked" was a misnomer. Samuel Gowon didn't *ask* for anything.

There was no way she'd be able to focus her mind. She'd simply tell him she hadn't been able to get very far in the book because she wasn't feeling well. She'd been plagued with migraines for her entire adult life; it had always been a reliable excuse, if used sparingly.

No, if she said she had a migraine, he'd come up with a remedy, some mystery pharmaceutical his Research & Development team had cooked up in their chemistry lab.

It would be better to say she was distracted with some vague situation on Capitol Hill, some frustrating interpersonal thing of which Samuel had no interest. He'd quickly shift the conversation back to himself.

She glared over at the cover of the biography, dreading the moment she'd have to pick it up again.

It was to be the first book published in physical form in years. As a part of his outreach campaign, he was reopening libraries across the country, citing the discord in culture being a result of the lack of access to written works.

Of course, all written works provided were going to be handpicked for inclusion in the library collections. Originally, library closures corresponded with a social program that provided a base tablet for every American that included access to the same library catalogs, just electronic. This was incredibly popular with roughly half of the population. As distrust of government grew, fewer people utilized them, and then infrastructure failure made recharging them impractical.

Samuel's justification for bringing back libraries had very little to do with the welfare of the public, specifically of children, as it was depicted in advertisements. It was simply a way to engage with people who had not participated with the government's social health programs. Parents might be reluctant to inoculate their children or send them to government schools, but a library was nostalgic from their own childhoods perhaps and seemed benign enough. There were play areas and movie halls and comfortable seating; which would seem downright luxurious based upon the living conditions of the majority of Americans. What was the harm?

He'd been pleased with himself when he explained his reasoning, that to catch vermin, sometimes you have to leave out a bit of cheese.

*   *   *

In The Loop w/ Christopher Loop: The Beginning of the End

"Do you know the moment I knew we were in trouble in this country? There's been a lot of moments, a lot of times I've said to myself we are really in a lot of trouble here, but the time when I thought to myself, we're not coming back from this, was when the opioid crisis was in full-swing, human trafficking was growing rampant, we were having devastating wildfires, inflation, there was corruption literally at every level, the cities were in ruins, tents, feces everywhere, gender ideology was taking hold of and the government had the nerve to look us in the eye and tell us they were taking away paper currency, coin currency. From then on, there would only be digital currency. A digital dollar. A simple keystroke could erase a person's bank account, or hold it hostage to force conformity. Make no mistake: a simple keystroke can erase any one of us.

"Today, we must confront a grim reality—a tyrannical regime that has seized control, eroding the very principles upon which our country was founded: life, liberty, and the pursuit of happiness. The very foundation of our great nation was built upon the idea of limited government, where the power rested with the people, not with a few elites in the District. But Gowon seems to have forgotten this fundamental truth, as he continues to encroach upon our personal freedoms at an alarming rate. There is barely even the illusion of personal freedom. The elites, the tyrants are feeling more and more confident to openly share their true intent–and that's truly terrifying.

"It's crucial to understand that the erosion of our freedoms did not happen overnight. It was a gradual and calculated process that began with the encroachment on our Second Amendment rights—the right to bear arms. The government sought to disarm the people, making us vulnerable and dependent on their authority. And when the right to defend ourselves was stripped away, it opened the door for further assaults on our liberties. As they say, without the Second Amendment, we have no means to defend our First Amendment rights—the freedom of speech, religion, and expression. The government was quick to label any dissenting opinion as 'hate speech' or 'disinformation,' using it as an excuse to silence those who dare to question their authority.

"The ever-expanding regulatory apparatus suffocated the entrepreneurial spirit that was the driving force in our economy. Small businesses, the backbone of our nation, were strangled by burdensome regulations and excessive taxation. In an unprecedented act, the government seized family farms and businesses.

"As the dominos continued to fall, the stranglehold on our nation tightened. The government's reach expanded, intruding into every aspect of our lives. Our once free society was slowly transformed into a surveillance state, where privacy became a distant memory, and our personal choices were dictated by those in power. Free speech became a thing of the past. Feelings trumped free speech and even truth became subjective. Let's be very, very clear: There is one truth and it is the truth of the Almighty God.

"Gone are the days when individuals could pursue their dreams, bask in the glow of liberty, and find happiness through hard work and determination. Instead, we now live under the heavy hand of the government, where the pursuit of happiness has been replaced by the pursuit of compliance to their oppressive policies.

"And let us not forget the government's blatant disregard for our Fourth Amendment rights, as Gowon and his entire regime supports widespread surveillance and data collection on innocent citizens. The right to privacy is a cornerstone of our freedoms, yet Gowon seems determined to erode it in the name of 'security.'

"In this dystopian reality, the government now openly decides who lives and who dies. The sanctity of life, a cornerstone of our values, has been disregarded as they exercise control over medical decisions and healthcare access. Our once sacred right to make choices about our own bodies has been stripped away, and the government now plays the role of a cold and heartless arbiter, deciding the fate of the innocent.

"We have arrived at a point where the values that once defined us as a nation are not just under siege; they exist only in rare instances. Our once great country, founded on principles of liberty and freedom, now stands on the brink of collapse under the weight of tyranny.

"We cannot allow the flame of liberty to be extinguished. We must be the guardians of the principles that make America the land of the free and the home of the brave. The road to restore our great country is not an easy one, but it's one we have to take, at any cost.

"Let us demand that our voices be heard, that our rights be respected, and that our government be held accountable. Together, we can reclaim our country from the clutches of tyranny and restore the promise of life, liberty, and the pursuit of happiness for all.

"The road ahead may be arduous, but history has shown that the fight for freedom is always worth it. We will not cower in fear, for we are Americans, and we will not surrender without a fight. God bless you all, and may God bless the United States of America."

6

songbird

"What, may I ask, are you doing?"

Essie furrowed her brow, attempting to blow the hair out of her face. She was furiously wiping at the bathroom sink basin, attempting to dislodge several globs of toothpaste speckled with hair shavings. "What does it look like I'm doing?"

Miles chuckled. "I'm sorry, I'll rephrase: Essie, why are you cleaning my bathroom?"

"It's filthy. You realize I left you a whole year's supply of cleaning products under the sink, right?"

"Wait, the cabinet opens?"

"*Oh*, Joel."

"*Hey*," he said in a warning tone. "I love you, but don't you start first naming me."

"Does it make you feel like you're being scolded?"

"No."

"Oh, then I won't use it anymore," she said with a sly smile. "What made you start going by your middle name?"

"I don't know, it was weird to have the same name as my dad? *I* didn't choose to go by Miles; it's just what I was always called."

"So you don't mind 'Joel'?"

"No, it's just weird. It's my name, but it doesn't feel like my name."

She nodded. "I get it. My first name is actually 'Magdalena.' If people started calling me that? *Weird.*"

"Your first name is not *Magdalena.*"

"It does allow for the nickname Maggie, which I don't hate."

"It's *not* your name, is it?"

"No," she said with a shake of her head, as the stray lock of hair continued to fall in her eyes. "Esther Evin Natale."

"Evin?"

"Yep, named for Luther's grandpa."

"*Wait*, how long have you known Luther?"

"Longer than I've known anyone."

Miles frowned. "That seems weird."

"I was adopted, Miles. You knew that, didn't you?"

"Wait, is *Luther* your dad?"

She looked up at him with sympathy, pursing her lips.

"I meant foster dad."

"Well, not officially, but he did take care of me for a little while when I was young."

"Huh." Miles leaned against the counter, now having watched her tackle the sink, the toilet, and the shower, the only assistance he'd provided being to pull the shower curtain to one side of the tub.

She smiled lightly. "What?"

"That's so strange to think of–that your dad isn't your biological dad."

"He's my dad in all the ways that matter."

"Do you know anything about your biological parents?"

Essie arched her eyebrow.

"Probably not. You were just a baby, right?" Miles looked at her with affection. "I'm sorry, Ess. I don't think I ever realized you were adopted."

"Don't be sorry, Joel. I pretty much won the adoption lottery."

He paused, smiling lightly at her persistent use of his first name. "*Still.* How old were you when your dad adopted you?"

"Almost three."

He appeared to be debating about asking his question again, about her memories of her parents. "I have a random question."

"Well, I probably have a random answer."

"What's with all the mention of birds in the Bible?"

She glanced up at him, suppressing a smile at the reality that Joel Miles Kent would be reading the Bible considering as children, he had likened a belief in God to a belief in the tooth fairy. "Would you be referring to all the doves?"

"Doves, eagles, sparrows...I read this passage that was something like: I am like a seagull of the wilderness; I am like an owl of the desert. I lie awake, And am like a pigeon alone on the housetop."

"'*I am like a pelican of the wilderness; I am like an owl of the desert. I lie awake, And am like a sparrow alone on the housetop.*'"

"Do you have the entire book memorized?"

"Not even close. I was reading Psalm the other night though."

"He meant he's lonely, right?"

"That's how I interpret it. He was using the imagery of the birds being out of their natural habitat to talk about how isolated and out of place he feels."

"Yeah, I felt that. I don't know. Maybe it's just what I've been reading, but there seem to be a lot of birds."

She chuckled.

"I do have to say, Psalms is a lot better than the chapters where it just goes into lineage. So and so had his first son at 140 and lived 910 years."

Essie smiled. "I can't keep those names straight. I tend to skip those sections, knowing there's no way I'm going to remember everyone."

"Speaking of *names*, I did read the book of *Esther*."

"Yeah?" she said, turning on the shower, rinsing the cleaner off the tiled walls.

"Oh, I thought that was the design of the tiles."

She twisted her expression, shaking her head.

"You're named for Bible Esther, right?"

"More or less, yes."

"It's a good story."

She nodded. "It is."

"The name still sounds like you're 90 years old though. It's good you go by Essie. It fits you better."

"Yeah, Bible Esther was a *Queen*. She'd never clean your bathroom. She'd send her least favorite servant to do it."

He grinned. "How did you get your call sign? 'Canary'? Is it the singing thing?"

She shrugged, spraying a foam over the mirror. "The thing about me is I can have a dark sense of humor. Maybe it's not even humor. I can just be really dark."

"Okay? I sort of picked up on that with the zombie babies prank at the safe house. Otherwise, I'm not really seeing it."

"Are you familiar with miners?" She asked, using the microfiber cloth to wipe down the mirror, needing to use extra force to dislodge some toothpaste bits.

"As in children? Well, I used to be one."

"No, people who work within a mine. Coal miners."

"Ah. No familiarity whatsoever."

"Okay. Well, coal mining can be really dangerous; there's a lot of concern about carbon monoxide."

"Okay?"

"Birds are really sensitive to environmental changes so miners used to carry canaries down into the mines with them. If the canary started having issues, or you know, *died*, it was a clear sign that they needed to get out."

He frowned. "*Okay*? Seems weird. What does that have to do with you?"

Josh stepped into the apartment carrying a pack of beer and peered down the hallway to where Miles stood straddling the threshold to the bathroom. He frowned. "What are you doing, Miles?"

"Watching Essie clean my bathroom while she tells me how she got her call sign."

"*Essie?*" Josh called down the hall.

"*Josh?*" she hollered back.

"Why are you cleaning Miles's bathroom?" He placed the beer in the sparsely-filled refrigerator, becoming slightly concerned about the prospects for dinner.

"Because there were bacterial colonies developing and he's not allowed pets."

Miles laughed. "It wasn't *that* bad."

"I hope you're teaching him *how* to clean. You know what they say."

"If you give a Miles a clean bathroom, he keeps it clean for a day, if you teach a Miles to clean–"

"He probably still only keeps it clean for a day," Miles interjected.

"At least you admit it," Josh remarked, leaning in on the door frame. Essie was just tucking the cleaner under the sink, along with the rubber gloves. Her cheeks were flushed from exertion. "Looks good."

"Clean enough to poop in here now?" Miles asked.

Essie scrunched her nose. "Ew. But yeah. I still wouldn't do much else. You still need to clean this floor."

"Yep. That is *definitely* something I'll be doing."

"*Dude.*"

"Fine. *Thank you*, Essie."

She washed her hands at the sink, then hesitated to touch the bleach-stained towel hanging on the towel bar. "I'm impressed there's a towel there, to be honest, or *soap*, but I think that's the same towel you hung up there when you moved in."

He shrugged. "Probably due for a wash."

"It's been five months, Miles."

"But I'm only using it when my hands are clean. Well, and I use it when I wipe my mouth after I brush my teeth."

She cringed. "Do you have paper towel?"

"Do I *have* paper towel—" Miles gave a throaty chuckle. "No."

Josh frowned. "Okay, new rule: Miles doesn't host."

Essie shook her head. "*No.* He needs to take pride in his place and be a good host. The best way for him to do that–"

"There are Tupperware containers coated with fuzz in the fridge. I'm pretty sure one of them was moving," Josh interjected.

"Contain*ers*?"

"Yep."

"Do they have turquoise lids?"

"I think so? That's bluish green, right?"

She twisted her chin in Miles's direction. "*Seriously*, Miles?"

"Some of it's probably still good. I eat most of what you give me."

"How many containers are in there, Josh?"

Miles compressed his lips and shook his head forcefully behind Essie's back.

"Um, are you planning to look in the fridge?" Josh asked hesitantly.

"No, I can't deal with rotting food smells or mold. Oddly, disgusting bathrooms are okay. So? How many containers *are* there?"

Josh twisted his face. "There aren't *that* many."

She lifted her eyebrows.

"I mean, when you consider he's lived here five months?"

Essie glared back and forth between them, then nudged her way into the hallway. "Boys are gross."

Josh moved to speak, but she followed up with:

"Actually, Josh is tidy. *No*, not 'tidy.' He's clean, but he can be messy. *Messy*, I can deal with. Dirty? No."

"Are you really going to let the first issue of incompatibility keep us from being together, Essie?" Miles asked, winking at Josh.

She rolled her eyes and stormed off to the kitchen.

Three seconds later, they heard the sticky seal on the refrigerator door, followed by the door slamming, the beer bottles inside rattling.

"We're going to Josh's."

Josh winced.

"Learn to lie better, Josh," Miles said, annoyed.

"I'd actually prefer if he didn't do that," Essie said, already at the front door.

"So, who are you riding over with, Canary?" Miles asked with a heightened level of inquisitiveness as they made their way out to the parking lot in the rapidly darkening apartment complex.

Essie peered over her shoulder. "Well, I'm kind of mad at you for all the rotting food in your fridge. Some of those things I made specifically *for* you. It wasn't leftovers."

"Really? Like what?"

"The mac and cheese with the cut up hot dogs? Granted that's not exactly a culinary triumph, but I made the cheese sauce from scratch. You said that was your favorite meal growing up."

"Aw, Ess. That's sweet. I definitely ate that." He watched Essie walk determinedly toward the passenger side of Josh's truck. "Alright, I'll see you guys over there. No 'errands' on the way," he added in a low voice for just Josh to hear.

Josh rotated his chin toward him, narrowing his eyes. "Seriously, Miles?"

"You know, you both give the same angry look. Essie just flares her nostrils more."

Essie spun on her heel, glaring at him.

"See?" Miles said, pointing at her nose.

Josh quickly turned toward the driver's side, grinning.

"I saw that, Josh." She redirected her attention to Miles, taking a deep breath. "It was wrong what I said before about being angry with you—I'm not angry, just disappointed. I have higher expectations for you than this, Miles."

"But you know what I'm like, Essie."

"Exactly."

He puffed out his lower lip. "You really do see the best in me, don't you?"

"Was there food being delivered here?" Josh asked.

"Food?"

"You invited us over for dinner."

"I thought if you host, you don't cook."

Josh sighed. "But you're not hosting now, *are you*?"

"Well, darn it with your logic. I'll grab some pizzas or something and head over."

*   *   *

Miles tossed his crust to Fenway, who had become more fond of him with each scrap he threw her way throughout the course of the evening. "Essie, did you finish explaining your call sign earlier?"

She furrowed her brow.

"It really is about the coal miners cruel use of the canaries? If so, I don't get what it has to do with you."

"Not exactly," she said, suddenly hesitant about the subject.

"It's the Phoenix Initiative work, right?" Josh asked, trying to be helpful–and vague–and bring the conversation to a close.

"Oh, so if the antidote doesn't work in one of the tests? I guess I get that." Miles stood. "I'll be back. Nature calls."

"Then you're heading the wrong way. You can't be trusted in civilized facilities," Essie quipped. "Nature's *that* way."

He smiled, leaned down and kissed the top of her head. "You're cute."

She shook her head as he disappeared inside, then continued to sway the porch swing. Fenway laid beneath her with both paws wrapped around her foot.

Josh shrugged. "He's not wrong."

"Ugh, he's like the ultimate man-child. Didn't he say he wanted to date a nice girl?"

"He did."

"Well, a nice girl is going to have standards that may include that he be competent in basic life skills like cleaning."

"I kind of think his standards for said 'nice girl' are *you*."

Essie laughed to herself, shaking her head. "Well then, he's in trouble."

"You forget I walked in on you cleaning his bathroom."

"Did you not hear me lecture him?"

"No, I heard it. But I'm willing to bet you're *going* to clean out his fridge."

"I am *not*."

He lifted his brow. "I guess time will tell. But my point is, you love him despite all his shortcomings–maybe he thinks a nice girl will also cut him slack–or in your case, a *lot* of slack."

She scrunched her nose. "He should still make an effort," she grumbled.

He cleared his throat, checking to be sure Miles was still occupied in the bathroom. "Alright, so where did your call sign come from, if not from the obvious? I'm curious."

"Well, you know I can be dark about things."

He winced. "For the sake of time and argument, I'll say yes."

"Even after coal miners stopped using canaries, the phrase 'canary in a coal mine' was well-known. It was used as a reference to something that was a warning of things to come, of greater dangers or threats ahead."

He narrowed his eyes.

"I chose it because what I am is the result of some evil scientists with darker intent. Therefore, I'm a warning of what's to come."

"That's how you see yourself?"

"I was in a dark place when I chose it."

"Is that how you see yourself?"

"Kind of. In a way."

Josh pressed his lips together, took in the scenery–the bright, glowing moon illuminating the currents of the river, the shadows of pine trees that lined the water.

"*What?*"

"It just seems to me that if *you're* a 'warning' of things to come–" He shook his head. "Warning is the wrong word. You could *only* be a sign of something good."

"You're biased."

"Why? Because I *know* you?"

She gazed across at him, her silver eyes shimmering in the porch light.

Miles stepped back onto the porch, blocking the sightlines between the two of them, yawning widely. "Am I interrupting something?"

Essie sighed, leaning back on the swing. "What's *your* call sign, Miles? I don't think I ever heard it. Gunner is Gunner. Corey is Martian. Collectively, Luther calls you the Three Musketeers for some reason."

"Viper."

"*Viper?*"

"Yeah. You know, from *Top Gun?*"

"I remember Maverick and Goose."

"Viper was the instructor."

"I remember Ice Man."

"Well, I'm Viper."

"And what does the call sign mean to you?"

"I don't know. It sounds cool."

"A viper is a venomous snake, probably with quick reflexes?" she offered in a questioning tone.

He shrugged.

"Oh no," Josh said, leaning back against the swing, "you're thinking of a new call sign for him, aren't you?"

"It just doesn't *fit.*"

Miles narrowed his eyes. "No. No, no, no, no, *no.* You picked Josh's and he sounds like an 80-year-old retiree with a fishing hobby."

"If that's the case, he'd be seriously underestimated by the enemy."

Josh lifted his brow. "Another definition for 'angler' is a scheming person. You weren't very happy with me around the time you would have made up my call sign so I wasn't sure–"

"I told you. I wanted to give you a scary call sign and an anglerfish is a terrifying predator."

"So is a shark."

"Or a bear," Josh added, cheeks tightening. "Actually, you would have picked it *before* I joined MET. They used the name when they got me out of Long Beach. I don't *think* you were mad at me then."

"Fine," she said with a sigh. "I picked *Angler*. Not Angler*fish*. I chose it because when I was brainstorming, I randomly thought of going fishing with you, Gabe, and our dads. I remember standing in knee-high water beside you feeling totally content. The memory made me really happy. *That's* why I picked it."

"How many Hail Mary's do you need to say to repent for that totally unnecessary lie?"

"That's Catholicism, Miles."

"*Oh.* That's not you?"

"No, that's not me."

"Alright, fine. Name me."

Josh chuckled. "No pressure."

"Sugar," she declared, almost immediately.

"*Sugar*," Miles repeated slowly. "Alright, let's hear the justification."

"Well, you're energizing and fun, you are under-appreciated, you have underrated value, but ultimately, you're best in moderation."

He considered her explanation, not committing to a facial expression. "I'm honestly not mad about that name. The 'moderation' part stings a little. You can be mean, Esther Natale, you really can be." He nodded, glancing out toward his truck. "Well, it was nice of Gunner, Corey, and whoever else was invited to this shindig to make me the third wheel, but I should get some beauty rest. Essie, may I give you a ride home?"

Esther's attention jolted over to Josh, who smiled slightly at her. "*Actually–*"

Miles dropped his shoulders. "I was the third wheel, please don't make me be the chastity belt."

Her jaw dropped.

"Oh dear, this could be awkward. Essie, a *chastity* belt is—"

"I know what it is," she interjected. "I'm confused though. You gave me such flack for the proxy costume–implying *whatever* it is you were implying–and yet now I *need* a chastity belt?"

Josh held up his hand. "Also? Unsettling mental image."

Miles ignored him. "I didn't know you very well then."

"And now that you know me better, you've assessed that I require a chastity belt?" She winced. "Thank you for this conversation, by the way. It's not awkward at all."

"You're a good girl, Essie. Probably the best I'll ever know."

Her eyes narrowed. "I'm *flattered*?"

"But even good girls can be swayed by temptation. Now get in the truck before Josh works those green eyes."

Josh shook his head, his cheek propped up by his fist.

"His eyes are brown."

"See? It's already started. Does he already have you in his trance?"

He clapped his hands. "Essie, look at me."

"I *am* looking at you," she said, arching her eyebrow. "You're heading out then?"

Miles froze, eyes darting back and forth between them. "Wait, *are* you staying out here? *Is* she staying out here?" he demanded of Josh.

Josh nodded patiently.

"Are you two a couple?"

Josh gave a small shake of his head, blinking slowly.

"Wait, wait, wait, so–*what* is happening here?"

"Don't worry about it," she said quietly, hugging him.

"I *will* worry. I'm so confused."

"Goodnight, Miles. I'll see you tomorrow."

*　　*　　*

The first night Essie spent at the cabin had happened naturally. They were sitting on the porch swing reading together and she fell asleep, head resting on his thigh. Josh had been uncertain about waking her and suggesting they move inside–for obvious reasons, the primary being how that would sound out loud–but the chill of the night air gave him no choice but to do just that. The failure of the space heater inside then led to a brief deliberation. He anticipated she'd just head home, but when she'd struggled to keep from shivering, she'd climbed into his bed. Before he knew it, they were snuggled under the covers for warmth. It felt like one of those building moments, their limbs intertwined, but within what felt like seconds, he felt her warm breaths against his neck. They had the slow, steady rhythm that told him she was already asleep.

The morning had admittedly brought some awkwardness–for Josh, at least. It seemed far more natural for her to reach for him, to be affectionate. It was how she'd always been with him. It felt far different for him to do the same, at least given the circumstances. It felt like any move on his part might give the wrong impression, put unintended pressure on her, seem...provocative? She had slept far past the normal start of her day— and his, stirring only when the sun was high enough in the Eastern sky to shine through the horizontal windows at the top of the wall.

When she opened her eyes, blinking toward the morning light spilling into the room, he could hardly breathe; it felt like literally any movement on his part was up for interpretation.

She furrowed her brow, pulled in her breath, and buried her face in his chest. "I made you late for work, didn't I?"

"It's only 7. I don't have anyone actually scheduled for an hour."

"Really?"

"Oh, my dad is going to give me such a—*look*. I have to call him," she murmured, propping herself up on her elbow, her hair a golden disheveled mess.

"I called him last night."

"You did?"

"*Well*, you fell asleep at 8:30."

"But he's usually asleep by then," she said with a smirk. "Wait, I slept *ten and a half hours*?"

"You did."

She blinked, furrowing her brow. "I guess I'm sleeping here from now on." She rolled onto her back and whimpered. "Is this what it feels like for normal people without debilitating insomnia? You just fall asleep? Take a multi-hour mental and physical vacation?"

"Pretty much?"

"Sign me up."

"Well, hopefully it's the same experience tonight."

She took a deep breath. "I was kidding, Josh. I can't sleep out here."

"Why?"

"Well, for one thing, it's not proper, right?"

"We're *sleeping*."

"Yeah. But if people knew I was sharing a bed with you--"

"Who has to know?"

"Okay, but it's not fair to you."

He frowned. "How so?"

"It's just not—with how things—" She pinched her eyebrows together.

"Essie, you are my best friend. I would do absolutely anything for you."

"Yeah, but—"

"But nothing. You need to sleep. If sharing a bed, literally just sharing a bed, helps you sleep, then why wouldn't we?"

"Well if you're going to just make perfectly logical sense, I'm not sure I can continue this conversation."

He grinned. "How do you feel?"

"*Well*, guilty, anxious, a little bit scandalous."

"I mean after sleeping 10 ½ hours."

"Oh, I feel awesome." And then she smiled a really endearing smile--eyes creased, lips and cheeks tight, reminiscent of her at a much younger age.

Essie had managed the difficult conversation with her dad, saying the arrangement was, at least, a temporary solution to her sleep troubles. Ultimately Matteo had agreed it was reasonable, emphasizing that #1 Essie was old enough to make her own decisions about what was best for her, and #2 that it was really important to him that she get sleep.

*   *   *

They had watched Miles pull away from the cabin, still looking extremely concerned about the arrangement. Josh had felt inclined to warn her that news would spread through their small group, as Miles lacked any sense of decorum, but that felt like it would be putting pressure on her to define what was going on between them. He also considered that bringing this up would likely lead to talking about Gabe, since there was some established pretense that both he and Gabe were romantically interested in her, that they had some sort of love triangle situation. If she gave too much thought to this, it might result in the end of the arrangement, as she wouldn't want to make Gabe uncomfortable.

While it caused some anxiety, not knowing where he stood with her, he really, really loved falling asleep holding her, waking up holding her. If it ended at some point, if she decided she was looking for something else, someone else after all, he would deal with that then. For now, he wasn't going to do anything to jeopardize it.

"Is it weird?" she asked suddenly, staring toward the hidden horizon. "That I stay out here?"

"*Weird?* No."

She lifted her eyebrow, turning to face him.

"Well, I mean, I don't know anyone else with an emotional support human."

67

She rolled her eyes, allowing a small smile.

"How are you feeling during the day? Now that you're sleeping?"

"Better."

"Well, that's good enough for me."

"I don't want to disrupt *your* sleep though."

"You don't have to worry about that," he said, pulling her into a hug, noticing she was starting to stiffen with the cold. "It turns out that you're my emotional support human, too."

The silence that followed made him question everything. He regretted saying that. It was too much. It made light of the trauma that was the cause of her insomnia. He thought of explaining that he slept better with her there, but that wasn't actually true. He woke repeatedly throughout the night, something he'd never had trouble with before. He'd wake worried he was inadvertently stealing covers, that his hand placement was inappropriate, that he'd accidentally shoved her off the bed. Several times he'd woken up just to check to be sure she was actually there.

"Is that why you stroke my hair? Do I possess the quiet, supportive presence of a Golden Retriever?"

He tightened his arms.

"Are you *laughing*? Are you trying not to let me see that you're laughing?" she said, struggling to loosen herself from his hold.

He kissed her on the top of the head and took a step away, aiming himself toward the cabin door.

"What's so funny?"

"You called yourself a Golden Retriever. That's really cute, Ess."

She narrowed her eyes, her mouth slanted into an amused smile, her freckles prominent across the bridge of her nose.

"Too bad it's too many syllables for a call sign."

She laughed. "Think I should use it as my Fight Club name?"

He pursed his lips. She'd recently started going back to the gym to do mixed martial arts training, saying that it was a good release for her pent-up anxiety. "'Next in the ring is the one, the only, the incomparable and unconquerable *Golden Retrieverrrrrr*,'" he bellowed in his best announcer voice, presenting her to the invisible crowd as he swung open the screen door.

"I know you're sort of mocking me, but I'm totally going to hear that the next time I enter the ring. And you know what?" she said, accepting his invitation to lead the way inside. "It's gonna pump me up."

"*Yeah,* it will."

She twirled around as he shut the front door, an old, shabby wooden thing cut slightly too large for the frame. It tended to groan loudly as it scraped against the floor–he'd been meaning to sand it down. Their eyes met just as he turned the lock. For some reason, the act of simply locking the door felt incredibly intimate. He imagined her moving forward and crashing into him, doing her best to clobber him, get a wrestling advantage. What started off as playfulness would quickly evolve to something else entirely. Or maybe she'd simply throw herself at him in a non-wrestling, very not platonic manner.

His heart beat heavily in his chest, the tension building.

She didn't leap toward him, as he imagined she might. Just the opposite. She approached him slowly, like a predator tracking her prey. As she closed the distance, he realized her eyes were not fixed on his. There was a nearly imperceptible jumpiness to her pupils, but her attention was focused on his neck, just below his ear.

She shook her head slightly. "Don't move."

"What is it?"

She stepped around him, opened the creaky front door again, and propped open the screen door. "Now step slowly back on the porch," she coaxed in a soothing tone.

He did as she said, narrowing his eyes. "This better not be a prank."

Esie tugged the screen door closed behind them, making sure Fenway stayed inside. She lifted her hand, holding her thumb, index and middle fingers close together as though loosely holding a chopstick, her eyes fixed on the same spot beneath his ear. "Don't flinch when I do this," she warned, briefly meeting his eye.

"*Okay.*"

She changed her approach at the last second, choosing a scoop instead of a pinch to remove, presumably a bug, from his skin, closing her opposite palm over the top of it. She had made a move toward the porch railing, cocooning the creature in her hands, seemingly intending to set it free, but she stopped abruptly, muttering as she flicked it to the porch floor and proceeded to stomp on it repeatedly with her boot until it was a splatter on the wood plank.

He burst out laughing. "What was *that*?"

"A blister beetle, I think?"

"Were you really going to set it free?"

"Well, it hadn't done anything at that point," she whimpered, examining her hand.

"You really *are* a Golden Retriever, aren't you?"

She puffed out her lower lip.

He descended upon her, finding a bubbled red sac already formed into the folds of her palm. "Why did you touch it?"

"Because it was sitting on your *neck*. I was afraid it was going to excrete its nasty little toxins." She looked up, cocked her head to one side. The way her golden brown hair flopped about made him grin. "Is your neck okay?" she asked.

"Yeah, I'm fine. Are you seeing your hand right now though?"

"Yeah, this is gross."

"Let's wash your hand and then I'll wrap it. Does it hurt?"

"Relatively speaking, it's nothing."

"Well that's not saying much."

"Will you grab something to wash off the porch first? I don't want Fenway licking at it."

Josh was silently appreciative for her expansive knowledge of a wide variety of subjects, including beetles. It wasn't a surprise really. There'd been incidents in the region where dead blister beetles wound up in hay and the cantharidin toxin wound up killing the horses and livestock who ate it. He knew she was an absolute stickler for inspecting hay before she fed the animals.

He reached for the glass of amber-colored liquid Miles had left behind. "That's weird. Miles isn't usually wasteful with liquor."

"I'm trying to get him to quit–or at least cut back."

He recalled her first attempt to encourage Miles to consume less alcohol: at the campsite on the way back to the Ark, she'd literally downed the rest of the bottle of–whatever it was they were passing around– knowing full well that alcohol had no effect on her; she just didn't want him to drink it. When Miles found out about her tactic, he had likened her to Elizabeth Swann burning up all of Captain Jack Sparrow's rum.

Josh held up the glass to better inspect the level of the liquid; it looked like Miles hadn't touched it, the melting of the ice causing a dilution of the color on the top. He dumped the liquid over the splattered insect, thinking the alcohol would have some nullifying effect on the poison. "We'll keep Fenway inside; I'll do a better job cleaning it up tomorrow."

"Montana has some really crazy insects. No wonder they don't advertise them."

7

candidate

*You are cordially invited to a charity fundraiser celebrating the
Leadership of the Ark Council and its prestigious members.*

*Saturday, July 18th
6pm-12am
formal attire*

Luther leaned back in the task chair, rubbing at his eyes, surveying
his desk covered with maps and strategy notes, things he once termed "war
plans." It felt foolish now, like a game of self-important make-believe.
None of it mattered anymore. Whereas before, the politicians, the officials
praised his name, once they'd positioned themselves advantageously, they
began to question his motivations, they accused him of being guilty of all
he'd been working against.

A chime on the computer alerted him that Annette had signed on.

SecureChat Session-user3892cc7hu1192

How are you?

Fine. What's this I hear about showboating non-elected officials?

I'm not sure what the fundraising is for exactly.

That's actually pretty obvious. It's for their pocketbooks. Can take the politicians out of the District, but can't take the District out of the politicians.

Unfortunately, that seems to be true.

I get the feeling they're wavering about their red line stance.

That's my impression.

There will never be another opportunity like this. You realize that, right? If we lose, that's it. Things will get so much worse. We'll lose everything.

I know.

*If not for you, none of this
would have happened.*

*I mean that in a positive way.
We wouldn't have gotten this
far.*

*You should get to see this
through.*

*Change their minds. There's
no going back.*

I don't think I have clout in the
Arks these days.

*If not for you, the Arks
wouldn't exist. If not for you,
most of the people at the Arks
wouldn't be at the Arks. If not
for you most of the people
would be dead. How can you
possibly doubt your value?*

*Step up and be a leader. Use
your words, your passion, your
authenticity.*

*The same way you built the
Arks.*

People were afraid then.

They should still be afraid.
Now more than ever.

Just so you know, they should
be questioning you. Where
you got the pathogens, how you
developed the antidote. This is
groundbreaking, mind
boggling stuff that's never
been done with anything close
to this success. They have a
right to ask questions about it,
but you're taking it
personally.

Well they're making personal
accusations.

Yeah. And?
Are you guilty of any of the
accusations?

...

The answer is no. No, you're
not.

Whether I'm guilty or not
doesn't seem to matter much.

They're putting your feet to
the fire hoping you'll do
exactly what you're doing.
Just so you know.

*They're intimidated by you
and they should be. They
know you should be leading
them, not the other way
around.*

I'm not a leader.

Yes, you are.

*Most of us have to invent an
origin story to compel people to
trust us—you have the story,
people should trust you.*

*Tell your story. Throw your
name in the ring. For all
you've done, people don't
know your name, but they
should.*

*Good people don't go into
government.
Right? That's why we ended
up here.
Let's see what happens if they
do.*

You're a good person.

Are you sure about that?

What I supported, what I helped fund, what I advocated for, destroyed millions of lives. I supported things that set humanity back, not forward.

If it weren't for you, there wouldn't be an Evin. Without Evin, none of this would have happened.

Everything she's done has been her own doing. I can't take any credit for her.

I know this wasn't what we planned for you.

I don't want that plan anymore. I'm not the leader we need.

I went into politics for all the wrong reasons, mainly for the money, the power, because I had something to prove.

I'm where I am now for one purpose.

What's that?

You said you couldn't figure out someone close enough to Creature. Well, now you do.

That's why you're there?

Just so you know, if you let these schmucks destroy our chances, I'll still carry out my end, but what is it they say happens if you cut the head off a snake? Isn't there something in the Bible about it?

Greek mythology. Hydra.

Ah.

I know what you're saying though. Two heads will take its place.

There will be no reconciliation of the country.

Will you be able to live with yourself knowing you could have done more?

*   *   *

<u>*In the Loop w/ Christopher Loop: Conspiracy Realists*</u>

"I remember as a youth associating the idea of conspiracy theorists with that homeless person on the street corner covered in filth wearing a tin foil hat, ranting and raving about the government spying on its people, about people going missing, 'what about the children?!' So easily we wrote her off, but the older I get, the more I think, you know, Bitzy may not have been so crazy after all.

"Being called a conspiracy theorist now should almost be taken as being synonymous with being told you have common sense. It can almost be an occupation title. Imagine the job posting: Company seeking individual with basic observation skills. Must have elementary knowledge of biology and math.

"Think about it. There have been people getting degrees in gender ideology–literally making shit up with no basis in anything but feelings. Honestly, I'd rather hear Bitzy's theories on who killed JFK. Even JFK, Jr., though that one's a little more obvious, isn't it? I'd like to hear her thoughts about Epstein's Island, how he wound up dead, how his associate who trafficked young girls to be assaulted by royalty, celebrities, politicians, received probation, while Martha Stewart went to prison.

"Let's put a team together of big thinkers who ideally excel at puzzles and chess, to come up with theories of what the government and the dark forces of the world–and I purposely group those two together–are trying to do. *To Catch a Killer*, am I right?

"Now, when Gowon was 'elected' President, we were told he was the most popular candidate *ever*. Do you think someone actually thought we'd believe that?

"Let's consider Samuel Gowon's first address to the nation:

"Subjects of this great nation, I stand before you today not as a mere ruler–"

The video switched from the speech footage to Christopher Loop sitting in his studio, leaning forward over his desk. Christopher narrowed his eyes, staring at the camera. Slowly, he shook his head. "Roll the rest of it."

"--but as a visionary leader who is ready to guide us into a new era of prosperity and security. I understand that some of you may have concerns about certain measures I am proposing, which might seem like giving up personal freedoms. But let me assure you, these sacrifices are necessary for the greater good and the strength of our beloved nation."

"This is like a socialist buzzword Bingo game, but here's a gigantic spoiler: Any 'leader' who uses the phrase 'greater good' is not thinking of anybody's 'good' except their own."

"As a leader, my primary duty is to ensure the safety and well-being of the nation. In times of uncertainty and external threats, tough decisions must be made. We find ourselves facing challenges that demand swift action and unity, and that requires putting aside personal interests for the collective welfare."

Christopher frowned. "Does the 2020 Coronavirus ring a bell? Yeah. It should. Those who don't learn from the past are doomed to repeat it. Well, enough people didn't learn so we repeated history and things became much, much worse." He nodded and Gowon's speech continued:

"Imagine a nation where every citizen can walk the streets without fear, where we can sleep soundly, and where prosperity reaches every corner of our land. Such a vision can only be realized when we come together as one, willing to make sacrifices for the greater good.

"Yes, there will be changes, and some of you may feel that your individual liberties are being constrained. But remember, true freedom lies in the stability and order that our actions will bring. Without discipline and control, chaos reigns, and freedom becomes an illusion, a fleeting dream shattered by the harsh realities of a disordered world.

"I must stress that this is not a power grab, nor is it about subjugating our people. On the contrary, these measures are meant to empower our nation to stand tall against those who would seek to harm us. By giving up certain personal freedoms, we are protecting the freedom of our nation as a whole.

"We live in a time when threats can come from anywhere, and we must be prepared to face them with unwavering determination. To do so, we need a strong, centralized authority capable of making swift decisions, *unburdened by the constraints of individual freedoms that could hinder progress.*

"Throughout history, leaders have risen to meet the challenges of their times, making tough decisions to safeguard their people. And while I understand that change can be uncomfortable, I implore you to trust in my vision and the path I have chosen. For it is through unity and collective sacrifice that we will forge a powerful and prosperous nation that will endure for generations to come.

"Let our nation rise above individual desires and embrace the greater cause—the cause of a safe, prosperous, and powerful nation. Together, we shall weather any storm and emerge stronger than ever before. Let history remember us as the generation that made the tough choices, not for personal gain, but for the love of our nation. United, we will triumph. Thank you, and may our nation flourish under our resolute leadership."

Christopher stared blankly at the camera. "This is the most popular President in the history of our country? Now, let's switch gears and talk about his Lady MacBeth–"

Annette lifted her chin, eyes wide.

"--Former Speaker of the House, current Vice President and First Lady Annette Gibbons, or as dictated by the hostile woke takeover, First Partner. She really took the public arena by storm didn't she? Running against the man who allegedly assaulted her, rising to power quickly, undergoing artificial insemination to have the authority to talk about working guardians, formerly known as mothers. She went into labor in a very public manner, and alleges the baby died due to complications with her pregnancy. This event served as a springboard for her to then advocate for artificial wombs, abortion. Seems legit.

"Now, Annette Gibbons did not ride up from poverty. She was actually raised by an upper middle-class *conservative* family. Yes, that's right. The author of the 'actuallyIdo' hashtag, who said a warehouse filled with artificial wombs was a better environment for a preborn baby, was raised in a conservative household. Now, this wasn't filthy rich money. Nothing like what she's come into working for the Left. She rejected her family's money and their politics when she left home, didn't have a dollar to her name. Just debt. Current net worth? $2 billion. That doesn't just happen, does it?

"I referred to her as Lady MacBeth. Who was the Shakespearean character? Well, she used manipulation to convince her husband to kill the king to seize power so that she could revel in the power along with him. She's considered *more* evil than her husband–

"Spoiler: It's nearly impossible to be more evil and cunning that the person who has murdered more people than Ze-Dong Mao, Hitler, Leopold II, Stalin, Tojo combined—in fact, he's killed more people than the #2 through 20 genocidal maniacs in history *combined*. I don't think the country could take if Gibbons was equally evil. *That* said–she has more than her fair share of skeletons in her closet. With a net worth of $2 billion? How could she not?"

Annette turned off the television and stepped out onto the dark balcony. She sat herself in the patio chair overlooking the Ginsburg Monument, the federal buildings in the distance. The border of the District was very distinct and since the establishment of the Arks, heavily guarded, an impenetrable border wall that was constructed overnight. Samuel had spoken about it at press conferences without any sense of irony. In a private moment of candor afterward, he shook his head and joked that he was grateful Donald Trump wasn't around to mock him.

The District was a bustling place that had never known rolling blackouts or energy conservation restrictions that limited when and how people could leave their homes. There were shortages of nothing, at least prior to December.

The areas outside the border of the District were another story, faced with rapid deterioration. Once prosperous suburbs were left half-empty by the mass exodus of people to the Arks, as well as the latest depopulation vaccine. The homes, neighborhoods, strip malls, schools left behind were being taken over by the homeless and those who were looking to upgrade their living accommodations. Crime had skyrocketed. Most businesses were shuttered.

Samuel had talked about the fallacy of the overpopulation claims. It was another gimmick, another way to divide the country. People villainized those who chose to have children as not caring about the future of the world, claiming there wouldn't be enough oxygen, not enough land, not enough trees. He cited studies that had been erased from public record that concluded that there was more than enough land, that each person or family could be provided twice the amount of land needed to grow food to sustain them and it would only use up the land mass of one continent.

When she asked why he supported the effort, he shrugged and simply said: "You have to choose your battles." It was something he had regretted, though he'd never admit it.

There had been over 70 million doses of the vaccine dispensed. Effects took place immediately with the body reaching active death stages within about 30 minutes. Most bodies were cremated in mass or piled onto cattle train cars to be shipped to landfills well outside city limits.

There had been no reason to track the bodies after the individual received the injection.

That was part of the strategy, to have the government underestimate the strength of the Arks by tens of millions of people.

Annette peered over her shoulder to the blank television monitor, considering her earlier conversation with Luther. She tightened her jaw.

8

others

Miles adjusted the knot of his tie as he walked into the church lobby. He shook the hand of Isaac, one of the associate pastors greeting people at the entrance, his movements stiff. The pastor, a red-haired man in his mid-thirties was actively trying to engage him in conversation, but Miles appeared far from his typical confident self.

Over at the hospitality table, Josh filled his stainless steel travel mug. He was just dumping a packet of sugar into his black coffee to cover the burnt flavor of the grounds when he saw Essie emerge from the door that led to the Sunday School classrooms. She was wearing a flowing floral dress with a belted waist, along with her favorite pair of cowboy boots, her golden hair loose in waves.

The pastor speaking to Miles waved to her and she moved quickly toward them. Miles had just turned in her direction, his hands dropped uncomfortably at his sides when Essie crashed into him, throwing her arms around his neck.

A smile expanded across Miles's face as he closed his arms around her.

Distracted by a young couple just walking into the church, Isaac let them be.

When Essie took a step back, Miles began fidgeting with his tie again. She shook her head, swatted at his hand, and moved to touch his very shiny, combed hair, which startled him quite a bit, though based upon the amount of product, it was more likely the hair would cause harm to Essie rather than the other way around. It looked like something that might snap on the top of a Lego minifigure. She approached Miles cautiously with a flat palm, like how one might approach a skittish animal, and lightly made contact with his hair.

Miles glanced around at his surroundings; the lobby scarcely occupied as most had already gone into the sanctuary. He looked increasingly uneasy again–

And then Essie placed her hand on his cheek and spoke softly to him.

He pursed his lips, nodding in response to what she was telling him, his body visibly relaxing. His eyes lifted as Josh approached.

"Looking sharp, Miles."

"And why do *you* get to look like a country bumpkin?" Miles demanded.

Josh nearly choked on his coffee, rotating his chin to Essie. "Do I look like a country bumpkin?" he asked quietly.

Essie turned on her heel and took in his outfit, which consisted of dark wash jeans, his standard cowboy boots, and a dark button up with rolled sleeves. She pressed her lips together, her cheeks reddening. "You both look very handsome."

Miles scoffed. "Oh *please*, he's not even wearing a tie."

"You're right," she said, clearing her throat. "He's *not* wearing a tie." Her cheeks pinched upward.

Miles glared in disgust, his attention shifting between the two of them. "Get a room," he muttered. "Oh, *wait.*"

Essie was startled at his remark, glancing toward the sanctuary where the worship band was starting the next song.

"Hey, I was *teasing*," he said, nudging her.

She nodded, but her mind was clearly elsewhere.

"We should probably go in," Josh suggested. "Do you want a coffee, Miles?"

"No, I'm edgy enough. Clearly."

Josh lifted an eyebrow. "Ess? Milk and sugar with a splash of coffee?"

Her cheeks tensed. "Yes, please." She grabbed Miles's hand, resetting herself, visibly expelling whatever thoughts had taken over her mind. "I'm happy you're here, Miles."

"Yeah, only *you* could get me to come to church."

Essie lifted her eyes to Josh, pressing her lips together. "We'll save you a seat," she said, taking a step toward the sanctuary.

*   *   *

The congregation had just completed their greeting of one another after the close of the first worship song. Miles turtled his shoulders and rigidly shook the hands of those in the pews in front of and behind them. He nodded nervously down their pew. To his right were Essie and Thomas. To his left were Josh, Gunner, Gabe, Corey and Renee, who had just slipped into the pew after the first set of worship songs.

Miles's hand lifted to check his tie.

Essie was exchanging a handshake with Thomas, who didn't appear keen to greet anyone else. She placed her palm gently on his back as she said something quietly in his ear, then resumed an upright position.

A moment later, Thomas tapped Essie on the arm, made purposeful eye contact, and smiled. "Thank you, E."

"What are you thanking me for, T?" she asked, her lips tight.

Thomas narrowed his eyes. "Don't call me that."

The way he said it made Miles immediately forget his own nerves; he had never heard anyone speak to Essie so gruffly.

Essie furrowed her brow. "*Oh*, I was just saying it to be–"

"I *know* why you were saying it, but it makes it sound like you're trying to be hip and cool. You're *neither* of those things."

Her bottom lip protruded as she turned toward Miles.

"Hate to break it to you, but if you're not hip or cool at 20, you'll never be hip or cool," he whispered.

"Thanks, Miles. Very helpful." She glanced over her shoulder at Thomas, who had occupied himself with the weekly bulletin.

Miles could see it wasn't the remark so much that bothered her, but the tone, the dismissiveness. She'd mentioned Thomas before, telling him how he had been a part of the Children's Ministry that she'd led at her old church, that he had a particularly challenging way of communicating at times that put a lot of people off. She'd also implied that she wasn't typically affected by it. Watching her reaction, Miles could tell he was witnessing an exception to that, as she pressed her lips together, furrowed her brow, clearly suppressing some emotion.

Miles reached for her hand and gave it a light squeeze. "Being hip and cool is highly overrated," he whispered. "I'd rather be whatever word they have for someone like you."

The corners of her mouth slowly lifted. "Thanks, Miles."

He nodded, feeling a sense of pride for putting a smile on her face.

"Of course that would mean more coming from someone with first-hand experience of being hip and cool."

His jaw fell open and he actively suppressed a grin. "*Obviously*, but beggars can't be choosers."

She smirked.

"No wonder your dad calls you a turd."

"What's wrong?" Josh asked, leaning toward them.

"Essie's having a mid-life crisis."

"*Hey*," he said, pointing at her sternly. "Pull it together. You have 30 years before that's supposed to happen."

She took a steadying breath, smiling. "I'm fine."

"*Yeah*, you are," Miles murmured.

She elbowed him lightly in the ribs.

"E, why isn't your dad giving the sermon?" Thomas asked in an agitated tone, suddenly tugging on her opposite arm.

Essie turned forward and watched a young man, no older than her, securing his microphone around his ear as he bounded up to the altar. He had a creamy complexion, an easy, lopsided smile, and a voluminous spiked haircut that seemed to be defying the laws of gravity.

"Good morning, everyone," he greeted, holding his hand over his earpiece. He winced, adjusted his volume. "Is that better?" he asked in a softer voice.

There were a few affirmative responses.

"Let me try that again: Good morning, everyone."

"Good morning," the congregation responded.

"That's better. Alright, well I'm sure you're wondering who the *extremely* attractive young man is standing at the front of the church."

There were some light chuckles throughout the congregation.

"Well, you should know by now. *That's* the incredibly talented and charismatic Pastor Matteo Natale," he said, turning on his heel and motioning to Teo, who froze momentarily, his eyes wide as he carefully placed his guitar on its stand.

There were a few nervous hoots, then Luke released a cat call whistle.

"Miss, you are in *church*–" the pastor scolded, squinting his eyes toward the pews, half-heartedly searching for the source of the whistle.

Teo's cheeks tightened as he filed out from behind the music stands, following the bass guitarist, who had tattoo sleeves, always wore a top hat, and prior to the government commandeering the healthcare system, was one of the most renowned neurosurgeons in the world.

"Actually, if you wouldn't mind pausing here, Pastor?"

Matteo pressed his lips together into a smile, raising his thick eyebrows as he joined the young man in front of the altar.

"I just want to take a moment to acknowledge the tremendous impact *this* man is having on the community. This has been an unprecedented time and Pastor Matteo has risen to the challenge, building an incredible church here with the life groups, the prayer teams, really creating a family, a support for everyone in this community. I don't live around here, but I've heard about Pastor Matteo and I can tell you that in other towns, they are hoping to create even a little bit of what this man has managed here. I hope you all realize how blessed you are to have this man as your pastor, talking the walk, walking the talk, and really living the way of Jesus. Can I get an Amen?"

"Amen!" Thomas shouted, along with several others.

"That was weak. Amen on 3. One, two, three–"

"AMEN!" The congregation bellowed at once.

The man shook Matteo's hand, patted him on the shoulder, and finally let him take a seat in the front pew.

"It's about time he gets recognition," Luke said, not terribly discreetly from a few rows back.

Essie had her hand braced over her mouth. She sat more upright watching her dad situate himself in the front pew, settling her hand back in her lap. Her eyes did a brief scan of the right-hand side of the church, finally pausing on a man in the second to last pew. He had a soft, almond complexion, a wide-set rounded nose and hooded brown eyes, a scar across his chin. It wasn't strange to see Luther, as he and her dad had become close friends, but it was unusual for him to make an appearance in disguise, in this case as Frank King with the help of the facial overlay.

Essie had used the technology herself during her trek into Denver to retrieve Gabe, registering for medical services under the identity of Emily Seger, a young woman who had died during one of the church attacks in Colorado, as well as Juliet Boggs, who was beaten and raped in front of her parents as punishment for their unflattering publications about the government, and Natalie Burgess, a 20-year-old girl who a medical "ethics" board determined did not qualify for a heart transplant, despite a compatible match being available. Facing the threat of her family members' government assistance being taken away, Natalie opted for medicated suicide.

Essie didn't know who Frank King had been; Luther had been evasive about answering her questions, but he had been a very handsome, gentle-looking man in his mid-forties.

When Frank met her gaze, it was Luther's eyes looking back at her. He gave her a light smile, which she returned before turning back around.

"Is that who I think it is?" Josh whispered, leaning behind Miles.

She gave a light nod, lifting her eyes to the young man at the altar, who was talking about how thankful he was to be joining them, that his home was in a city, though he didn't specify which one. He complimented the open lands in the area, the mountains, the lakes. "And I understand you have glaciers not very far away from here? That's just amazing.

"Anyway, by now you're probably wondering who the far *less* attractive young man is standing where Pastor Matteo should be?" He paused. "No whistle for me? That's hurtful."

The congregation laughed and Luke released a sharp whistle.

"Ah, there we go. I'll take it, even though it's a pity whistle. Well, my name is Timothy Hesch. I am a youth leader and formerly, I was a surplus frozen embryo donated for scientific research." He paused again. "That's a real conversation starter right there, huh? Yes, I was actually grown in an artificial womb in a human factory warehouse. I sort of envision something like Costco, but sinister. No giant packages of comfort plus toilet paper, thirty-pound cans of nacho cheese, reasonably priced clothing, or food samples there."

There were a few uncomfortable chuckles.

He motioned to a middle-aged man a few rows back. "I'm very distractible, Sir, I apologize. To his wife, he's like: 'Why is he talking about Costco?'" He furrowed his brow. "Yeah, I've heard about that hot dog combo." He nodded. "A buck fifty." Timothy laughed to himself. "Where was I?' Yes. As I was saying, as a wee embryo, I was placed in the candidate pool for a research project that PETA would have shut down immediately had the researchers been using adorable little Pugledoodles or whatnot instead of children.

"When I was in the third-trimester lab, which was basically a giant room lined with glowing orbs containing babies–yeah, Sir, now I'm understanding how my Costco comparison was in poor taste." He lifted his eyes. "Let's take a second, actually, to acknowledge the horror of this." He glanced around. "Human babies being grown in a lab. Rows of them. Really a terrifying mental image."

Josh glanced across to Essie, who was sitting rigidly between Miles and Thomas, taking very shallow breaths. He reached for her coffee cup, which had gone slack in her hand. She startled, as though waking and looked over at him, her eyes unblinking. He desperately wanted to put his arm around her.

It would cause too much commotion with Miles in between them, trying to get him to discreetly change spots. She wouldn't want to draw unnecessary attention.

And then, as though he'd read his mind, Miles slid his arm along the top of the pew behind Essie's neck, resting his hand next to her shoulder. He twitched his fingers at the loose strands of her hair near her ear with his fingertips briefly, just until he'd gotten her attention.

Josh couldn't tell what expression was on Miles's face as she looked at him, but he could see her breaths deepen, and though she still had some tension in her jaw, her posture visibly relaxed.

"I was rejected from being included in the experiment data due to having the markers for Down Syndrome. The nuchal translucency test indicated I had abnormal amounts of fluid in my neck and was doomed to have this condition that would make basic tasks, communication, functioning really challenging. If I was being grown the old-fashioned way, they would have advised my mother to terminate the pregnancy. In the situation I was in, had there not been money to be made, they probably would have literally pulled my plug, but since they had the opportunity to sell me to another lab for experiments or for parts, they graciously allowed me to live—for a while.

"Lucky for me, God had other plans other than a sinister government lab, and by His grace and through the work of a *true* guardian angel, I was saved from that situation and put in the custody of my adoptive parents."

Essie peered over her shoulder.

Timothy paced along the altar, lifted the microphone closer to his mouth. "You can give that an Amen if you'd like."

"Amen," the congregation said in unison.

"Now, I'm not supposed to mention him by name and he made me promise not to spend time talking about him, but how many of you know of a man by the name of Luther Graham?"

About one-third of the congregation raised their hands.

Essie remained still.

"That's actually more than I expected. Everyone knows the bad players in the situation we find ourselves, with the Arks versus the U.S. Government? There are many individuals responsible for the Arks, but none of them are owed more gratitude than Luther Graham. He's the person who literally made all of this possible, facilitated resources, coordinated a strategy, as well as arranged transportation from all around the country to the three Ark locations for pretty much everyone who wasn't already residing in those areas. If that weren't enough, he's a doctor and helped develop what is being hailed as a one-size-fits-all vaccine for just about any disease, any ailment you could imagine. If not for him, most of us would not be here, probably not be alive."

This seemed to be new information for many. Several people scanned the pews around them, uncertain about what Luther Graham looked like, wondering if he might be asked to stand to get recognition.

"Many on what I'll call, 'our side' knew about the labs, knew about the babies. Believers in Christ. They knew. Doctors, scientists, government officials–they saw what was happening and did nothing. Now I get feeling uncertain, scared, but I also know that God calls upon his people to be brave, to be steadfast, to stand up for those who cannot stand up for themselves. And that's exactly what Luther did.

"Luther was a medical student when he happened upon the government-funded baby mill. Renowned medical schools were providing academic credit in exchange for students working in the research labs and performing experiments on preborn babies. That's not what was advertised in the brochure or in the course catalog, I'm sure. But suddenly Luther found himself in that lab, in that warehouse full of glowing orbs containing nearly fully developed babies, babies that were going to live very, very short, horrific lives. He could have run away; I wouldn't have blamed him for doing that. What was he supposed to do? He was just a kid trying to make his way. He didn't come from monetary wealth; he didn't have the resources to do anything. Right?" Timothy paused, taking a reflective breath. "You know, sometimes it feels like God leads us to situations that are just too much for us to handle. It's frustrating, Man. It's like, why did You lead me here when I can't do anything?" He lifted his brow. "Does God make mistakes?"

"No," came a murmur from the congregation.

Timothy held his hand to his ear. "Does God make mistakes?"

"*No.*"

"No. God doesn't make mistakes. God led him to that lab. God meant for Luther Graham to step into that lab."

Essie's nose twitched, her shoulders rising and falling more overtly.

"God does that. He puts us into situations with the opportunity to do something meaningful, life-affirming, life-changing, and in this case, lifesaving. He's like: You want to do something meaningful with your life? This is what I need you to do. He leads us there, but the rest is up to us. We don't *have* to take that opportunity. We don't *have* to rise to the occasion. But I wouldn't be standing here today, I wouldn't be alive today if Luther hadn't done just that. He chose to be brave.

"This scared kid who had to fight for everything he had in life–God put a different path at his feet–and y'all, it wasn't some pleasant, paved path. If you were in the forest, this would be like the dark, foreboding, overgrown path filled with every manner of demon along the way. No one in their right mind would choose that path. But Luther did. Luther trusted in God, he looked at that path, knowing that whatever lay ahead on that path was going to test him. It would test his faith. It would push him to his absolute limits. It might even kill him." He took a deep breath. "Does everyone realize that no matter what happens to us here on this earth, whatever suffering, heartache we endure, at the end of our path, is Jesus Christ? Is life everlasting, eternal life in Heaven. That's what awaits us. No matter what we choose to do, as long as we have our faith in our

Lord, Jesus Christ, we get to live forever in a place without suffering, without fear. So I invite every one of you–be bold in your faith, in your life. Maybe you feel God through the work of the Holy Spirit calling on you to do more. Listen. God has a purpose for you and you might say, Timothy, I'm scared. I don't know what's on the path that God is calling on me to take.

"To that, I say this: You know where it ultimately leads. And do you know what phrase is repeated 365 times in the Bible? Come on now, what's the phrase?"

"Do not be afraid," Thomas shouted.

"Well, Sir, I like your enthusiasm," Timothy said, smiling widely. "And you're absolutely right. Do. Not. Be. Afraid.

"I'm going to do rapid fire here with some Bible verses:

"'Deuteronomy 31:6: Be strong and courageous. Do not be afraid or terrified because of them, for the LORD your God goes with you; he will never leave you nor forsake you.'

"'Psalm 34:4–5: I sought the Lord, and he answered me and delivered me from all my fears. Those who look to Him are radiant, and their faces shall never be ashamed.'

'Psalm 23:4: Even though I walk through the valley of the shadow of death, I will fear no evil, for you are with me; your rod and your staff, they comfort me.'

"Who doesn't love Psalms?" He continued on, standing alone at the front of the church without a Bible in his hands or any notes to help remember the words. "'Psalm 27:1: The Lord is my light and my salvation; whom shall I fear? The Lord is the stronghold of my life; of whom shall I be afraid?'

"'Psalm 46:1–3: God is our refuge and strength, a very present help in trouble. Therefore we will not fear though the earth gives way, though the mountains be moved into the heart of the sea, though its waters roar and foam, though the mountains tremble at its swelling.'

"'Isaiah 41:13: For I, the LORD your God, hold your right hand; it is I who say to you, "Fear not, I am the one who helps you.'

94

"Back to Psalms. 'Psalm 91:4–5: He will cover you with his pinions, and under his wings you will find refuge; his faithfulness is a shield and buckler. You will not fear the terror of the night, nor the arrow that flies by day.'

"'Deuteronomy 3:22: You shall not fear them, for it is the LORD your God who fights for you.'

"'Joshua 8:1: And the LORD said to Joshua, 'Do not fear and do not be dismayed. Take all the fighting men with you, and arise, go up to Ai. See, I have given into your hand the king of Ai, and his people, his city, and his land.'

"'Isaiah 35:4: 'Say to those who have an anxious heart, 'Be strong; fear not! Behold, your God will come with vengeance, with the recompense of God. He will come and save you.'

"'Isaiah 41:10: Fear not, for I am with you; be not dismayed, for I am your God; I will strengthen you, I will help you, I will uphold you with my righteous right hand.'

"I'll repeat for the ones in the back: 'Fear not, for I am with you; be not dismayed, for I am your God; I will strengthen you, I will help you, I will uphold you with my righteous right hand.'

"'Jeremiah' *was a bullfrog,*" he sang suddenly and dramatically to surprised laughter, then continued, speaking quickly: "Jeremiah 42:11: 'Do not fear the king of Babylon, of whom you are afraid. Do not fear him, declares the LORD, for I am with you, to save you and to deliver you from his hand.'

"'Matthew 10:26: 'So have no fear of them, for nothing is covered that will not be revealed, or hidden that will not be known.'

"'2 Timothy 1:7,' shameless plug, '...for God gave us a spirit not of fear but of power and love and self-control.'

"'Hebrews 13:6: So we can confidently say, 'The Lord is my helper; I will not fear; what can man do to me?'

"'Isaiah 43:1-2: Fear not, for I have redeemed you; I have summoned you by name; you are mine. When you pass through the waters, I will be with you; and when you pass through the rivers, they will not sweep over you. When you walk through the fire, you will not be burned; and the flames will not set you ablaze.'

"Can I get an 'Amen, Hallelujah?'"

"Amen, Hallelujah," the congregation called back.

The Worship Band began to play, though Josh hadn't paid any attention to them getting situated behind Timothy.

"Praise God. Thank you for having me. Have a blessed day, a blessed week. Why don't you rise to your feet and we'll lift our hands and our voices to praise our Lord and Savior?"

*   *   *

Danny took in the sight of Esther being trailed by Josh, Miles, Gunner, and a late-arriving Gabe, grinning. "You have quite the entourage of young men, Essie."

She glanced over her shoulder. "That's my security detail."

He smiled at her, nodding approvingly.

"I actually think they have potential as a rock band–don't they kind of have that look?"

Danny did not look convinced.

"A rock band?" Miles asked, furrowing his brow.

"Yeah, you all are the rock band and I'm like the–"

"*Oh*, Essie–" Miles remarked with a sad shake of his head.

"What?"

"First a proxy, now a groupie," he said, giving her a wink.

"I wasn't going to say 'groupie.' *Manager.* I'd be your *manager.*" She twisted her expression in exasperation.

"Actually that tracks. You'd be good at keeping us in line," Miles agreed. "Except you're the talent in our little group based upon what Josh has said—I got a little preview of it on the drive back to the Ark. The singing, not your potential as a proxy costume model."

"Miles? *Really*?" she sighed, watching the group of men dissipate. Gunner and Gabe drifted toward the hospitality counter, despite the fact their plan had been to go get breakfast, while Josh had been pulled into conversation about a herd of buffalo, which honestly, she was pretty interested to learn more about.

Danny smirked. "I thought the brief stint as a *proxy* would just be between me, you, Gabe, and the Big Guy," he said, eyes shooting toward the wood beams in the rafters.

"Yeah, well, it wasn't my decision to share it."

"Forget-Me-Not over-shared," Miles explained, helpfully.

She narrowed her eyes. "Stop calling him names, Miles. It's not funny."

He nudged her arm and shook his head in sadness. "She promised to model the costume for us and then never did."

She rolled her eyes.

"*Oh*. Well, if you're okay showing them, I could get you a still frame image from the security footage." Danny frowned questioningly.

Miles's eyes lit up. "Security footage of *what*?"

"Miles, you are at *church* and I never said anything like that," Essie scolded. "And *you*," she said, turning to Danny. "Why are you offering this guy security footage, number one. Number two, why do you *have* security footage?"

"The monitoring systems keep an archive of anything we look at. Nobody reviews it though."

"And you can't just delete it?"

He shook his head. "It's marked for deletion, then it waits in a queue for someone else to review and delete."

She nodded slowly. "Great."

"I was keeping an eye on you in the housing complex." His eyes floated in the direction that Gabe had gone. "I wanted to make sure you were safe."

She twisted her expression. "Wait, was that *you* activating the camera in Gabe's room?"

"*Yeah*, sorry about that. Like I said, just trying to make sure you were safe. That was made more difficult when someone duct taped the camera." He said this in a vaguely inquisitive tone. "Probably a good move considering."

"Considering *what*?" Miles asked, intrigued.

"Considering that they could get spied on at any moment—and Essie had turned off the facial overlay to talk to Gabe," Danny remarked sternly, irritated suddenly by Miles's presence.

Miles frowned. "Is this an example of the 'best in moderation' thing?"

Essie raised an eyebrow, grinning.

"I'll be quiet."

She looped her arm around Miles's arm, gave him a gentle tug toward her. "I'm not sure I ever really thanked you for all your help with that, Danny."

He shrugged. "You did the hard part. You were out there getting it done, pulling off a minor miracle as I understand it. I was back here hiding behind a computer."

"If not for you, I wouldn't have gotten into the housing complex."

"Which ultimately had no impact on you getting Gabe out of Denver."

"Yes, it did."

"No, it *didn't*," Danny said with a dismissive tone a few notches off how Thomas had spoken to her.

Miles frowned, watching Essie take the impact of his words.

She peered over to a group across the vestibule. "Hey Danny, the guest pastor?"

"Tim."

"You know him?"

"He's my cousin," he said shortly, nodding. "That's what our parents said anyway. We were adopted around the same time." He gave an affirmative jump of his brow.

She seemed suddenly uneasy.

"Essie, what he was talking about sounded a bit *familiar*," Miles offered, putting his arm around her shoulder.

"Familiar to *what*?"

"Oh, Essie played a prank on me, saying she lived in some zombie government lab."

Danny furrowed his brow. "Zombies huh?" he remarked.

Essie snapped to attention. "I'm sorry, I just realized that I haven't introduced the pair of you officially." She shook her head, breaking from her daze. "Danny, this is Miles. Miles, Danny."

The two young men shook hands.

"What's this zombie origin story?"

Miles waved it off. "Oh, she was just trying to mess with me."

"*Trying*?" she asked incredulously.

He turned to Danny, rolling his eyes. "She told me she needed to eat my arm to meet her nutritional needs. She was giving me like, a dead-eye stare. It was absolutely terrifying."

Danny grinned.

"You forgot to mention that prior to this you were being a complete–" She glanced over her shoulder, then lowered her voice to a whisper. "*Assclown*."

Miles curled forward, suppressing a laugh. "Yeah, I can't deny that."

"So, I said what I said," she said with a small smirk.

"Wow," Danny said flatly, seemingly unamused. "How long had it been since you'd fed on human flesh?"

"Days, Danny. *Days*."

He shook his head. "How did you find the strength to resist?"

"Not you, too," Miles groaned.

"What's going on?" Josh asked, stepping toward them.

"Esther roped Danny here into her zombie baby story."

Josh frantically looked at his watch. "Wait, did you feed before church? We should probably get going."

Miles rolled his eyes. "Nice to meet you, Danny, but I'm leaving before these two really get going. We're going to the diner across the way, right?"

Josh started to step away with Miles, then paused and peered over his shoulder.

"I'll be there in a few. I think we have 5, if you want to grab a table. Danny, did you want to join us for breakfast?"

"Oh, thanks, Essie, but my Claira and I are going to meet for brunch."

Josh held up his full palm to Miles, who had continued on, seemingly to indicate the number of people in their party, then moved to rally up the others. He was swept into conversation with the same associate pastor who had greeted Miles, and they walked slowly out toward the parking lot.

"*Claira?*" Esther asked, cheeks tightening.

"She's a security analyst–we've been seeing each other for a couple months now."

"Aw, I'm happy for you, Danny."

"Thanks."

"Does *she* have clearance to delete the security footage?"

Danny pressed his lips together. "What's your story these days? I haven't seen you for a while."

It was true. They had gotten in the habit of seeing each other pretty much every day when she was doing the Phoenix Initiative antidote runs. Since being back and getting involved in the day-to-day at the ranch, they just hadn't had a reason to cross paths, especially since he ordinarily attended the later service. "Things are good," she said, her voice catching.

"*Yeah?*"

"It's an adjustment. In some ways it's been easier, obviously, but in others–"

"You feel like you lost a bit of your purpose?"

She considered this. "Yeah, I guess that's part of it. I also still feel that post-run sickness."

He frowned. "Yeah? Like what?"

"Just a lighter version of it. I feel fatigued, nauseous, achy pretty much all the time. I shouldn't complain about it. It's probably head stuff." It had lessened when she had started to get sleep at night, but the symptoms had started to re-emerge over the past week.

"Have you talked to Luther about it?"

"He ran tests. Everything seems fine."

"So, it's like land sickness."

She furrowed her brow.

"People tend to get seasickness when they occasionally go out on a boat, but the people who live out on the water for an extended time, when they come back to normal life on land, they get land sickness."

"*Oh*. Maybe?"

"Are you still having nightmares?"

She scrunched her nose. "That's nothing new though."

"I kind of hoped they'd go away when you stopped being a lab rat."

"I had nightmares long before that."

"Yeah, but they got worse being a lab rat."

"It'll probably just take time."

"It's been five months."

She pulled in her breath. She hated lying, but she couldn't very well have a conversation in the church lobby with its pronounced acoustics about how she was sleeping at Josh's. "There's been a lot to process."

"You and Angler over there–"

She lifted her eyes to the open outer doors where Josh was just walking back into the church lobby, shuffling his boots over the door mat before entering. He looked taller, broader; his jawline more chiseled. They'd spent so much time together, she hadn't noticed how the nature of his work, the manual labor, had slowly expanded his muscles.

At some point, his face had matured; he still had a boyish charm to his smile, his eyes, but there was no mistaking he had put some life between himself and the boy of their childhoods, worry and severity presenting as lines in his forehead, a crease between his eyebrows.

She had the sudden need to make him smile, laugh; she wanted to pull him into some playful antics; maybe take off for him at full speed and leap into his arms.

She assessed the potential landing spot if he lost his footing and thought better of it. He'd definitely get hurt or they'd topple into some unsuspecting elderly person.

Perhaps just the arms about the neck thing and then kiss him passionately? She could feel her lips stretch upward at the thought of it.

Danny cleared his throat, startling her. "How much time do you plan on taking?" he asked, grinning.

She frowned, straightened herself. In that instant, her mind considered when their sleeping arrangement might end, and the return of the nightmares, her thoughts becoming entangled with the images, the sensations, the fear that had plagued her for as long as she could remember. Her breaths became shallow as the loneliness, the nothingness threatened to swallow her.

Josh smiled politely as he approached. "Figured I'd head over with you whenever you're ready, but I don't want to interrupt."

Her breaths deepened.

"I actually should get going," Danny said conclusively. "Good to see you both. *Essie*, maybe we can try to figure something out with those nightmares?"

Esther shifted her attention to Danny, narrowed her eyes.

"You should take your own advice about the Sim being used for good–it seems to be helping Gabe," he offered.

Josh raised his eyebrow, looking across at Esther, who was avoiding his gaze.

"Say 'hello' to Claira for me. We should get together sometime; I'd love to meet her."

Danny offered a fist bump to each of them, smiled affectionately to Essie, and wheeled himself toward the doors. Essie stepped closer to

Josh, watching Danny leave. There was something about being in close proximity with Josh West. It was like sitting near a campfire; being close to him just filled her with calm and warmth.

He leaned his head toward her. "Do you want to talk about it *now*?"

It had been unexpected. Weeks of no nightmares and then, suddenly, a few hours before sunrise, she'd burst from sleep screaming. When he'd tried to comfort her, her whole body was drenched in sweat and shivering. It took twenty minutes before she found she could speak.

"Essie," he whispered gently.

"What?"

"We should talk about the nightmares," he said quietly. "We've said we're going to, but then we never do."

She cleared her throat. "You know, it's not recommended to get emotionally vulnerable 30 minutes prior to eating."

"That's not a thing, but I see how it would make sense." He lifted a hand in greeting to his dad, who was heading out to the parking lot.

When Josh dropped his arm to his side, she reached a hand like a claw toward his bicep. "This shirt seems to be made of quality materials to contain these muscles, but how is your *skin* managing this, Joshua?"

His cheeks tightened. "Nice change of subject."

She shrugged. "I think it's a legitimate question actually."

He took a deep breath. "Bountiful breakfast, then maybe we can talk about the nightmares?"

She looped her arm around his and straightened her posture, peering over at him. Even with stretching her back and a slight heel in her boots, he was still effortlessly 4 inches taller than her. She wasn't quite sure when that happened either.

He raised his eyebrow.

"Breakfast first, then we can talk about the nightmares," she agreed.

* * *

The tone at breakfast had taken a considerable amount of time to recover after a large military convoy rumbled down the main street of town. There was a lot of discussion about if they were taking up offensive or defensive positions, if the vehicles, the soldiers, were being relocated for a specific reason. It seemed unlikely that the vehicles would be moving about just for the heck of it.

While Miles had provided enough comedic relief to pull things back into a light-hearted direction, giving an account of one of the MET team extraction trips, a preview for the news on the restaurant televisions had efficiently turned the mood sour again. The preview showed Gowon giving a speech. Garrison Chase, a prominent news anchor, provided narration, making mention of the Gowon Administration claim that Ark leaders were guilty of treason against American citizens. It was not a new claim, but he promised to share never-before-released evidence of the Ark leaders' decade-old efforts to inflict infertility on the country's population through use of food additives, which *may* have been a reason the government seized so many farms and food processing plants. Garrison then invited the audience to listen to President Gowon's remarks at a World Leaders Summit in Shanghai.

"Look at that woman," Miles remarked, indicating Annette Gibbons, who was standing just behind Gowon. She was pressing her thin lips together in a controlled smile, eyes blinking with the rhythm of a metronome. "They have her up there like a Stepford wife. I thought she was part of that whole 'Spinster for Life,' anti-marriage club. Now look at her."

"Before I could appreciate her standing up for what she believes in, but this seems like a switch for her," Gunner remarked. "Keeping in mind I was adamantly against everything she stood for."

"It's bizarre having her look adoringly at a man with a creep factor just so far off the charts," Miles said, shaking his head.

"*She* has a creep factor off the charts," Gunner muttered. "You realize she pushed through funding for those experiments Timothy was talking about."

"Gowon was a tech guy before, right?"

"Yeah, one of the richest guys in the world, but somehow, he got involved in vaccine production, artificial wombs, artificial intelligence. Most of what he dabbled in was artificial-something. Should have raised some sort of red flag, don't you think? But no, he was praised as a 'humanitarian.' Pretty sure he got the Nobel Prize?"

At the press event, there was a disturbance near the stage and a guard familiar to Josh stepped up beside the Speaker of the House. A swarm of guards and officers seized hold of three young protestors, while the main guard for Gibbons stepped back into position, nodding to her reassuringly.

Josh narrowed his eyes, confirming that the man had the same stature, the same profile, the same deep skin tone, the same stern expression as the man who had accompanied Essie to the meeting place in the forest, just before they arrived at the Ark.

Demetri.

At the time, Josh had accepted that there was information that he just couldn't know, and he trusted Essie when she told him that Demetri was an ally, that he worked with Luther, but as the events ran through his mind again, it occurred to him that Demetri was also the one who had kidnapped her. He was the one who wrestled her into the backseat. He was the reason Josh had aimed a gun at Essie that day. If Josh had kept his promise to shoot her if she were captured, she would be dead, and that man would be to blame.

The camera angle shifted. Josh looked across to Gabe to see if he'd recognized the man, but he was actively avoiding looking at the television monitors. Miles and Gunner were both no longer paying attention, Miles was expressing his disbelief that people still thought they could protest their way to having a more reasonable government overlord. Josh then peered over his shoulder to where Essie had been sitting quietly beside him during the exchange. To his surprise, she immediately met his gaze.

"You rode over to church with your dad, right?" he heard himself ask.

She nodded.

"I was going to stop by and check on my mom—I could give you a ride home?"

Miles contorted his face. "You should act like you're going in *opposite* directions if you want to hide the fact that you're secretly a couple." His expression turned to remorse when he met Essie's eye.

"Why would they need to hide that?" Gunner asked.

Gabe raised his eyes.

"Gabe, want to come along?" Josh asked, wincing internally. "Go see mom and dad?"

Miles widened his eyes. "Well, that just got awkward."

"*Miles*," Esther growled, though just before he said it, she'd briefly had a facial expression that conveyed that she felt similarly.

Gabe furrowed his brow. "I was just going to walk back over to the church for life group."

Miles slapped him on the back. "Are you going to a support group for men left emotionally scarred by Esther Evin Natale? Because if you are, I should probably join."

Josh was about to put his friend in his place when Essie chimed in with the most words she'd spoken since they'd placed their orders:

"Hey, *Miles*," she said in a doting, sing-song voice. "There's a life group for adults under 30."

"So would that be, like, *just* us?" he asked, motioning to the other occupants of the table. "Because the average age in that church?" He widened his eyes, providing no further elaboration.

She frowned at him. "You realize there are two church services, right? The 11am service is usually a younger crowd."

"There's a later service? Then why'd you make me get up so early?"

"Because I wanted you to come to church with me," she said innocently. "And ranch work starts at 4:30."

Josh chose not to remark that she'd been sleeping well into the 6 o'clock hour as of late. She'd prep food for the animals the night before and her dad would cover if she hadn't gotten back.

Miles narrowed his eyes. "You're not messing with me, right? Josh, is 11am the young single lady's service?"

Josh frowned.

"Never mind. Wrong person to ask," he said, leaning back in the booth. "It makes sense—probably all recovering from Saturday night."

"Church-going girls aren't typically out partying on Saturday nights, Miles," Gunner murmured.

His shoulders slumped. "Yeah, it's kind of an early to bed, early to rise crowd around here, isn't it?"

"There's an entire group of twenty-something girls who meet up at sunrise on Sundays to go for multi-hour hikes. Guess who goes to the 11am service–and *then* life groups?"

"I sense a trap."

"Maybe a group with an abundance of athletic young women isn't your thing," she challenged, arching her brow. "There's a Senior Singles group. Is that more of the demographic you're looking for?"

Miles grinned. "I feel like you're baiting me into joining the life group with some reverse Psychology methodology, but you've sparked my interest. By all means, point me in the direction of the ladies. The *young, athletic* ladies," he added for clarification.

9

two by two

The truck cab was nearly silent from the diner parking lot until the moment they arrived at the ranch, but it hadn't been tense. It was a patient silence, both understanding that the conversation that needed to take place wasn't going to happen while one of them was driving. They rode with both front windows down, Esther allowing the wind to whip her hair about, letting the sun soak into her cheeks.

The only uncertain moment had been when they arrived at a vacant ranch. Matteo wasn't home yet, as he typically spent the early afternoon leading life groups. Despite spending considerable time alone together, there were times when the thought of not having a buffer felt more intimidating.

"What time are you supposed to be at your parents'?"

"Anytime. They don't know I'm coming."

She froze thoughtfully, then nodded, glanced past him toward the picturesque hills and mountains. "Will you come sit with me at the overlook?"

"Yep," he said, giving her a brief smile.

They fell into step with each other for the walk. His eyes kept glancing across at her. At first it was because she just looked so—*enchanting*—with her billowing dress, her cowboy boots, her loose, flowing, albeit probably severely tangled hair. She'd worn the boots for years, but he'd only recently learned that when she got them when she was fourteen, she'd specifically picked them for the design that reminded her of fishhooks, which made her think of him. He'd been standing on his parents' front porch a few weeks earlier watching Essie climbing onto the back of a bowing Bree, slipping her leg over his bare gray back, when his mom shared the story, remarking about how she was surprised they'd held up so well. Glancing down at the design now, catching her peering across at him, he felt his chest inflate.

Once they stepped into the open field, no longer blocked from wind gusts by the barn, the walk had become a chaotic whirlwind for her. Quite literally. She had to keep her palms over the bottom hem of her dress to keep the fabric from rising up and twisting about her waist. This resulted in her having no way to address the wind aggressively whipping her hair in all directions.

"Do you have a hair tie?"

She presented her wrist, where she always kept a spare hair tie and Josh immediately went to work to tame her hair into a messy knot at the nape of her neck.

They continued on.

Josh followed her lead to sit along the edge of the overlook, which for the moment had a layer of grass. They used the petrified tree trunk as a back support and for the first few minutes they both gazed out toward the valley of ranches and protected lands. He forced himself to be silent, waiting for her to speak, even as she released her hair from his amateur attempt at a bun and expertly pulled it into a high-top knot. He was struck by how elegant she looked with her hair up. For a few moments, he watched a loose strand of her golden-brown hair flutter over her cheekbone.

She stretched forward, taking a cleansing breath of mountain air. Just as she resumed an upright position leaning against the tree trunk, he heard her say quietly: "Annette Gibbons is my mother."

He wasn't sure what he thought she was going to tell him, but her being the daughter of the Speaker of the House was certainly not it. "*Okay,*

I was not expecting that." He raised his eyebrows. "I need more information."

The details flowed out in a steady stream: how Annette had joined a program she thought was providing healthier starts for babies, that she decided to have a baby to be an example for other women, to advance her career, but had a change of heart about being in politics at all. She told him how they had told Annette her baby had died, which had sent her on a path to push for artificial wombs and ironically more research initiatives.

She had changed paths once Luther contacted her and informed her that her baby had been stolen and used in the research she had helped fund. Essie wavered with details as she spoke about the six years Luther and Annette had worked closely together, though she speculated that they'd had an intimate relationship based upon what she had observed. She had been kept in the dark about what information Annette had been providing to the Ark, but shared what Luther had said at one point about Annette being a key factor in the success or failure of the Arks.

Esther gave a small shrug, indicating she was finished speaking, but then sat more upright again. "Oh, *and* she had me kidnapped at the mechanics shop's restroom and brought to her family's cabin so she could meet me and tell me all this. You recognized Demetri in the coverage of Gowon's speech, right?"

Josh nodded slowly.

"Kind of goes without saying, but once again, I really appreciate you not shooting me."

He pressed his lips together, reading that there was more she had now thought of to say, which was just as well because he would have had a difficult time speaking; he had felt his chest twist uncomfortably at the reminder that he'd agreed to shoot her. He thought of the moment he held up his gun and took aim, eyes unable to focus on anything but her silver eyes locked onto him, eyebrows raised pleadingly. Her reasoning was valid, that if she were captured, she'd be subjected to torture and experimentation, a fate worse than death. He'd seen the videos of her from when she was a little girl; he knew what would await her. And yet, he couldn't bring himself to shoot her. He couldn't live with the knowledge that he'd ended her life.

To know she wasn't in danger after all, despite the theatrics of the kidnapping, wasn't comforting.

She tapped her boot against his. "I shouldn't make light of that. It wasn't fair what I asked you to do."

The alternative scenario came to mind—if she had been captured and tortured—and he could have saved her from it.

It was selfish what he did. It turned out to be the right call and maybe there was some spiritual guidance with that, but ultimately--

"*Hey,*" she said shortly—and then he felt the sting of her backhand across his cheek.

He startled, eyes wide, coming to full awareness. "*Ow.*"

Essie clamped both hands across her face. "Oh my God, I didn't mean to do that. *Josh?*"

He pressed his tongue against the inside of his cheek.

"I'm sorry. I could see you were stuck in your head and you weren't responding to me and I was overwhelmed and I didn't know what to do--"

He chuckled, shaking his head. "I think I needed that, actually."

"You did?"

"Thanks for not winding up; the smack was probably more delicate than it could have been."

She pressed her lips together, looking indecisive about whether she would burst into tears or laugh. "You're okay?"

He nodded. "Yeah. I'm fine."

She was sitting upright on her knees, reluctant to resume her previous, reclined position alongside him. "I don't know what I was doing--I don't *smack you.*"

"Yeah, that was new for you."

"Can I hug you?" she asked, a pleading look on her face.

"Yeah, of course you can."

She threw herself at him, wrapping her arms solidly around his neck. "I'm sorry."

"You don't need to be sorry. You were in the middle of telling me something really important, why don't you continue?"

She sat back on her heels, frowning.

He patted the ground beside him.

"I think I was finished?" she said apprehensively, leaning back into the tree trunk. "I mean, it was a lot. Finding out this woman I had hated is my--I called her an *ostrich*."

"To her face?"

She laughed. "Long story. It was in a conversation with Luther. Her call sign is Bluebird and I didn't think that was fitting."

He threw his head back. "You have very strong opinions about call signs."

She took a deep breath. "*Anyway*, it helped in a way, to know I wasn't completely willingly handed over to the experiments? But–it was– *a lot*." She made a motion with her hands to indicate her brain exploding.

He nodded again. "You believe her?"

She considered this, the expression on her face indicating a slight edginess about her conclusions being doubted. "Yes. Luther confirmed our DNA matches." Her eye flickered as she seemed to realize her answer may not have addressed the question he was asking.

"Why did she have you kidnapped if she was on good terms with Luther?"

"She wasn't exactly seeing eye to eye with him at that point. Not about Ark stuff, but–"

"Why weren't they seeing eye to eye?"

"He told her I was dead."

Josh frowned, staring out to the mountains as he worked through his analysis of the situation. "Because he was protecting you."

She nodded, taking a deep breath. "I'm not sure if Luther's still her 'handler' or 'contact' or whatever at the Ark. Luther's never really been forthcoming with that information."

112

"He knew the whole time that she's your mom?"

She shrugged. "I don't know. I'm assuming, yes?"

"He *did* save you. She must be really grateful for that."

"Yeah," she said quietly.

"But he didn't tell her about you—and he also put you through the antidote runs."

"We actually didn't discuss that. She knows about it though. I mean, I'm assuming."

He frowned. "What's she like?"

Essie twisted her mouth. "Less confident than I thought. I mean, I know the situation impacted that, too, but she just seemed sad and kind of lost. At Calvary I saw it with the pre-teen girls especially--the uncertainty? Trying to figure out who they are and then being okay with who they are? It felt like that's where her mind was."

"So her marrying Gowon—was that part of some sort of long-game?"

"I asked her about it. She wouldn't elaborate, but she said something about how in chess, you have to set a trap early." Esther tensed her face. "She hates him—Gowon. That much was very clear."

Annette had been able to maintain a calm demeanor through much of her vague explanations, but when Essie had called upon her own dark humor, alluding to how Gowon could be depicted as an animated villain if only he could pull off a catchy villain tune to endear him to audiences, Annette had stiffened and there seemed to be something raging behind her eyes. Essie could feel the disdain for him radiating off her skin like a fever.

"Does your dad know about her?"

Essie blinked, the image of Annette dissipating from her mind. "Not unless Luther told him, but I think I'd be able to tell if he knew."

"You don't want to tell him?"

She shrugged. "I'm not sure he needs to know that—I don't want it to change anything for him."

He moved to protest but backed off.

113

"It's relevant, but it literally changes nothing. It's not like I'm switching off going to see her for holidays or anything. It's literally informational only."

Josh took a deep breath. "So who else knows?"

She turned her chin toward him, lips pinching upward. "You."

He nodded slowly, gave her a small smile. "It took you a long time to say anything."

"I know." Essie leaned forward, stretching her back again.

"You said it helped to know, but it has to feel–strange, right?"

"Yeah, it does," she said quietly. "I don't really feel an attachment to her. I mean, I have sympathy about what happened and I appreciate whatever it is she's doing. I always knew I had parents who had my DNA, obviously. I had to come from somewhere. She may have ultimately regretted getting pregnant for political gain–" Essie shook her head. "--but I have a difficult time with a lot of it, how and why she set down that path in the first place."

"Yeah."

"I'm worried about her. I'm worried about everyone, but she's right there, right beside that psychopath. I don't see her making it out of this. Whatever *this* is."

"Maybe she's slowly poisoning him."

She frowned. "I'm a pastor's daughter–should I feel *comforted* by that thought?"

"Well, Gowon *is* pure evil. It feels like God would support it." An uncomfortable sensation began to build in his stomach. "Essie, how did she find out that you're alive if Luther didn't tell her?"

She twisted her torso, gasping with satisfaction when she managed to summon a very loud crack from her spine. "Ah, that's better. That's been bothering me since my ride this morning." She took a deep breath. "She saw me–when I went to the District initially to ask Luther about running tests to see if we could extract something from my blood to make some sort of antidote–"

"*Wait*, so it was *your* idea? For the antidotes?"

"Well, I didn't know the science of it completely, but I knew the general idea for how vaccines and other treatments had previously been created."

Josh frowned, gazing out toward the horizon.

"What's wrong?"

He pulled in his breath. "I thought Luther convinced *you* to do it in the beginning."

She lifted her eyebrow. "No, he was *adamantly* against it from the get-go." She took in his facial expression, his tensed body. "Josh, you can relax. No matter whose idea it was, I'm not doing it anymore."

They were quiet for a few moments before Esther broke the silence.

"It's not like a parent/child connection with her–it feels more like she's a character in a novel that I can sort of sympathize with, but there's a disbelief that she's real. Does that make sense?"

"I think so."

She sighed. "Before we said goodbye, she pointed out that I didn't ask who my biological father is."

Josh waited for her to continue.

"The truth is it never occurred to me to ask. I told her that. I didn't want to know. I didn't think it'd be helpful to me, selfishly speaking. There's very little chance he was or is a good person, to be involved in the experiments, to be involved with Annette?"

He nodded.

"I mean, I have *the best* dad on the planet, no offense to your dad."

He shook his head. "No argument there."

"Your dad is pretty great though."

"Second to your dad is still a pretty high accolade."

"I didn't want to risk having that information of who my 'biological' dad is to, I don't know, take anything away? It just didn't feel important for me to know. I think I thought I needed to know—before. It had started to bother me that I didn't know, but in hindsight, I feel like I could have lived without this information."

Josh nodded.

"Like I said, it's helpful, selfishly, to know I wasn't willingly handed over when I was born, that she didn't know what they were really doing–*allegedly*," she added with a tense shrug.

"*But?*"

"What happened to me and to all the other babies–" She pulled in her breath. "It wasn't okay, like not at all okay or justified."

"No. It wasn't."

"Selfishly   though–?"

Josh leaned in close to her ear, speaking softly: "I'm going to respectfully request you stop referring to your feelings as being 'selfish,' Ess."

"I can be selfish."

"Anyone can, but I think you could give yourself a lot more grace than you do."

She sat more upright, gazing across at him, processing his remark. Suddenly her cheeks tightened and she turned away, scrunching her nose.

"What was *that?*"

She shook her head, moving to tuck her hair behind her ears, forgetting she'd tied it back.

"As I was *saying*," she began again, clearing her throat. "What happened to me wasn't okay–" She frowned. "--but my dad wouldn't be my dad without it happening. I wouldn't have gotten to live the life I've lived since. I wouldn't have met you, your whole family. I probably wouldn't know Jesus like I do. Granted, I've had a complicated relationship with Him as all this has come about."

He furrowed his brow.

"The day Calvary was attacked, the kids were asking me about what happened at St. Dominic's Church—that was the big chapel in town—"

He nodded, attesting he remembered.

"They asked why God hadn't protected those people, why He lets bad things happen." She cleared her throat. "At the time, I gave an answer about God giving us free will, which allows us to choose our own path, that it also allows people to do evil, that it allows bad things to happen. I thought I understood the concept." She lifted her eyebrows. "But *then* I was spooning a sarin gas canister–well, *first*, I was bleeding out of my eyeballs, my spine snapped in half, and *then* I was spooning a sarin gas canister—"

He winced. "Wait, wait, wait, your spine *snapped*?"

"Yeah, pretty sure. Weird sensation. Luther said it wasn't possible–like, *stern*, no ifs, ands or buts, just not a possibility so I don't know. Maybe it was something else entirely."

He frowned. "It's not like him to just rule something out like that."

"Exactly. It's that sort of blatant denial that it's even a possibility that makes me highly suspicious that it's exactly what happened."

"It does seem suspicious," Josh agreed, frowning, thinking of the rapid bruising and healing of her hand after Lilliandil bit her, however, it seemed to be a drastic leap to go from a bruise to repair of a spinal cord. "When did you bring this up to him? Back after it happened?"

"A few months ago." She waved the thought away. "Once I found out about the lab and everything from those first few years, I discovered that I really didn't understand what I was teaching the kids. It sounded nice, you know, that God promises a blessing from every tragedy, every evil, that something good will come from it? I believed it because that's what I had been taught, but that belief hadn't really been put to the test.

"I felt *betrayed*–that's the best word I can think of to describe it. I had grown up with this faith, this belief in a 'good, good Father,' this loving God, and all of a sudden, my world was rocked. I couldn't understand why He would allow me to go through all that. I looked around at the state of the world and I was confused and angry. I didn't understand why, if God is all we believe He is, He wouldn't have intervened."

Josh thought of how on the drive to the Ark, they'd passed through a town where they happened upon a family who had been slaughtered along the side of the road. The last surviving member of the family was an infant with tufts of dark hair. Essie had lifted the baby, nestled her in her arms, and sang to her quietly until the baby's final breath. She had broken down as Miles took the baby's body away: sobbing, screaming, demanding answers from God. It was the first time Josh had ever seen her armor falter so openly, the first time he had ever witnessed her questioning her faith. It suddenly occurred to him that it was only six months since that day.

"I stopped relying on God and I started taking matters into my own hands. I was going to be a crusader or something." She rolled her eyes. "I had closed myself off from hearing anything He was trying to tell me, but when I found Gabe in the city–"

Josh's eyes lifted.

"I had gotten access to his–whatever you'd call it–cabin? Dorm room? I knew a lot of what he had been through. What everyone was saying about how he might not be himself anymore? There was reason to think that way with what he had been subjected to." She shrugged. "So, I was waiting in his room. He was coming back from a really intense Sim training session. It was supposed to be this 'upgrade' program?"

Josh nodded.

"He came inside, not knowing I was there, sat down on his bed and he prayed for forgiveness." She lifted her brow, nodding. "After everything he'd been through, he was still calling on Jesus–and there I was, having lived most of my life being absolutely blessed by God and I had turned away from Him."

"I'm going to put up a strong defense on behalf of my client."

Her lips curled up. "Are you my attorney now?"

He rolled his eyes. "I'm not sure why I said it like that."

She shrugged. "It's kind of funny." She slowly turned her hand, presenting the air before them. "Proceed, Counselor."

"Essie, you were going through a *lot* and you didn't have anyone you felt like you could turn to."

"I could have turned to God," she murmured. "It's what I should have done."

Josh dropped his chin to his chest, internalizing an objection.

She pinched her eyebrows together. "God was talking to me a lot during that trip—or trying to, but my mind was all shaken up." She took a deep breath. "When I held Vivian, the baby by the lake?"

He lifted his eyes and gazed across at her.

"All of my doubts about God, about my faith just came rushing back. I *didn't* understand." Her eyes shifted to where his tanned, muscular hand now rested on her knee. "*But,* when you hauled me into the lake and everything just quieted down, I kept hearing the same phrase over and over in my head." She made gentle eye contact. "'God is good.' 'God is good.'"

He nodded slowly.

"The evil things, the painful things, the tragic things? That's not God's doing. All the good things? The beauty? The love? The rugged best friend holding me in his arms when I needed to break down? God's had a hand in making all of *that* possible. God *is* the good." She shrugged. "And in the back of my mind, I heard Him tell me: '*She's with Me now, Little One. She's with Me.*'"

He gave a light smile. "When you talk to God, God calls you 'Little One'?"

Tears had filled her eyes. She ran her thumb underneath them, mopping at the tears. "It's silly, probably. It's probably something in my own mind that came from the *Narnia* series with how Aslan calls Lucy 'Dear Heart.'" She furrowed her brow. "Actually, *no.* I remember He called me that, in my mind, long before I'd ever heard of Narnia. When I was at the lab, then later when I first met my dad. Before I knew anything about God."

Josh shifted uneasily.

"I have this really vivid recollection of when I first met my dad. I'm not sure I ever told you."

He shook his head.

"Can I just–" she began, twisting her mouth. "I feel like I keep using that phrase: 'I never told you.' You should know, I didn't keep things from you because I didn't want you to know." She squinted toward the mountains, considering her next words carefully. "I didn't want you to see me differently–and I didn't want to feel differently." She winced, seemingly displeased with how she was explaining things.

"It's okay, Essie. I wish you had talked about it so you weren't dealing with it on your own, but I think I can understand why you didn't want to."

She frowned, unconvinced.

"You were telling me about when you first met your dad," he prompted gently.

She nodded. "I was in the back seat of his pickup truck. Luther had moved me from his car to my dad's truck while I was sleeping."

"You didn't get to say goodbye to Luther?"

"I don't think so. He's not great with goodbyes. Even now." She took a deep breath. "When I woke up, I was startled because I didn't know where I was–so I guess it wasn't exactly a 'meeting' or an introduction. I just woke up and he was there." She threw her hands up dismissively, folding her leg so she could turn in his direction. "My stories are weird. Nothing is normal. It's all so dramatic."

He squinted one eye. "I can't really deny that."

She smiled tightly. "This is at least a good story. I like this story."

"Good," he said with a smile.

"*So*, I was pretending to sleep. I was listening to all the noises as we drove, trying to figure out what was going on, who he was, where we were going. I remember listening to him breathing, but his breaths weren't familiar to me. That sounds weird, but I was very hyper aware of sensory details."

Josh lifted his hand and tucked the loose strand of hair behind her ear, letting his fingers linger there momentarily.

"I could feel the air shift whenever he glanced back toward me. I could tell he was nervous. I remember hearing bits of words, but I didn't know what he was saying. I figured out later that he was whispering a prayer in Italian."

He nodded.

"The energy of his nervousness started to set me at ease a little bit, actually, but I was still unsure. It was jarring–I fell asleep in Luther's car–and I had built this trust in Luther–and then I woke up in a stranger's truck. Granted, it was my dad, so I had literally nothing to fear, but–"

"You didn't know that."

She shook her head. "So, I was still pretending to sleep, not really sure what to think. Then a voice in the back of mind whispered *'Open your eyes, Little One.'*"

Josh smiled lightly.

"So I did--and *there* was my dad, focused very intently on safe driving practices. You know, ten and two." She demonstrated with both hands and sniffled, cheeks tightening. "I remember he glanced over his shoulder at me. He was *so* startled to see me looking back at him, he sort of wavered the truck on the road. When he steadied himself–and the truck–he looked back at me and he gave me this small, but exceedingly kind smile–" Her own smile broadened. "--and a calm just *washed* over me. I knew I was safe. Everything else was behind me. I knew I was safe."

Josh exhaled deeply. He imagined Essie at the age she was when he'd met her–deep dimpled cheeks, big, round eyes, exuding sweetness and innocence. He thought of the torture she'd endured, how she'd heard God speaking to her–he imagined in a comforting tone, calling her "Little One"--he thought of how He'd had her pass from Luther, who adored her, to Teo–and he felt a deep appreciation, a gratitude to God filling his chest for making it all possible, for bringing her into his life. "I love that moment, thinking what that must have been like for you having God reassuring you that it was going to be okay."

She wiped her eyes again. "Yeah, I kind of think of it like there being a little 'ta-da' moment," she said, her voice soft and lifting at the end. "Like God was presenting my dad as a gift to me–which he *was*. 'I know you've been through a lot, Kiddo, but ta-da! I'm going to make it up to you.'"

They were both quiet, and simultaneously turned to gaze out toward the mountains.

Finally, Essie cleared her throat. "Meeting–" she hesitated, frowning, "*Annette* made me realize how amazing my dad is, how blessed I really am–and that God did that. He brought us together."

Josh nodded.

"I remember this visiting pastor at Calvary doing a sermon about blessings in Heaven, like eternal life is bought and paid for, it's ours, but that in Heaven, we're rewarded for our suffering and for our good deeds we do *here*."

Josh furrowed his brow.

"I wasn't sure how I felt about that. About having different classes or levels of Heaven? My dad didn't agree with the message because he didn't feel like it was founded in scripture, but this pastor had an interesting way he applied this way of thinking in his life. He was talking about how he had faced a really horrible cancer diagnosis. The way he dealt with that was saying it was a win-win for him. If he beat it, he'd get to live more years with his loved ones. If he died, he'd be with God in Heaven and God would bless him greatly in his eternal life." She nodded slowly. "It's kind of a great outlook, isn't it? Even taking out the idea of 'extra blessings' in Heaven."

"Yeah, it is. A similar idea to what Timothy was saying today about being brave because no matter what happens, all paths lead to Jesus."

She nodded. "So I took what the visiting pastor said about extra blessings and applied it in terms of my own life, how God has blessed me. It seems to me like He's *really* trying to make it up to me, what I went through. He's just been pouring the blessings out on me–and I'm grateful, I really am. It's just—I'm still human, I'm still working through the mental gymnastics—*and* the grief of what happened, Luther calls it 'trauma' but that just sounds *so*–" She shook her head. "I know it's crazy to still be sorting through it because it was so long ago."

"Ess."

"I can be a really slow learner."

"*Ess.*"

"It took me an exceptionally long time to learn how to ride a bike."

He started to argue then retreated. "Yeah, that did take a while. Yet somehow you were riding Bree without a saddle the first day you tried."

She shrugged. "If you believe what that guest pastor at Calvary was saying, about getting blessings here *or* in Heaven, I kind of feel like I'm stealing from the blessings from my eternal life self. I mean, I don't really agree with what he said because the idea of *some* people just barely getting into Heaven—he said something about people walking around with their clothes smoking because they barely made it through the flames of judgment—"

"Yeah, he lost me with that image."

"Right? If some people are just lucky to be there and others are getting showered with blessings, it would create a class system in Heaven that I don't feel like Jesus would be cool with."

Josh smiled. "I agree."

"But whatever the case, I *do* feel like God blesses me a *lot*, way more than I deserve."

Josh contorted his face, looking across at her with an expression of utter disbelief. "Have you *always* been this—?" He hesitated to assign an adjective, chuckling to himself.

She wasn't fazed, as there was clearly more on her mind. "*That* made it easier to accept, more than anything else."

He frowned. "What did?"

"Stopping to appreciate all the blessings in my life? I think it must have really pained God to have me go through all that I did, which is why he's blessing me so much. And given the options of a) the life I could have had had I not been a lab rat, or b) the life I have?" She held out her hands, weighing the options. "There's no question. I'd go through it all over again." She concluded her sentence lightly, with a shrug and a small smile.

He shook his head, took a deep breath, thinking of the words he wanted desperately to share with her when they were at the cabin after she'd saved Gabe. He heard himself saying them before he'd even made a conscious decision to speak: "You are the bravest, most selfless, most magnificent person, Esther Natale."

She tensed, her eyebrows pinched together. "Josh, I'm *not–*"

"Hey," he interjected, "that wasn't a question."

She pursed her lips.

"I haven't told you that and I really don't know why. I've thought it for a very long time."

She twisted her expression.

"I kind of feel unworthy to be in your presence actually."

Her chin jumped up. "Oh, stop it."

"No, really. God puts this angel on earth, this girl who puts so many saints to shame–"

Esther rose up on her knees, moving toward him, threatening to cover his mouth. "Saints are Catholicism, Joshua."

He smiled widely, undeterred. "--and *I'm* entrusted–"

She froze just at the moment he thought she might kiss him. She gazed into his eyes, searching for something within them.

In the split second before they both heard the tires on the drive in the distance, he saw a flicker of something in her eyes. Fear? Pain? He couldn't be sure, but it stirred up an uneasiness in his chest.

She stretched her neck, squinting her eyes toward the house.

"Is it your dad?"

She nodded, cupping her hand to her ear. "We have to go," she said abruptly, clambering to her feet.

"What's going on?"

She offered her hand to help him up. "Your mom's having the baby."

*　　*　　*

"Do you really think she wants me in the room? I don't want to see *that*," Josh remarked a few minutes later as they walked quickly toward the house.

"This is a big deal for her, Josh."

"I've delivered horses and cows. It's not pretty, Ess."

"What? Are you saying you won't be there at the birth of *your* children?"

His pace slowed. He had no idea the tone of one syllable could have such an impact on him, not until the moment her tone suggested a future for him separate from her own.

Essie glanced over her shoulder.

"That's different."

She stopped walking, turning fully toward him, her eyebrows arched upward. "What's wrong?"

Josh took a breath, shaking his head slowly. He was being ridiculously too sensitive. It was a *word*–did he expect her to say *our*? "Nothing."

She nodded and they continued on.

Teo turned on his heel as they approached, all three moving determinedly toward the driveway.

"Do you want to ride over together?" Josh asked, climbing into the cab of his truck. Receiving no response, he looked up to see Essie conversing quietly with her dad, a frown taking over her face.

Matteo shrugged, said something too low for Josh to hear over the sound of the engine, then rounded the front of the truck, climbing in the passenger side.

Essie climbed up on the sidestep of Josh's door, her eyes very round. "I'll meet you at the hospital." She ran her hand briefly across his forearm in what seemed to be a reassuring way before jumping down.

"The shifter's being finicky," Matteo called out his window as she climbed into the driver's side of his truck. "You have to really muscle it from first to second."

She nodded, turning the ignition. She reversed the truck, tossing an ample amount of dust toward the barn, and took off toward town before Josh had even considered shifting into reverse.

"Where's she off to?"

Matteo cleared his throat uncomfortably. "To get Gabe."

10

nurture

While the majority of people doted over five-year-old Esther, likening her wild, waves of golden hair to that of a princess, Sara West included, Sara had been one of the first to recognize the challenges of it. Whenever Esther came to stay at the farm, she'd have to spend a considerable amount of time detangling it, dozens of stubborn knots hiding just under the shiny top layer as Matteo tended to only brush the very top, not wanting to inflict pain upon his young daughter.

Essie sat cross-legged on the ottoman of the couch, fists smashed into her cheeks. She stared at the television as Sara prepped her hair to be brushed out, parting it into sections.

Josh and Gabe had agreed on a movie for once, though Essie had been surprised when the first scene came on, as it began with what seemed to be the reading of a typical princess story, something they were typically opposed to.

"'She waited in the dragon's keep in the highest room of the tallest tower waiting for her true love and true love's first kiss.'"

Essie frowned at Josh suppressing a laugh.

A large green hand reached for the storybook page, ripping it out. "'Yeah, like that's ever going to happen,'" the narrator mocked, the scene switching to an exterior shot of an outhouse. "'What a load of–'" A toilet flushed and an ogre stepped out to a catchy melody, stretching, and tugging his underpants from being wedged into his backside.

Essie giggled loudly.

"See, I told you you'd like it," Josh said, shooting her a smile.

"Oh, you kids," Sara remarked, running the brush through the bottom layer of hair first. Despite the nest of knots making it what should have been a painful process, Essie appeared to be distracted by the movie.

The truth was that Essie was wincing internally, trying not to make Sara feel bad for the task she had to perform. Plus, Essie very much enjoyed the feel of the brush gliding through her hair once it was tangle-free, the satisfying noise the brush made, how Sara's hands delicately handled her hair, sending a lovely, tingling sensation up her neck.

Some time later, around the point in the movie when a talking donkey announced he'd be making waffles for breakfast, Sara had parted Essie's hair into two halves, and was beginning on the right braid. The natural tilt of Essie's head to that side provided a helpful view for the starting point of the French braid. Sara's hands quickly laced the glossy locks and secured her hair with a simple purple hair tie. She adjusted herself on the couch, giving a final brush to the left side.

Essie leaned toward her.

"Doesn't that feel nice?" Sara asked.

Essie smiled tightly, giving a small nod.

"You have such beautiful, thick hair."

"Thank you."

Sara took a deep breath and gathered the loose hair at the crown of Essie's head, began the second braid. Once she was finished, she gave Essie's shoulders a gentle rub and kissed the top of her head. "All set, sweetie."

"Will you brush my hair again later?" Essie asked, peering over her shoulder.

"Well, I braided it so it shouldn't get tangled."

"I just like when you brush it. It feels nice."

Sara placed her palm on her chest. "Of course I will."

Essie smiled. "Can I get down now?"

"Yes."

Essie immediately dropped to the floor and crawled onto the air mattress that was covered with blankets and pillows. She settled her head on

Josh's pillow, curling herself toward him so she could have a better view of the screen.

She took a deep breath.
Or she would have if there was any oxygen in the air.

It's better not to feel.
It's better not to think.
It's better not to remember.

Everything was dark.
The room was silent.
She should have been able to hear herself gasping for air, but there was nothing.
There was no light, no sound, just nothingness that stretched on forever.

11

intention

"So, many of you probably don't realize I have a daughter. I know, I know. I *never* ever mention her."

There were some appreciative smiles, but overall, the sanctuary was very quiet.

"I'll just clarify–I'm being sarcastic. I have a beautiful, intelligent, funny, talented daughter who I mention all the time. She's 20. Yeah, I saw that reaction. When people meet her for the first time, they're a little surprised she's 20. A young person from our youth ministry turned to me after meeting her and said: 'Are you *that* old?'" His face turned severe. "Yes. Yes, I am."

Miles peered over his shoulder, checking the nearby pews for Essie, even though she'd told him she was working with the Sunday School classes. It was just the first time he'd sat through a service without her.

Josh glanced over at him, raising an eyebrow as he saw Miles tapping his thumb nervously on his knee.

"Essie has a calming influence. I get antsy," he explained, taking a deep breath.

"Yeah, she's like a Golden Retriever, isn't she?" Josh said quietly, grinning to himself.

"You don't wear ties and you liken her to a dog. Honestly, besides your rugged good looks and obvious deep emotional connection, I don't know what she sees in you," Miles said with a grin, redirecting his attention back to Pastor Matteo. He made a conscious effort to stop fidgeting.

Matteo's eyes gleamed over the row. "I tell a lot of stories about my daughter. Most of them are positive; she's taught me a lot over the years and she had so many really adorable moments as a child. I like to brag a bit about her talents, her wisdom that far surpasses her years, or even *my* years. *This* is not one of those stories."

Miles furrowed his brow.

"*This* is the story about how my daughter accidentally adopted a— you know what, I don't want to give away the end."

Miles turned to take in Josh's expression.

He clearly knew the punchline already, his mouth turning upward.

"When we lived in Colorado, I was pastor at a church there, she and I lived in the house that was attached to the back. It was really convenient because I could jaunt over to the church when things came up. Well, the need came up for me to take one of these impromptu jaunts. The plumbing in the main church building was a bit wonky and frequently caused pipe bursts and toilet overflows and I wasn't *just* the pastor, I was a Super Mario Brother." He held his fist in the air. "Any gamers from back in the day?" He grinned. "Wahoo!"

Several congregation members chuckled.

Miles actually laughed out loud in surprise. He hadn't gotten to know Matteo growing up, but he'd never picked up on his sense of humor. It made sense, he supposed, given Essie's nature.

"Essie was maybe seven and I was going, like I said, maybe twenty yards away. At most. What kind of trouble can a seven-year-old who is obsessed with reading get into when you're twenty yards away, right? Well, it turns out, *a bit*, but I didn't know that.

"So I left. She had been given clear instruction to stay in the house and continue reading as she had been. Well, soon after I left, she remembered she needed to water the plants outside. Not really a big deal, the plants were all on our front patio area. Actually, without her intervention, we would have had a major fire hazard on our hands. She's the resident green thumb.

"So she's outside watering plants...and she spots the most *adorable* little kitten you've ever seen over by the parking lot wall, just all by itself. Tan, probably a 'tabby'? Well, Essie had it in her mind that the kitten was lost and alone and needed her. I wouldn't disagree with her on that; any animal would be blessed to have Essie dote on it. *Anyway*, the kitten apparently came inside the house willingly, Essie got some whole-grain cereal for it, some water, some milk, though she explained later that she'd read that cats have a difficult time digesting milk, despite popular belief that it's their main source of hydration. She used that phrase: 'main source of hydration.'

"Once she'd given it food and something to drink, obviously she thought it would enjoy relaxing and having story time, so she carried it up to her room."

"What? Was it a bobcat?" Miles whispered.

Josh shook his head, lifting his brow.

"So here she was, my sweet seven-year-old daughter reading to this potentially lactose intolerant 'kitten.' Meanwhile, I was helping with this emergency plumbing situation up in the main building that was taking way longer than I expected. Finally, I told them, hey, I need to go check on Essie. I should probably just bring her back over here with me. Keep the pipe off, I'll be back in a few minutes.

"I got home and I'm a mess and the house is quiet. If you've been in a house with children, there's such a thing as 'too quiet.' I ran upstairs, opened her door, and found Essie had fallen asleep snuggling with this 'kitten' bundled up in her blankets.

"By now, you've probably drawn the correct conclusion that this wasn't a kitten. No, no, my daughter had taken in, fed, read a story to, and lulled to sleep, a–" He paused for dramatic effect. "--mountain lion cub."

The congregation laughed.

"Seriously?" Miles said, nudging Josh.

"Yep."

"So this mountain lion cub had really taken to Essie. Like most animals, with the exception of a Mustang mare we have out here at the ranch, it sensed that she's good and kind and would be an endless source of treats. This cub did *not* get this sense about *me*, however, evident when it woke up and began growling(?), snarling(?) at me. At this point, of course, I had no idea how it got in the house. I mean, I had a vague idea based upon the fact Essie had been snuggling with it, but I certainly didn't know how I was going to get it *out*, especially when the cub freed itself from the blankets and climbed on top of Essie, who was somehow still sleeping, and took up, shall we say, a *defensive* position?

"Claws literally came out, which is what woke Essie because they dug into her–which obviously hurt. Essie didn't even have that big of a reaction, but it startled the cub enough and suddenly it didn't trust her so much anymore. It jumped to the floor, but now it was prowling, primed to attack.

"My first thought was to get Essie out of the room, but she was fixated on calming the 'kitten' down. She'd already come up with a name–Marlo–after a beach she'd read about because the sand was the same color as the fur. So she's explaining her name choice and how she found him all alone, and that she doesn't know why he's so grumpy, maybe his tummy hurts? This is when she explained the whole cats are lactose intolerant thing." Teo paused, pressing his lips together, letting his eyes float about. "Marlo, in the meantime, is making this antagonizing high-pitched growl, which is making it difficult to even hear what Essie, my seven-year-old zoology professor, is saying.

"Long story short, I convinced Essie to make her way over to me. This was expedited when Marlo suddenly sprinted at her. Essie came crashing into me at the top of the stairs and I slammed the door shut. I told her I'd need to call a veterinarian and of course this was the end of the world. She was worried they would hurt him. It was not a comfort to her when I told her he would probably be tranquilizing Marlo.

Anyway, we were waiting for the vet to show up and we could hear Marlo being very, very destructive upstairs. Mountain lions do *not* like being confined into a bedroom, just so you know. Of course, Essie felt very maternal hearing these noises of his. She was very worried about *him*. I actually had to walk her up to the main office, pull up a photo of a mountain lion cub to convince her that's what he was. And I remember her reaction to seeing the photo was: '*Oh*, that explains a lot actually.'

"Essie had every intention of doing good, right? She thought she was doing right by Marlo. Should she have talked to me first? Probably. From her perspective, she just saw a helpless kitten who she could help. She certainly didn't *mean* to bring a mountain lion into the house. Oh and he destroyed her bedroom. It was a mess. Ripped her bed covers to shreds, peed on her bed, the floor? And mountain lion pee is about 100x more potent than house cat pee in case you're wondering."

A few people winced in disgust.

"Essie thought she was doing the right thing, she thought she was doing good, but her actions ultimately didn't help Marlo, it didn't help Marlo's mom, it definitely didn't help the condition of our house, and Essie could have wound up really hurt.

"Oh and I see the same concern on some of your faces as I've seen on Essie's face when it comes to animals. Marlo was captured without needing to be tranquilized, but he was very, very angry about it. He was then promptly reunited with his mom, who was just on the other side of the wall. And I'm sure is living happily in the Colorado mountains," he said with a shrug.

"Okay, so, cute story, but what can we learn from this? *Well*, it can teach us that having good intentions is one thing, but it's important to set our intentions on the right course. For Essie, she's always been drawn to helping those who are lost or in need. She was being drawn to help, she just needed to have some direction on how she could do that–and *should* do that.

"In the Bible, God includes instructions for how to live our daily lives:

"*Ephesians 4:21-32 – Since you have heard about Jesus and have learned the truth that comes from Him, throw off your old sinful nature and your former way of life, which is corrupted by lust and deception. Instead, let the Spirit renew your thoughts and attitudes. Put on your new nature, created to be like God—truly righteous and holy. So stop telling lies. And "don't sin by letting anger control you." Don't let the sun go down while you are still angry, for anger gives a foothold to the devil. If you are a thief, quit stealing. Instead, use your hands for good hard work, and then give generously to others in need. Don't use foul or abusive language. Let everything you say be good and helpful, so that your words will be an encouragement to those who hear them. And do not bring sorrow to God's Holy Spirit by the way you live. Get rid of all bitterness, rage, anger, harsh words, and slander, as well as all types of evil behavior. Instead, be kind to each other, tenderhearted, forgiving one another, just as God through Christ has forgiven you.*

"He wants us to succeed, to be happy, to experience so many blessings here on earth. The thing is, it can feel a little vague, right? To be a good person, to do good, to try to live like Jesus? You might *intend* to be a good person, to serve Jesus, but while we talk about this being a 'living' text, it doesn't always feel like it.

"I've spoken with people who say: Teo, I just don't hear God. I go to church, I read the Bible, I pray, but I don't hear God. He feels so far away.

"To that, I usually ask: How much *listening* are you doing?

"Intention in faith is not about mere routine or going through the motions. It is the deliberate choice to live our lives in alignment with God's will and purpose. Having intention in our faith requires us to approach our spiritual walk with mindfulness, purposefulness, and sincerity."

Miles straightened himself in the pew as Matteo's eyes drifted over him.

"By setting aside time to pray and meditate on God's Word, we open our hearts to His guidance and discern His purpose for our lives. In prayer, we communicate with God, laying our hopes, fears, and desires before Him, and ask for His direction.

"But be mindful of how you pray. This isn't like the idea of sitting on Santa's knee and laying out your wish list."

Miles chuckled.

Matteo smiled kindly. "I'm not going to tell you how you should pray, but what I'd suggest is to ask for guidance, but don't expect God to immediately answer. He *might*, but also understand that God doesn't always answer the way you expect or at the time you want. Remember from the Lord's Prayer: 'Thy will be done.' Let me repeat that: 'Thy will be done.' Not Pastor Matteo's will be done." He paused to take a sip of water and began pacing again.

"So how can we be intentional in our faith? We covered a few—reflect, meditate, pray, *listen*," he said, counting them out on his fingers, then holding his hand up in the air. "What else?" His eyes began bouncing around to different congregation members.

"Love like God," Josh whispered.

Matteo froze. "I heard the word I'm looking for." He smiled, waiting for the word to be repeated.

"Love," the man sitting in front of Josh echoed gruffly.

Matteo nodded. "*Love*--others the way God loves us."

Miles furrowed his brow.

"Love is at the core of our faith. We are called to love God and to love one another as God loves us. God doesn't love us passively—it's a constant. That's the purpose of the 3 in 1—Father, Spirit, Son. The Holy Spirit is part of this entity. It's the part that's supposed to compel us in our lives. Our love shouldn't be passive. We should be *actively* seeking ways to show kindness, compassion, and empathy for those around us. We should serve others selflessly. By doing so, we also serve God.

"Okay, so love others," he said, counting on his fingers again. "Next, be accountable. Surround yourself with fellow believers—encourage and support each other. If you're not in a life group, join a life group. We've talked about before about how church community can't be solely based upon our experience in this sanctuary. The community comes from having a circle of believers around you, supporting you in your life, your walk with Jesus. It's amazing how the experience of being in groups like this can deepen your connection with God and with those around you. Keep yourself rooted in God's will. Read the Bible. Have a heart that seeks after Him with genuine passion, knowing that as we draw closer to God, He will draw closer to us."

*   *   *

Essie finished tidying up the empty classroom, sliding the study Bibles onto the shelf, piling the bean bag chairs along the wall, and cleaning up snack wrappers. The quiet was a stark contrast to the decibel level she'd experienced for over an hour when about a dozen 11-14 year old girls had occupied the room. She'd volunteered to help out when it was determined the only youth pastor available to work with them was male. She was just meant to be observing, but after she watched the girls continuously huddle together and giggle about Pastor Jake, Essie had stepped in.

She'd engaged the girls in discussion by asking them for help in preparing Sunday School lessons for the class one age group lower. With everything going on in the world, all the uncertainty, she asked them to consider what they would have found to be helpful to talk about. This ultimately had the intended effect of getting them to open up about their experiences before and since arriving at the Ark and by the end, Pastor Jake was merely an accessory in the classroom.

She stretched her back, coaxing out a light crack, and closed the door behind her. She moved with purpose down the hallway, thoughts fixated on coffee, when she heard a familiar voice bellowing out of the next classroom. Peeking through the window, she confirmed that Miles was, indeed, inside. The classroom was set up with vintage school desks lined up in even rows; it was rarely used for life groups unless there were no other spaces available. Based upon the general appearance of the occupants of the room, it was the young men's group, age 18-30, which was being mentored by one of the associate pastors, a red-haired man who looked a bit like Ed Sheeran, according to Renee.

The classroom was full with several men scattered around on spare chairs. Occupying the front row of desks—and looking comically large for their chairs--from left to right--were Gabe, Gunner, Miles, and Josh.

Miles was being very animated with his hands. She hadn't quite determined what he was talking about, but Josh was shaking his head, suppressing a laugh.

As he finished his story, Miles looked up and saw her standing at the window. He smiled tightly. "Speak of the *devil*!" she heard him exclaim, her reaction bringing him substantial amusement. "No, seriously, all good things."

Josh smiled tightly at her.

She pursed her lips and waved quickly. Just before she darted away toward the lobby, she thought she saw Miles make a gesture like a claw.

12
spin

It felt juvenile and unprofessional now to have elected to go by a nickname professionally. In her defense, Millie Meyers had previously held a position in the People's House that didn't receive much attention from outside the cabinet. She enjoyed the work she had done as a speechwriter on principle. She absolutely loved writing and there were fewer and fewer opportunities for "creative" or "scholastic" work with the advent of artificial intelligence, so she was grateful to have writing be at the forefront of her work, even with the sometimes challenging work hours, thankless rewrites due to a change of policy or circumstance.

It was surprising that speechwriters hadn't yet become obsolete with the advanced artificial intelligence available, especially with Samuel Gowon's interest in the technology. The running joke was that even he recognized that he needed a hint of humanity to him, even if it was only in the words he read off a teleprompter.

Her mother, a really influential District lobbyist, who had carted her to rallies and protest marches as a child, had admittedly helped her acquire a position with the People's House directly out of college. She was undoubtedly Millie's top supporter and harshest critic. Most of the things she critiqued about the speeches she wrote were actually edits Gowon had made in the moment, a certain way he enunciated things that altered the overall message. She once made the mistake of telling her mother this and found herself sprawled across the floor, her skull throbbing, her cheeks swollen and bruised, and no recollection of how she'd ended up there.

She hadn't made the mistake of airing her grievances or criticisms out loud again.

The truth of the matter was that she felt proud of being a part of history, her words flowing to the world's ears, even if it was through the voice of the President, who had the charisma of a moldy crust of bread.

Millie had arrived that morning to a chaotic West Wing. There was a distinctly manic energy. There were far fewer people than normal, but it was the sort of emptiness that felt eerie more so than peaceful. The people who were there were clustered together conspiratorially outside the normal places she was used to seeing them.

Her cropped white hair slid over the contours of her cheeks as she poked her head into the workroom typically used by news correspondents. It was empty except for the Public Relations Coordinator's desk, which was occupied by Avril, administrative assistant for Communications, the daughter of a Congressperson, who she'd had forced social activities with since she was a young child.

Avril was hunched over her phone, continuously sliding a slender, manicured thumb upwards, scrolling through an endless tiling of photos.

"Avi, what's going on?"

There was no indication the woman heard her, eyes fixed on the faces on her phone screen. "They released footage of The Taken."

"The Taken?"

"Garrison Chase released information about the people who were kidnapped or killed by the Insurgents. It was an exclusive."

Of course it was, Millie thought. *Garrison Chase is basically state television.* She rolled her eyes, having disagreed with the forced vernacular of "insurgents." It didn't convey the message she felt like they were intending. Gowon and his cabinet seemed to be teetering about how to describe them. When asked direct questions about them, answers supported the idea that this was a small group of people. Insignificant. These "exclusive" news releases completely contradicted this idea, talking about the insurgents poisoning food and water supplies, causing power outages, and now, apparently kidnapping or trafficking a substantial number of people.

It made her job that much more difficult. The more contradictions she noticed, the more and more she felt like she had stumbled into the role of creating propaganda and while she was a vocal advocate for the Party's primary missions since elementary school, it was all starting to sound stale.

Most of her classmates had gone into roles within the government, but she'd heard stories about some escaping the confines of the District, going "off the grid," though based upon what she knew about surveillance along the border of the District, she doubted they got far.

Millie watched as Avril continued to scroll through videos, allowing each to play for a second or two until she had determined if she recognized them. She remembered when this type of scrolling on social media was accompanied by funny sound clips or sentimental songs, but now it sounded to be snippets of horror movies. Two seconds of screaming, move to the next. Two seconds of choking noises, move to the next. Two seconds of crying, move to the next.

Avril's eyes narrowed. "No, no, no, no," she pleaded, stopping on a video of a young man with shimmering blue eyes sitting on a clinical exam table, sweating profusely.

Millie recognized him as a movie actor who seemed to have a natural disaster or end of the world film released seasonally. There was light conversation pouring from the phone's speaker and then a sudden gasp, like someone breaking the surface of water after nearly drowning.

Millie moved around behind the woman's shoulder, her view of the phone screen slightly obstructed by Avril's stringy teal hair. "He's *suffocating*," Avril narrated softly to no one in particular.

"Millie Meyers?"

She startled, finding it challenging to clear away the image of white foam bubbling out of the mouth of the former movie star. In the doorway stood a willowy young man without an ounce of unnecessary body fat. His skin was pale, his cheeks gaunt, and he wore a metal headband over his forehead and temples. His eyes did not make eye contact, instead they were fixed to the left.

"Millie Meyers?" he repeated.

Avril glanced over her shoulder, seemingly out of annoyance for the disruption.

"Yes. I'm Millie Meyers."

The young man nodded once, a quick bob of his head. "Millie Meyers, the President would like to meet with you."

"I'm sorry?"

There was a pulsation of lights beneath the device and he continued to stare to the left, right cheek twitching. When the lights stopped, he nodded. "Millie Meyers, follow me."

*   *   *

Millie washed her hands in the restroom just outside the Press Room. She was due to make remarks in three and a half minutes.

She held her hand under the soap dispenser then froze, frowning.

She'd already used soap.

She quickly rinsed off her hand and inserted her hands into the automatic drying contraption.

Her heart clenched in a way she'd never experienced before and suddenly her eyes jolted up, fixed on her reflection.

She blinked.

The face staring back at her was hers, but it was like she was seeing this version of herself for the first time. Her hair was different, dyed its natural dark color, and fell in waves. Her makeup was heavy, but meant to look natural. Her lips looked more plump than she'd ever seen. She wore a simple tailored pant suit in a rich navy color with a silk button up shirt beneath. Her People's House credentials were prominently displayed over the left chest pocket of the blazer.

All of it was bizarre. It was her, but not her. She had no recollection of changing her appearance. Hell, she didn't have any recollection of stepping inside that bathroom.

90 seconds.

She lifted her hand to her cheek, finding her reflection matched the movement. She also found her fingers manicured, gleaming with a neutral polish. Millie lowered her hand, examining her nails, the moisturized, smooth skin.

Her eyes suddenly fixed upon a band of shimmering diamonds on her left ring finger.

You're married to Dakotah Brink. The two of you were childhood best friends turned lovers and recently eloped.

Millie narrowed her eyes upon the ring. *I don't know anyone named Dakotah,* she said silently. She felt a sudden sharp twinge in her temple.

Twenty seconds.

She blinked, shook out her shoulders, and reset herself in front of the mirror. She gazed into her reflection, took a breath in, and smiled lightly, imagining the faces of the press corp.

She gave a quick nod, turned, and walked confidently across the hall.

13

best

Matteo watched as Sara gently placed Hannah Marie West in Essie's arms. She was the youngest infant he'd seen so close since before he moved back to Colorado, more than seventeen years earlier. Most couples had experienced trouble conceiving, as Luke and Sara had, or faced miscarriages and stillbirths, as he and his wife, Rachel had. There were children younger than Essie at Calvary, but they had moved to town from elsewhere.

Hannah was a tiny, finicky little bundle with full, pursed lips and spiraled blonde hair. He'd spent a considerable amount of time holding her already, realizing he'd never held a baby of her age before, as Essie was nearly three by the time she'd come to live with him and he hadn't "met" either of the West boys until they were at least a few months old. He'd been overwhelmed by how endearing Hannah's little noises were, how holding her had an intoxicating, lulling effect.

Esther appeared nervous as she pulled Hannah close against her body, running her fingers along the back of the blanket in smooth, rhythmic circles. Her mouth moved to speak a few times, but she stopped short each time, finally tightening her hold on the baby with her right hand so she could blot tears from her eye with the left. Her lips curled up at the corners as she took in the features of Hannah's face.

Sara stopped to place her hand on Matteo's arm as she circled around to the kitchen. "Something about seeing your baby hold a baby, hm?"

He pressed his lips together, gave a short nod. "It's how it should be, right?"

"You could still have more children, Teo. We're all old, but we're not *that* old. Clearly." She lifted her chilly palm to his cheek, looking down at his face affectionately.

He raised his eyebrows and sighed. "You should sit down, Sara. Put your feet up."

"I will, I will," she said, continuing on her way. "Just going to get some tea."

"You gave birth five days ago. *Sit*," Luke ordered, herding her from the kitchen back into the living room. "I'll make your tea—and I'll do it just how you like it."

Matteo smiled as Sara took a seat beside him on the couch, resting her head on his shoulder. "He won't, but he'll really, really try," he murmured.

Sara smiled tightly, settled carefully into the cushion, her body still giving her sudden jolts of pain when she moved indelicately.

Esther tucked Hannah more snugly against her as the baby started to fuss. She released a soft *shhhhh*, but Hannah continued to squirm.

"She *can't* be hungry," Luke remarked.

"No, she just likes to be in motion," Sara replied, sliding to the edge of the couch, intent to stand and reclaim her infant.

With far more confidence than she'd shown so far, Esther rose to her feet, gently stroking Hannah's back as she proceeded to move about the room. She began to quietly sing as she did this, occasionally kissing the top of the newborn's head.

Gradually, Hannah eased back to sleep. As this happened, Essie smiled victoriously and continued to circle the room.

"She's never even held a baby before, *has she?*" Sara whispered.

Matteo shook his head. "I'm not sure when she would have had the chance." He'd heard of several babies being born to members of the congregation recently, but most kept the newborns home until they were a few months old. In anticipation, Essie had been working with the Youth Pastor to set up a few Sunday School classrooms to accommodate infants.

It was just as Luke was delivering his wife's tea cup that the front door swung open, and Josh entered, carrying a few bags of groceries. He stepped quickly to the kitchen, eager to place the bags on the counter. When he looked up and saw Esther holding his baby sister, he froze abruptly. As he watched her, his shoulders slowly lowered and his eyes became very round, his expression slightly dazed. When Essie's path around the house led her toward him, his lips curled up. "*Hi,*" he said in a breathy syllable.

"*Hi,*" she echoed back, eyes bright. "Nice haircut."

"It was time."

She smiled tightly. "You have a very adorable baby sister."

"You should see my emotional support human."

She scowled half-heartedly at him, cheeks reddening.

As her path weaved around the dining room, he followed behind her as far as the kitchen table, avoiding the watchful eye of his mom, who wore a knowing smile. He took a hard right down the hallway, presumably to use the bathroom.

Esther was just making her way back toward the living room area when Hannah released a very full burp–which accompanied a fair amount of her last nursing session.

Sara jumped to her feet. "Oh, I'm sorry, Essie. She was very enthusiastic at her last feeding. I knew she was having too much."

Esther scrunched her nose as Sara peeled the now sleeping baby away, wincing as she took in the sight of the warm, creamy goo seeping down the front of her shirt. It had a pungent, thick odor to it. She had her arms locked in the position they had been in while holding Hannah, afraid to move, but no one seemed to be coming to her rescue.

146

"I have some extra shirts in the nursery I use for such an occasion," Sara said somewhat dismissively. "Bottom drawer of the dresser." She waved her hand toward the hall, immediately moving to clean up her baby, who, other than a smudge on her chin, was entirely free of vomit. She checked the floor around her feet. "Wow, I guess she managed to only get you, sweetie." Pleased by this, Sara carefully sat back on the couch, easing Hannah onto her chest. She propped her feet up on the coffee table.

Essie made brief eye contact with her dad, eyes wide and disbelieving, before turning on the spot and moving stiffly down the hallway.

Unlike the Wests' farm in Colorado, Esther was not very familiar with their house at the Ark. As a child she spent so much time at the farm, finding all the nooks and crannies of infrequently accessed closets and rooms during games of hide and seek. There were certainly fewer acceptable opportunities to explore other people's houses and develop that sort of familiarity as an adult.

The Ark house was much smaller, just the one story, but for being such a small house, there were quite a few door options down the one and only hallway: the furthest door on the right led to Sara and Luke's bedroom, the next was a closet, followed by the small den and the only bathroom in the house. On the left were the accordion doors for the laundry, another storage closet and the nursery. Hannah's door stood out from the rest in that it had a decorative tulle wreath with the letter H hanging on it. She pushed open the door and pulled in her breath.

Josh was wearing far less clothes than just a couple minutes earlier—he was, in fact, wearing only his boxer shorts as he unfolded a fresh pair of jeans. To her fascination, the muscles she had jokingly admired on a number of occasions in his arms continued into his back. His tanned skin had a chiseled look about it, like carved stone.

It was as Josh rotated to face her, attempting eye contact—like a normal person—that Esther's eyes widened and she immediately spun around toward the doorway. In a much higher octave than was typical for her, she burst out with: "*What happened to your clothes, Josh?*"

He chuckled to himself, hearing his dad laugh through the wall, and quickly pulled on and zipped his jeans. "Sorry, I was just changing clothes. My dad is allergic to cats and I was out at a farm that has dozens of them that are rather fond of me."

"*Oh*. Okay," she said, nodding approvingly, pressing her lips together, voice still unnaturally high. "I thought you were in the bathroom."

"There's only one. I didn't want to occupy it if–"

She furrowed her brow, squeezing her eyes tighter. "No, yeah, that's thoughtful of you."

"Essie, you can turn around."

"I think I remember your dad having allergies," she said, continuing to nod unnecessarily with her eyes still closed. "So you keep extra clothes here just in case?"

He finished pulling on a clean t-shirt. "Yep."

"That's thoughtful of you."

"Essie?" he said quietly.

"Yeah?"

"You can look now."

She turned cautiously, wincing as she opened her eyes. "Sorry. That was a really weird reaction I had just then." *Especially considering you share a bed with the man.*

"Your voice got *really* squeaky," he teased, grinning.

"It *did*," she said, clearing her throat. "It did. Sorry. I just came in here for a shirt. Hannah–" She tugged at the hem of her shirt.

"She tagged you, huh?"

"To say the least. Your mom said she keeps spare t-shirts in the bottom drawer of the dresser?" She motioned to the dresser behind him.

He bent down and retrieved a heathered navy shirt, which according to the date on the chest, which also featured a collegiate crest from his mom's school, was twenty-three years old. "If you want to, you can throw your shirt in the bag with my clothes. I'll make sure it gets back to you."

148

She nodded, peering around the room nervously.

"I'll let you have some privacy," he said, his cheeks tight as he side-stepped around her.

*　　　*　　　*

Esther had been sitting in the rocking chair on the porch beside her dad, gnawing persistently at her thumbnail for thirty seconds when he turned to her and said: "So Josh is back in contention."

She frowned. "*What?*"

"I'll admit I am *not* very good at figuring out where you all are with this whole love triangle situation. I know you and Josh have been spending a considerable amount of time together," he began, lifting his brow in a way that conveyed all the things he wasn't going to mention, including that she'd been sleeping at Josh's cabin for a few weeks at that point. "—but the last time we had an extended conversation about the West boys, it seemed like Josh had put himself out of contention for romance."

"Daddy."

"I suppose things never had a chance to reach the pique of drama when the three of you were younger."

"Are you *enjoying* yourself? Look at you."

He shrugged. "I guess I'm just happy to see you experiencing something that's a fairly normal teenager problem."

She declined the opportunity to remind him that she was no longer a teenager. She had started to take opportunities she may have previously used in jest to maintain silence. He attributed this to her maturity growing, the hard edges of the world softening her further, but as he watched her gaze toward the hidden horizon, he thought there may have been some sadness there.

As she blinked, seemingly coming out of a trance, he considered the possibility that she was simply experiencing a split-attention. "It's not a love triangle," she said finally.

"It's not?"

"The concept of love triangles makes no sense because the points don't all connect. If anything, they should call it a love V."

"I'll buy that logic," he agreed, pursing his lips. "Is it a love V?"

"*No*, it's not."

He nodded.

"But you *knew* that."

He pursed his lips. "The crocodile hunter won you over after all, eh?" His eyes gleamed over the intricate tattoo on her forearm, specifically the hat resting on Bree's back.

"A long time ago actually," she said matter-of-factly. "But you knew that, too, didn't you?"

He gave a short nod.

"Which is why you're always leaving the room or the front porch when he comes over. You're not exactly subtle. He's going to start to think you don't like him." She lifted her brow.

"You know, I'm *not* really worried about that."

"Don't gloat," she said with a smirk. "And by the way, that was a *painful* Australian accent."

"Better than your Italian one."

"No fake accent is better than my Italian one."

He grinned.

"Don't gloat," she muttered.

"I'm not." He tightened his lips. "Does he know?"

She sighed. "I think based upon–whatever *that* was in the nursery–he has a *vague* idea that I have feelings for him, yes."

"That's lust, not love. It's part of it, but–"

She cringed. "Daddy, please don't say the word 'lust.'"

"Fine. *Eros*."

Her jaw fell open. "Stop enjoying this so much. You are a *pastor*. *And* you're my dad."

"Fair enough," he said with a nod. "You haven't told him though? Surely this has come up with you staying at his place?"

She pressed her lips together, eyes panning across the landscape. She shook her head. "I mean, *yes,* but I've been able to suppress it. That little outburst though?"

"What's holding you back from being a couple? That's like the million dollar question around here."

She frowned. "There's just–a lot on my mind. Adjusting to living here. Adjusting to a semi-normal life? It's just taking me a long time to adjust mentally to everything. I'm using the word 'adjusting' too much." She shook her head. "It's just been a lot."

He nodded. "That's fair."

"Things haven't really felt 'normal' since I was fifteen. I think I've needed time to figure out what that feels like, who I am without all the other stuff. I've needed to find my way back to God, too."

Matteo gazed across at her just as she lifted her hand to the cross pendant around her neck, gently ran it between her fingers. "That's good. That you recognize you need that time."

She stretched her back, took a breath. "Josh has been really good about letting me have some breathing room."

He nodded.

"—and just being a support for me."

Matteo took a deep breath. "*Well,* you just take all the time you need."

The silence swelled.

She smiled tightly, then shook her head. "It's seriously been like– what was that phrase in the olden days? 'The elephant in the room'?"

He nodded. "That *is* what we said in the olden days."

"We're around each other all the time and I can feel him just– *waiting* for me, you know?"

"I *do* know. But you shouldn't rush yourself."

"I know."

He grinned. "Just a warning though–and this should have no bearing whatsoever on your timetable, but after taking care of Hannah a few times, I might be getting grandkid fever. Just a heads up–no pressure."

Her mouth fell open. "It is *not* Biblical times, Daddy. You're not as young as you once were, but you'd be a *very* young grandpa. An awesome grandpa," she said, raising her eyebrow, "but very young."

He shrugged.

"If you want a baby so much, go trot yourself down to life groups, or to the pub even, and find yourself a charming lady (who isn't too close to my age or too close to menopause, whenever that happens), and have an adorable baby you love slightly less than me."

"I hit the jackpot with the first kid. Any new one would just be a disappointment."

She raised her eyebrows, considering his assessment. "I think a new baby would have a fighting chance of being the favorite. I can be a real pain in the ass."

He nodded. "*Yeah.*"

She glanced over her shoulder through the front window then sat forward rigidly on the chair. "Are you almost ready to head home? I'm thinking I should probably stay at the ranch tonight."

He shook his head. "I'm watching Hannah so Sara and Luke can go out for a couple hours."

"It's 7pm. I'm surprised you're not in bed yet."

He grinned.

"I just—I didn't know you were planning to stay."

"I just decided to actually."

She pressed her lips together. "You're trying to set it up so Josh drives me home."

He furrowed his brow. "You two are alone together *all* the time. Why's it such a big deal for him to drive you home tonight?" His voice lifted at the end.

She released a long exhale.

"You know, it's not *that* far. You take the truck, I'll just walk back later."

"If you were a younger man, I might be okay with that."

He was happy for the jesting; maturing and sensitivity be damned. "*Turd*."

"Gotta take care of those joints, Daddy," she said, patting his knee. Through the front window, she could see Josh snuggling his baby sister on his chest. She cleared her throat, running her hands briskly over her arms to warm herself.

"In all seriousness, you *should* take whatever time you need—" Matteo waited for her to make eye contact.

She raised her eyebrows. "*But?*"

"But I think you need to talk to him," he said softly. "If you're not ready, tell him that. I don't know what conversations the two of you have had." He furrowed his brow. "But it'd probably feel better if you were on the same page about it."

"Yeah. It would."

"That way maybe you could still get some sleep tonight."

"It's weird for you, I know. It's honestly just sleeping. When I stay out there?"

He lifted his brow. "You're 20 years old, Essie. You can make decisions for yourself. But if it makes you feel better? I believe you—*especially* after—" He grinned, glancing back toward the window, but stopping short of saying anything more.

She buried her face in her hands. "That was a surreal little moment, I'm not going to lie. I've known him for 17 years, but I *still*–" She sat upright and scrunched her nose, making a swirling motion with her hand over her stomach.

"Butterflies?"

"Yeah," she practically whispered. She seemed to be continuously suppressing a smile.

He nodded slowly. "*Now*, not to take anything away from what you're feeling--I know things are much different now."

"But?" she said, frowning.

"But when you came to see me before you left to get Gabe from Denver, I was actually worried about the dynamic between you and Josh.

What you said about it feeling like he abandoned you, like he only cared about you *sometimes*?"

"Yeah."

"That's not a feeling I want you to have. Ever. Things seem *different* now, but I feel an obligation as your dad–"

"And primary spiritual counsel?"

He smiled, wavering his hand. "--to check in with you about it."

She lifted her eyes.

"Has that changed?"

Essie nodded slowly. "A lot of it was me. *Most* of it was me. When I was little, it was easier to compartmentalize the negative so I could just be happy and carefree with Josh. Once all of the stuff from *before* came to the forefront and I was having to deal with the memories, the nightmares, the– *discomfort* of the antidote sessions with Luther–I still tried. I wanted it to just be us without all that and that just wasn't a possibility. I kept most of it from him. I didn't speak up. I didn't open up and tell him I was struggling so much. I thought if I let any of that leak in, I would never feel the joy I felt with him again."

Matteo planted his foot, momentarily pausing the rocking of his chair.

She shrugged. "I needed him, I needed his support during all of that, but I just refused to let him in in the way I needed. I refused to tell him I needed him."

"That must have felt miserable. You isolated yourself for years, Essie."

She nodded, swallowing hard. "I mean, he was away at Mandatory for some of it."

He tilted his chin to the side. "Do you let him in now?"

"Yeah."

He pursed his lips. "And?"

She shrugged. "He's *Josh*. He's supportive, he's easy to talk to. He's perfect, basically." She tucked her hair behind her ears. "It's really inconvenient sometimes."

"No one's perfect," Matteo said in a soft, warning tone.

"No, I know that," she remarked with a roll of her eyes, a tightening of her cheeks. "'Perfect' isn't actually perfect. It's just the sum of who he is terribly, irritatingly perfect for the sum of all the chaos and sass I have to offer over here."

"You know, I *think* that you have this amazing self-awareness, and then you say things like that."

"Oh, I'm just being a turd," she muttered, rubbing her hands over her arms again. "I'm not all terrible."

"What are you afraid of?" he asked softly.

Essie wiped roughly at her eyes. "It's going to sound really selfish."

"That's okay."

She peered over her shoulder to the window and took a deep breath. "I'm afraid I won't be able to give him children."

Matteo blinked. "*That's* what's holding you back?"

She shrugged. "It's not *just* that, but it factors into the equation of if things are going to work out between us. *And* if things don't work out between us and he's gone from my life–" She swept at her eyes, reset herself in the chair so she was facing further from the window. "I can't imagine Josh not being in my life. Like, I'd survive. I know I'd survive. It's not some totally codependent situation, but I just–I mean, in my emotional devastation, I'd probably wind up with someone like Miles–and that'd *maybe* be okay?"

"Bite your tongue, young lady."

She smiled lightly. "Miles isn't a bad guy. He just acts immature sometimes. Can't totally blame him for that. His sister did the best she could after their parents died, but she wasn't much older than him. She indulged him a lot, kind of babied him, and then when *she* died–" She shook her head. "Forget I said that about Miles. That wasn't nice. I adore Miles. I was just using humor to make myself feel better about an entirely hypothetical situation." She exhaled deeply. "And anyway, it wouldn't make me feel better–because I'd know Josh was in the world and we weren't together."

He furrowed his brow. "I'm a little surprised."

"About?"

"You mentioned Miles next–if things didn't work out with Josh."

"I was joking."

"Still."

"You thought I'd say Gabe?"

He shrugged.

"Don't get me wrong, I love Gabe—as a *friend*, an older brother, but—" She shook her head. "Look who I'm talking to. You're the one who told me five years ago that Gabe and I weren't compatible."

"Did I?"

"Yeah. Yeah you did."

Silence filled the space between them. Matteo allowed the quiet to stretch, waiting for Essie to air the words her heart wanted so desperately to say.

Finally, she sat more upright in her chair, stretching out her back. She glanced over her shoulder again. When she didn't immediately turn back around, Matteo followed her gaze. Josh, still holding Hannah on his chest, had locked eyes with her and was smiling lightly. Essie's cheeks tightened and she turned back around, taking a steadying breath.

"I *love* Josh," she said in a quiet voice. Her mouth tightened with some relief, but tears were pooling in her eyes. She glanced erratically out the corner of her vision at her dad, waiting for him to speak. "I always have."

"Loving someone is the scariest thing we do," he said softly. "It requires us to open ourselves up to the possibility that we could lose that person at some point. Whether that's because the relationship doesn't work out–or if something happens to them."

She wiped at her eyes with the hem of Sara West's old college t-shirt.

"But I'll tell you, kiddo? Love is always worth it."

Her chin rotated toward him. It wasn't often he spoke about Rachel.

"I knew my love for you was immense–"

Essie watched her dad's expression deteriorate.

"--but *nothing* could prepare me for the fear that something could happen to you." He swallowed hard. "I felt it when you were little, for sure. All throughout your life, actually. There's a constant worry as a parent.

"When I thought you might not make it back here, when I thought something might happen to you when you went to Denver? That was a fear I would never have been able to prepare for." He shook his head. "Would I have chosen not to love you to avoid that feeling? That fear?"

Essie raised her eyebrows.

"Hell, no. That aching feeling, that worry, that gut-wrenching fear? It just speaks to how much you mean to me. And Essie?" He patted his chest. "Non ci sono parole per descrivere quanto ti amo." *There are no words to describe how much I love you.* "Non ho mai amato nessuno quanto amo te." *I have never loved anyone as much as I love you.*

She smiled, eyes glistening in the light pouring out from the window, the weight of his words resonating in her chest. "Dio deve amarmi molto per benedirmi con te come mio papà." *God must love me a lot to bless me with you as my Dad.*

His jaw tightened, his eyes panning out to the dark horizon. "I shouldn't have razzed you about grandkids. Just to be clear, I was teasing– *mostly.*"

She shook her head. "I know no one knows if they can have kids– with what went on over the last few decades. At least I know *theoretically* I can."

"What do you mean?"

"I had Luther run tests to make sure."

"Then why 'theoretically' can you have kids?"

She took a breath. "My body destroys anything it sees as a threat."

He frowned. "You think your body would see a baby as a *threat?*"

She gave a small shrug. "I know a baby is totally different from a pathogen or a parasite–those are talking points from the people who 'shout their abortion,' but what I *am*? What my body does? Is the result of *their* goals. The female body was designed by God to nurture and protect new life."

He raised his eyes.

"What if mine is more selfish than that?"

He felt a lump in his throat. "There's not a selfish thing about you."

"That's not true."

"It's mostly true. It's truer for you than anyone else I've ever known." He sighed, leaning back in his chair. "Have you prayed about this?"

She nodded.

"And?"

Essie gave him a light smile, though tears had started to spill over her eyelashes. She began to murmur the lyrics to the first hymn she performed with the Children's Ministry when she was three. "*Trust in the Lord with all your heart, and lean not on your own understanding.*"

She was the only child to add her own choreography, placing her hand on her hip and wagging her finger in the rhythm of the syllables of the chorus. "I provided the silence when I was praying, for God to answer me–and that song started playing in my head."

"Proverbs 3."

"Yep."

He took a deep breath, shaking his head. "I don't think I can add any wisdom to that. I believe God has a plan to give you a future beyond all that you've done already."

She leaned back in her chair, clearing her throat. "My advice still stands if you want a baby, Daddy. You can skit-skat to the singles group."

He tightened his lips, accepting that the serious portion of their conversation had concluded. "So where do you think you'll have the wedding?"

She stood, started across the driveway toward the ranch at a determined pace.

"Don't tell me you haven't thought about it."

She cupped her hand to her ear, her cheeks tight. "*What?* I can't hear you."

"We spotted a bear family down the road earlier tonight."

She rotated on her heel and aimed herself back toward the Wests' front door. By the time she had reached the porch, Matteo had stood. Essie deviated from her path abruptly and walked straight into his arms.

"What's this for?" he asked, closing his arms around her.

Her breaths were staggered. "Perché ti amo, Daddy. Perché ti amo." *Because I love you, Daddy. Because I love you.*

He kissed the top of her head.

Twenty minutes later, Sara was prodding Luke down the hallway ordering him to put on his "dress" jeans, Matteo laid happily on the couch with Hannah sleeping on his chest, and Essie was making her way out to the driveway where Josh was waiting to drive her home.

14

ti porterò

Essie always remembered Luke describing Matteo's office at Calvary Church as reminding him of a principal's office, or maybe a psychologist's office. When she'd first heard him say it, she didn't have a familiarity with either. She just knew she very much liked to spend time there.

The office was quite small and dark, as the narrow rectangular basement windows were covered with an opaque film tinting. Most of the furniture in the room was large and ornate and looked like it belonged in a medieval castle. There was the tufted leather sofa and its chenille throw pillows, a high back floral patterned chair with curved wooden arm rests, a heavy table centered beneath the sofa and chair, as well as his desk, which took up a third of the space. The desk had clanky brass drawer pulls and the wooden legs were carved with tremendous detailed patterns.

Her dad typically used a laptop, which took up a tiny section of the deskspace. He had a few small stacks of papers, a nearly empty coffee mug, and a simple white stone frame, which contained a photo of him carrying Essie when she was three years old. Luke took the photograph when they went to a Christmas tree lot her first Christmas after coming to live with him.

They were both heavily bundled in hooded jackets. Essie had on a pair of wool gloves, her hand braced on his arm staring wide-eyed over his shoulder toward a selection of trees, the twinkle lights sparkling in her eyes, her expression awestruck. Matteo was smiling across at her with an equal amount of wonder.

She adored the photo. Looking at it filled her chest with warmth, seeing a candid view of how affectionately her dad looked at her when she wasn't paying attention.

She remembered blinking slowly as she took in the scene around them, and then she remembered meeting his eye. His smile widened considerably as they looked at one another–and then he gave her a kiss on the forehead and told her he loved her.

She remembered being overwhelmed in that moment, feeling so much at once. She had tucked herself against him, head burrowed under his chin, and said: "I love you more."

It's better not to feel.
It's better not to think.
It's better not to remember.
Thoughts are the enemy.
Feelings are the enemy.
Memories are the enemy.
The nothingness is peaceful.
The nothingness is safe.

The first blow made direct impact with her right jaw. She wasn't sure what hit her, but it was heavy. solid, and constructed of metal. The second felt like it caused an explosion in her left eardrum. Something warm pooled in that ear. The third made her skull echo like a clock tower bell and everything faded to black.

The nothingness is peaceful.
The nothingness is safe.

15
fiction

Unveiling the Layers of Annette Gibbons

"The life of Annette Gibbons, the esteemed Speaker of the House and First Lady, had been one of twists and turns, a narrative woven with strands of determination, resilience, and transformation. To understand the woman behind the powerful titles, one must delve into the roots of her journey - a journey that began in the affluent conservatism of a small town in Oregon.

"Annette was born wrapped in the comfort of an influential conservative family. But even from a young age, she found herself wrestling with the weight of expectations that accompanied her status. Raised in the shadow of her older sister Mikayla, she often felt like her own identity was being overshadowed. And then there was her name - Annette - a name she often found incongruous with the spirited soul she felt within. It was as if she had been assigned a moniker that didn't quite match her true self.

"As her frustration with societal norms in her hometown grew, Annette began to reject not just her name, but also the values and principles her family upheld. The day after her high school graduation, she left behind the comforts of her childhood home and set out on a journey of self-discovery.

"*Enrolling at the University of California-Berkeley, Annette chose to study communication, a discipline that aligned with her newfound passion for advocating change through dialogue. Her time at Berkeley proved to be pivotal, her enthusiasm for justice and equality igniting a fire within her, and she began to discover her voice that would eventually inspire generations of women that followed her.*

"*It was a fateful day at a protest rally in San Francisco that etched its mark on Annette's life. Her experience of being brutally assaulted shook her to her core, leaving her grappling with pain, fear, and anger. The perpetrators included a prominent Republican congressman, a man whose political ideologies stood in stark contrast to her own. Despite the trauma she endured, Annette found the strength to stand up and tell her story, to face her attackers in court and demand justice. Her testimony shattered the facade of power, bringing to light the darkness that could lurk beneath.*

"*This harrowing experience did not break Annette; it galvanized her. Her determination to rise above the pain and the odds propelled her to run for office. Her story of survival and her fierce advocacy for justice drew people from all walks of life, transcending political affiliations. This led to her running in direct opposition to the very congressman who had assaulted her. It was a victory that symbolized the strength of the human spirit against adversity, and a moment that exemplified the power of change.*

"*As a Congresswoman, Annette wasted no time. She channeled her unwavering determination into an ambitious agenda, using her platform to advocate for the rights of women, the marginalized, and those who had been silenced for too long. Her tenure was marked by landmark legislation relating to reproductive equity, abortion rights, and the groundbreaking legalization of artificial wombs. Her passion and resilience were undeniable, and her commitment to justice was unwavering.*

"In a testament to her dedication and the impact she had made, Annette Gibbons was voted as the Speaker of the House at the start of her third term as Congressperson. This new role catapulted her to a position of even greater influence, allowing her to shape policies and legislation that would have a profound impact on the nation. Her journey, from a small-town upbringing to a powerful political force, served as a beacon of hope for those who believed in the transformative power of resilience and determination.

"Annette Gibbons is viewed as one of the greatest living role models for children, as a woman who rejected convention, triumphed over adversity, and used her voice to amplify the cries for justice that often went unheard. Her name has become a symbol of strength and change, embodying the essence of a woman who refused to be defined by circumstances, and instead, carved her path with courage and conviction."

Annette stared at the last line of the writing sample:
...carved her path with courage and conviction.
It was lies. All of it.

She turned to her computer and began to tap out a biography that was better grounded to reality. Things started off well, as she immediately thought of a title that resonated with her.

Falling Up

"Annette Gibbons had been born into a world of kindness and faith, nurtured by loving parents and an older sister, Mikayla, who all held steadfast to their Christian beliefs. Growing up in a close-knit family, she had spent her summers at her grandparents' cabin on a serene lake in Marion County, Oregon. These cherished moments formed the foundation of her childhood, creating what should have been an unbreakable bond with her family.

"Annette's path diverged sharply from her family when her sister Mikayla married at eighteen and started a family. Annette felt a growing sense of

resentment towards her sister's choices, growing uneasy about a similar lifestyle for herself. As time passed, that resentment extended to her parents and the extended family, accusing them of living a life she saw as cultist and stifling.

"Annette's restlessness reached its peak. The day after her high school graduation, she left her childhood home without even leaving a note and moved to the bustling campus of the University of California-Berkeley. Enveloped in the vibrant atmosphere of college life, she delved headlong into sorority activities, protests, and clubs.

"Her impressionable nature led her down a path of radical political beliefs, and she eagerly participated in controversial protests that sometimes spiraled into chaos. Annette's academic performance suffered, leaving her buried in student loans and debt. The haze of protests was often accompanied by heavy drinking and drug use, leading to moments of recklessness that would haunt her.

"It was during one such moment that Annette's life took a turn she could never have foreseen. Awakening beside a busy intersection with a fragmented memory of the night's events, she found herself facing a reality too grim to ignore. Social media posts exposed the unthinkable - Annette had been sexually assaulted while unconscious during the protest. Shocked and traumatized, Annette's life seemed to be spiraling out of control. In her lowest moment, she was visited by a group of public relations specialists who saw an opportunity to capitalize on her story. It turns out, a Republican Congressman named Victor Lance was garnering attention for his efforts to bridge the gap between political parties. Since the photographs of her gruesome assault did not depict specific attackers, the PR specialists suggested she come forward with accusations against Congressman Lance, aiming to flip a historically red congressional district.

"*The accusations triggered a brief and sensational public trial, with Annette providing compelling, but fabricated testimony that captivated the nation. Riding the waves of public sympathy, she followed the advice of the PR team to run for office, ultimately unseating Congressman Lance herself.*

"*Her ascent to power continued as she was voted Speaker of the House after two terms in Congress. Each success came with an unsettling realization that the programs, the bills, the budgets, she was supporting went against her beliefs, but she accepted this as a means to an end, knowing it was her ultimate destiny was the presidency. The weight of her aspirations led her to become complacent in the face of a political machine that saw her as a pawn to further their agendas.*

"*Yet, the darkest moment of Annette's life was still to come. A team of public relations representatives convinced her to become pregnant, not for personal reasons but as a strategic move to further her political image. She was persuaded to participate in a genetic optimization trial, offering up her unborn child for experimentation. Blinded by ambition and manipulated by those around her, Annette agreed to the trial, not realizing that by doing so, she was committing her unborn child to a horrifying fate.*

"*Her conscience finally stirred just before her planned labor, set to unfold within the hallowed halls of Congress. As she reflected on her life and the choices she had made, Annette realized that the path she was on was not one she wanted for herself or her child. Determined to break free from the clutches of those who controlled her, she decided to leave the political landscape behind and return home.*

"*However, escaping the District was not so simple. Her captors had invested too much in her political rise and more importantly, into her unborn child. She was forcibly drugged, her labor induced, awakening later to be told that her child had died during birth. In reality, her child had been stolen away to endure nightmarish genetic experiments, a fate more horrifying than she could have ever imagined.*

"As Annette Gibbons stood at this crossroads, she faced not only the demons of her past choices but also the tangled web of power and manipulation that had ensnared her. The journey ahead held the chance of redemption, but also the looming threat of an even darker truth waiting to be uncovered."

*   *   *

Christopher Loop lifted his phone, narrowing his eyes upon the incoming number. He cleared his throat, turned his ear away from the loud conversation taking place to his left. "This is Chris."

"Are you armed?"

He frowned, trying to decipher the voice on the other end of the line.   He'd programmed the number into his phone with a code name for Annette Gibbons, but after six years, he never expected the name "MJ Watson" to ever show up on his phone. And yet, there it was.

She'd had a rocky press conference in the Oval Office, wrapping up a rather "off" week for her. There'd been a number of incidents where she'd lost her train of thought, where she'd stopped blinking for an excessive amount of time, eyes wide, clearly struggling. Sometime after the press conference and after having a private meeting with Gowon, she'd staggered out of the Oval Office, struggling to breathe. Christopher had accompanied her to the south exit, avoiding the awaiting press. After talking her through some breathing exercises to help her recover from what seemed to be an anxiety attack, he bid her farewell.

They'd encountered each other again outside the South Lawn gardens in an under-utilized parking area. It seemed intentional on her part. She had the look of someone with information to share, or at the very least, someone who was desperate for an ally. He'd offered her a ride home out of politeness, knowing very well she'd never be able to accept, even if she was itching to share information with him. He had felt legitimately concerned for her when she expressed her intent to take a walk. The guards certainly never would have let her leave on foot, but he was aware of snipers situated outside the District who were primed to take out anyone from the Party who put themselves in their crosshairs. As they stood in the secured parking lot, he found himself stepping into the most advantageous sightlines to block the shot. He certainly couldn't warn her about the snipers.

When she'd declined the ride and directed her feet back toward the White House, he'd made a show of leaning down to pick up "her phone," just in case any security guards were paying attention, and had slid the burner phone into her blazer pocket. She watched him do this and hadn't said anything, so he had anticipated he'd be getting a call. He lost quite a bit of sleep waiting for the phone to ring, afraid he'd miss it.

"You said you don't go anywhere without your unicorn bubble wand," she added for clarification and to hint at her identity.

He had to remind himself of the conversation they'd had. He warned her about walking around the streets outside the White House, how he concealed carried and still didn't like walking around after dark. She had then remarked about gun laws, which resulted in some surprising back and forth quips about the ridiculousness of gun restrictions, which included mention of unicorn bubble wands(?) It sounded bizarre, but he found his mouth curling upward at the memory, at her unexpected playfulness with him.

His shoulders eased. "Yeah, that's right." He chuckled. "*This* is a phone call I didn't think I'd ever receive. I don't think they make charging cords anymore for such a relic."

"It was turned off."

"Ah."

"I figured there was probably a GPS tracker in it."

"It wouldn't do much good anymore, would it? From what I hear, you don't leave the White House." He regretted speaking so loudly, but no one around him seemed to be paying much attention, much too focused on the soccer game on the monitors.

"This is true."

She didn't correct him about the current official name of the building, which seemed to be a positive sign. The "People's House" sounded asinine considering none of the implied "people" would be allowed to set foot inside.

"Well, it's turned on now. What does your device there say about my whereabouts?"

"I wasn't–I got a text on my other phone. Wait, can you see me right now?"

"Of course not. *I* can't see you and you *aren't* tracking my location."

Through the ear piece, Christopher could hear the same Irish jig playing through the speakers of the pub where he was sitting. The app on his secondary phone confirmed his suspicions. His eyes scanned the occupants of the high top tables behind him.

"Colder.'"

He turned the opposite direction.

"No, you forget. I'm the Ice Queen."

He turned the opposite way again.

"Colder."

He locked eyes with a brunette with wispy fringe. Her facial structure looked a little different, but there was something familiar in the shape, the color of her eyes. "*This* is unexpected."

"Are you staying nearby?"

"Well my house is in upstate–" He stopped short. "That's not what you asked, is it?"

"No."

He nodded slowly. "I'm staying just around the corner. At the Lincoln."

She stood, taking one last swig of her drink. She wore a pair of black high-waisted, tailored dress pants, a billowing white V-neck silk blouse and lifted her eyes to meet his gaze as she passed him, moving elegantly toward the exit.

The District sidewalks seemed far more bustling than usual as Christopher stepped out into the evening. Much had been done over the past six years to rid the District of undesirable residents. The area had the feel of a high-end entertainment complex, catering to the ultra-powerful and ultra-rich.

Annette was already ten yards ahead. She didn't look back as she made the turn that would lead to his hotel lobby.

It probably wasn't wise to enter into a meeting with the President's wife, who just so happened to have been appointed Vice President after Rose Bingham's sudden passing, attributed to previously undiagnosed cardiac condition.

It wasn't that he feared for his life; he was fairly certain if Gowon wanted him dead, he wouldn't send his wife. He'd actually been surprised he hadn't been taken out yet; it had started to negatively affect his confidence that he was having any impact on the world. The country was literally crumbling and sometimes he felt like he was simply an end of the world sports commentator.

With that thought, he quickened his pace.

He caught up with her at the elevator bank only because she paused to read through the information on a daily cocktail hour that took place in the rooftop garden. She trailed him into the elevator, where he pressed his thumb to the control panel. "Welcome back, Mr. Loop. And *guest*," the elevator said in a questioning tone. "Shall I add–*Melanie Siever*–to your reservation?" Christopher glanced across at Annette. "No, Elevator AI Lady."

"OK, let me know if you change your mind. Guest safety is our top concern."

The elevator chimed at the ninth floor. "Have a pleasant evening, Mr. Loop. Ms. Siever."

Christopher led the way to a door halfway down the hall. He pressed his thumb to the lock.

"Good evening, Mr. Loop. Good evening, Ms. Siever," the door announced.

Annette paused, glaring at the source of the voice.

He put his index finger to his mouth and moved inside, holding the door open for her. Once they were both inside, he fixed a mechanism to the backside of the door, tapped a few buttons, then nodded affirmatively as it activated. He pulled out a palm-sized device and proceeded to pace around the room.

"We're clear," he finally said. "You'd be surprised where I've found bugging equipment and cameras."

"I probably wouldn't be surprised."

He frowned.

"Windows? Mirrors?"

"Yep."

"Sewn into sheets."

He furrowed his brow, motioning to the leather sofa. "Why don't you take a seat? Would you like a drink? I'm not sure what you were having downstairs."

"Something strong over ice will do."

"I probably don't have ice, but I can run down the hallway."

"Something strong will do."

He nodded. "You've got it." He opened a mini bar whiskey bottle and emptied it into a rocks glass. "I can get ice. It's not a problem."

She shook her head, accepting the glass. "What's the mechanism you put on the door?"

"It blocks out signals, listening devices, Bluetooth, wireless connections, scanners, and provides soundproofing."

"They should make body suits with that."

He lifted his eyebrows. "I have them on the walls, ceiling, and floor."

She nodded. "Smart."

"I'm not naive enough to think I can't still be spied on or killed no matter where I am or what devices I have, but I'd like to think I can give them a bit of a challenge." He suddenly remembered his faltering confidence and realized he probably sounded like a pompous asshole, or worse, a fool. "Not that I'm making any sort of impact on things, right? I'm just complaining into the void."

Annette furrowed her brow. "Not into the void. Your viewership is higher than ever."

"Oh. We don't really get the same feedback or statistics anymore. It's hard to know who's watching."

"The data exists."

"Ah."

She shrugged. "Why do you continue to do what you do, if you think you're not making an impact?"

"What am I doing? Pissing off politicians?"

"I mean without sponsors, contracts, with social media regulations, you can't be making anywhere near what you used to."

"No. I'm living off what I was able to make before."

"Why do you still do it?"

He took a deep breath. "To feel like I'm doing something, I guess?"

"You must feel like you could be taken out at any moment."

He shrugged. "No more than anyone else. I'd feel a little safer with whatever you have there?" He motioned to her face. "Is that a prosthetic or makeup?"

"Off the record?"

"Off the–yeah. I'm not recording anything. You kind of caught me off guard. Not that I would have recorded anything if you hadn't caught me off guard." He frowned.

"This is you off guard?" she said, glancing over at the door.

"That's all a part of normal life. This is all feeling very surreal though. I'm actually starting to think I'm trapped in one of the government simulation programs. Just hoping I don't wind up like poor Millie Meyers."

She narrowed her eyes. "The new Press Secretary?"

"Yeah. Up there spewing Gowon propaganda?"

Annette, as Melanie, appeared a bit distracted by his assessment. "Why do you say '*Poor* Millie Meyers'?"

He pressed his lips together. "I'll just say, that's not the Millie Meyers I know."

Annette frowned. "Is she a spy?"

He winced. "Not exactly. Fine, I'll just say it; I can't say anything that will put her *more* in harm's way. Gowon chose her for that role for a reason–to send a message–or rather, a threat."

She lifted her eyebrows, encouraging him to continue.

"For a few years now, there's been a Gowon 'insider' posting on dark web, secure 4chan boards, sharing details about prominent District residents, congresspeople, speculating about the plans of the Gowon Administration, issuing warnings about different initiatives, speaking out against the Party. Some in the channels had recently identified her as the author."

Annette stared toward the floor, clearly processing something.

"They could have been wrong about her identity. It's not like she confirmed anything, but if they weren't wrong? From what I've seen of her, Gowon's made some significant advances in mind control that far exceeds what we saw in Mandatory enlistees."

"The Sim programs didn't control enlistees, it just drove them insane."

Christopher nodded slowly. "I thought perhaps he was using some kind of mind control simulation on you."

She blinked.

"I picked up on something from you–that you found him, his policies, all of it–intolerable. And *then* you were suddenly a power couple."

She twisted her mouth. "I can see why you would think that." She tilted her chin to the side, pointing out the translucent button behind her ear lobe. "This is an overlay. It maps the face and projects an image over it."

"It's better than that deep fake AI from years back. Wow."

She nodded.

"May I?" he asked, reaching his palm toward her face. "I mean, that's probably not appropriate. Sorry. It's just a technology I haven't seen before."

She watched him reel back his hand. "You don't seem that surprised to see me."

"Well, I see you all the time around the hallways, in press conferences."

She nodded again.

"And right now, technically, I'm not seeing *you*, am I?"

Annette tapped the button and the overlay disappeared, revealing a crossword-like pattern of veins at the surface of her cheeks, bruises under both eyes."

"Annette, what happened to your face?"

She straightened her posture.

"I'm sorry. Should I not call you that?"

"No, it's fine," she murmured, shaking her head, looking confused. "There's just a tone people usually use when they say my name."

"An infliction in the syllables?"

"Yeah."

"I've noticed that. It makes your name sound harsh." He furrowed his brow. "I didn't use it?"

She shook her head. "You have a soothing way of speaking."

He leaned toward her, examining her face. "What *is* all this?"

"'Enhancements.'"

"Agree to disagree."

"This is the least of it."

"What do you mean?" he said, his eyes widening.

"It's not important."

He started to argue, but she cut him off.

"I do find it ironic that the men who get heralded as feminists are probably the most disgusting, women-hating creatures on the planet."

"I wouldn't doubt it."

174

She cleared her throat, raked her fingers through her red hair. "Do you prefer to be called 'Chris' or should I call you 'Mr. Loop'?"

He twisted his expression. "*Chris*. Please. And it's okay that I call you 'Annette'?"

She took in a slow breath. "Yes."

"Okay."

"Chris, are we still off the record?"

"Yes."

She took another sip of her drink, swallowed hard, then placed the glass on the coffee table. "First–I've been wondering–When you helped me that night–when I was having an anxiety attack–"

He nodded encouragingly.

"I've never given you any reason to show me kindness."

He frowned.

"Why did you?"

He leaned back into his seat. "I think you're confusing kindness with decency. My parents raised me to help those who needed it."

"Even if they represent all you stand up against?"

His mouth stretched. "Even then."

She nodded, centering her gaze upon him. "The Arks have enough control over vital resources, enough firepower, enough soldiers, to challenge the Gowon regime."

He frowned. "Gowon has been putting a lot of press out there minimizing the significance of the Arks. The average viewer would think they've seized hold of a strip mall."

"The Arks have control over most territory from Lake Michigan to Washington State, everything south for hundreds of miles. They have California, south of Huntington Beach. They have all of Florida plus Alabama, Louisiana, Georgia, and the bottom half of South Carolina."

Christopher's jaw fell open. "I knew they had a lot more territory than was being let on because of reports at 'border stations,' but–"

"They have control of satellites, power grids, nuclear weapons, they have a vault of military vehicles, ships, and planes. They have tremendous foreign ally support."

His jaw fell open. "What allies?"

She gave a tight shake of her head.

"How did they manage to get control over all of those things?"

"Key people in key places."

"Including you?"

"No."

"No?"

She shook her head. "I tried and failed to gain the support of my fellow congress*persons* and senators. That was a big part of my role. Originally, the plan *was* to have me sitting in the Oval Office–as the President–at some point. Although that scenario aimed to avoid the predicament we find ourselves in now." It was so definite, conclusive, the way she was speaking. She seemed so resolved.

"Wow. That's not a part of the current plan? For you to be President?"

"I'm not meant to lead. I know that now."

He cleared his throat. "So the Arks are going to stage a coup?"

"No. They *should*. They really need to. But they won't."

"Why? If they have the resources?"

"The Ark Leadership is gutless. Those in charge have no intention to do what has to be done to dismantle the Gowon regime. They're in it for themselves and because of them, millions more people are going to die."

His shoulders sank. "So you're saying there's no possibility for reconciliation."

"Absolutely not. Ark Leadership expects Gowon to be fair and reasonable."

"And Gowon–"

"Is a terrorist and at this point, I feel that I'm qualified to say, 'Devil Incarnate.'"

Christopher Loop's eyes widened in disbelief. "So it's really been a keep your enemies closer situation for you. For more than six years?"

She nodded. "There have been a lot of horrible things rumored about my *husband*. Detestable things."

"They're all true."

She lifted her eyebrows. "They don't even scratch the surface."

"So why are you doing this? What's in it for you?" He frowned. "I didn't mean for that to come out the way it sounded, but why do this? Why commit to this? Why put yourself through this?"

She took a deep breath. "Samuel Gowon killed my daughter."

His eyes darkened. "He did *what*?"

She revealed the truth behind her pregnancy early in her political career, which had launched her into supporting the use of artificial wombs, since her baby was thought to have died as a result of one of the "many vulnerabilities of primitive reproduction." Her breaths constricted as she described what her daughter had endured, how difficult it was for her to accept that it was her daughter in the videos showing a toddler being tortured in a medical lab, that this revelation in Luther's initial contact was what caused the anxiety attack that Christopher witnessed outside the Oval Office.

"You had just found out that was your daughter," he whispered. "*That* day?"

She tensed her jaw and nodded. "Your 'decency' meant a lot to me that day. And now," she added.

Her eyes were fixed on his hand, which rested over hers in her lap.

It took several moments for him to realize he'd reached for her. When he did, he didn't move away. Just the opposite. He began stroking her hand.

"Annette," he said softly, but firmly. He waited for her to meet his eye. "Do you have–have you had anyone to talk to about any of this? I mean, you've obviously had contact with the Arks, right?"

She nodded and shook her head in close succession. "No one I could talk to about this, but everyone's had to take on more than they feel like they can–"

"*Annette*," he said in almost a whisper.

Her lips pulled upward briefly and she took a steadying breath. When she spoke again, it was in a low, warning voice: "If the Arks fail to act, millions more people will die and this country will *fall*. There will be no going back."

"Is there something we can do?"

She lifted her eyes, which looked both more vulnerable and more fierce than he'd ever seen. "We need to force the Arks to act."

"Okay," he said solidly, furrowing his brow. "How do we do that?"

16

the narnian

It had reached the time of year when the warmth of the sun struggled to counteract the chill of the shade. Esther purposely positioned Bree so she could use the benefit of the sun on her back.

Bree could occasionally be fussy about the prospect of being groomed, but he had trotted along the fence line, neighing eagerly as Esther entered the paddock.

Essie began with the soft round brush, sweeping it across his haunches, the bristles making a satisfyingly crisp noise. She felt Bree enclosing her in the curve of his neck, tucking his muzzle into her lower back.

Bree had a spectacular speckled mane. Each strand had a unique pattern of color. Nothing was quite as lulling as brushing through his washed, silky mane, and she loved when he leaned his head indulgently in her direction, craving more. Essie hoped it was as enjoyable for him as it was when Sara brushed her hair when she was a child.

Esther had always loved how curious the Percheron horse had been with her, taking aggressive inhalations of her hair, sometimes even chomps. He liked to interrupt her when she was reading, drop his head into her lap, nudge her for attention. He was more dog-like than anything in that way. For as needy as he could be at times, he reciprocated, never tugging away if she hugged his neck too long or laid against him in his stall.

It's better not to feel.

It's better not to think.
It's better not to remember.
Thoughts are the enemy.
Feelings are the enemy.
Memories are the enemy.
The nothingness is peaceful.
The nothingness is safe.

The nothingness is peaceful.
The nothingness is safe.

A hand clamped around each of her shoulders. The air seized in her lungs. The sun was gone. The ranch was gone.

The nothingness is peaceful.
The nothingness is safe.

17

praise

"May I ask you a question?" Renee asked, turning to Essie, who was gathering up the sheet music from the scattered music stands. She sat down on the top step of the altar, organizing music into the folder for each instrument. She'd taken on the role of arranging sets for the Worship Band a couple of months earlier. At first people had been concerned about her age, being only 15, but they quickly observed a higher rate of attendance for band practices and members were suddenly punctual. It turned out Renee garnered a lot of respect for her talent, but also for the fact that most people were pretty scared to get on her bad side.

"Of course you can," Essie replied, handing off the music. She then retrieved her dad's Taylor guitar from its haphazard placement on the stand and slipped it delicately back in its case, feeling a bit of regret for allowing a sixteen year old boy to use it for practice. She had outwardly winced every time he bumped it against the music stand, which was literally every time he shifted his feet.

"What happened to you at Calvary? For real?"

Essie frowned as she clicked the locks closed on the case. She moved toward the altar step and slowly sat down beside Renee. She took a breath. "What do you remember?"

"I remember you putting us in that supply closet. I didn't fully understand what was happening at the time, but I knew you were trying to save our lives–and Thomas made that a thousand times more difficult."

Essie nodded. "He was upset."

"Because he thought you were going to die."

"Yeah."

Renee cleared her throat. "I went back for you. That day."

Essie frowned. "*What?*"

"We finally got the return vent open and everyone started climbing through." She picked at her cuticle, narrowing her eyes upon it. "Once everyone was out, I opened the door back into the classroom."

"*Renee.*"

"My parents didn't believe me when I told them what I saw."

Essie furrowed her brow. "I can only imagine—"

"Don't do that," Renee said firmly.

"Do what?"

"Feel sorry for me because of what I *saw*."

Essie readjusted herself on the step, ran her fingers through her hair. "You were 11, Renee. You shouldn't have seen that. I'm sorry you did."

"*What* did I *see* exactly?"

"I don't know."

Seeing Renee immediately become agitated, Essie put up her hand. "I honestly don't know what you saw. I'm not trying to be evasive. If you ask me a question, I'm going to answer the best I can."

"And tell me the truth?"

"Have I *ever* lied to you?"

Renee furrowed her brow, searching her memory. "No."

"Just try to understand that I don't have all the answers. And what I was experiencing could have been very different from what you would have seen."

Renee nodded and took a steadying breath. "When I opened the door, you had just collapsed on the floor. Then I watched you crawl on top of the canister."

"Yeah, I remember that part."

"Your skin was peeling off and you were crying blood, Essie."

Essie released a breath, shaking her head, remembering warm sludge coating her eyes, making it difficult to see. When the gas started to saturate through her shirt, it felt like her stomach, her skin was on literal fire. "I really wish you hadn't seen that, Renee."

"Yeah, it's all the nightmare fuel I'll ever need, but that's not my point. It was sarin gas, Essie. *Right?*"

"That's what I was told."

"How did you survive that? There's no way you should have survived that. They said you were dead. Everyone from Calvary thinks you're dead."

Essie took a steadying breath. "What were you told?"

She tensed. "It doesn't really matter what I was told, does it? I'm asking *you*."

"I'm just curious. We haven't talked about this. When you were coming here, did they tell you anything about me?"

"They said the doctor missed the fact that you had a very faint pulse," Renee said, rolling her eyes. "Never mind that you were bleeding out of your eyeballs and your skin, your *flesh* was melting off."

Essie winced. "That's actually true. The thing about my pulse. From what I was told, they actually *did* think I was dead."

"They said that your dad had freaked out about what had happened and wanted to get you as far away from there as possible."

Essie wavered her hand. "More or less. Probably more."

"Thomas believed them, my parents believed them, but they didn't *see you*." Renee looked at her with wide, round eyes, needing to know. There seemed to be more hinging on Essie's answer than Renee was letting on. Looking in her bright blue eyes, Essie realized she couldn't possibly lie to her. Renee was only fifteen and a part of Essie hated the idea that she'd snuff out the last bit of childhood she had, but she realized with regret that Renee's childhood had probably ended long ago with the attack on St. Dominic's Church.

She thought of her own search for the truth about her life. She would have been able to sniff out a lie, a false story, even a euphemism when she asked Luther for details, and detection of any of those things would have destroyed her trust in him.

Renee was the same way.

She couldn't lie to her.

*   *   *

Essie had tried to be brief. She had tried to trim out unnecessary details. As the silence swelled in the church sanctuary, she still worried she'd made a mistake being so forthcoming with the truth of the situation.

Renee straightened herself, fixed the stack of sheet music that had been in her lap, tapped it on the tile floor and set it aside. She sat uncomfortably for a moment, gnawing at the inside of her lower lip, staring down at her knees.

Essie allowed the silence to persist.

"You've always been like a big sister to me," Renee finally said, sniffling. "Ever since we started coming to Calvary when I was five. Everyone has always focused so much attention on Thomas, of course, and I get it. You gave attention to everyone, but you really made me feel like I was special."

"Renee, you *are* special—"

Her hand shot up again. "Let me finish."

"Sorry."

"They told me you died. They told everyone you *died*. But then— there wasn't a funeral. They had a moment of silence. That was it. Your dad came back to help move people to the Arks, but you were just *gone*, and nobody cared. I didn't mean that. People cared. A *lot*. They were just so caught up in their own fear and everything else going on." She shook her head. "It wasn't enough. What you meant to me, what you meant to everyone, what you had done—I mean, you saved *all of us*—it wasn't enough what was done to honor you and I didn't understand. I hated everyone for it."

Essie blinked slowly, trying to imagine what it must have been like back in Wallace for the congregation, for her dad. She had stonewalled him during the time when he was traveling back and forth. What must that have been like for him to have people console him about his daughter, keep up appearances that she had died, but not be able to fully experience the relief that she was actually alive because she wasn't speaking to him? "I'm sorry. I didn't think about what it was like for anyone else."

Renee pinched her eyebrows. "Don't do that."

"Do what?"

"Are you on a perpetual apology tour, Essie?"

"What do you mean?"

"You saved my life. You saved the life of my brother. You saved the lives of all those kids at Calvary. You didn't *know* you would be able to survive that. You *thought* you were going to die trying to save us. *Correct*?"

Essie shrugged.

"Don't–" Renee drew up her shoulders in what Essie was sure was a very accurate, but unflattering impersonation. "You *did*. And I don't blame you for freaking out or not knowing what to do with the information–you say I'm only 15 or whatever, but you were only 16, Essie. When you saved our lives? You were *my* age. I don't blame you for freaking out about the fact that you're what?" She lowered her voice, noticing it starting to echo. "I'll just say *special*, okay? It doesn't cover it, but whatever. I'm sorry for being angry with you when I saw you here. You didn't need that."

Essie suppressed another apology, and waited for Renee to continue.

"The truth is, I thought it was all fake. I thought you had faked the whole thing and didn't tell me."

"*Faked* it?"

"No one should have survived what I saw. That much I knew. I was 11; I came up with something that made a little bit of sense to me. Even if it didn't *really* make sense." She frowned. "The truth doesn't even make sense."

Essie nodded. "It bothers me that you went through all that, Renee."

"Ditto," Renee said, raising her eyebrows. She took a deep breath. "You're from the same type of place as Timothy, the visiting pastor from a few weeks ago, aren't you?"

Essie wasn't surprised that Renee would be able to put two and two together, but it was surreal to have another person know the truth. "I think we're from the same exact place." She stopped there; there was no need to mention Danny. It was a strange thing to think of. This wasn't like the happy synchronicity to discover that you were born or grew up in the same hometown as someone; based upon what she had gathered when she walked through the abandoned lab that occupied the eighth floor of Glory Hospital in Denver, what she had seen in the photos and videos, Danny and Timothy, along with hundreds of other babies were being "grown" just outside the pressurized door from where she was put through excruciatingly painful experimentation. No one should begin their life or live any portion of their life in such a place; it was difficult to find a sense of camaraderie about it. There was no reminiscing about–did you ever go to that restaurant? Do you remember that store? Did you ever know–?

"He's not–*special*–not like you though, right? He wouldn't have survived, say, what happened at Calvary?"

It occurred to Essie that Timothy and Danny were rejected from the experiment. All of the babies Luther was able to save were rejected for one reason or another from the experiment, mostly due to having "undesirable" traits. Timothy had the markers for Down Syndrome. Danny had a neural tube defect. Both were conditions that "scientists" were looking to eradicate from the world. There just weren't the same opportunities to save the others, the ones allowed to be "born." They were removed from their artificial womb orb and immediately subjected to the experiments. Most survived hours or maybe days.

Luther had managed to save the rejected babies by creating a "dummy" lab under a shell corporation and by outbidding competing labs on auctions on the dark web. Digital currency wasn't as challenging to obtain with the right tech-savvy ally, as it turned out. Those in charge of the lab "inventory" didn't bat an eye that the digital footprint of the lab buying up their rejects had them with connections in China and Russia. It probably helped them blend in with the rest. Once auctions were won, Luther would handle delivery himself, trading comparable artificial wombs for ones holding third trimester babies. One by one, he'd initiate their birth and place them in a foster or adoptive home, tending to any medical needs. For being rejected due to "comorbidities," Luther said very few actually needed medical intervention of any kind. For those who did, like Danny, Luther had managed to pull together a network of medical professionals.

Suddenly Essie thought of Otis Doyle, who played bass and electric guitar with Worship Band. *Dr.* Otis Doyle, world-renowned neurosurgeon. She'd seen he and Luther have fraternal exchanges. It made sense now that they had once worked together.

Essie thought of Danny–brilliant, computer and tech guru Danny. He'd helped produce the antidote, he could hack any computer, he had broken down the intricacies of the Sim program. He'd be a tremendous asset to Gowon's cause, if he worked for his side, and yet he was rejected from the experiment. He was literally thought unworthy of life because of something that had done nothing to stand in his way of success. Medical researchers were certainly working to eliminate the occurrence of conditions like neural tube defects, but not in the way they'd have the public believe. They weren't fixing genetics to keep it from occurring; they were killing babies with the condition before they could be born. It made sense. Like Thomas. The government stripped away healthcare benefits from his entire family because his parents did not comply to selectively abort Thomas.

Of course, the government got a bit more forceful as time went on. Sterilizing the general public and only allowing monitored reproduction would ensure that the government could control the genetic lines that would be passed on.

"*Essie.*"

187

She jolted to awareness. "No. He wouldn't have survived."

Danny, Timothy, any of the others–they wouldn't have any memory of the lab, nothing beyond subconscious things from when they were in the "wombs." They would have no memory of the sounds of crackling, wheezing lungs, the cries, they wouldn't recall hearing a shriek escape from their own throat against their best efforts in response to physiological responses, they wouldn't remember the unrelenting brightness of the overhead lighting, the task lights, they wouldn't remember the ceaseless pain, they wouldn't remember the pungency of the smells lingering in the air–the bodily fluids, the burning of cauterized flesh, the hint of antiseptic soap.

Essie watched Renee's hand reach over and cover hers. She hadn't realized she was trembling.

"You remember it, don't you?"

Essie took a deep breath, finding it still came out in a staccato rhythm. She cleared her throat, swallowed hard.

"You're the only one like you."

She nodded. "I think so."

"That's why Timothy can go around and talk about it and you can't."

"Yeah."

She twisted her expression into a sort of scowl. "What was that *like* for you?"

"What?"

"After Calvary. When you found out where you came from, that you're *special*. What was that like?"

Essie thought of staying out at the West's farm, of the sleepless nights sitting up in the loft in the barn forcing herself to read, even though her mind didn't want to settle on the words on the page, the fictional worlds no longer welcoming to her, no longer an escape. She thought of how she'd avoided her dad, avoided Sara and Luke West, how she had shut off any communication channels with God. Days ran together. She hardly ate. It was confusing to feel so absolutely hollow inside, but also on the verge of tears in every waking moment. "Lonely."

Renee squeezed her hand. "I won't tell anyone. The truth about what happened? It would be dangerous for you, right? For people to know?"

Essie nodded.

Her eyebrows pinched upward. "Thank you for telling me."

"Renee, I'm s–"

Renee scowled.

Essie closed her mouth and nodded again for lack of anything else to do.

"You were going to teach us a song that day."

She could see her guitar leaning against the wall covered in decal stickers she'd picked up each time they'd make the trek to the West farm. The strap was handmade for her by a woman from the congregation who'd never missed a chance to squeeze her into a hug, which was an intense experience since she wasn't a small woman and she had a startling amount of upper-body strength.

Della.

She always dressed like she was going to Easter service and smelled of lavender-based perfume and wintergreen candies.

All at once, Essie really ached for a hug from Della.

She wondered silently if she was still alive, not because she was particularly old (probably only late-50s when she last saw her) or of poor-health, but because of all that had gone on in the world. She hoped she'd made it to the southern Ark with the rest of the congregation. She hoped she was doing well.

It was strange. All the worry she had devoted to making Luther try to create some sort of universal antidote, then do all those runs to extract the plasma to manufacture it–and she suddenly felt like she had so little to show for that time in her life. She did nothing to directly check on the people she cared about for all those years, the people who cared for her.

Surely there had been an opportunity to do that. Surely she'd had the time.

"Essie?"

"Yeah."

"Now I know what my mom means when she says I'm stuck in my head."

Essie frowned.

"What is it? Right off the top of your head. Don't think, just say what's on your mind."

"I wish I knew what happened to Della."

"*Della.*"

"She memorized like entire books of the Bible and recited them at service? She ran toy drives. She–"

"I remember Della. She babysat Thomas and me a few times."

"I should have handled things differently. I went my own way and I feel like I let people down. I just *left.*"

"There you go with your apology tour again."

"No, Renee, it's not that."

"What is it then?"

Essie turned her chin away, wiped at her eyes.

Renee leaned her head forward, trying to get a look at her face. She took a deep breath then scooted closer until their hips were touching. She looped her arm around Essie's elbow, and waited.

"*I miss her.* I miss so many people from there. There were people who really did feel like family to me and I lost all those relationships. Just like that."

"Are you just now realizing that?"

Essie nodded, sniffling. "I knew it, but I just didn't let myself–I didn't have a choice–" She pulled in her breath, searching the floor around her.

"What are you looking for?"

"A tissue box."

Renee released her arm and pushed herself off the tiled step. She hurried down to the first row of pews and returned with a full box. She watched Essie smother her nose. "Oh, stop being polite. Just blow your nose."

"Now I know why people are afraid of you."

"Yeah, yeah."

"But thank you for the tissues."

Renee waited impatiently for Essie to finish blowing her nose, then rolled her eyes. "I know I intimidate people. I probably need to dial it back. People are going through a lot." She sat back down on the step. "It's just I can't stand how even after all that's happened, people are wishy-washy. They're afraid to act. To be bold, like what Timothy said. I thought the point of the Arks was to take a stand, stop living in fear. No matter what the consequences."

"I feel targeted by that statement."

"I didn't mean you, but now that you mention it? Why don't you sing in church, Essie? You won't even sing in rehearsal and you've heard the other vocalists I'm having to work with. There's Liza, who sounds like an out of work porn star with the 'ooohs' and 'ahhs' and 'oh yeeaaahs' she randomly throws into songs."

"Renee! How on earth do you know about—"

"When we were kids and still had access to the internet, Thomas would search for information about things he'd heard about but didn't understand." She widened her eyes pointedly. "Then there's Sage—and Essie, how are people expected to get lost in the message, the words of the music, if they're getting distracted by pubescent vocal squeaks?"

Essie smiled lightly. "I sang with you at Christmas Eve Service."

"That was different. I didn't give you a choice. Essie, you're *choosing* not to sing. Why?"

She shrugged. "I don't know."

"Then sing."

"I can't."

"*Why?*"

191

"Because I–" She stopped short and shook her head.

Renee lifted her eyebrows insistently.

"Because I don't feel like I should be leading anyone in worship when I'm just now reestablishing a connection with God."

"*Wait*," Renee said, sitting more upright. "You fell away from your faith?"

She nodded. "Yes."

"When?" Her eyes were very round.

"Right after Calvary."

"That was 4 years ago, Essie."

She lifted her eyebrows. "I know."

"*Essie*," Renee murmured, those two syllables carrying more sympathy than Essie had ever felt from her. "How did that happen?"

"After Calvary, I stopped hearing Him. Or I stopped listening. Probably the latter."

"But you've come back to your faith, right? I guess it makes sense now—you weren't coming to church at all. For years, right?"

She nodded.

"When did you start moving back toward God?"

Essie scrunched her nose. "Just before Christmas."

"This *past* Christmas?"

"Yeah."

"Wow. So did you stop believing altogether or–"

"No. I just lost my way. God was trying to talk to me, but I didn't want to hear Him. I felt really alone and each time I thought He might be sending me some reprieve, it felt like it was taken away again. It was really frustrating and discouraging."

"You needed to turn to *Him*."

Essie frowned.

"What reprieve were you hoping for?"

Josh. I wanted Josh. "My best friend."

"Josh."

"Yeah. He was at Mandatory and then as soon as he came here, he joined MET."

"Not the reprieve you were hoping for."

"No, but he didn't know."

"Maybe God was trying to get you to stop ghosting Him."

"What's *ghosting*?"

"My parents use the word. I guess in the old days that meant you were ignoring someone."

"Well, with that definition, I guess I was ghosting God. Wait, so you're saying you think that God was *keeping* Josh from me?"

"Or vice versa, yeah."

"What do you mean?"

"Maybe God was keeping *you* from Josh, also."

"Why?"

She shrugged. "I don't know. Maybe you both needed to go through some things and that wasn't going to happen if you were together."

Essie stared intensely at the grooves in the stone floor, thinking of how desperate she felt to see Josh, but when she did, it didn't feel quite like she thought it would. It was like drinking gallons of water and never quenching a thirst. "So you're saying God could have kept us apart–on purpose."

Renee nodded.

"So I'd move closer to God. So I'd start listening to *Him*."

Renee widened her eyes as though to say *duuuuh*. "When did you start talking to God again?"

Denver. The night I watched Gabe pray to Jesus, even after all he'd faced. "December 19th."

Renee pursed her lips. "That's precise."

Essie nodded.

"Did you get the reprieve you needed after that?"

"Yes."

"After months and months of going without."

"More like years, but yes."

"When did *that* happen?"

Essie thought of the night after the lake when Josh came to her and declared that he would be whatever she needed him to be, that he was there for her no matter what. "That would have been December 21st–*Ohhh.*" She looked up questioningly.

"See what happens when you follow what *God* wants you to do?" Renee smiled tightly. Her eyes lifted to the lobby where some of the life groups were starting to let out from the Sunday School classrooms. "We're going to try something." She pushed herself to her feet, kicked off her heels, and jogged down the center aisle. She closed the double doors for the sanctuary then considered the long windows on either side of the doors. "Okay, I wish we had blinds or something, but that'll have to do." She hurried back up to the altar. "Stand up."

"What are you doing?" Essie protested, but she found herself standing obediently.

"*We* are singing." She checked the switches on the microphones, moved around to the open laptop.

"*Renee.*"

Renee bobbed her head in mockery, widened her eyes. "*Esther.*"

*   *   *

As the last notes faded, Essie took a deep breath. She slowly opened her eyes. Tears had soaked through her lashes and were pouring down her cheeks. She turned to look across at Renee, who smiled knowingly.

"We rehearse Sundays after service, as you know, then Wednesdays and Fridays."

"Renee."

"I know you might not be ready to sing during service yet and that's okay. Just come sing at rehearsals at least."

"Renee."

She shook her head and turned away. "I have your guitar from Calvary. If you want it."

Esther tilted her chin. "You have my guitar?"

"I've tried to teach myself how to play, but I'm not very good." She was refusing eye contact, her jaw tight.

"Would you like to learn?"

She shrugged stiffly.

"Well, if you *would*, I'd be happy to teach you."

Renee nodded, eyes still lowered, though her cheeks tightened. "OK."

Essie wiped at her eyes, taking a deep breath. "What can I help with? Do we need to clear out the instruments?"

"No, we can leave most of it, but I've got it. You can get going. I know you have a zoo of animals to tend to."

"Are you sure?"

"Yeah."

"Thank you, Renee."

"For what? Being a bossy witch and not taking no for an answer?" Despite her jesting, her voice was thick.

"Yes."

Renee paused. "Maybe you can give me a guitar lesson before Worship Band practice on Wednesday night?"

"Yeah. That sounds good."

Renee nodded tightly, then rotated away.

Essie furrowed her brow, turning toward the aisle. When she heard Renee say her name just as she crossed the halfway point, she barely recognized her voice. She turned on the spot in time for Renee to come crashing into her chest.

"Thank you for saving my life," she said in one long gasp. "And thank you for not being dead."

Essie chuckled, thinking to say that she really had no say in the living or dying thing, but thought better of it. She squeezed her arms around her, her face buried in Renee's hair.

*　　*　　*

As she left the sanctuary, Essie's mind was still fixed on Renee, Calvary, the path she had taken away from God and back again. She reconsidered her answer, about when she had come back around to her faith. The moment with Gabe, when she'd watched him pray struck something within her, but it wasn't until after holding that baby by the lake until her final breath, that she really faced her crisis of faith. She cried, she screamed, she reached a level of emotion that she never had before, and hoped to never reach again. It was cathartic. She needed to reach the point of total vulnerability and surrender–and the moment she did, the moment she thought she'd collapse from exhaustion, God had Josh ready to be there, to catch her, to hold her until her mind, her heart settled. Once they did, she suddenly felt the warmth in her heart, God's presence, that had been missing for so long. She felt Josh's arms wrapped around her, compressing ever so slightly.

Essie was grateful for a silent lobby and the fact that she wouldn't have to overwhelm her mind with any other competing thoughts or conversation as she left the church building.

It was just as she took full appreciation of this that Gabe stepped in her path.

She stumbled forward, catching the tip of her boot in the tile grout, but he managed to steady her.

"I didn't mean to startle you."

She reset herself, taking a step back so he would release her arms. "Sorry," she murmured, but winced, thinking of how Renee had pointed out her proclivity to apologize. "I mean, *thank you*. Thank you for catching me."

"Are you okay?"

Essie frowned.

"You look like you've been crying."

196

Her hand flew instinctively to her cheeks. "*Oh*. Happy tears mostly."

Gabe pinched his eyebrows, some trepidation in his smile.

"It's totally a thing."

"Were you running off somewhere?"

She hadn't given it any thought where she was going when she left, but she had been walking with a steady, resolved purpose, hadn't she? She had a plan before he'd taken her off guard.

Josh. She had decided she needed to find Josh.

At this time of day, he'd probably be rounding to the priority veterinary cases he'd been working with. He'd mentioned a filly at the Nguyen's ranch, who had been off her feed for a couple of days. The Roercks had a pregnant goat. Josh had teased her about taking one of the kids as payment for his veterinary services, a gift for her, of course. Then there was a bison at the ranch off Hudson–what was wrong with the bison? Something with his horn?

She pictured Josh standing in one of the barns in question, focused intently on what he was doing when she walked in. He'd slowly look up and just by the expression on her face, by the determinedness of her gait, he'd know why she was there.

"--would that be okay?"

Her attention snapped back to present and she felt herself nod, not knowing what she'd just agreed to. Gabe certainly looked pleased about something. He placed his hand on the small of her back and guided her to the stairs. She knew the stairs led up to the choir/pipe organ loft set above the main sanctuary, but she wasn't exactly sure why they were going there.

As she stood upright in the loft, she glanced over the railing toward the altar. Renee looked to be close to leaving. She glanced up just as she reached the center aisle and narrowed her eyes, glancing between Essie and Gabe in confusion.

Gabe spoke Essie's name and she turned her attention back to him, following his lead to sit on the front pew.

She asked about the life group he'd attended, purely speaking from familiarity and a little automation. In turn, he told her about the journaling project they'd been doing for the group, lifting the notebook he had been carrying. He'd also been journaling his sessions with Danny, the Sim reversal program. He'd found the program somewhat helpful, but he was finding that the memories lacked the emotional depth he expected they had when the Sim took them in the first place. He could watch them and commit them to memory, but it didn't feel like the memory really integrated in his brain. It was like watching a movie about his life.

"How did things go with your parents?" she heard herself ask.

The image came to mind of the last time she was at the West's house when she'd walked in on Josh wearing only his boxer shorts. She felt her cheeks warm. She actively suppressed the smile she felt reemerging on her face because Gabe's tone and his worried expression didn't seem to align with what she was feeling.

"I tried to just put it past me and move on, but it was out there already and my brain decided to torment me with it–"

She nodded. "There was a woman who worked with the Children's Ministry at Calvary who said 'you can't put the toothpaste back in the tube.'" The words emerged automatically, but sounded bizarre coming from her. She needed to focus on what he was saying and not her own thoughts.

"Yeah, exactly. That's a funny way of putting it, but it's true." He took a deep breath. "So that didn't go as I would have liked, but–"

"You're trying, Gabe. That's what matters. 'I think you could give yourself a lot more grace than you do.'" She sat stunned for a moment. Those weren't her words. Josh had said those precise words to her on the overlook. Her heart thumped heavily in her chest. She suppressed another smile.

"You think too highly of me, Essie."

She shook her head. Josh would probably be spending the most time with the filly who wouldn't eat. The Nguyen's house was a mile or two northeast, a street away from the zoo sanctuary. It would make the most sense to stop there first. It was the closest. Actually, there was something significant about the bison's horn. Was it infected? Josh had said he'd started him on antibiotics. That would take a day or two to kick in, which meant if he was making rounds, he was either with the filly or the pregnant goat. She was pleased to have narrowed the potential places she'd need to go.

"I'm grateful," Gabe said, resetting himself, looking more serious.

Josh had the satellite phone. She could always call to see where he was. But that would spoil the element of surprise. She really liked the idea of finding him on her own, feeling the rush of accomplishment, of excitement mixed with the swirling of butterflies in her stomach as she set her gaze upon him and started to close the distance.

"I missed that," Gabe said, gazing over the balcony. "Hearing you sing?"

Essie nodded lightly, confused because she seemed to have missed a change in topic. She wondered if she needed to stop for gas, what time it was, what the state of the weather was outside.

And then Gabe was leaning toward her.

He was running his fingers along her cheek.

He was kissing her.

Her initial thought was utter confoundment, baffled by the act of Gabe kissing her; it just didn't make sense in the context of her thoughts, what had transpired that day, what emotional journey she had taken in just the past hour.

Her mind then assessed that Gabe smelled different than he used to. There was a hint of antiseptic soap that seemed to follow him around, cling to his clothes.

It was as he turned himself toward her, slid closer, that it occurred to her that she wasn't dreaming. This was happening. He was kissing her and she was allowing it. She'd gone slack-jawed with the shock so she wasn't exactly reciprocating, but she wasn't discouraging him either.

In the next moment, she felt her body rear back, she felt her hand slap him across the cheek with such force the noise echoed through the sanctuary and caused a pins and needles sensation in her palm.

She slid to the far end of the pew, breaths heavy and unsteady, glaring at her trembling hand. The distance from him allowed her to be swallowed up by the chilly air conditioning, which alerted her to the fact that she had fresh tears in her narrowed eyes.

"Essie, *you*–" he began to say in what seemed to be an accusatory tone, looking confused. "I'm sorry. I thought–"

She shook her head, staring at the vague handprint-sized pink splotch on his cheek. "I shouldn't have slapped you. I–" She thought to say she was sorry, but Renee's disapproval of her constant need to apologize caused her to stutter. Instead of saying it, she shook her head again.

"*Oh*. Essie, I–"

"I need to go."

He nodded. "Essie, I'm sorry."

She stood and turned on her heel, startled by the proximity of the balcony railing, as she was suddenly feeling dizzy. She took the long way around to the stairs to avoid crossing paths with Gabe, gripping the back of the pew for extra support. She moved quickly on the stairs despite a persistent fear that she was one unbalanced stride away from a really unfortunate and painful fall.

Fortunately, just as she felt her balance fail, as her boot slipped on the slick lobby flooring, she collided into someone.

"Woah, Girl, it's not even drinking hours. You okay?"

Her arms were being steadied; she felt confident in the embrace she had literally stumbled into. Her vision was still terribly blurred and unfocused and noises were distorted, so much so that she couldn't decipher who was speaking to her.

"I've got you, Essie. You're alright."

Her hand lifted and rested on his cheek. She took a steadying breath and blinked. "Miles."

His hazel eyes, his mop of sandy colored hair came into sharper focus. "Yeah, what's going on?"

"Will you get me out of here please? I can't breathe."

He frowned. "Are you about to faint?"

"Miles, *help me*," she whimpered in a weak voice she didn't recognize. Any second Gabe would come downstairs and see her even more panic-stricken than in the loft. She'd already probably wrecked their friendship, but seeing her so upset would make things a thousand times worse.

"Yeah, of course," he said, setting his water bottle on the counter. He put his arm tightly around her waist and guided her toward the parking lot. "I'm parked over here."

Inside the cab of the rusted vintage Bronco, Essie immediately tossed herself across the front bench seat, hoping she'd go unseen by anyone coming out of the church.

"Alright, Essie, *what* is happening?"

"Just close the door and get in on your side. Please." She tucked her legs.

"Oki doki. This is highly unusual behavior, even for you," he said, but did as he was told. As he closed the driver's side door, he took a deep breath, cautiously placed a hand on her shoulder, which rose and fell in great heaves as she still struggled to catch her breath.

Essie lifted her eyes to look at him, her cheek smashed into the leather seat next to his leg.

"Can you really not catch your breath right now?"

She shook her head.

"Well, sit up. It's harder to breathe when you're lying down."

"I can't."

"Why?" he asked, looking over the dashboard in time to see Gabe exiting the church. Miles put his hand to his face, scratching at his cheek to hide the fact he was speaking to a psychopath lying on his bench seat. "Does this have something to do with Gabe? Because I'm his ride."

She gasped–with her already strained breathing, it came out like a tight wheeze.

"OK, calm down. I'm kidding. I mean, I *would* be if he weren't going to Sim reversal therapy with Danny." He rolled down his window. "The block party barbecue's at 6, right?" he called out, then gave a thumbs up. His chin rotated in her direction. A quip of some kind seemed to be on the tip of his tongue, but he suppressed it. Instead he ran his palm over her back in encouraging, rhythmic strokes, practiced some audible deep breathing, and waited until she seemed to have settled.

He waved to who she presumed was Gabe and/or Danny, then sighed, shifted the truck into reverse and pulled out toward the main road through town.

A few minutes later, Essie was seated at a picnic table outside a retro drive-in burger restaurant. She watched Miles speaking to the carhops, girls in cheerleader skirts, cropped shirts, and roller skates. He wasn't demonstrating any of the behavior she would have expected of him. While she couldn't be sure because he was wearing mirrored sunglasses, he didn't seem to be dropping his chin enough to be prowling with his gaze. His body language also didn't strike her as being remotely flirtatious. He looked as casual as if they were discussing the weather.

The moment their order was ready, he was efficient, gathering the tray and nodding a farewell.

He placed a milkshake and a cup of fries before each of their seats, then set the tray out of the way, sitting beside her on the bench. "You have to try this. You take the fry and dip it in the shake. You've never tasted anything like this. It's amazing."

She frowned.

"Seriously. These are hand-spun, super thick, super cold shakes, and then the fries they cut fresh, too. They grow the potatoes like *literally* down the street." He pried the lids off their shakes, took a moment to tuck her hair behind her ear, and gave an encouraging nod.

She did as he instructed, scooping a considerable amount of chocolate ice cream onto the thick and crispy, heavily seasoned fry. Her eyes widened.

"Good, right?"

"What *is* this sorcery?"

"It's the hot and the cold, the salty and the sweet. The opposites just somehow go together."

"Really, really well."

"Now just imagine if *you and I* got together."

Her cheeks tightened.

"I'm just kidding," he said, focusing his attention on fry dipping efficiency. "I mean, if I'm being completely honest, I'm probably 90% kidding, 10% totally, totally serious." Noticing her watching him, he lifted his eyes and smiled tightly, leaned toward her and kissed the top of her head.

*   *   *

Sometime later, after Miles dropped her back off at the church, Essie sat in the cab of her pickup truck, taking slow, deep breaths, the air conditioning still blowing warm air at her face, taking an agonizing amount of time to cool down.

It occurred to her as she stared straight ahead at the exterior details of the church building, that she had planned to find Josh. A spark of panic seized hold of her heart that she was supposed to be somewhere. She had to remind herself that it was only a plan for her. Josh didn't know about it; he wouldn't be expecting her. She didn't need to be in a rush anywhere. After what had happened, it probably wasn't the day to carry out the plan anyway. It would seem cruel to go this long without a declaration of her affection for Josh, only to decide to finally say something *the day Gabe declared his affection for her.*

She took a deep breath, unable to keep the moment from returning to mind, of him kissing her, of her allowing it, of her slapping him.

That's right. She hadn't just rejected Gabe, she'd physically assaulted Gabe.

She took another breath, focused her thoughts on simple observations, appreciating the details of the world around her that typically went unnoticed and unappreciated.

There was a deserted feeling to the church in the mid-afternoon, life groups long concluded, most off to wrap up their weekend elsewhere. There was one other car in the parking lot that belonged to one of the ushers, who sometimes used the church computer to play Solitaire, a favorite pastime of his, or write emails to family in one of the other Arks.

As Essie exited the truck, slamming the door behind her to be sure it closed, she took in the details of the church: the brick Midwestern exterior, the traditional arched stained-glass windows, the prominent, towering steeple. She was grateful when she found the door unlocked.

She passed through the lobby area, avoiding looking at the stairwell that led to the choir loft and slipped through the carved wooden door leading to the sanctuary. Her eyes lifted to the cross hanging over the altar as she slowly made her way down the aisle. When she reached the threshold to the altar, she didn't hesitate as she expected she might. She climbed the steps and retrieved her dad's guitar case.

*   *   *

It wasn't unusual to see the old orchard pickup parked alone at the church, but Josh found himself steering into the parking lot just the same. He parked alongside it, a handful of spaces from the front entrance to the church and took a deep breath. He seemed to recall that it was parked in the same place that morning. If Teo had driven back to the church, he surely would have parked in one of the front spots so it stood to reason that either Essie had gotten a lift home for some unbeknownst reason *or* she was still there.

He got his answer the moment he stepped inside the church lobby, hearing the gentle strum of a guitar. He quietly made his way into the sanctuary.

She was standing on the bottom step in front of the altar, eyes closed, arched forward as she strummed delicately on her dad's guitar, playing through a melody a number of times. She was playing entirely from memory so she occasionally paused mid-note and adjusted her finger placement before continuing.

He had just identified the chorus when she started the song from the beginning and quietly began to sing the words to *"Gratitude."*

She was subdued with her vocals and she wasn't using a microphone, but her words resonated deep within his chest. He took a seat in the back pew, pulling in his breath.

All my words fall short
I got nothing new
How could I express
All my gratitude?
I could sing these songs
As I often do
But every song must end
And You never do

So I throw up my hands
And praise You again and again
'Cause all that I have is a hallelujah
Hallelujah

And I know it's not much
But I've nothing else fit for a King
Except for a heart singing hallelujah

Hallelujah

I've got one response
I've got just one move
With my arm stretched wide
I will worship You

So I throw up my hands
And praise You again and again
'Cause all that I have is a hallelujah
Hallelujah

There was an unmatched intimacy to the moment, how she kept her eyes closed and surrendered to the simplicity of the melody, to whatever images came to mind, to whatever emotion stirred within her. Seeing this unfiltered version of her was incredibly endearing, but the thing was, it was how he had always known her. With some people, when you rolled back all the facades they built up around themselves, there was an insecure, neurotic mess beneath. Essie wasn't that way. When no one was around, when she wasn't trying so hard to be all that people expected her to be, when she wasn't being clever or silly or strong, this was her:

A gentle, beautiful child of God.

And I know it's not much
But I've nothing else fit for a King
Except for a heart singing hallelujah
Hallelujah

Her fingers strummed the guitar strings more forcibly, the melody beginning to build, and he watched her lips gently curl upward as she anticipated the upcoming chorus.

So come on, my soul
Oh, don't you get shy on me

Lift up your song
'Cause you've got a lion inside of those lungs
Get up and praise the Lord

Oh come on, my soul
Oh, don't you get shy on me
Lift up your song
*'Cause you've got a lion **inside of those lungs***
Get up and praise the Lord

She released a breath, the intensity and volume of her voice startling her a bit. She played through the chorus again with just the guitar before continuing.

Come on, my soul
Oh, don't you get shy on me
Lift up your song
'Cause you've got a lion inside of those lungs
Get up and praise the Lord

Her smile broadened briefly. She allowed the melody to soften, playing through the chorus a couple of times with just the guitar. Her voice was quieter as she continued:

So I throw up my hands
Praise You again and again
'Cause all that I have is a hallelujah
Hallelujah
And I know it's not much
But I've nothing else fit for a King
Except for a heart singing hallelujah
Hallelujah

As the song ended and the last chord she played on the guitar faded, she opened her eyes and took a deep, satisfied breath.

The corners of her mouth continuously tugged upward as she tucked the guitar carefully into its case, stood with the case in hand, and started up the aisle. Her eyes remained lowered in her thoughtful recessional–until she was two rows away.

When she looked up and saw him, she stopped walking immediately, her mouth falling slightly ajar.

He gave her a light smile, which, after considering his presence for a few   additional moments, she reciprocated.

18

unspoken

It was apparent that Essie had not slept. When Josh arrived at the ranch to help her set up to host a birthday party for a six-year-old from church who had never had one, her eyes were puffy and shadowed, irises glassy, pupils dilated.

"I should have come by earlier to help," he remarked, silently scolding himself. "The place looks great though."

She smiled weakly, turning on her heel to take in the decorations: the chalkboard sign, the balloons, the streamers. There was an unsteadiness to how she did this.

"How can I help?"

"I was going to give Digory and Trufflehunter baths so they're nice and clean for the pony rides."

"I can help with that."

No matter how many times he'd heard the names, the name Trufflehunter just sounded bizarre to him. He'd asked enough times that his brain automatically pictured their fictional counterparts, all animals to the ranch being named for characters in the *Narnia* series. Both Digory and Trufflehunter she had described as being very wise, the latter being an old, talking badger, fitting considering the nonfictional Trufflehunter was a docile black and white painted horse.

She cleared her throat, which was froggy and strained. "Josie really loves unicorns. What are your thoughts about me fashioning a horn for Truff? Sort of a non-traditional unicorn."

"I think you'd do a fantastic job."

"But?"

"But I'd rather have you nap than spend hours on something that poor horse is going to hate."

She gently turned his wrist to check the time on his watch. "I probably don't have time, do I?"

"You have four hours."

"I have time."

"That's not the point. It's potluck style, right?"

"Yeah. My dad has his chili going in *two* crockpots, your mom is making something delicious, I didn't ask questions, Miles is supplying pizzas, as he 'does not cook–'" She held her palm to her forehead, searching her mind. "A few others from church are bringing things–coleslaw, mac and cheese, hot dogs, ice cream. Josie's mom made cupcakes."

"What else *has* to be done?"

"Darryl's going to come by at 2 to set up the dunk tank. He might need help? *Oh,* he's also bringing a bounce house? Do *you* know what that is?"

He furrowed his brow. "No, but it sounds fun."

"For pony rides, we should probably have more than just Digory and Trufflehunter, right? Jadis is too temperamental. Hwin's too skittish. Bree's ginormous."

"And he hates everyone but you."

She considered this. "He doesn't hate everyone. He just has trust issues."

"Caspian?"

"Ooh, he'd look very regal with a unicorn horn. And he's done really well with people."

"No unicorn horn."

She sighed. "*Fine.*"

"OK, so I'm hearing that Digory, Trufflehunter and Caspian need baths sometime between now and 3pm, preferably by 2:30 so they have a chance to dry and get saddled."

She nodded, exhaling deeply.

"I'll handle that so you can just cross it off your list."

She blinked slowly, staring off toward the horizon.

Josh lowered his chin. "Essie, are you feeling okay? You seem really off."

She hesitated in her reply. "I don't feel right. I don't know what it is."

"Do you feel sick?"

She shrugged. "Yeah, a bit. I feel nauseous and kind of dizzy. I'm just really tired probably. I haven't slept."

"In how long?"

"It's been a rough week, sleep-wise."

"You haven't slept all week?" She stopped sleeping at the cabin the night he found her singing in the church sanctuary six days earlier, citing that Renee had questioned her about the arrangement and she wanted to be a good role model.

Though the claim was plausible, Essie had never been a very skilled liar except in poker.

It seemed more reasonable to think that what he'd witnessed at the church had been a reaffirmation of her faith—and maybe she didn't feel quite right about their sleeping arrangement at this point.

He was grateful for her reconnection with God, but he'd be lying if he said he wasn't disappointed about the turn of events—and that he wasn't secretly hoping she'd come to some resolution about it that absolved her of feeling guilty about it, if that was, in fact, her reason.

"I nap," she offered, scrunching her nose. "When I can. I mean, I haven't *not* slept in the past week." She frowned. "Did that make sense? The words feel all jumbled in my mind."

"Are you having nightmares again?"

That had been something alleviated by her sleeping at the cabin: No nightmares—with one exception. He wasn't sure what it was, if it was having someone, anyone in close proximity, or if it was him specifically, but the arrangement had all but resolved her insomnia.

It didn't make sense that she suddenly change the arrangement. There hadn't been anything that had happened between them that would justify a change. Even the incident at his parents' house hadn't kept her from staying at the cabin.

Something had happened that he didn't know about and it made him extremely uneasy that she'd felt the need to lie to him about it.

She sighed. "*Yeah*. Lots of nightmares, anxiety, impending doom stuff," she said, waving the words away like swatting at gnats. "I just can't settle my mind for some reason."

He tucked a loose strand of hair behind her ear, letting his hand linger over her cheek.

She pressed her lips together, leaned her cheek against his palm. It felt cool despite the warm day, like she'd been sitting directly in front of an air conditioning vent. "I was doing better. I felt like my mind was getting to a better place and then all of this started happening."

He decided against making the case that her getting quality sleep trumped her being a "good role model." The role model thing was a lie; there'd be no reason Renee would know about the arrangement, unless Miles had offered up that information—but Miles had been different, showing a strong loyalty to Essie, especially in the past week. When Josh had mentioned her deciding not to stay at the cabin anymore, Miles hadn't razzed him like he'd expect he would. He'd furrowed his brow, taken a long swig of beer, and said: "We didn't know how to tell you, Bro."

"When's the last time you napped?"

She scrunched her nose. "I nodded off at the lookout this morning. Not for very long—a couple minutes. The lion roaring woke me. *That* was surreal."

"Let's go lie down for a while."

She shook her head. "My dad doesn't know I haven't slept. I don't want him to worry."

Despite Josh being fairly confident Teo would be aware she was having trouble sleeping, he didn't question her. "His truck's gone."

"Yeah, he went–*oh*, right." She stared off toward the driveway, looking confused. "He had some meetings at the church. He won't be back until the party."

Josh watched her closely. If he didn't know better, he'd think she was intoxicated with her slow processing, her unsteady movements.

"I guess I *could* lie down," she conceded. She took a step toward the house then stopped. "You don't have to stay though. I'm sure you have other things you'd rather be doing."

"Honestly?" He thought of teasing her, that he wouldn't be taking off his shirt for their nap, given how alarmed she had become the last time she saw him shirtless, but any way he phrased it sounded pompous. Besides, her eyes looked lost and unfocused; she might not immediately get his reference. So instead, he motioned toward the house and heard himself say: "Well, I *love you* so there's literally nothing–"

She turned on her heel, eyebrows lifting.

"--I'd rather be doing," he finished, uncertain of how to reverse course out of the situation. The words just flew out.

As she stared at him, her breaths slow and heavy, he realized what was throwing him off the most about her appearance: the silver irises of her eyes, which typically shimmered intensely in the late morning sun, had turned a muddy shade of brown.

Her body began to sway.

*   *   *

"I'm just going to ask the question that's occurred to every single one of us," Miles remarked, glancing around the firepit, long after the last birthday party guests had gone home. "*Essie*, where are all your female friends?"

213

She motioned toward Renee, taking another sip of water.

"No, she's like your baby sister. Okay, not *baby* sister, but you know what I mean."

"I don't know, Miles. Do you have any theories about my missing female friends?"

"Do I have any theories," he scoffed. "Of *course* I have theories."

She lifted her eyebrows. "And they are?"

He considered this. "Okay, I have no theories. You're awesome. Anyone should love you and want to be friends with you. Male *or* female."

"Aw. That's really nice, Joely." Her silver eyes sparkled in the light of the firepit.

Corey lifted his chin. "What did you just call him?"

"Nothing," she said shortly, frowning. "I can have a nickname for Miles. It's not weird."

"Wait, is your name *not* Miles?"

"See what you started?" Miles said, peering over at her. He sighed. "Miles is my middle name. Joel is my first name. Essie has special permission to call me Joel. Not *Joely*."

She grinned. "I have special permission now? You're making my whole day."

He grimaced. "Okay, fine. Joely's fine, but only when you say the little 'aww' part with it. Because that's adorable."

"When did *you two* become best friends?" Corey asked incredulously.

"You know what, I don't think I could ever assume that title for her. *But* she had very little difficulty dethroning the rest of y'all." Miles shrugged. "I'm just sayin'. Maybe return a call. Maybe whip up a from-scratch baked macaroni and cheese with butter cracker crust and cut up hot dogs. Maybe I find that comforting at 2am when I can't sleep."

She furrowed her brow. "Did you actually eat it?"

"Did I eat it? Of course I ate it."

"What about the other food?"

He smiled widely, then turned abruptly away. "So *Corey*. You're paying particular attention to the other female at our campfire. What's happening there?"

"No, no, *no*. Don't you start your shenanigans or match-making, Miles. Renee is only 15," Essie teased.

"*Oh*, is Miles going to be the name you use when I'm in trouble?"

"She's not your mom, Dude."

Miles tried to maintain an upbeat demeanor, but he couldn't prevent the downward slope of his mouth so he simply nodded, riding out the wave of sadness.

Josh watched Essie discreetly give Miles' hand a squeeze.

It was difficult to believe that only a few hours earlier she had collapsed into his arms. He had carried her into the house and found her vitals entirely normal. He managed to stir her awake briefly, then tucked her into bed.

In her exhaustion and haze, she had tugged on his arm, encouraging him to join her.

He obliged and she slept two hours, clinging to him like a koala bear holding onto a tree limb. She had then startled awake, immediately asking if Darryl had arrived yet with the dunk tank.

Despite her earlier episode, she had looked remarkably more refreshed after a rest, and had zipped around finishing up party preparations, then ping-ponged herself around being a gracious hostess, pony ride leader, game host. He'd witnessed her running back and forth to the house, retrieving a lemonade for Thomas, who wasn't keen on any of the other drink offerings at the party, then another for the birthday girl, who saw the one she'd retrieved for Thomas. Miles had been standing beside Josh at the time, remarking that next Essie would offer to squeeze the lemonade fresh. "There has to be a lemon tree orchard nearby," he quipped.

Even after all the activity and exertion, she looked perfectly normal sitting next to the firepit, which is to say she looked radiant and happy, her wild, unruly golden-brown hair twisted into a messy knot on the top of her head.

Even still, he was having a difficult time easing his mind that the episode was nothing.

"I have an idea," Renee said excitedly. "Why don't we have everyone share three things that no one else here knows?"

"Renee, I'm just going to say that might be difficult for this trio over here," Miles said, wagging his finger between Essie, Josh, and Gabe.

Essie narrowed her eyes upon him, surprised there wasn't any additional commentary about a love triangle with his observation.

"I'm mature now, Essie," he said, reading her thoughts. He smiled sheepishly, placed his still-full beer bottle on the ground, and ran his palm over her arm. "You did an awesome job with this party, Essie. Seriously. I did not know a children's birthday party and a ride on a pony was what my heart needed."

"You really did a great job," Corey agreed.

There were some nods around the firepit.

She smiled tightly, glancing over at Josh. "I had help."

Josh furrowed his brow. "Yeah, can't let you share credit. This was all you. You made this happen."

Essie scrunched her nose. "Thank you all for coming though–and for bringing what you did."

"It was nice. I can't remember the last birthday party I got to go to. I had to have been Josie's age," Renee remarked.

"You did good, kid," Miles said, reclining back in his camp chair.

"*What* is going on with Miles?" Corey asked, frowning.

Gunner shrugged.

"Alright, Blondie," Miles said abruptly. "Three things we don't know about you. Since you came up with the idea, why don't you go first?"

"*Oh*," Renee stuttered. "*Okay*." She sat more upright, crossing and uncrossing her legs. "Well, as most of you know, my brother has had a lot of medical issues. What you may not know is that when he had a lot going on, my parents had me live with my grandparents for the better part of two years."

"How old were you?"

"3-5."

"How was that?" Corey asked, tilting his head.

"Oh, they spoiled me rotten. I got to do whatever I wanted."

"*That's* why you're like that," Miles remarked.

Essie glared at him, suppressing a laugh. "I didn't know that, Renee."

She shrugged.

"Okay, what's your next one?"

"I donated a kidney to Thomas four years ago."

"Well now I feel like an asshole." Miles held up his hand over Essie's face. "Don't say it."

"I wasn't saying anything." She pushed his hand away. "You donated a kidney?"

"Yeah. He's always had a lot of infections and then they figured out he was going into kidney failure. Being his twin, it was pretty likely I'd be compatible." She smiled lightly. "Luckily, it went well. Thomas hasn't had any issues."

Miles nodded. "That's awesome."

"I'm also dyslexic."

"Renee Bethany Shaw, how did I not know that?"

"I've gotten pretty good with different compensatory strategies. It makes me feel good that people don't notice." She shrugged, then nodded to Miles. "I guess those are mine."

"Oh, shit. I'm next. Okay, well, this could be difficult because I've been spilling my soul to my girl over here. And I can't use the name thing." He became fidgety in his chair. "Shit. Alright. Mac and cheese with cut up hot dogs *was* my favorite meal until I became lactose intolerant."

"Miles!"

"I still ate it. No problems. My GI tract must have figured things out. Or, you know, things are less processed up here? Anyway, number two–"

Corey sniggered.

"Pun not intended. *Second,* I never learned to read properly so the Bible, which Essie is helping me get through, is actually my first chapter book."

"Oof."

"Yeah. Tough read, tough read. That one might not qualify–did you figure that out, Ess?"

She shook her head. "I knew you struggled with it, but I did not know it's your first chapter book, so I think we can count that."

He gave a nod. "Uh, third, I share a birthday with my dad so I have a really hard time on that day." He pressed his lips together uncomfortably.

Essie continued to eye Miles.

"Go on, Essie," Renee coaxed.

She scrunched her nose. "Yeah, this is tough. These guys know a lot and my dad tends to over-share in his sermons. *Okay.*" She glanced over at Josh, wincing.

He wanted to tell her telepathically that she could use something that he knew, just to get her turn over with.

She instinctively reached for her necklace, something she did when she was nervous at times. "I've worn this cross necklace since I was 2. It was given to me by Luther's mom, Loretta, who was absolutely wonderful to me. *Lola,*" she added fondly.

Miles sat more upright to get a better look at it. "It's pretty."

She nodded. "Possessions aren't really important to me, but I do have a few things that are sentimental; if they were lost or broken, I'd be pretty heartbroken." Essie sat more upright. "Number two, when a book makes me sad or is particularly scary or haunting, I put it in the freezer."

"What? Why?"

"It's silly. It's something my dad suggested when I was little when a book really bothered me so there was a separation, like the book couldn't get me."

"That's why I found a book in the stinking freezer," Miles muttered.

"Did you really?"

"*Never Let Me Go.*"

"Oh. Leave that one there. Holy moly."

"What's it about?"

"These kids grow up in a boarding school, but they're not actually 'normal' kids. They're clones raised knowing that when they grow up, they'll be forced to donate their organs."

"So what do they do?"

"What do you mean?"

"Do they fight back? Escape? Run away?"

"They tried to delay it from happening."

"And?"

She shrugged. "They did nothing. They accepted their fate."

"They all *died*?"

She lifted her brows. "Hence why it's in the freezer."

"Ugh, I want that book *out* of my freezer," Miles said, wincing. "Alright, what's your third?"

She furrowed her brow, clearly struggling.

"What's on your tattoo?" Renee suggested, her voice light.

"Somebody knows this one though, right? You've all probably seen it."

"There are a lot of details in there though. I definitely don't know what everything represents."

Essie took a deep breath and tugged up the sleeve of her raglan shirt, held up her arm so everyone could see. "The tattoo in question."

"Don't take this the wrong way, but you don't seem like the type to have a tattoo at all," Corey remarked.

"Let alone one this big and prominent?" She smiled. "Well, having a tattoo wasn't originally my choice. The government was really into them for a while. So this started off as a data matrix code tattoo that they could scan to get my information when I was little. You can still kind of see it in the grass shading. About a year ago, I was tired of looking at it and decided to design a tattoo to cover it up, or at least work it into the design."

"You could have had it removed," Gunner remarked.

"Yeah, I know. I thought about it, but I figured even with that, there'd still be a scar. So I designed this. On it there are things that represent God's blessings in my life, all designed to create the outline of a cross."

Miles tilted his head to the side. "What's on it?"

"Well, the tree from Josh and Gabe's childhood house, complete with the swing. That's where I met them for the first time. Then there's my dad's guitar, Bree, the hat's for Josh."

"What kind of hat is that?"

Her cheeks reddened. "It's an inside joke. It's silly."

Miles glanced up at Josh, smiling lightly.

"There's a ribbon in Bree's mane."

"There's a ribbon?" Josh asked, leaning in. "I haven't noticed it."

"Remember I used to try to braid his mane and he hated it, but he just put up with me?"

"Yeah, I don't remember you using ribbons though."

"The ribbon was to represent Renee."

Renee's chin jolted upward. "*What*? I'm in your tattoo?"

"When you first started coming to Children's Ministry, you wore a pink ribbon. No matter what you were wearing, you always had that ribbon in your hair."

Renee pursed her lips. "I can't believe you remembered that."

Essie nodded slowly. "That ribbon meant a lot to you. The Childrens Ministry leader at the time got quite the earful when it went missing on the playground. I think you wanted arrests made."

"I don't remember that."

Essie suppressed a laugh.

"Oh I remember you telling me about this," Josh said, eyes wide. "Was this a really special ribbon?"

"I don't—did I really make that big of a deal about it?"

"Yes."

"Well, still. What made you put that on there?"

"I don't know. I remember at the time it meant a lot to you and I thought it would sort of be nice if the mystery was solved. Like, *see*, it's not lost, it's right there in Bree's mane," she said in a light voice. "That's silly probably." She rolled her eyes. "*Anyway*, then there's the wildflowers Josh and Gabe's dad would pick for their mom, and sometimes me, also Luke's cowboy boots, a stack of books, my dad's Bible." She took a deep breath.

"Who's the stack of books for?"

"I intended it for Gabe," she said, looking up apprehensively.

He nodded lightly.

"Since he was really the one to teach me how to read." There was more she wasn't saying. Her eyes flitted over to Josh and she gave a light smile.

Miles leaned forward. "Is that an itty bitty elephant sitting on the swing?"

Josh's cheeks tightened.

Tucked behind the rope of the tree swing, as though playing peekaboo was a sweet plush elephant.

"Gelato?" Gabe asked.

"Oh, is that for Gabe, too?"

Gabe shook his head, lifted his brow toward Josh.

"Josh gave me a little elephant stuffed animal the day we met. It's probably silly to have it on there," she said, pursing her lips.

Miles leaned toward her. "You're using that word a lot. I do not think it means what you think it means," he remarked softly, lifting his brow. "I think you are very attached to what you refer to as 'silly.'"

She cleared her throat, nodding.

"So where am I?" Miles asked.

"Well this was before we really bonded, Miles."

"I understand that. It just seems wrong that I'm not there somewhere."

"Well, no. I misspoke. I do have something for you."

"You do? Where?"

"You see Bree there?"

"Yes."

"You see this spot by his tail?"

Miles sat back in his seat, cheeks tightening. "You mean his ass, Essie? Are you calling me a horse's ass?"

She grinned.

"I told you she could be mean. No one believes me."

"That was awesome," Corey mumbled.

"I don't think you're a horse's ass, Miles. Not even a little—*well*—
"

He shook his head, smiling. "It's fine. I can be. That was a clever jab, Girl," he said, offering a fist bump.

She shook her head as they tapped knuckles. "Maybe the tattoo needs an update."

Miles sat up immediately. "What would you get? For me?"

"I don't know. I'd have to think about it, Joely."

"That wasn't the deal."

"*Aww*, Joely."

"There you go."

"I'd have to think about it."

He smiled tightly.

"So that's it for me I guess," Essie said, sweeping the hair from her eyes.

Josh nodded, leaning back in his camp chair as the attention turned to him. It was certainly challenging to think of things that were semi-interesting that Gabe or Essie or even Miles wouldn't know, but he finally settled on: "I was a southpaw, but I crushed my hand in some farm equipment when I was young so I had to learn to write with my right hand since my fingers didn't heal quite right."

"One of these two would know that."

Gabe frowned. "I have no recollection of that."

"I was 4, I think."

"Essie?"

She shook her head. "I didn't know him then and I was never told about it. Your handwriting is *remarkably* good, Josh."

"Thank you," he said with a small smile. "Alright, so, around the same age, we had a dairy cow who stopped producing milk. Dad was going to send her to the butcher, but before he could do that, I set her free."

"You set her free?" Essie asked, her eyes very round.

"Yeah, dad was *not* happy with me. I couldn't sit for a week after the whooping he gave me."

"Are you being–what do you mean?"

"Dad had some pretty rough punishments early on with us. Mom never liked it. They'd fight about it a lot."

Gabe lifted his brows. "I remember that."

"Wait, the cow or the alleged child abuse?" Miles asked.

"It wasn't child abuse, but it wasn't something I'd ever do with my kids," Josh said, shaking his head. His heart lurched as he committed the same offense as Essie that had bothered him so much–implying a future separate from her. It was ridiculous. He hadn't. He just couldn't very well say "our kids." He glanced over at her and smiled.

"Gabe, can you make a ruling about the cow? Does this unknown fact count?"

"I don't remember the cow."

"Alright, there's two," Miles said. "Did you ever see the cow again?"

"Oh, she probably got picked off by a mountain lion," Josh said reminiscently, shaking his head. "I used to come up with stories in my head about where she wound up. None of those ended with her getting eaten, but that was probably wishful thinking."

Essie twisted her expression. "I don't remember your dad punishing you guys like that."

"He stopped."

"Before I came along?"

"The exact time you came along?" Josh speculated, furrowing his brow, checking with Gabe for confirmation.

Gabe nodded.

She considered this. "Maybe it was because he and my dad were spending time together again?"

"*Maybe,*" Josh said, pressing his lips together.

"Alright, one more," Miles prompted.

Josh shrugged. "Alright, perhaps a little ironically after my second fact—my third fact is that at Mandatory, I randomly found out I have an allergy to meat substitute."

"*Really* not going for emotional depth with that one, are you?" Miles muttered.

"Sorry to disappoint you."

"Like you get a stomachache or—?"

"No. Same level as like a peanut or shellfish allergy."

"Bizarre, but uninteresting. *Gabe?*"

Josh chuckled.

Gabe cleared his throat. "Well, I have the advantage over Josh in that I had a couple years head start on him."

"But you also had your memories wiped," Miles pointed out, then retreated, seeing Essie's pained expression. "It was rude how I said it—I didn't mean it that way, but it's accurate, right?"

Essie took a deep breath and turned her attention to Gabe.

"I was struck by lightning when I was three. Not directly, but the bolt hit a tree out by the barn and it traveled through the ground to me."

"Is that why you're so twitchy?"

Essie widened her eyes at Miles, who clapped his hand over his mouth.

"Sorry. I wish I could help it. I was mostly kidding."

"Try harder, Miles," Essie mumbled.

Gabe shrugged. "Nah, the bastards at Mandatory Sim training did that to me."

Essie rotated her chin back to Gabe, her expression a mix of regret and encouragement.

Gabe gave her a small smile. "I lost my hearing in my left ear. Not sure when that happened. I could hear fine before Mandatory from what I remember."

"You could," Essie affirmed, frowning.

"And last, I once drove our tractor into the house."

"Wait, *what*?"

"The front porch. No one was out there. I was out by the barn with Dad and he left the key in it."

"Did he whoop your butt, too?" Miles asked.

"*Yeah*. It was bad enough that we went and stayed with Mom's sister for a few days."

"Dad really had a temper back then, didn't he?" Josh reminisced.

Gabe nodded.

Everyone was quiet for a few prolonged moments, staring toward the fire.

"Gunner?" Renee prompted. "It's your turn."

He cleared his throat, lifted the brim of his baseball cap and scratched at his head. "I was brought up in what I guess was foster care. Some wildfires swept through the town and most of the adults were killed so me and the rest of the kids wound up at this, like, old school building that was converted for living? Dorms and a cafeteria and a hospital or medical clinic, what have you?"

Essie raised her chin.

"There were special tests and training—none of it seemed right. Kids weren't coming back. Some were coming back to the dorms beaten up—both girls and boys. Things were happening to them they didn't want to talk about, or were told not to talk about. Some would stop talking altogether. They just weren't right in their minds anymore. Some of us decided it wasn't a good place for us all to be so one day we took off. We got as many out as we could, but not all of us made it."

"Where was this?"

"A few hours outside Denver, I think? It was called HAVEN. All caps. Not sure what the letters stood for."

"So what'd you do once you escaped?"

"We came across this, like, big group of people living out in the woods, you know, 'off the grid.' It was up north. We must have been up in Wyoming. Lots of ex-military. Anyway, that's where I learned how to shoot, where to drive, fly."

"*Fly*?" Miles asked.

"Planes, helicopters."

"I did not know you have that particular skillset."

Gunner nodded, satisfied that he'd completed the task, scratching at his beard.

"You got pulled from Mandatory though, didn't you? Then you joined MET? How'd they get you if they were living off the grid?"

"Heat mapping. The government raided the place, wrangled up some of us, mostly the kids and teenagers, killed everybody else. Since I knew how to fly, they put me into the military; the rest went to Mandatory. I did a few tours overseas. I got pulled from the base out there on the coast though, a couple years back. Not sure why *I* was picked, but I'm grateful. Wish some of my buddies had been so lucky."

Miles nodded. "This was a great idea, Renee. Very light campfire talk."

Corey sighed, shaking his head. "Dude, don't talk to her like that."

"Oh. I have an autistic brother. He can't hurt my feelings."

"So how *old* are you if you've done all that?"

"28." Gunner glanced around as though checking to be sure it was still acceptable for him to be there.

"Hey, we found our campfire elder!" Miles pointed out.

Gunner raised his beer bottle.

"Last but not least," Miles said, nodding to Corey.

"Alright, well, all of you have met my two little sisters and my mom, but our family used to be a lot bigger. I had my dad, two older brothers, one younger brother and my baby sister. Not Mormon—people like to ask that--just a big family." He cleared his throat. "We lost the five of them over the course of about a year. Mysterious illnesses," he said shortly.

"Shit, Man, I'm sorry," Miles said regretfully.

Essie reached over and briefly rubbed Miles's shoulder when Corey's eyes were lowered.

"My other two facts I'll keep a little lighter."

"Thank *God*," Miles muttered. There was a half-second delay before Essie walloped him in the arm.

"So, number two, I've collected rocks since I was little. From each new town, somewhere I actually spent time in, not just like a pit stop."

"How many rocks do you have?"

"Right around 100." He frowned, searching his mind for a third fact. "I speak six languages? Is that a good one?"

"You *do*?"

"Yep."

"You should be a translator with the Ark. There's been major security concerns with AI translation."

"That's what I do."

"You *do*?"

"Yeah. I started a couple years ago translating for Luther."

"So you know some of the top secret hoopla that's gone on."

He took a sip from his cup. "Couldn't say."

Miles narrowed his eyes. "Wait, so you speak 6 languages and do top secret work, but you mentioned your rock collection first?"

"The rock collection's more sentimental to me."

"So, what languages do you speak?"

"Spanish, Mandarin, Cantonese, French, and ASL."

"How did you learn so many languages?"

227

"My dad was half-Chinese, my mom's family immigrated from Mexico, my little brother was deaf. I took a couple years of French in school and then when I needed a distraction, I became fluent."

"Oh."

"The pay's good; I just can't let them find out my age or they won't let me work so much."

Gunner furrowed his brow. "How old are you?"

"*Sixteen*," Corey said cautiously.

"Well Blondie's 15–hey Essie, can we matchmake these two? They're only a year apart," he asked excitedly, pointing out the pair of them.

"You're only 16 and you were doing MET missions a year ago?" Josh asked incredulously. "How'd you even get involved with those?"

"I signed up? You guys did the actual field work stuff, I was just intel," he said with a shrug.

"I thought there was a minimum age. Like 18."

"Yeah, I lied."

Miles chuckled.

"I have a family to support."

Miles leaned in close to Essie's ear and whispered loudly: "I'm liking this guy more and more for Blondie, what do you think?"

She gave him a tight smile, putting her index finger to his mouth.

Miles nodded, turning back to the group. "Is it just me or are we like old whatever age we are? Like, when our parents and grandparents were in their teens and 20s, they were playing video games and partying and being stupid on social media as like, *influencers*. And most of us have spent much of our lives actively trying *not* to get murdered by the government."

"In their defense, their lives were being threatened by the government, too. They just didn't know it."

"They say ignorance is bliss," Miles said with a lift of his brow.

There was a collective exhale followed by repeated head bobbing.

"Great game, Renee. *Really*."

Renee laughed along with everyone else. "Honestly, I thought it'd be fun."

"Actually, I feel like I know all of you better," Miles conceded. "So I think it was a good suggestion, Blondie."

She smiled.

"And to think, after that, we learned that *Josh* is the most boring person in this group."

Josh shrugged overtly.

"Animal doctor at 22, MET operative and total badass operative at that, really, really respectable guy, handsome as all get out—and the guy goes with food allergies, setting a cow free, and hurting his hand. Seriously, Dude, get some stories," Miles said with a good-natured smirk.

*　　　*　　　*

"Just set them in the sink, Josh," Essie said, letting the screen door slam behind her, having just said goodbye to most of the group.

"I'll help wash them later."

"Well, you *better*. I'm terrible at washing dishes. Just ask my dad."

Josh smiled lightly. "You seem to be feeling better?"

"Yeah. This was nice. Having this group? It's nice to have *people*, you know?"

"Yeah, but I kind of meant if you're feeling better from earlier. Before the party."

She stood at the edge of the kitchen in her distressed and very dusty overalls, the frayed hems catching under her heels. Compared to nine hours earlier when she had fainted into his arms, she looked far more alert, her silver eyes bright and sparkling in the light of the kitchen chandelier. "Yeah, I'm not sure what that was about. Maybe that's how my body handles natural viruses. There was a little who had the sniffles at life groups childcare. His mom just thought it was allergies though."

He nodded slowly, choosing not to challenge her assessment.

Essie cleared her throat. "Do you have to be up early tomorrow?"

Josh shrugged. "The usual time."

"I want to talk to you about something," she said, her forehead deeply furrowed.

He felt his heart jolt upward into his throat.

"It could wait until tomorrow though."

He pursed his lips. "If you want to talk about something, we should talk about it."

She nodded. "OK. We'll talk tonight." She gave a small smile and turned down the hallway.

When Josh returned to the firepit, Miles was getting to his feet.

"Are you heading out?"

"Yeah, I can't be the fourth wheel. It's my lot in life to provide chaos, not balance."

"Aren't you going to say 'goodnight' to Essie? She should be right out."

"*GOOD NIGHT, ESSIE!*" he shouted, his voice bellowing into the night.

The bathroom window slid open forcibly. "*GOOD NIGHT, MILES!*" she shouted back.

Miles shrugged and extended his hand for Josh to shake.

As Miles drove away, Gabe returned from refilling his coffee at the carafe on the foldout table leftover from the party, having gone to visit Lilliandil and her colt.

Josh added another log to the fire, poking around unnecessarily with the placement of wood. He started to wonder about the nature of the conversation Essie wanted to have. She had smiled when he agreed to stay, which led him to believe it was something positive.

Or maybe she was feeling relief to be able to get something off her chest? That didn't mean it was something positive for him. It didn't mean it was anything about him.

The fainting episode was bizarre, how her eyes had turned a muddy shade of brown? Maybe there was something she had found out from Luther about her condition. Maybe the antidote runs, all she went through as a child were having long-term repercussions. Maybe her body was shutting down.

No. If it was something like that, she wouldn't have used the words "impending doom" earlier, out of consideration for him. It was very possible not sleeping for several days would have caused her to faint. There didn't need to be anything beyond that.

Maybe she was back to doing antidote runs, or other experiments.

No, she wouldn't have lied about it. She wouldn't be living at the ranch if that were the case; she wouldn't want her dad to witness her recoveries.

It had to be about things between the two of them. It had to be.

Maybe the smile was sympathetic. Or nervous.

No, it wasn't like her to smile nervously. Her facial expressions tended to be straightforward and true to the emotion she was feeling. She only smiled when the corresponding emotion made her happy. It was a tremendously reliable and comforting thing about her.

He tried desperately to picture the expression on her face before she had turned down the hallway so he could perform further analysis of it.

Meanwhile, his brother, literally the only thing between him and what could be a momentous conversation with Essie, leaned casually back into his camp chair, sipped his coffee, glanced out to the mountains hiding in the darkness, and looked in no rush to leave.

In his fleece-lined flannel jacket, jeans, work boots (he'd finally acquired a pair of practical footwear), his shaggy brown hair, he looked like a much more severe version of their dad.

Josh felt his jaw tense as he pictured Esther throwing her arms around Gabe's neck when he rescued her from the dunk tank seat.

It was nothing. It was endearing. It was a relief to not have her submerged in cold water after her body temperature had dropped so low earlier. (He would have rescued her himself had he not caved to an adorable child who wanted another ride on Trufflehunter–and in fact, Gabe *had* looked questioningly to Josh before running to her aide.) But then in another moment, to see her place her hands on the sides of Gabe's face, gaze so seriously into his eyes?

He hadn't imagined that.

Was she planning to tell him that she had chosen Gabe? Was that why Gabe seemed to have no intent on leaving despite the late hour? Was Gabe staying so he could support her if Josh had a poor reaction to the news? Would she *really* have Gabe present for that conversation?

On the other hand, he hadn't imagined the energy during his own interactions with her. He hadn't imagined the deepening of her cheeks whenever the two of them had made eye contact throughout the day, everyone else falling out of focus. He hadn't imagined the laughter they'd shared when he attempted to teach her how to two-step, how she'd grinned widely up at him from under the brim of one of his old cowboy hats, wearing the boots with the fish hook design that apparently reminded her of him. He hadn't imagined how tightly she had held him as she slept before the party.

He hated that he was so tormented by the situation. This jealous, anxious person wasn't someone he wanted to be. He just didn't entirely understand why she was so reluctant to move forward. Something was definitely troubling her; she hadn't had such problems sleeping at night since–

He frowned. Before their recent and short-lived sleeping arrangement, she'd always had problems sleeping at night, except for when she had Gabe when they were kids. She'd never overcome that, had she? She just made do. During the Phoenix Initiative antidote runs, she'd be in the thick of recovery throughout the night, usually heading to bed after a full breakfast. On off-days, she worked out at night, she trained, then took cat naps during the day.

With few exceptions, she'd never slept consistently at night except when she had Gabe to comfort her.

Or himself, he conceded—when he came back from Mandatory, when he returned from a trip with MET, on the drive back from Denver, at the safe house and then camping, and of course their recent, short-lived sleeping arrangement.

—but was he just a substitute for Gabe?

He took a deep breath, tried to quiet his mind, but it did little to settle the erratic rhythm of his heart.

What if her heart was truly pulling her to Gabe, not him? How would he respond? Could he control his reaction enough so he wouldn't destroy their friendship?

He wasn't sure what that would look like, to have her in his life, but not be together, or rather, have her be with Gabe. He wasn't sure it was even possible to have that work, but he knew he would never forgive himself if she told him something he didn't want to hear and he destroyed any chance of keeping her in his life by having a knee jerk response. He needed to prepare himself for news he didn't like and he needed to have a supportive, winning message ready.

He took a deep inhalation, tried to take himself back to the mindset when they were traveling back to the Ark. It was around a campfire very much like the one he'd been staring into for the past several minutes. He needed to be whatever she needed him to be. That was all there was to it. There was going to be no changing the way she felt so he'd simply need to accept whatever she decided.

He glanced up at the house. She'd immediately closed the window after issuing a goodbye to Miles and for at least ten minutes, according to his watch, there'd been no sign she was about to appear.

He took a seat abruptly and heard himself murmur: "Essie's not the type of girl who's going to respond well to us competing over her."

Gabe looked up, frowning, his cheek propped up by his fist.

"And neither one of us wants to lose having a relationship with her, romantic or otherwise."

"*Correct*," Gabe said slowly.

"Can we agree to just let the cards fall where they will? Respect her choice?"

His brother cleared his throat. "That sounds reasonable."

Josh nodded. "Good."

"Good," Gabe repeated. He glanced over his shoulder to the house, then leaned forward, lifted his brow. "Is the general impression that this is some sort of love triangle, like what Miles said?"

"It doesn't make sense, I know. It can't be a triangle if two of the corners aren't connected. It'd be more like a love arrow or something."

"No, it's *just*–"

Josh braced himself for the worst.

"It's blatantly, *blatantly* obvious that you love Essie. You've loved her for most of your life."

Josh lifted his brow.

"Equally obvious, though apparently not to *you,* is the fact that Essie loves you."

Josh considered this, finding it impossible to generate words.

Gabe shook his head. "If I'm being totally honest, if she looked at me the way she looks at you?" He pursed his lips, suppressing any further elaboration. "*But* she doesn't and I have to be okay with that. Which I am."

Josh stared at him. "Oh."

"*Oh,*" Gabe echoed, giving him a kind smile. Gabe was apparently one who *could* have emotions and facial expressions that contradicted each other. Not far beneath the forced smile, he could see a tremendous amount of hurt.

"The two of you spend so much time together. I thought–"

"Nothing like the two of you. In duration and context, I'm sure." He considered his next words. "There was a time that I'm pretty sure I was the one comforting *her.* These days it's the other way around–and it's been pretty one-sided these days, if I'm being honest."

Josh nodded slowly, his observations of the pair of them aligning with Gabe's assessment.

"She was only 14 when I left for Mandatory the first time," he said in a disbelieving tone.

It was difficult for Josh to picture Essie at that age anymore. So much had gone on for her in those years. The overall-wearing girl with hair braided by their mom, muddied cheeks still with the roundness of childhood, big, sparkling silver eyes that had easily negotiated for desserts or later bedtimes seemed to exist in a different world.

"Before she found me in Denver, I hadn't seen her in four and a half years, Josh."

Josh sighed. "Wow. I didn't realize it had been so long."

Gabe nodded. "She's still Essie–but she's changed so much. She's been through a lot, I can tell. It's heavy on her shoulders."

Josh released a long breath. "It's been a lot. St. Dominic's getting bombed? She was going to three funerals a day for weeks. The attack on the Children's Ministry? Saving those kids' lives and then never getting to see them again?" *Putting herself through hell with the Phoenix Initiative,* he added silently. *Learning that she was tortured for the first nearly three years of her life.*

Josh watched the color drain from his brother's face and suddenly he realized that Gabe had been speculating. He really didn't know anything about what Essie had gone through since he'd been gone.

"There's no way you would have known, Gabe. She wrote to you all the time, I know, but I don't think they were letting anything get through."

Gabe shook his head. "I kind of feel like she's all I have–from before Mandatory?"

"That's not true, Gabe."

He gave a shrug. "She's the only one who treats me the same now as before I left."

Josh fell silent as he reflected on his own distrust of his brother since returning from the city. He remembered declaring at the cabin that he would not be giving Gabe a firearm for the treacherous journey back— *without* any consideration that Gabe was sitting just inside the single-pane window from where he'd said it. In his defense, Essie had just quietly and casually requested, as she polished off a second plate of diced potatoes, that

Josh shoot her if they ran into trouble on the way to the Ark. He wasn't exactly in the frame of mind to be tactful.

"Gabe, I probably haven't been the support that I could be. I know at the safe house, I–"

Gabe put up his hand. "Josh, you had more important things on your mind than sparing my feelings." He sighed. "Mom and Dad had been treating me like a ticking time bomb."

Josh furrowed his brow. "What do you mean?"

"They were terrified of me being near Hannah. I don't totally blame them. I have reactions to things. I mean, I *get* it."

"What kinds of reactions?"

Gabe released a long exhale. "It's difficult to be around babies—after what I saw, what I did."

Josh narrowed his eyes, realizing he wasn't entirely sure what Gabe had faced when he lived in Denver. "You worked in a medical clinic? They had you training to be a doctor, right?"

"I functioned as a doctor for all intents and purposes, but nothing they had me do felt like medicine or healthcare. I did health screens, but things at the clinic were mainly procedural. Nothing was intended to *support* life."

"Like the sterilization procedure."

Gabe lifted his eyebrows. "Yeah. And euthanasia. And abortion, but considering many of the babies were capable of surviving *on their own*—it seems there'd be a different word for *that*, wouldn't there?"

"*That's* what they were having you do?"

"Essie didn't mention it?"

Josh glanced up toward the house and shook his head.

"It makes sense, I guess," Gabe said with a sigh. "She's trying so hard to have me fit here, which isn't easy considering I wasn't really fitting in before I left home in the first place. I still have a hard time processing what she did for me, getting me out of the city, risking her life. I mean, if she didn't have the antidote, she would have died. *Right?*"

Josh narrowed his eyes, shifted his attention to the fire and gave a short nod.

Gabe dropped his chin to his chest.

All at once, the interactions he'd observed between Essie and Gabe had entirely different meaning. His inner speculation that she could be falling in love with Gabe over these months at the Ark now seemed completely ridiculous.

Her mission had been to save Gabe; that didn't end when she got him out of Denver; it was only the start of it.

Josh glanced over his shoulder toward the dim lights inside the house and sighed. "You mean a lot to her, Gabe."

Gabe released a breath. "And she means a lot to me, but I never risked my life for her. And here she saved my life, *literally* saved my life, and I–" He let his voice trail off, shaking his head.

"I think she knew you would."

Gabe frowned.

"You were given a direct order to sterilize her, Gabe, but you wouldn't do it." He lifted his brow. "They would have probably killed you for not following orders if they knew."

Gabe considered this. "I *couldn't*. There was no way I could knowingly do that. To *her*," he added. "I'd done those before and I didn't even remember her name at that point, but—"

"You'd never hurt her."

He took a deep breath, electing not to argue or continue.

Josh felt an impulse to thank him, but it didn't feel right. What Gabe did was for Essie, not him. Besides, thanking him for not doing something barbaric felt patronizing. Josh reached forward, nudged the firewood around the basin with the poker. "What's going on with you, Mom and Dad? You were dad's right-hand guy when we were growing up."

Gabe cleared his throat. "Before I left for Mandatory, Dad and I were at odds. He wanted me to take over things at some point–that was before the government started running all the farms and ranches into the ground. I had seen how they had struggled financially, and I wanted to do something to help them, to change the trajectory for me, for our family. I thought becoming a doctor was the solution, since we didn't have many medical clinics or anything in town, though now I know why."

"The government had taken those over, too."

"At the time I thought I could provide what seemed to be a needed service in the community *and* I could probably make a decent living.

"I had found some medical training programs and I was working out how I could pay for it, but I didn't exactly present it well to them. Dad flew off the handle about cost, about the family business, about me thinking I was better than the work he had chosen for himself. When I was given the opportunity to be in the medical program at Mandatory, I thought it was fate. I thought I'd be able to get through it and I'd have some sort of degree. I'd be able to bring that back home and things with Dad would get better.

"I was having a hard time facing them when we got here after what I had done in the city. Essie got me to go to the hospital when Hannah was born, but I–I had an anxiety attack when I was holding her. It kind of freaked them out. I tried to make it better when I went over to their place a few weeks ago."

Josh remembered the nervousness in his brother's expression as he climbed out of his car carrying three large, poorly wrapped baby gifts. Essie's eyes had lit up seeing him and she had glanced back toward the house a considerable number of times before finally getting into the truck so Josh could drive her home. "It didn't go well?"

"Matteo was babysitting so they could go out. All of a sudden, Mom wanted to stay back. Dad thought it was because she didn't trust me with Hannah–"

"He said that?"

Gabe nodded slowly. "She was upset, mainly because she didn't want me to think she'd think that; she said it was because she wanted to spend time with me. I actually did believe her, but the thought was already out there and it really messed with me. I couldn't get out of my head about it."

"Gabe, she's been a disaster with you gone. She's said a thousand times that it doesn't matter what any of her kids do, she'll love us no matter what." He frowned. "Dad's protective. You know that."

"He was actually fine leaving me there with Matteo and Hannah."

"Oh. Well, that's--"

Gabe glanced across the drive toward the distant lights of their parents' house, where someone, undoubtedly their dad, was out in the barn. "I'm heading over there tomorrow. We talked when they were here today. I held Hannah actually, showed her the horses."

Josh smiled lightly. "It sounds like things are moving in the right direction."

"I hope so. I'm trying. Essie got me to go to a support group they have at church. I'm now in three life groups, but this is a good one for me, I think. She was right, as usual. It's helping, talking to people who went through similar training and experiences. Church is helping, too. I feel like God is calling me closer, you know?"

Josh nodded. "Yeah."

"And I'm getting better about at least attending social gatherings. Like today. I'm still not great with interactions though."

"*Well*, you never were a great conversationalist."

Gabe's chin popped up. He smiled in a distantly familiar way. "Jackass."

"You'll get there, Gabe. Moving on from what happened in Denver. I know you will. Growing up, everyone depended on you and that put a lot of pressure on you. It's okay that you need to lean on other people more right now."

Gabe nodded, staring into the fire. "That's what Essie tells me."

Josh lifted his eyes once again to the house, catching a glimpse of movement inside. His heart began to race.

Through the kitchen window came the sound of a chair crashing to the floor.

There was a momentary delay before both men bolted from their seats and took off for the house.

It appeared Essie had just stepped out of the bathroom when she collapsed. Her body heaved on the hardwood flooring as they reached her, her breaths catching in her chest. Her eyes weren't focusing, the muddy brown irises staring blanking toward the ceiling.

Her hand was braced over her right side. Noticing this, Gabe unbuttoned that side of her overalls, tugged her shirt up, revealing deep purple bruising across the entirety of her abdomen, stretching to her back.

Her lungs made a constricted shriek as her chest arched upward– and then her body dropped to the floor.

19

phoenix

When they arrived at the hospital, Gabe spoke with a confident level of authority, directing the stretcher team, firing off directions to medical staff who swarmed them as they entered. Someone even fetched him a set of scrubs, which he rejected, focused on getting Esther set on an IV the moment they reached an ER suite. He moved about with familiarity, calling for IV vitamin K, fresh frozen plasma, O- blood, lab work. He quickly drew a blood sample and handed it off for processing.

When he glanced up to find Josh standing rigid and horror-struck, he took a deep breath, began to explain his actions:

"She's bleeding internally, but before we can take a closer look to see what's going on, we need to try to stop the bleed so we can stabilize her." He attached an oxygen mask to her face, which immediately fogged.

Josh's eyes panned to the monitors.

"Heart rate dropping," Gabe called out. "We need 1 mg epinephrine."

Josh watched as a nurse tugged Essie's overalls over her hips, down her legs. She jabbed the syringe of cloudy colored liquid into her muscular thigh. He flinched involuntarily, seeing that the bruising continued down into her legs.

"Dr. West?" the nurse said to Gabe, motioning to the deepening purple hue. She draped a paper blanket over Essie's torso, rolling the overalls and placing them on the counter.

The monitor beeped a warning.

"What the hell is happening," Gabe muttered, moving to retrieve the portable ultrasound from the technician just entering the room.

"We'd expect to see her heart rate going up, not down." He lifted the ultrasound wand, applied the gel and placed it on her bare stomach, pushing the shirt further out of his way. "How soon can we get a CT?"

"I'll see what I can do."

"What is going on in there, Kiddo?" Gabe asked once the nurse exited the room, narrowing his eyes on the screen. He gently moved the wand across her abdomen.

The room was decidedly quiet as Josh stepped forward, placed his hand over Essie's forehead. Her face, her lips, were eerily pale. Her skin was cool to the touch.

"Wait, what the *hell*?" Gabe stammered, resetting the ultrasound device.

"What's going on?"

"The blood is receding, but I have no idea where it's going."

Josh's satellite phone made a chirping noise in his pocket. The moment he answered, Luther was demanding an explanation of what had happened, having missed Josh's earlier call.

After going through the events briefly, Josh concluded with: "We're in the ER with her."

Luther sighed. "Tell me they didn't run her blood."

*   *   *

To say Gabe was reluctant to have Essie leave the hospital in her condition was an understatement.

On the phone call, Luther had put in very firm, very clear and well-enunciated words that Essie needed to leave the hospital immediately, that the blood sample needed to be retrieved immediately, that it needed to be like she was never there. *Immediately.*

Josh didn't want to ask why, but did anyway. When he'd received the answer and Luther had signed off from the call, saying he'd be there as soon as possible, Josh knew he didn't have a choice in his approach with Gabe.

There were a half-dozen people who knew Essie was involved with the development of the antidote, but were under the impression it was in a testing capacity only. Only three people, other than himself, knew that Essie was the one and only source of the antidote: Luther, Matteo (he assumed), and Danny.

Now, there was a fourth. It took very little persuasion for Gabe to be convinced. He immediately set off to try to recover the blood sample.

Luther arrived fifteen minutes after hanging up with Josh, wearing scrubs and a new facial overlay. The face was familiar to Josh, as it had a strong resemblance to a movie actor from decades earlier, whose movies his parents liked to watch. His mom had a crush on the actor, going on about his "symmetrical" features, how there had been a study done with babies and it was shown that babies are most drawn to faces that are symmetrical, which is why he *scientifically* had the most visual appeal. Luke liked to tease her about the *science* making her gush over him, that her infatuation was out of her control; she had absolutely nothing to do with it.

Luther, resembling Denzel Washington, spoke calmly, confidently, identifying himself as an Infectious Diseases physician named Dr. Bryan Marshall. He immediately sent the nurse assigned to Essie on a quest to put those who came into contact through a decontamination and isolation process. He told her that there was a highly contagious gastro-intestinal virus suspected, which as he explained later when things had de-escalated: "When there's poop involved, people act fast, don't want details, and don't ask questions."

As soon as the nurse left, he went to work, sealing off Essie's IV line for transport. He lifted IV medication bags carefully off the rack. He pulled a blanket from the wall cabinet and draped it over her. He eased the oxygen mask from her face, let his palm linger over her cheek.

Gabe returned, having been unable to retrieve the blood sample before it was deposited for digital testing.

Luther released a long breath, then directed Gabe to gather up extra medication, determining that Vitamin K and fluids were unlikely to do harm. He disconnected the blood transfusion line from the donor O-blood, however, scowling angrily at its presence.

Ignoring Gabe's objections to moving Essie, Luther instructed Josh to lift her, which he did with as much tenderness as he could and still keep a solid grip on her. It felt a bit more precarious not having the security of her arm around him. Luther checked the corridor then signaled for him to follow quickly. They crossed to a stairwell with a direct parking lot exit, where Luther had strategically parked his SUV.

Josh slid into the backseat, holding Essie against him.

"You drive," Luther told Gabe, climbing in the opposite side of the back seat. He lifted her legs, let them rest across his knees.

Josh checked her positioning on the bench seat, making sure the seat belt locks weren't jabbing into her hip.

"Where are we going?" Gabe asked.

"Her house. Where she should have *stayed*," he muttered impatiently.

"Luther, there was nothing that should have set this off. She was having convulsions, she couldn't breathe."

The desperation in Josh's voice seemed to defuse Luther. He nodded and patted Josh on the arm in consolation. He then pulled aside the hospital gown, examining her stomach. "How does this look compared with when it first happened?"

"Better than it did, but Luther, what *did* this?"

Luther pressed his index and middle finger gently to her wrist, closing his eyes as he focused on counting.

"When Gabe was doing the ultrasound, he said it looked like the blood was receding?"

"Yeah."

"What does that mean?"

Luther didn't respond.

"She's going to be OK, isn't she?"

Luther nodded without opening his eyes, taking deep breaths, running his thumb gently against her wrist.

"You said she would be in danger if they ran her blood."

"I have Danny trying to make her blood sample disappear from the database."

"Because it'd be connected with the antidote?"

Luther's eyes opened abruptly and shot a glare toward the back of Gabe's head.

"He knows."

Luther twisted his mouth angrily.

"Gabe's my brother. I trust him," Josh said firmly.

Gabe glanced up to the rearview mirror then took a steadying breath.

"We added superfluous blood plasma to the antidote. It would take some work to isolate singular strands of DNA from the antidote and make that connection to her. If they're *looking* for matches, that's another story since her blood sample is now in the database." He exhaled angrily.

"Are you worried about someone doing a genetic test?"

Luther's eyes widened threateningly, again jumping toward Gabe. Josh shook his head.

"That's been taken care of on the other end."

"Then why is she in danger?"

Luther dropped his head to peer through the windshield to check their location. "We're almost to the ranch. We'll talk about this once we have her settled inside."

Josh checked their surroundings, verifying the proximity. The drive to the hospital seemed to have taken considerably longer. "Do you know what did this to her?"

Luther sandwiched Essie's hand between his palms, gently massaged her cool skin. "When we get there, I want to get her set up on some fluids, probably a catheter, which she's going to hate me for, but oh well. Then I want to do a quick ultrasound. She seems to be in full-recovery mode so then we'll probably just need to wait it out."

Josh nodded.

"We'll let her dad watch over her, but you and I need to talk."

*   *   *

Luther Graham looked very much out of place sitting on a hay bale in the barn. He kept peering around, taking in the setting, his nose twitching as he picked up on odors that Josh hardly noticed anymore. He cleared his throat, swept a gnat off his arm, and straightened his posture.

"When Essie went to the medical clinic in Denver, Gabe injected her with saline instead of the sterilization serum," he began.

Josh nodded.

"She had mentioned it to me and I didn't question it at the time because I didn't think there was a *reason* to question it. We had run tests to make sure she hadn't inadvertently been given the serum. There was no telling if the serum would have the same effect on her that it does on everyone else, but everything was fine."

"She was worried about–" Josh stopped short. "Gabe thought it was saline. Was it not?"

"At the time, everything seemed fine. It seemed like he was telling the truth." Luther shook his head. "But now? I don't think it was *just* saline."

Josh's chin swiveled toward the barn doors and back. "You think he gave her something else?"

"Not on purpose, no."

"What was it?"

He took a deep breath. "About ten years ago, there was a de-population effort. One of many. The idea was that people would come in for routine exams and receive an injection in place of a routine vaccine or flu shot. They could have used actual vaccines, but why waste supplies?" The hay bale shifted and he reset himself, looking less confident in his chosen seat. "The injection contained a nanotech device that proved to be undetectable unless you were looking for the exact signature for it. We're talking something one hundred times smaller than a pin tip."

Josh narrowed his eyes.

"Once injected, it would seek out the closest major artery. The device would then self-replicate."

"This was tech."

"Yes."

"That would clone itself."

"Yes."

"To do what?"

"Once the device reached normal body temperature, a timer would activate, counting down a specific amount of time. Some were set for two weeks, some for three, some for a month. When the countdown ended, the device and all its clones would literally detonate, causing the artery to burst open and the person to bleed out.

"The deaths were brutal and took place over the course of just a couple of months. The original plan had been to spread out the deaths over a longer period of time, a year or so, but the criteria that clinics were instructed to use was too inclusive: Age 50 and older."

Josh narrowed his eyes.

"20 million people were estimated to have died from this depopulation campaign. The government claimed that a bovine flu outbreak had managed to cross species. There was another push to go to what they termed 'plant-based,' even though most of that food was just processed chemicals. 3D printed food became popular. Lab-grown meats. They needed to shift the focus and have someone, or some*thing*, to blame. In this case, cows."

"That's when the government came in and took our healthy cows."

Luther nodded. "These Neanderthals were eating steaks during this time, make no mistake about it."

"It wasn't just middle-aged and older who died from the 'bovine flu.'"

"No. They had to shift to have the 'flu' impact younger populations as well to tame suspicions that this was manufactured to kill off the most expensive portion of the population."

Josh blinked. "She was injected with this."

"Yes. But I honestly believe that Gabe didn't know. These vials truly did look just like plain old saline."

"He would never have injected this on purpose."

Luther pressed his lips together. "Just bad luck then. A leftover supply."

"You said once activated, it would detonate within a few weeks."

"I *did* say that, but that's in the average person."

"You're saying her hyper-immunity or whatever you want to call it put off the detonation until now?"

Luther winced. "Something like that."

"So, she's been living with a ticking time bomb inside her for six months."

"It's a theory, but everything seems to align and support it. Everything except the timeline, but I have a hunch on that."

"Okay?"

"The device was meant to be given like a vaccine in the upper arm, but sterilization is administered–"

"Like artificial insemination."

"Yeah, I guess they use that a bit with horses, right?"

Josh nodded, his jaw tight, not caring for the connection between the method for artificial insemination and the procedure performed on Essie.

"Based upon what I could see on the ultrasound, it may have implanted inside the uterine wall. The device is meant to be attracted to major arteries and the uterine artery is the main blood supply of the reproductive system." Luther considered his next words, seeing the confusion in Josh's face. "I'm going to go through my theory quickly and

I'll warn you, it's not going to make any sense with what you currently know."

"*Okay.*"

"I suspect that Essie's body recognized the device. It may have been trying to break it down initially, but with the duplication that would have been taking place, I think what happened is that her body produced and built up adipose tissue around the device. Adipose tissue is—"

"Body fat."

"Right. So, body fat is responsible for body temperature regulation. Now, Essie doesn't have a lot of body fat, but the device wouldn't have been very large, even after cloning itself, so it probably just wouldn't have looked like anything more than a little bloating. I certainly didn't notice anything unusual when I did the tests with her."

Josh shook his head.

"I think this buildup of tissue insulated the device and prevented it from reaching the triggering temperature as quickly."

"Her body temperature was really cold earlier. She didn't seem to be feeling well."

"When was this?"

"Ten? She actually fainted."

Luther's stare intensified. "I wish you had called me."

"She hasn't been sleeping. I just thought--She seemed better after she napped for a couple hours–"

Luther nodded.

"She wasn't herself. She seemed very out of it this morning–she was confused, wobbly, not really processing things."

"I imagine having this going on inside of her would feel a bit like having an impending illness–you know, like you feel the flu coming on?"

Josh nodded. "Something she hasn't really experienced before."

"Right. Well, no, actually. In the antidote runs, she'd sometimes wake up feeling sick like that. She wouldn't want to eat or do anything else, she'd just go home and crawl into bed." Luther cleared his throat. "Those weren't great days. For me or for her. I hated seeing her like that."

Josh took a breath. "So, ever since this was injected, she's probably been feeling like that?"

"I'd assume so. Maybe not as severe, but yeah."

Josh shook his head, the weight of the word "detonation" finally settling in his brain. "What damage did it cause?"

"Based upon what I saw in the ultrasound, it seems that the source of most of the blood pooling in her abdomen was from the tissue itself, but there was some significant damage to her organs. If we had more sophisticated equipment, we might be able to differentiate new cell growth, which would indicate freshly repaired organs."

"Repaired organs?"

"Regenerated organ cells."

Josh narrowed his eyes. "That doesn't sound like an *immune* response."

Luther took a deep breath. "What do you know about stem cells?"

Josh frowned. "Not much. I mean, I know there was a lot of research done years ago. They studied salamanders, how their cells are different, how they can regenerate in all different ways. Scientists, doctors used embryonic stem cells to develop treatments, vaccines–"

"Do salamanders have pluripotent or omnipotent stem cells? I can't remember."

Josh shrugged, no longer wanting to talk about salamanders.

"Never mind. It doesn't matter, my brain just wanted to know. Anyway, twenty, thirty some odd years ago, there was a push in medical research to figure out how to reprogram specialized adult cells to behave like embryonic stem cells."

"Human induced pluripotent stem cells," Josh recited, picturing the section in one of his Biology textbooks.

"*Yes*," Luther said, impressed. "If they could reprogram the genetics of adult stem cells, it would essentially allow the body to heal itself. In clinical trials, it worked to some degree, but the benefits were temporary. The new cells were accepted by the body initially, but were eventually destroyed by the body's native cells. Think of it like probiotics."

"The bacteria in probiotics is transient, right? It helps while it's in the body, but–"

"For lack of a better term, it's just passing through."

Josh nodded.

"In cancer patients, tumors could be eradicated temporarily by the reprogrammed cells, but as soon as the induced cells died off, the tumors came back, often more aggressively. It also led to genetic mutations. Therapies were offered to those who could afford the maintenance treatment, but they would need to continue indefinitely, and the side effects were significant, a lot of cardiac and pulmonary issues.

"As a result of all this, scientists had two goals. They wanted to: 1) see about making the reprogramming permanent, and 2) see if they could reprogram *all* the body's cells. To do this, it made the most sense to them to start with individuals who already had pluripotent stem cells."

"Babies."

"More accurately, preborn babies in their earliest developmental stage. Researchers worked to maintain cellular structure in first trimester babies by constantly reprogramming cells as they attempted to convert into more specialized cells."

Josh narrowed his eyes.

"It didn't go well. There's a lot happening in the first trimester specifically and they quickly overwhelmed the cells. In the next round of trials, they decided to have a less frequent intervention and developed–I'll call it a smart serum."

"*Smart* serum?"

"It was task driven. It used tumor cells." Luther resituated himself on the hay, leaning forward over his knees. "Tumor cells are excellent carriers in the body. Destructive, obviously, but they can get in anywhere. The baby's induced pluripotent stem cells were implanted inside the tumor cells. The tumor cells were then injected weekly back into the baby using ultrasound guidance. The idea was that the tumor cells would invade existing cells and the reprogrammed cells would replicate with them.

Eventually, recognizing the threat, the stem cells would destroy the tumor cells. Theoretically."

"That sounds complex."

"It was a disaster. Some babies were born with only certain organs possessing pluripotent cells, which didn't turn out well. It would be like upgrading one component in a computer, but not anything else. Most babies had major problems with their growth and development. Many were born with rampant tumors. The ones who managed to be born without these issues faced aggressive genetic therapy. Their bodies continuously tried to convert cells to multipotent or unipotent, specialized for their place in the body, while the therapies sought to block this from happening. Ultimately this put too much strain on their little bodies." He paused abruptly, the word "little" bringing to mind images he'd rather forget. He took a breath. "Babies who lived beyond that initial stage didn't do well once they were exposed to threats meant to test their cells' resilience and response. Their cells overcompensated when threatened. Their bodies just couldn't regulate."

Josh blinked slowly. "Essie doesn't *just* have hyper-immunity, does she?"

Luther shook his head. "*All* of Essie's cells are pluripotent. *All* of the cells in her body behave like embryonic stem cells. That's why her body heals itself."

"So the antidote didn't *just* work because she generates antibodies."

"The reason it's so effective is that her blood stem cells are also pluripotent. When used in treatment, they act as carriers of the antibodies that treat the condition, respond to the antigens. The cells in the patient, in turn, mimic the behavior of her stem cells."

"The recipient's specialized stem cells behave like pluripotent stem cells?"

"Temporarily, yes. Her stem cells essentially train the recipient's cells to defend the body in whatever way they need. It's not just limited to the issue at hand. Any problems the body is facing. Once the threat is neutralized, the body is healed, the cells revert to their specialized behavior. But there's one thing that really sparked my interest–there are a lot of things, probably some more pressing honestly, but this piqued my curiosity after a conversation with Essie's dad actually."

Josh lifted his eyebrows, encouraging him to continue.

"Over the past few decades, there's been a 76% decline in births. Meanwhile, the rate of stillbirths, miscarriages, ectopic pregnancies, and infertility has skyrocketed. That wasn't random."

"It was another depopulation effort?" Josh asked rhetorically. He considered how his parents had wanted desperately to have a big family, but they could never manage to conceive another baby after he was born. He thought about how Matteo and his wife faced repeated losses that eventually caused Rachel to sink into depression and take her own life.

"Have you noticed the sudden baby boom?"

Josh pulled in his breath. "You're saying the antidote is fixing whatever had been–what would the right word be? *Broken*?"

Luther nodded.

"The antidote started to be re-engineered to be a full-spectrum vaccine, correct?"

"It hasn't been approved fully for that yet. The Ark Council approved its use for emergency, life-saving situations, as well as a less-concentrated version for general 'immune boosting' purposes, while they 'confirm efficacy, safety,' etcetera, etcetera." He rolled his eyes. "I'd respect having safety and quality assurances if that's what I felt like they were doing. This is just bureaucracy, which is kind of ironic."

Josh frowned.

"Beside the point," Luther said, visibly getting his mind back on track. "Most people who hadn't already gotten the concentrated version in an emergency situation received the diluted version, the 'immunity booster' when they arrived at the Ark as a precautionary measure. It was optional, of course, but people had seen with their own eyes their family members, friends literally be brought back from certain death by the antidote. It seemed like a good idea to take *any* version they could get."

"Luther, my mom and dad tried for my entire life to have more children and they never could. Now I have a baby sister. You're *saying*–" He cleared his throat. "Whatever was wrong–was healed. Because of the antidote/booster that only exists because of you and Essie."

Luther frowned. "I really hesitate to accept the amount of credit you're giving me." He shrugged. "It's been her. Without her tenacity, we never would have even pursued an antidote, vaccine, 'immunity booster' in the first place."

Josh chuckled to himself, buried his face in his palm. "How is this possible, Luther?"

Luther shrugged. "Nothing the government, scientists, the medical community has done has come close to this. At this point, no one's looking at reprogramming stem cells anymore. They haven't looked at it in at *least* fifteen years. It was a very controversial, very expensive endeavor that had very little to show for it. The government maintains 'embryo farms' where they harvest stem cells to be used in regenerative 'medicine,' for anti-aging treatments, nothing for the general public, this is all elite stuff for the rich, famous, and powerful. They've streamlined that whole process with clones."

Josh dropped his chin.

"I'll clarify that these are first trimester clones/babies created *only* for stem cell harvesting. They're not actually allowing clones to be 'born.' They serve their purpose *and*–"

"That's a chilling thought, Luther."

"I've seen worse," Luther replied, swallowing hard, lifting his eyes toward the barn door.

Josh took a deep breath, picturing the video clip showing a two-year-old girl being forced to inhale a deadly gas, clamped by the waist, the ankles, the wrists, to a metal table. He remembered how she was so resolved in her situation. She had twisted her mouth, her cheeks, to try to shift the mask from her face. Then there had been a moment when he could see her accepting that there was nothing she could do, and she took a deep inhalation.

A quote from a sermon Teo had given recently suddenly struck a different note with him. He was talking about grief, opening up about his wife's death, and he said: "There are situations you just want to escape, emotions you just don't want to feel, but the truth of it is this: Sometimes the only way out is through."

He thought of the toddler clamped to the table. He had to remind himself that the child in those videos who appeared to be, *was* in a place, a situation with unthinkable horrors, pain, suffering, a place without any hope—was the same little girl he met a few months later. She was the same girl who adored everything about life at his family's farm (except anything that had to do with animal suffering)--she loved the dirt, the horses, the hard work, loved the wide open sky, loved the dinners around the table. She was the same girl who smiled with her eyes, who always wanted to be outside, who marveled at things he often overlooked, who had a refreshing and seemingly unspoiled viewpoint of the world. She was the same exceedingly kind girl with a razor sharp wit and frequently self-deprecating, sometimes dark sense of humor. She was the same girl he'd loved since the day he met her, who embodied just about everything good and beautiful he could possibly imagine in the world.

"I still have a difficult time comprehending what happened to her as a child, Luther."

"I do, too," Luther said quietly. "And I was there."

Josh took a deep breath. "Now to know the impact she's had? That my baby sister wouldn't–" It was unfathomable. All of it.

"Josh, what Essie's body does? Its capabilities, its healing power, its resilience? There's no worldly explanation for it. The nature of their experiments were sloppy at best, but even *if* the experiments were run perfectly, there's no way it should have been successful. There's no way *if* it was successful that her body should have retained its cellular structure after they stopped interventions. The odds of that actually happening–"

"One in a billion?"

Luther shook his head. "Try adding about twenty zeroes to that denominator. There are too many factors that had to be in place for it to work in the first place, let alone continue to work. This is just not in the capability of science."

"So you're saying–" Josh said, then frowned. "What are you saying?"

"I'm saying that God intended Essie to be just as she is. To do what she's done."

"To give us a chance? To fix what was broken?"

Luther shrugged. "Maybe? Maybe there's more to it that we just don't know, can't see yet."

Josh nodded slowly. "If this could cure infertility–I mean, that wasn't the intent, Essie wasn't exposed to a pathogen or something that specifically caused infertility. What you were saying before–it seems like her cells identify *any* issue, *any* problem in the body?" He lifted his brow.

Luther nodded. "If we can obtain data points for diseases, it would be interesting to see what's happened over the past couple of years. What will happen over the next decade, two decades."

"So, your theory is that anything the cells identify as an issue–cancer, organ failure, brain damage–could be repaired simply by a one-time blood transfusion using her blood?" He said this with trepidation, as the idea absolutely boggled his mind, but Luther gave a light smile.

"Kind of like God is gifting us back a little bit of the Garden of Eden, if that's the case, huh?"

Josh sighed, watching Bree, who was starting to investigate Luther's back pocket. "So, her body, right now, it's *literally* repairing, regenerating organs?"

"And blood vessels, muscle tissue–"

Josh released a breath. "Luther, this *is*–"

"Incredible? Mind-boggling?"

"*Terrifying.*"

Luther froze, then nodded slowly. "Yeah. It is."

"Before the concern was that Gowon, the government, if they discovered who she is, what her body does in terms of *hyper-immunity*, she'd be in danger because they could weaponize it in some way–"

"And/or use it to benefit themselves," Luther said with a shrug.

"Right, but this discovery, her existence, her one in a ten to the thirty-something's power of even existing as she is–" He furrowed his brow. "Whether their intent is good or bad, it won't matter. She won't be Essie to any scientist or any doctor other than you. If someone else comes to this same conclusion and finds out who she is–"

Luther nodded slowly, his face severe. "That's why I don't want anyone looking too closely at her blood."

20

anew

Essie spent three full days recovering at the ranch before fully waking and was entirely unconscious for the first 24 hours.

That part was surreal and terrifying, but being that it mirrored the recovery period after an antidote run, just significantly longer, Josh felt far more at ease than he would have been otherwise. It was the other aspect of it, the conversation with Luther, that plagued his mind if he let his thoughts linger there too long. So instead, he focused on supporting Luther's efforts to ease the wait for Teo.

Matteo hadn't been desensitized about the recovery period like they had. He simply saw his daughter in a state of unconsciousness and complete vulnerability. He hadn't studied science and didn't have a working knowledge of medical vocabulary, so they explained each term, each principle in layman's terms. He didn't know the recovery signals to look for, so they pointed them out for him, explained what they thought the next signal might be, and what it would mean on her recovery timeline.

Luther had encouraged Matteo to complete tasks such as keeping a cool washcloth on her forehead, then warming her blankets, changing out the IV fluids bag, all things that probably weren't having a tremendous impact on her comfort level, but were nevertheless keeping him occupied. Having some sense of schedule also provided a sense of control, which seemed to be helping him.

For her recovery, they had set her up in the corner of the tufted leather sectional with an abundance of pillows and blankets supporting her in a semi-reclined position. There had been consideration that her bedroom would be more comfortable, but the couch supported the optimal angle for oxygen and blood flow, plus the living room had the advantage that all three of them could be situated nearby to keep an eye on her.

Luther had set her up on IV fluids, twice-per-day transfusions of her own stored blood, a catheter, and oxygen. Initially the sight of the mask on her face troubled Luther, probably stirring up the memories from his first encounter with her, but he justified that a flow of good oxygen could only help and would likely shorten her recovery time.

He had assessed that the blood she was given at the hospital likely hurt more than it helped, as her body's cells needed to make sense of the incoming red blood cells on top of what they were already doing.

The justification that there were more places for all three to sit turned out to be unwarranted given the fact that they each had taken to pacing, Teo more than anyone. He rarely sat down for longer than a minute or two at a time before suddenly thinking of something he needed to be doing.

In the first 24 hours, Essie didn't adjust her position or make any sounds associated with sleep. Any movements, any noises seemed to be physiological reflexes to the things happening internally. Small grunts and squeaks would escape her throat, low vibrations would emerge through her stomach. Teo had a difficult time being convinced that the noises weren't hunger, that she didn't need nourishment. Luther very nearly started her on tube feedings that first day just to pacify him but had stayed firm that having to absorb or break down nutrients would just complicate things internally for her. With more authority in his voice than he ever used with Teo, Luther told him that he'd plan to start a nasogastric tube at 48 hours if she was still not showing signs of waking. While not their most pleasant interaction, Teo stopped verbalizing his concern; he would instead check the clock, convinced that 48 hours had most certainly passed.

Luther ushered Matteo to get some sleep in the mid-afternoon, suggesting they should have a coverage plan so there was someone always alert and keeping watch on Essie. As soon as Matteo was out of the room, Luther put his hand to his head and released a long sigh. "Maybe I should put in a feeding tube. Give her something more to work with energy-wise."

"But you said you think it would put more of a strain on her system."

Luther nodded distantly. "That's what I'm afraid of. She's already dealing with a pint of garbage blood, she doesn't need tube feeding sludge on top of that."

"I didn't know, Luther."

"I'm sorry. I'm not blaming you. You'd never do anything–" He stopped short, shook his head. "I just thought I was done seeing her like this. And I never wanted her dad to see this."

Josh glanced up at Teo's closed door and took a deep breath. He was seated in one of the dining chairs, which he'd situated directly in front of the couch facing her, his legs stretched beside her hip, his body slumped against the couch's chaise lounge next to her feet. He was not the least bit comfortable, despite his casual positioning, but he was satisfied that he'd be able to feel her movement when she woke up if he happened to nod off.

Essie had been very pale since she collapsed, but her cheeks, her nose, her earlobes were beginning to acquire pink pigmentation, likely due to increasing body temperature.

Luther leaned over the couch, placed the backside of his hand over her forehead. "I know she's in pain and I can't do a damn thing about it," he muttered, checking down the hallway for signs of Matteo. He moved across to the relocated coffee table and extracted a device from his bag.

"What's that?"

"A technology borrowed from Communist China," he said grudgingly. "They started using it a decades ago, but for the usual purposes." He gently placed the narrow, brushed steel band over Essie's head. It had the appearance of a high-tech crown, resting just over her eyebrows. The underside illuminated upon making contact, the lights pulsating. After a few moments, the lights underneath turned off and an indicator panel on the front turned a bright shade of red.

"What *is* that, Luther?"

He explained how the device scanned brain waves and assigned a color based upon the brain activity it measured and the associated feeling or emotion. The assigned color could have different levels of saturation based upon intensity of the brain waves. The Chinese government had a variety of applications for the technology, most notably in the education system. Beginning around 2021, school children in many schools were required to wear the devices, which tracked their brain waves throughout the school day. Reports were generated to be analyzed by the school and provided to parents–obviously also shared with the government for unspecified purposes. The color display was also used by teachers to recognize when children were distracted or otherwise not engaged in class. Eventually the technology was advanced to include transcripts of their thoughts throughout the day.

"I never had a mood ring, but I imagine red isn't happy."

Luther shook his head and explained the interpretations of the colors: Purple was happiness. Blue was calm/relaxation. Green was primarily neutral, but could indicate some discomfort if the color gradient leaned toward Yellow, which was agitation and/or mild to moderate pain. Red was fear/stress and/or severe pain. Black was extreme distress.

"Can we try giving her a pain med?"

"We *can*, but her body metabolizes things so fast. I didn't want to give her anything before because her heart rate was already low."

"Well, her vitals are stable and this would tell you if the pain med has any effect, right?"

Luther immediately moved back to his bag, returned with a small clear bag, which he added on the hook with the half-empty fluid bag. He made the connection to the IV port line and adjusted the settings until he saw the liquid begin to drip into the tubing.

Josh gazed at Essie, whose blank expression was unchanged. For a normal person, pain relief should come pretty quickly, peaking 5-10 minutes after starting the medication, but there was no telling what impact, if any, it would have for her. He thought of how she'd used epinephrine to give her body enough of a jolt to be able to get Gabe to the pickup truck to get him out of the medical clinic and on the highway out of Denver. For anyone else, it would continue working for 25-30 minutes. For Essie, it wore off in less than 5 minutes. Then again, her body was powering down to deal with a lethal dose of fentanyl. Without that influence, perhaps the adrenaline dose could have lasted longer.

After a few quiet moments, the front light indicator on the scanner turned off and the underside lights turned back on, pulsating rapidly.

Red. Just after illuminating, it turned back off again and pulsations resumed.

"Come on, come on, come on," Luther beckoned quietly. He checked his watch.

Yellow.

Off.

Yellow.

Off.

She started having a rhythmic tightening in her chest, like suppressed hiccups.

"Luther? Her hands," Josh said urgently, dropping his feet to the floor, and leaning toward her.

Essie's hands were clenched into fists with such force that her arms were shaking.

Luther glanced up at the device just as the underside lights dimmed.

Black.

Off.

Black.

Luther clambered to switch off the hydromorphone drip and disconnected the tubing from the bag for good measure.

Josh had taken her right hand and was gently stroking the delicate skin of her wrist. "I'm here, Essie," he whispered. "You're going to be OK. I'm right here."

Her chest rose and fell heavily, her breaths tensed, and her hands remained clenched.

"Luther, she's sweating a *lot* all of a sudden."

The device was once again trying to get a reading. Meanwhile, Luther checked the monitor stand positioned on his side of the couch. "104.6."

Her cheeks, nose, earlobes had turned bright red and there was a visible beading of sweat on her forehead.

Black.

Off.

"Do you think it's the device? When it reads her brain waves?"

Black.

Off.

Black.

Off.

Luther glared at the persistent lights, then abruptly pulled the device from her head, disassembled the battery compartment on the underside of the device.

Within seconds, her body temperature was dropping and her body had relaxed considerably.

Josh continued to stroke her wrist. "There you go," Josh whispered as the muscles in her arms eased and her body sank a bit deeper in the pillows. "How are her readouts?"

Luther checked the monitor. "Better."

"Maybe the pain meds worked after all? I don't know what the hell that device was doing. You're sure it was just *reading* brain waves?"

Luther looked down at the device in his hands. "You know what? Fuck China." He tossed it surreptitiously toward his bag, then began the process of reconnecting the hydromorphone drip.

A few minutes and several insistent flicks of the drip tubing later, and the two men watched Essie's chin slide toward her right shoulder. Her body seemed suddenly intent on shifting to her side.

"What do we do here, Luther?" Josh asked as she wedged her face awkwardly into the stack of pillows beside her, her right knee now aiming at the floor.

"Can you lift her?"

"Can I lift her? Of course I can lift her."

"Let's get her into bed. She's trying to move to her right side, which is a good instinct. That side puts less pressure on the heart and helps stabilize blood pressure and heart rate."

Josh stood, keeping a hand on her hip to keep her from rolling off the side of the couch. He heard Luther shifting the dining chair out from behind him.

With Luther trailing behind, wheeling the monitor stand and keeping watch on the tubing lines, Josh carried her into her bedroom, where he attempted to place her as gently as possible in the center of the bed. It was just about the time he started to lower her to the mattress that her hand once again clenched into a fist, gripping a section of his t-shirt.

He was forced to sit down to keep from losing his balance. He glanced up to Luther for guidance, worried she was having another poor response to the IV pain meds.

Luther frowned at the monitors. "Well, the meds *seem* to be working," he observed. "Kind of wish I had started them sooner." He postulated aloud about why the medications would be allowed to penetrate her system, that perhaps if her body decided a substance was helpful in the moment, it would allow it. He was encouraged by a new theory, that in those situations, her body might metabolize a substance slower to extend the effects, if it was beneficial.

Josh patiently waited for him to finish his stream of consciousness, holding Essie against him.

Luther furrowed his brow, taking in the scene. "Sorry."

"Do you want to try to loosen her grip on my shirt so I can lay her down all the way?"

He moved to help but stopped short. "She seems to want you to lie down with her, Josh. Subconsciously, but still."

Josh frowned. "Is it OK that I do that? I don't want to put pressure on her–" He paused, confused by his choice of words.

"Freudian slip," Luther murmured knowingly.

"I mean since she's healing? I don't want to nudge into a tender spot."

"Yeah, I see what you're saying. Just try to keep her propped on her side rather than leaning forward onto her stomach against you."

Josh slowly eased her onto the mattress, making sure her cheek rested comfortably on a pillow and laid himself down so they were facing one another. As he did, she released her hand's flexion, her left side leaning more heavily toward him, her breaths slow and rhythmic, her arm dropping to the space between their bodies.

Luther nodded approvingly, helping with the bed covers.

"How are her vitals?"

Luther's eyes panned over to the actual numbers, but when he answered, he simply said: "Blue."

Josh took a deep breath. "That device doesn't come anywhere near her again."

"No. It doesn't," Luther agreed. He watched Josh place his hand over hers, kiss her cheek. Essie's body, her face had relaxed considerably. Luther nodded approvingly, patted Josh on the shoulder, and stepped toward the hallway.

*　　*　　*

Relief swept across Matteo's face when Luther informed him that IV pain medications seemed to be helping. Relief turned to confusion, which quickly resembled anger, or as close as Matteo Natale got to anger, when he asked why Luther didn't start her on pain medications sooner.

This was the conversation that Josh interrupted when he emerged from the bedroom just after 8pm. The vague aroma of tomato sauce and boiling water wafted down the hallway.

Matteo frowned, standing at the end of the hallway, eyes darting suddenly to the back of the empty couch. He took a step toward it to confirm his suspicion that she was no longer there. "I thought you said the couch was better for her?"

"Her body relaxed a lot with the pain meds. It seemed like she was going to be more comfortable in bed since she kept trying to turn onto her side."

His expression eased. "She's doing better?" he asked hopefully.

Luther suppressed something internally, patting his friend on the arm. "She is. *Right*, Josh?"

Josh rubbed roughly at crust buildup in the corner of his eye and cleared his throat. "Yeah. Even snoring a little bit."

"Is that her drool on your sleeve?" Luther teased, pointedly eyeing the side of Matteo's head, encouraging Josh to keep things light.

Josh briefly glanced at his shirt. "It's debatable. We'll just say it's mine." He frowned thoughtfully. "I just need to use the bathroom and then I'm going to replace the bags."

Luther immediately stepped forward. "*I'll* do that. Teo, how long does pasta take to cook?"

"Did you get it from the pantry or the freezer?" he asked, peering toward the stove.

"Freezer. It's the ravioli."

"2-3 minutes tops. It was flash-frozen fresh."

"Oh."

"How long has it been boiling?"

"Maybe 15 minutes?" Luther winced as he brushed by Josh, hearing Matteo express what sounded like very harsh disapproval in Italian.

*   *   *

Overall, things were significantly better for everyone once Essie passed the 24-hour mark, though Josh felt a bit more on edge about sharing a bed with her when Teo kept sweeping in and out of the room. Being the only permanent fixture in the room as Teo still felt the need to be busy and Luther had needed to take several phone calls, Josh had situated himself alongside her, but sat upright, leaning back into the headboard. He kept a book in his lap, giving the impression he was reading and casual, and not watching her sleep quite as much as he actually was. His left elbow was propped against the top of her pillow and he periodically indulged in stroking her hair and cheek.

She started waking intermittently around 2am. Josh glanced over and saw her gazing toward the dim beam of light pouring in from the hallway. She blinked slowly then closed her eyes again.

This continued throughout the course of the next day. At first, they would attempt to interact with her, but her gaze was glossy and unfocused and she didn't respond. They relocated her to the living room by the second evening, expecting that she'd be coming out of it soon. There she'd open her eyes, peer around the living room, saying nothing, attention focused vaguely on inanimate objects, her expression unchanged, and then close her eyes again. When this happened several times, they began to regret relocating her from the bedroom as they worried it was their occasional conversations disrupting her sleep. The trouble was they didn't want to put her through being moved again.

Early in the morning on day three, Josh woke, having sat himself on the floor in front of the corner of the couch where she was propped, to act as a human bumper to keep her from rolling to the floor and found she had draped her left arm over his shoulder, burrowed her cheek into his neck. This contorted positioning looked terribly uncomfortable for her so he had carefully encouraged her back onto the pillows.

That morning, she also began murmuring things as she drifted in and out of sleep. They figured it to be conversational, but she remained nonverbal when her eyes were open and she didn't generate responses to anything they said. By the afternoon, she had more expression in her face. She smiled in her sleep when Matteo sat and massaged her legs and feet (the most gratifying recommendation Luther had made).

When Matteo left for about thirty minutes to pick up dinner, Luther pulled out the portable ultrasound to make sure everything was healing properly. He remarked about how healthy everything looked, penning the phrase "better than textbook," when talking about her organs. He became decidedly quiet when he drew her blood, took a sample from the catheter collection.

Josh hadn't thought much of it; it seemed like a reasonable thing to do, but he recognized when the cloud of tension surrounding Luther finally dissipated.

"Things are looking better, I take it?" Josh asked.

Luther took a deep breath. "Yeah. Of course they are. I just wanted to make sure of something for when she inevitably asks."

"For when she inevitably asks what?"

Gathering up the materials from the tests, Luther stepped to the trash can and dropped everything inside. He moved to the sink to wash his hands. "She had been concerned about her ability to have children."

"Why?"

He released an extended sigh. "Part had to do with making sure Gabe hadn't actually used the sterilization serum, if his memory was skewed. We know the answer to that now, of course." He dried his hands on what Josh recognized as a dish drying towel. Teo would not be pleased if he saw him. "She was also concerned—since her body has, shall we say, *unique* ways of responding to things, how it would respond to pregnancy."

Josh furrowed his brow.

"My answer now is the same as it was when she first asked," he said with a shrug. "She has nothing to worry about," he added when he noticed Josh raising his eyebrows questioningly.

"That makes sense though. If you think her blood cells, her antibodies, all that, cures infertility–it would stand to reason–"

Luther's eyes darted to the couch.

"What?"

"She doesn't need to know that," Luther scolded quietly.

"You think she can hear us?" Josh whispered, feeling uneasy with the turn of the conversation.

"Possibly."

Josh considered all that he now knew about Essie that she apparently didn't. It made him extremely uneasy. "She doesn't know about how her cells work," Josh said flatly.

"*No.*"

Josh remembered Essie speculating that Luther wasn't telling her the truth about her body's abilities. When she told him that her spine snapped at Calvary, he had told her, in no uncertain terms, that it wasn't possible. "You've been keeping that from her."

"Yes."

"*Why?*"

Luther sighed. "I couldn't get her to stop doing the antidote runs when she thought it was just saving people from the government vaccine, or some limited other uses. I use the word 'just,' but it's ridiculous. She saved hundreds of thousands of people. Probably more. Not to mention, *everything else.*"

Josh was rendered silent by the reality of Essie's impact.

"If she knew a blood transfusion of her donated blood could cure–"

"Pretty much anything."

"She never would have stopped, Josh. She would be wanting me to drain 3-4 pints of blood from her multiple times per week."

Josh nodded. Whole blood donation guidelines were 1 pint a maximum of 6 times per year, but that would mean nothing to her. She'd push her body to its absolute limits.

Luther was right. She never would have stopped and there would have been no possible way of protecting her.

*　　　*　　　*

Around 10pm that night, Luther and Matteo woke from their respective seats to find Josh in the same place where he'd fallen asleep earlier, stretched on his back on the opposite side of the sectional, perpendicular to Essie. When he'd fallen asleep, he'd been sure to tuck his feet beneath the pillows propped behind her so he wouldn't accidentally kick her.

Now, she was lying parallel to him, wedged between his side and the back couch cushions, limbs haphazardly draped across him, the medical bandaging holding her IV in place struggling to stay attached.

Luther sprang into action, easing the strain of the IV line while also untangling the catheter tubing, which was wrapped around her leg. He winced, hoping her movements hadn't caused it to tug. Finally, he draped the blanket over the pair of them. His intent had been to provide some modesty for her with the catheter line, which was probably not necessary considering he'd used a solid black tube and ran it to a closed collection container, but what he realized he'd done, as he surveyed the pair lying on the couch, was to make them appear far more cozy, far more intimate.

Josh didn't appear to have been disturbed in the least by Essie tucking in beside him; in fact, he looked like he was enjoying the deepest sleep he had during her recovery. His chin was turned toward her and he had the appearance that he was inhaling the scent of her hair.

Luther lifted his eyes to Matteo, who had thankfully mellowed over the course of the 72+ hours.

Matteo's brown eyes were swollen and heavily shadowed, his waves of dark hair disheveled.

Luther stepped over to him and patted his knee, nodding pointedly toward the front porch.

Matteo rolled his shoulders and stretched after closing the front door behind him. He took a seat in the rocking chair opposite Luther and released an extended breath.

"I think it's safe for both of us to get some sleep, but I wanted to talk to you first."

His friend nodded, rubbing at his eyes.

"I said something to The Kid before," Luther began, having assigned the nickname affectionately to Josh at some point over the past three days when conversing with Matteo. "I know you've talked about this before. I just never really recognized it myself."

Matteo frowned. "What's that?"

Luther narrowed his eyes, gently rocking the chair, which gave the impression he was lightly nodding. "God meant for Essie to be your daughter. He meant for her to meet The Kid. She is precisely where she should be with precisely the people she needs."

Matteo pursed his lips, glancing over his shoulder through the window toward the back of the couch. He nodded. "Yeah."

"He did that. He guided me to that horrible group home situation at the dilapidated school where I wasn't going to leave her in a thousand years. He guided me to that specific gas station. He told me to look up at that exact moment and see the decal on your truck, to look up and see you holding the door open for the couple going into the restaurant–so I'd know you were polite and not some psychopath."

Luther had described the moment on a number of occasions, trying to explain how seeing the interaction was reassuring and confirmed something integral about Matteo's qualifications as a dad. Matteo had given him a bit of a good-natured challenge on his selection criteria several times before, but he didn't feel compelled to repeat that now.

"It's just incredible to me, Teo. You both were coming from these tragic situations–" His voice trailed off. "God really made something beautiful out of it. I don't know what The Kid's circumstances would have been if she hadn't come along, but–the affection they have for one another?"

"It's been that way from the beginning," Matteo said quietly. "Those two." He took a deep breath. "At Men's Group a few weeks ago, I learned something I never knew about Luke and Sara."

He described Luke's testimony, about how when the boys were young and they were struggling to conceive and Sara was consequently having other health issues, their marriage had become very strained. At that time, Luke didn't like to talk about their struggles. When Sara initiated these conversations, when she tried to talk about her feelings, he told her they had two healthy boys, she 'should just be happy.' "As it turns out, she was planning to leave him. She had set things up to have her and the boys stay with her sister.

"I didn't know this. I had just moved back to Colorado after Rachel–I called him and asked about coming out to visit. I hadn't gotten to see them since I moved back and I hadn't even told them about Essie. Well, evidently Sara had agreed not to move out until after the visit so they could keep up appearances since she knew I'd probably be having a difficult enough time as it was. So we went, they met Essie, who as you remember, at that particular age–I mean, she always has been, but particularly at that age?"

"Adorable."

"Yeah."

"As it turns out, that trip was a turning point for them. Sara saw the way Luke interacted with Essie." Luke had described scooping up Essie after she had fallen asleep in the barn while Gabe was reading to her. He'd described how she'd nuzzled into him, wrapped her arms around his neck, what an impact that had on him. After tucking her into bed, he'd gone to his own bedroom and cried. Sara walked in and saw him and at first she didn't think it was her place to comfort him given the state of their relationship, but she did anyway. "As it turned out, he'd always wanted a daughter. He didn't realize how much until he met Essie–and then everything else he'd been feeling but holding inside–"

"Just flooded out."

Matteo nodded.

"So if Essie hadn't come around, they probably would have ended up divorced?"

"Sara had already filed the papers. She had them dismissed the following week."

Luther leaned back in his chair, releasing a slow exhale. "Wow," he murmured. When he saw Matteo nod in agreement, he stopped rocking his chair abruptly.

"What?"

"Just thinking about that conversation I had with The Kid."

"About?"

He chuckled to himself, shaking his head. "He told me how his parents weren't able to have more children after he was born."

"Right."

"Now they have a baby girl."

Matteo nodded. "All of a sudden. You and I talked about that months ago, right? For years, it felt like there weren't any babies around, but ever since getting here–"

Luther smiled lightly. "*Yeah,* funny how that happened," he murmured.

"You don't think it has anything to do with–" Matteo peered over his shoulder again.

It was as Luther saw the correct conclusion register on Matteo's face that he resumed rocking his chair. "*Yeah,*" he said again, nodding. "It's really something when you can *see* the intricacy of God's plan."

*   *   *

When Essie woke on the fourth morning, she spent a few minutes silently watching the three men preparing breakfast. She had been lying on her side when she opened her eyes, uneasy by the amount of airflow brushing her cheeks, a suspicious amount of couch real estate spanning out before her, the blankets beside her were still warm.

She pulled her legs beneath her and pushed upward to get a look over the back of the couch; any noises she made were muffled by the sound of breakfast meats sizzling on the stove. She squinted in the morning light reflecting off the windshields in the drive.

It appeared Josh was just returning from the bathroom. He yawned widely as he stepped into the kitchen, asking if he could help. Matteo was checking on something in the oven and gave no response, while Luther looked very uncertain about his role, continuously flipping sausages and occasionally giving the contents of a saucepan a very brisk swirl. He shrugged indifferently.

Matteo stood and peered over Luther's shoulder to the cast iron filled with breakfast meats, then immediately evicted him from the stove area, tasked him instead with getting plates and utensils.

Josh posed his question once more and again received no response from Matteo.

She watched her dad whisper a choice Italian phrase, his motions uncharacteristically punctuated, and she chuckled.

All three men lifted their chins in her direction, their eyes wide.

Matteo abandoned the stove, unapologetically the first one to reach her side.

"Che bella vista," he said as he sat beside her. *What a beautiful sight.*

She smiled weakly, her wild golden-brown hair barely managed by a loose hair tie on the top of her head. "Sono abbastanza sicuro di sembrare un roadkill."

"Solo un pochino."

Her jaw dropped as he kissed her repeatedly on the forehead. "*Nice.*"

"What?" Josh asked.

"My dad agreed I look like roadkill."

274

"Don't mis-quote me. That's not what I said."

"Oh, right. I'm sorry. He said I look 'just a little' like roadkill," she said with an Italian accent, using complementary hand gestures. She grinned.

"Ti amo, ti amo, ti amo."

"Yeah, yeah," she murmured. "I love you, too."

Luther rounded the couch on the opposite side, offering her a cup of ice water.

"Oh, you've got to be kidding me with this, Luther. I don't think I've ever been more hydrated–" She cleared her throat. "--but yeah, my throat's a bit dry." She took the cup and had a sip, then another before handing it back to him. She settled back into the couch with a satisfied sigh. "Actually that feels better. Thank you."

He smiled, placed the cup on the coffee table. "I had to put in a catheter."

"Yep, I'm aware."

"How do you feel?"

Matteo spotted a washcloth on the coffee table and immediately grabbed it and took leave, presumably to re-soak it for her forehead.

She raised an eyebrow. "A few notches better than how I look?"

Luther winced. "*Yikes.*"

Essie grinned overtly at that, glancing up at Josh.

He sat on the edge of the cushion beside her and placed his hand on her cheek.

"I know what you're going to say," she murmured.

"*Do* you?" he asked, suppressing a smile.

"Yes. You're going to ask me how my quest to take back the One Ring is going."

His cheeks tightened. "Believe it or not, that was *not* what I was going to say."

She blinked slowly, leaning her cheek into his hand. The washcloth suddenly appeared on her forehead and Matteo was encouraging her to lean back, the excess water careening down her cheeks in competing lines. He was distracted, sniffing the air, then disappeared into the kitchen.

"This just enhances the look, doesn't it?" she said, pinching her eyebrows together, crossing her eyes to look upward at the dripping cloth.

Josh helped to fold and better situate the washcloth, mopping at the excess water with his sleeve.

"I don't have a fever anymore," she whispered.

He scrunched his nose, nodding.

"How's that washcloth?" Matteo called from the kitchen.

"Oh, it feels so nice. Thank you," she said, smiling tightly at Josh.

Luther distracted himself, peering inquisitively toward the kitchen, then moved quickly in that direction.

Essie took a steadying breath, closing her eyes as Josh resumed stroking her cheek.

"Here we have a *fine* specimen of the human species," he began in a thick, overt Australian accent.

Her eyes opened.

"Yes, definitely a female, but by the look of her, I'd say she'd been wrestling with a grizzly bear."

Her eyes creased as her lips pulled upward. "Must have been one of those bachelors," she whispered.

He suppressed a smile and continued. "It's unconfirmed, but rumor has it they were at odds over a plate of biscuits and gravy."

"Don't toy with me, Josh West. Are there biscuits?"

He lifted his brow. "Homemade. My mom sent over the dough." He smiled upon seeing her do a subtle fist pump, then he returned to his Australian accent. "Now, we don't want to overwhelm this magnificent creature, but let's see if she'll let us get closer." He leaned toward her and delicately kissed her forehead. "What'd'ya know? She's acting quite docile this morning, which isn't always the case, I can assure you."

Essie placed her hand on his cheek, rubbing at the stubble with her thumb. "Have you slept?"

"A bit."

"Hmm," she murmured, pursing her lips, clearly not convinced by his answer.

Just as the moment slowed, just as the room around them began to go out of focus, Luther burst into the scene.

"I am apparently unqualified as a chef," he announced, purposely mumbling under his breath so Matteo wouldn't hear.

Essie let her attention drift in Luther's direction as Josh sat more upright again. Her hand dropped to rest over her abdomen. "Better start developing your skills for other career tracks, Luther."

He suppressed a smile. "Any pain?"

"Well, I'm just sitting still. Things feel very tight right now though." She gestured to her stomach.

He nodded thoughtfully. "Do you remember what happened?"

She furrowed her brow. "Well, it *felt* like a miniature grenade was set off in my stomach."

He stopped nodding.

"Is *that* what happened?"

Luther shrugged. "More or less."

"Oh." She scrunched her nose. "I knew I shouldn't have had that chili dog."

21

phototropism

The Heroic Journey of Dr. Luther Graham

"Dr. Luther Graham was not your typical hero. He didn't wear a cape or possess superhuman abilities, but he had a heart of gold and an unwavering commitment to protecting the innocent. Raised by a single mother, Loretta Graham, MD, in the bustling city of Denver, Colorado, Luther's journey towards becoming a savior of hundreds of babies and children, as well as the architect of the Arks infrastructure that would ultimately change the course of American history, would be nothing short of extraordinary.

"Luther's childhood was filled with love and a strong sense of justice instilled by his mother. Loretta was a dedicated physician who cared deeply for her patients, often going above and beyond the call of duty to help those in need. She taught Luther the value of compassion and the importance of standing up for what was right, even when it meant facing adversity."

Annette sighed, switching to her notes page, where she was keeping a list of aspects of Luther's life, things that he'd done, that she wanted to make sure to mention in writing the op-ed. She added:

Talk about the "group home" he mentioned, where he considered sending E.

She found her folder with supporting documents, added the link in her notes. It could be another topic for Chris to cover on his show. Surely, he had more than enough examples of the evil that had taken over the government for decades, but what she'd learned about the facility had been particularly chilling.

The building had previously been a school, but over the years, with additional structures added, some re-work done to the façade, it had started to resemble a bleak, turn of the century apartment complex. It was established as a group home connected with the foster care system, funding by who else, but Samuel Gowon. As laws were rewritten in ways that allowed for certain pliability of interpretation, it had begun to devolve from that purpose. Children were funneled from foster care, from social services, an increasing rate of natural disasters leading to a rise in children being orphaned. They were brought into this facility, fed, provided education, medical care, and were then subjected to experimentation, a precursor to the Sim program used in Mandatory training. Like the Sim program, the effects were devastating, an alarming few surviving into adulthood. Some had managed to escape, only to be located later, put into Mandatory, some into government work, mainly menial jobs, a few were put into military service. As with the STRONG program and the experimentation that Esther was a part, the researchers kept constant surveillance.

Unlike the videos from STRONG, where the test subjects could only scream, unable to express their pain in words, the children at HAVEN could. Annette had struggled to recover after listening to teenage boys crying out in desperation for their mothers, begging for death, the young girls subjected to degradation and abuse.

Annette tensed her jaw as she made another note. It wasn't a necessary note, but she typed it out just the same, her fingers tapping heavily against the keyboard:

Luther drove by HAVEN with E and was suspicious, but he didn't have resources. Years later, when he gained access to records after the place had shut down. He cross-referenced the HAVEN files with government records to find out the status for all who'd been there. Hundreds of children dead. Only five survivors.

She mopped at her eyes.

He tracked them all down and made sure they made it to the Arks.

There was Trey Timmers, 15, a first-year Mandatory enlistee in Boston, Makena Wallace, 15, who was a part of a private "reserve" of proxies for the elites in the District, Kennedy Ellis, 18, in third-year Mandatory training in Chicago, twins Nathanial and Knox Lufton, 23, who worked as custodial staff for a government building in San Diego, and Leo Gunner, 26, an airman with the U.S. military.

Millions of people in the country, billions of people in the world...and Luther made sure those five were safe.

*   *   *

SecureChat Session-user175rt982cwl413

Any progress?

> No. I laid out the plan for them and they expressed that they were "choosing a different path."

Is that it then?
Did you ask for another opportunity to present the other information we discussed?

There have been other things that required my attention.

More important than this?

Evin.

What happened?

A complication from her time in Denver.

What does that mean? Is she okay?

Now, yes. But I hesitate to push the "powers that be" too much considering I haven't been keeping a low profile when it comes to her. I don't want them to start investigating and making that connection.

I appreciate the attachment that you have to her.

It's more than that.

You're protecting her. I get it. You're afraid those assholes in charge are going to want to study her.

Do you really think that's even on their radar at this point?

I can't risk it.

*Her immunity is something that was
cooked up in a lab 20 years ago. You
don't think they've come up with
something more advanced since then?*

You said yourself they haven't.

*Their interests lie elsewhere at this
point. Far from hyper-immunity.*

*This isn't what I need to talk to you
about.*

What is it? Are you okay?

*   *   *

<u>*In the Loop w/ Christopher Loop: Mass Exodus*</u>

"Ladies and gentlemen, this is a time of immense frustration and disbelief. Look around you—our suburbs and rural towns, neighborhoods, once thriving with life, now stand empty and desolate. The government, the mainstream media attempt to explain it away that people are taking advantage of the opportunities and benefits of city living, but here's a look at one such city."

Footage played driving through downtown Chicago.

"Opportunities? Benefits? Really? I don't mind having a little extra breathing space, but where did everyone go? We've heard rumors about what the spokespeople for the Gowon Administration has called 'communes,' but is that accurate? And if the number is larger than what they're letting on, what would trigger this many people to up and leave? What were they running away from? What did they know?

"If we were in a crisis that resulted in the deaths of eight times the number of people killed in the Holocaust, we'd know it, right? We'd know if our friends, our family members, our neighbors were being murdered, right?

"Politicians have been telling us for years that they wanted to optimize population control efforts. Perhaps this is one of the times when we should have believed them. Bovine flu, pandemics, tainted virus testing supplies, skyrocketing rates of infertility, historically low birth rates—we're talking all-time lows—and the most recent public emergency—mandated vaccines laced with lethal doses of opioids. Are you paying attention yet?

"Tens of millions of people are dead, millions more are missing, and it's becoming increasingly clear that the government is pulling the strings behind this nightmare. The government's agenda is no longer hidden in the shadows: They want to control every aspect of our lives, from where we live to what we think to who, if anyone, is allowed to have children. They want us dead or compliant.

"Theories and speculation might abound. For decades, talking heads such as myself have used the drama, the controversy, the bloodshed to spark ratings and viewership, but none of that means anything anymore, does it? No one cares about all that bullshit. If there's one silver lining from all of this, from the majority of our country being forced into poverty, into devastation, into an early grave, is this: We finally let go of the superficial stuff that doesn't matter. We rejected social media. We don't all have a cell phone cemented to our hand. Gone are the days of the selfie. Thank God for that. But this comes on the heels of genocide, of apocalyptic, end of the world nightmares. The worst parts of the Bible.

"It's time to call a spade a spade. We must confront the grim reality that our own leaders, the very individuals we entrusted with our well-being, have betrayed us, have been betraying us for years. This is not a time for political correctness or sugar-coated explanations. It's a time for raw, unfiltered truth. And this is not a time to be courteous or forgiving of these individuals who murdered our families, our friends. It's a time to force a change. It's a time to fight back with unyielding repulsion for this regime that orchestrated the nightmare we find ourselves. We must not let fear paralyze us. We must not assume that someone will swoop in and save us. We must save ourselves.

"I know you're afraid, I know you've already lost so much, but if we don't do something, all that we're clinging to, all that still exists that we love? Will be wiped away.

"Still not convinced? Let's talk about that. Let's look at where we've come from. How we got here. And then we're going to look ahead to the direction we're headed."

Christopher first focused on the topic of healthcare and medical influence: In the name of safety, there had been a sprawl of government oversight, mandatory reporting and testing. For decades, the government had quietly required hospitals to take blood samples from all newborns without the option for declination from parents, stored in a national database used in whatever research approved in 1,300-page Congressional budgets. A line in one of these documents, for example, had authorized the government to perform genome sequencing on any person who had blood work performed. Another line, another budget on the heels of a public health crisis, authorized government access to protected health information.

When privatized insurance was forcibly eliminated through surcharges, penalties, and regulations, people had to make a choice: To trust the government-run health system—or to not. At first, about half chose to trust it, out of necessity mostly. Emboldened by their expanding power, but facing financial crisis from the rapidly expanding social and health programs, the government began to establish medical panels that made care decisions to ensure the "sustainability" of the programs. Those who found their case being referred for "panel review," it was a death sentence. Individuals were typically given three courses of action: palliative/hospice care, no intervention, or euthanasia.

These "death panels" were viewed unfavorably by an overwhelming majority, even those in the Party so it was determined that population control measures needed to be put in place that were more difficult to detect. Additives were put into food, into the water supply, known to cause infertility.

Running parallel to depopulation efforts was "genetic optimization." Christopher promised to circle back to this topic.

"Our so-called 'President' has always had a fixation on artificial intelligence. It's no secret he thinks it superior to human intelligence, which is why he focused so much of his life before the White House with simulation technology meant to warp the human mind. We were forced to send our children for Mandatory government service and this technology was used to alter their thought processes, attempt to change their brain chemistry.

"It was mind control. Blatant attempts at mind control. For some, it worked. For most, it drove them insane. For others, the ones who got out–the lucky ones? They're still trying to put themselves back together. To come to terms with what they saw, what they did, what the technology made them see.

22

eros

"Daddy, I can fetch my own drinks," Essie said as her dad emerged through the screen door carrying two tall glasses of lemonade.

"It should probably be more hydrating with electrolytes or something though, right?"

"Nah," she said, accepting the glass and taking a satisfying sip. "The sugar is really, *really* good for me."

"It is?"

She grinned. "It's been a week, Daddy. How long are you going to wait on me, hand and foot?"

"Does it bother you?"

"Not *exactly*, but if your butler services are going to drop off at some point, I better prepare myself now."

He took a seat on the opposite rocking chair. "Well, while I don't want to go through *anything* like that again, it dawned on me the other day that you were never sick when you were growing up. I never had the opportunity to take care of my little girl when she wasn't feeling well."

She smirked. "Glad I could give you that experience?"

"Yeah, don't do that again."

"OK."

"Gabe stopped by last night after you fell asleep."

She took another sip of lemonade, peered out toward the mountains. The visibility over the past week had been incredible. She'd been tempted to take a ride on Bree, but all it took was a treacherous venture from the bathroom back to the couch, her body weak and exhausted by the time she arrived, for her to resolve that perhaps she just needed to rest for now.

Silence filled the space between them. At last, Matteo sighed. "I've been in the dark about a lot of things. I still am, I think. Nessuno dovrebbe sopportare così tanto." *No one should have to endure so much.*

Essie scrunched her nose.

"I'm grateful your body is even more stubborn than your mind."

She gave him a light smile.

The crunch of gravel under truck tires drew both of their attention to the driveway.

Through the dusty windshield they watched Josh shift into park, then begin to gather up some items in the truck cab. "It's amazing to see you kids all grown up," Matteo remarked. "It feels like just yesterday you were running around the farm, flying off the tree swing."

"Josh had far less facial hair back then."

"Yeah, he sprouts a beard like a Chia Pet." Reading Essie's confusion, he explained. "It's a silly thing we had in the olden days. You spread seeds and dirt over this pottery shaped like a pop culture icon and it sprouted–well, sprouts of whatever the plant was, but it grew like crazy."

"The olden days were a simpler time," she said with a longing sigh.

Josh closed the driver's door, his arms full. "Good *morning*," he said cheerfully, having not gotten to see either before he had to make his way to a nearby farm to assist with a stalled calf delivery. "How are the two of you today?"

"Good," Essie replied. "We were just talking about your bountiful beard."

His cheeks tightened, his dimples still evident beneath his facial hair. "I skip shaving for a few days and I don't hear the end of it."

"That is *not* 'a few days" worth of beard."

He lifted an eyebrow. "Two and a half weeks?"

287

"I tried growing a beard once, but gave up after a couple months," Matteo said, rubbing at his cheeks. "Apparently, I'm the only Italian man who can't grow a beard. My facial only grows to stubble length and then stops."

"Daddy, you should have seen Josh before we got to the Ark. Long hair, bushy, but sort of patchy beard? He could have played Jesus."

Josh raised an eyebrow. "I can't take that as an insult, being told I had a small resemblance to our Lord and Savior."

Matteo toasted him with his nearly empty glass of lemonade.

"I prefer to have an unobstructed view of the dimples, but I don't mind the beard, if I'm being honest," she said with a small smile.

Josh grinned. "Teo, my mom sends her love—and a lasagna." He placed the dish on the porch banister.

"Sara West fears no one, not even an Italian judging her lasagna."

"This Italian has eaten her lasagna. It's amazing."

"I also brought *you*–" Josh began, raising his eyebrow to Essie. He handed her a hardcover book. "--this."

Her eyes brightened and she seemed to be actively suppressing the width of her smile.

Matteo cleared his throat, pushing himself out of the rocking chair. "I should put the lasagna in the fridge."

"You can eat some of it, Daddy. Nobody will judge you."

"It's brunch time, right?"

"Well, we're drinking lemonade; that's a brunch beverage, isn't it?"

"I'm leading groups at the church today so I should really fuel up." He checked his watch. "Actually, I might need to take a small morsel of it to go."

"You wouldn't be running late if you didn't make such a fuss over me."

Matteo fixed his gaze upon her.

"But I appreciate you making a fuss over me."

Josh took a long stride to hold open the screen door for Matteo, who then carried the casserole dish excitedly into the house.

"Hey Daddy, Josh and I are going to take a walk," Essie said, holding the book to her chest, casually rocking her chair. She smiled as he took a step backward so he could see her through the screen door.

"You know what I'm going to say."

"I won't over-do it."

Matteo nodded in gratitude to Josh, then glanced back at Essie. "I love you. Ti amo."

"Ti amo. I'll see you when you get back."

Josh slowly closed the screen door, looking concerned. "You feel up for *walking*?"

"No, but it's been too long since I took a piggyback ride."

*　　　*　　　*

Essie started having second thoughts about her idea the moment she was situated on Josh's back. "Are you sure I'm not too heavy for you?"

"You're a lightweight, Essie," he said reassuringly, resituating his hands to be sure he had a firm hold on her upper legs. "Are you comfortable though?"

She wrapped her arms around his neck and rested her chin on his shoulder. "Yep. Giddy up."

He took a couple strides, mimicking a horse's trot, then slowed to a walk. "Yeah, I don't want to bump you around too much."

Bree and Hwin rushed to the exterior paddock fence as they strolled by. Josh walked close enough to the fence for Essie to give the Percheron a reassuring scratch on his cheek before continuing on. They were silent except for the scuffle of Josh's boots on the dirt path. After a few quiet minutes, they reached the first overlook.

There were several excellent overlook spots near the ranch. The one closest to the barn and ranch house looked over the main preserve lands, the exotic animal sanctuary, some cattle lands, corn and wheat fields, and the broad mountains in the distance. Others had more intimate views of the different landscapes. The glacier lake overlook was a few miles and several small hillsides further.

"Where to?" he asked, considering the different paths, trying to determine if one had fewer tripping hazards.

"Let's just take this view in for a bit."

He nodded, rotated on his heel and climbed to the overlook's higher elevation, which offered the best view of the mountains and a peekaboo view of glacier lake in the distance through the forest.

Essie stretched forward, hugging him and took a deep, satisfied breath.

He smiled audibly, leaned back and kissed her cheek. "Are you doing alright up there?"

"Uh-hmm," she murmured.

"Good."

"This is such a great view."

"Yeah, it is."

"I've missed seeing this every day."

"Well, you'll be out riding again soon."

"I know." Her breaths were shorter as she nuzzled her cheek against his. "Hey, Josh?" she whispered.

"Yeah?"

"Is this a good time for me to tell you that I'm in love with you?"

His boots shifted against the dirt, taking a more rigid stance. He rotated his chin toward her, cheeks tight.

She scrunched her nose. "I shouldn't have said it when I was riding piggyback. It's awkward, isn't it? I want to see your whole face and I'm limited to just this half. I mean, it's a great half. It has the more pronounced dimple."

"*Essie.*"

"Yes?"

"Do you want to get down?" he chuckled, trying to figure out the best way to have her slide off his back without accidentally dropping her, given her weakened state.

"Tree stump. 8 o'clock."

He moved quickly to the stump left behind by a tree struck by lightning the previous fall, then eased her legs down, ensuring she had adequate balance. He turned around, narrowing his eyes as he put an arm around her waist. "Could we start over and have you *repeat* what you just said, please?"

She tilted her head to the side. "I don't know. I'm not sure the eloquence will come through when I have to repeat myself."

His cheeks tightened. "*Try.*"

She shrugged, resting her wrists on his shoulders, enjoying the height advantage provided by the tree stump. "I love you, Josh West." She ran her fingers through his hair. "If you don't feel the same, it's okay. I mean, it's totally *not* okay." She twisted her expression. "For one thing, it'll be a *really* awkward piggyback ride back to the house and I'll definitely cry myself to sleep for the next several–"

He braced her face in his hands and kissed her.

In the heat of the midday, she felt chills shoot up her spine. Her mouth curled into a smile as their lips parted. "--hundred nights."

He kissed her again.

She winced. "Or *days*. You *know* I keep odd sleeping hours."

Josh tilted his chin, gazing at her with tremendous affection. "*Essie.*"

She raised her eyebrows. "You should know a few things before you fully respond."

"Okay?"

"I mean, the kissing seems to be a pretty good indication of where your mind is with this, but there are things I'd like you to know."

He took a half step back, positioning his hands around her waist again. "You have the floor—or stump."

"I don't know how many things exactly and these are in no particular order."

He nodded.

"First of all–It's always been *you*." She lifted her eyebrows with a knowing arch. "It's never *not* been you."

His smile widened against his best efforts.

"#2: I realized that growing up and even more recently, I tried to keep things from you. Not *from* you exactly. I tried to compartmentalize the bad things. I thought that if I told you about the memories, the nightmares, everything else, it would take away from the experience of being with you, which has always been when I'm happiest."

Josh swallowed hard.

"I know now that I can't do that. I shouldn't have done that. I want to share *everything* with you–good, bad, joy, pain, fear, tres leches cake, all of it. You make every day, everything better."

He placed his palm back on her cheek and whispered: "I would *never* get between you and tres leches cake."

She smiled tightly, gave a small shrug. "That's probably a wise decision, to be honest." She looked back and forth between his eyes. "I'm sorry it took me so long, Josh," she whispered, furrowing her brow. "I kept getting in my own way."

He stepped forward again and swept the hair from her eyes, breathing deeply. "Is that all you wanted to say?" he asked quietly.

She nodded.

"Okay then," he whispered, taking in the details of her face with intense appreciation. "My turn."

She suppressed a smile.

"I love you, Essie. I always have. I always will. From the moment I first saw you, all I wanted to do was be near you. Make you smile. What you've done for me? Far surpasses anything I could ever do for you."

Essie furrowed her brow.

"You breathe life into everything you touch. Including me." He shrugged. "And I don't deserve you, I know that."

Her eyes filled with tears.

"But oh, if you only knew how much I love you." He glanced up toward the sky and back. "*God* knows. He knows my heart. That's the only reason I think I'm standing here with you, *like this*, right now."

The silence stretched. She placed her hand on his cheek, taking in the details of his face. She swallowed hard, her bottom lip trembling. "I love you, Josh West," she finally whispered.

He rested his forehead against hers, took a steadying breath. As their eyes met, her smile began to stretch.

*   *   *

There was a stillness at the ranch in the late afternoon, just as the sun began to set over the western sky. There was something categorically different about the feel of the air at that time of day. That was how Essie was able to estimate the time of day without even opening her eyes. She quickly got her bearings, knowing she was snuggled beside Josh in the corner of the couch. She reminded herself as to what had transpired that day.

She had told Josh she loved him. It had actually happened. It wasn't a tremendous shock that he expressed mutual feelings, but it had altered the dynamic between them immediately. It had been more of a relief than anything overly impassioned, like a burdensome weight finally removed from their shoulders. They both seemed to be taking deeper, more satisfying breaths, and they embraced one another with a resolve that they would be satisfied to never have to let go. For a few prolonged moments, they simply gazed at each other in an appreciative, almost disbelieving daze.

It started off sweet and innocent.

Essie started kissing him in a playful manner, beginning with the tender bit of neck closest to his ear, invigorated by the fact that she was allowed to kiss him, that the restrictions of their relationship were gone. She kissed her way across his cheek, stopping to seek out his dimple, then

293

gave him an affectionate peck on the bridge of his nose, continuing toward the opposite ear. She centered herself again, smiling knowingly.

Then she tenderly kissed him on the lips. Once and then again.

She arched back, her mouth lifting at the corners. "What's that look?"

He pressed his lips together, shaking his head.

"Tell me," she persisted, lifting her eyebrows encouragingly.

"I honestly don't know what to say. I'm *so* happy. I don't think I've ever been this happy."

"Same."

His smile mirrored hers. "I know what my heart wants to *ask*—"

She tilted her head to the side, frowning, which was such a jarring shift in her facial expression that it made him laugh, his tell that he was teasing. "Oh my goodness, is *nothing* enough for you, Joshua?" she said in an exasperated tone, though her cheeks were tight.

He secured his arms around her waist.

"I know we've always kidded around with each other, but you don't tease about a *proposal*," she scolded, forcing a scowl. "Wait, *are* you teasing, or were you being serious?"

He shrugged.

"*Josh*? You shouldn't tease about a proposal or like, half-ask."

"You don't *want* me to propose."

"Not right *now*."

He grinned, falling silent.

She narrowed her eyes. "What?"

"Esther Natale wants to marry me—" he said in a sing-song voice, then whispered: "someday." He considered this. "I should have that printed on a t-shirt."

She lifted her chin as though to challenge, then rolled her eyes, cheeks reddening.

"You want to marry me," he persisted. "You've *thought* about this."

"Yes. Yes, I do. And yes I have. Want to make something of it?" Her jaw fell open as she realized what she'd actually challenged.

"*Well*–since you're now open to the idea–"

Her palm instinctively covered his mouth, then she frowned at her hand's placement. "I'm sorry. That was rude–*EWWW*," she exclaimed, reeling her hand back. "You *licked* my hand!"

"Here," he said, tugging her hand toward him and wiping it off on his shirt. "Better?"

"Yes."

"Good." He dropped to one knee.

"Stop it! Get *up*!" She pursed her lips, determined not to smile. "This is supposed to be a very serious moment, one we treasure for all–" She broke down in giggles as he slid his hand up her t-shirt and tickled her side. She folded over and he had to wrap his arms around her to keep her from toppling off the tree stump. "*Owww*," she half-groaned, half-laughed, clutching her side.

He immediately stopped, helped her stand upright again. She was still smiling.

"You want to marry me," he said slowly and indulgently. "Just not right now," he added. "And that's okay."

Her mind appeared to be reassessing, her brow furrowed and regretful. "*Well*—I mean, I guess it's sort of silly to know you want to be with someone forever and then *not*—"

He smiled victoriously. "Actually, just knowing that you want to marry me makes me a *very* happy guy. No pressure at all. I'm good with this. Status quo." He gave a sporting thumbs up.

She frowned, really doubting herself now. "I don't want to rush into it–and I don't know. I just think: 'For everything there is a season.' Right?"

"And what is *this* season?"

She took a steadying breath. "Spending time together. No planning weddings. No planning babies. Right now, I'm perfectly content getting to snuggle with you and kiss you whenever I darn well please."

There was a lift at the end of her sentence, questioning her assessment, as though to say *right??*

"That last part? Goes both ways?"

"Yes. Unless I happen to feel cross with you."

"So in your mind, we're already arguing?"

She lifted her brow.

He pinched his expression. "It *is* me, I suppose. I'm bound to do something to warrant you being cross with me."

She rolled her eyes. "Doubtful. You are irritatingly perfect these days."

"'*Irritatingly* perfect,'" he repeated slowly.

"Of course that was through rose-colored glasses of infatuation. Now I've claimed you as mine *so*—"

"We're fighting and the rose-colored glasses are off. The honeymoon stage really is brief, isn't it?"

"Well there you go with the marriage thing again."

He grinned, giving her a prolonged kiss, which ended with her hugging him snugly.

"What should I do when I cause you to be cross with me?"

He could feel her breaths against his ear as she pondered his question. "You should do something *so* charming and so very Josh West that I can't possibly stay mad at you."

"No flashy jewelry, no flowers?"

"*Flowers!*" she gasped, releasing him from the hug, but keeping her arms draped over his shoulders. "But only ones you pick yourself."

He nodded. "Okay."

"Actually, no. *Only* bring me flowers as a surprise if you've done absolutely nothing wrong. Never as an ornamental apology. Actually, you should also never try to charm your way out of trouble or to smooth things over. You should reflect upon your actions or words and then apologize sincerely." She gave a conclusive nod.

He gazed into her eyes, moved forward and kissed her delicately on the lips.

"And when I do something wrong, I'll do the same."

He nodded, electing not to tease her further. "Deal."

She let her palms slide across his upper arms, her lips lifting as she felt the shape of his muscles.

"What's *that* smile about?" he murmured.

"I'm allowed to smile. I'm happy."

"This isn't *just* happy. You look like you're up to trouble."

"Well, what can I say? I'm touching Josh West's bulging biceps," she whispered dotingly. She paused, letting her fingers explore the same muscle again. "*Wooow.*"

He chuckled under his breath.

She stretched her arms around his neck again, scrunched her nose. "You *know*, it looks like rain; we should *probably* get inside."

Josh took in the cloudless sky. If there was rain on the horizon, it was days away. "Yeah, that came out of *nowhere*, didn't it?"

"It *really* did," she said, grinning. She slumped her shoulders suddenly. "Actually, I have to level with you. I just made up the thing about a storm."

"*No.*"

"Yes," she said, regretfully. "I just want to be able to kiss you without anybody looking."

He glanced around, the only people in sight looking about the size of tiny ants over at the exotic animal sanctuary.

"It'd also be regrettable if we were kissing and suddenly got mauled by a bear."

He suppressed a laugh. "Good enough for me." He leaned down and in one fluent motion, scooped her into his arms, starting for the house.

"Would it be a hazard if I kiss you during the walk back?" she asked, giving him a gentle peck on the cheek. "Like *that* would probably be okay?"

His cheeks tightened. "Seems okay to me."

"*But* if I were to get a little more *enthusiastic*—"

She had gotten as far as lightly kissing her way across his cheek, her warm breath tickling his neck, when Josh turned his chin toward her and stopped walking. "You're *supposed* to be the sensible one."

Her forehead creased in total confusion. "I have no idea why you would think that. I have never assumed that role in our relationship. That's been *you*."

He considered her claim and scowled.

"'Search your feelings, you know it to be true.'"

He grinned. "Coming in hot with the *Star Wars* reference."

Her eyebrows jumped suggestively and she began kissing him again.

He reared his chin back after momentarily indulging, giving her a stern look. "Behave for the next 3 minutes."

She narrowed her eyes. "90 seconds, final offer. Walk fast."

He gave a nod, then moved briskly past the paddocks, across the drive, and up the front porch steps. He hesitated halfway through the threshold provided by the screen door.

"What's wrong?"

He took a steadying breath. "I have an angel on one shoulder and a devil on the other."

"And what am I up front here?"

He grinned. "*Mostly* angel."

She accepted his analysis and resumed kissing him, smiling widely as she felt him continue forward into the house.

"Becoming less angel-like," he teased, in between kisses.

Even with that observation hanging in the air, she forced her legs to the floor and twisted so their bodies were parallel. She wrapped her arms around his neck, attempting to draw him along with her as she moved backward toward the hallway. It was clear when she had convinced him to follow, as he secured his hands under her hips. Without prior thought to do so, she pretzeled her legs around his waist.

She couldn't think of the awkwardness of the moment had her dad shown up and seen her *assertiveness*. She pushed the thought away as Josh carried her down the hallway into her cave-like bedroom, naturally shaded during the day by a collection of pine trees on the west-facing side of the house.

Her thoughts stalled just before they reached her bed. "*Josh?*" she whispered urgently in his ear.

He immediately turned on the spot and retraced his steps toward the door, tightening his hold around her. He kissed her temple and murmured: "You're sensible."

"Was that a test?"

"No," he said shortly.

"Were you going to stop us if I didn't?"

"*Yep*. But only after kissing you for a *really* long time. We can do that out here though."

She whimpered quietly, burying her face in his neck as they reached the kitchen. She eased her feet to the floor, ran her fingers through his dark hair. "Is it patience? Is God teaching me to be patient?" Her forehead was creased.

He smiled lightly.

"You're who I want to spend my life with, Josh," she said quietly, but definitively.

"But?"

"But I suppose if I'm not ready for us to get married, for whatever reasons my brain has that I'm not clear about at the moment, I'm not ready for everything else that comes with it."

He cleared his throat, resting his hands on her hips. "Essie, I believe, and I've believed for a long time now, that God has been shaping me into the man you need me to be."

She furrowed her brow.

"I have to believe that if *we* aren't ready for that next step, it's God telling us we aren't ready, that He's not prepared us for it yet. Rushing into anything isn't going to make us better prepared."

She suppressed a smile. "You better watch that talk. There's already enough competition for pastor gigs in this town."

He continued, undeterred. "I believe what God has in store for us is far beyond anything we've experienced or imagined. But *He'll* guide us there. And I'll wait as long as it takes. He's already blessed me more than I deserve–just for the fact that I get to love you and have you love me back--" He squinted one eye. "--slightly less than I love you, but that's fine by me."

She fell silent for a few moments, lips pursed.

"What's that look?"

"I don't thank God for you enough. I mean, I thank Him for you a *lot*, He's probably honestly tired of hearing about you."

He gave a short, breathy laugh.

"What's so funny?"

He shook his head. "I don't think you realize–*Essie*, I wouldn't know God if it wasn't *for you*."

"What do you mean?"

"I let Jesus into my heart for the first time in my life after hearing you sing."

She frowned. "I need more information."

He tucked the hair behind her ear, took a deep breath and smiled. "This is a story I should have told you a long time ago."

And so Josh reminded her of the infrequent trek his family had made to Wallace for a weekend when he was thirteen; for a visit and also so his dad could help with some structural work on the church. At that time, Calvary had services on both Saturday evenings and Sunday mornings. They had intended to go to church on Sunday since it was a different pastor preaching on Saturday night, but as they finished an early dinner, Essie had quickly gathered her plate and glass and placed them in the sink. She stepped across the kitchen to her dad and gave him a sideways hug. He had kissed her forehead and asked her something in Italian, to which she shook her head.

"Where do you think you're off to?" Luke had asked, reaching out, attempting to pinch her.

She smiled tightly. "I'm singing at service tonight."

GRACE FINLEY

Sara had clasped her hand to her chest, checking the state of her damp hair, already in her pajamas. "Why didn't you tell us?"

Teo side-eyed his daughter. "I told you they'd be upset."

"I'm singing the same thing in the morning," Essie replied dismissively, heading for the door.

Josh's mom had, of course, gone on about it, but ultimately things moved on to the planned game night. As dishes were being cleared and cleaned and his dad disappeared for his notoriously long post-dinner visit to the bathroom, Josh had slipped out and gone to the church.

This was an unusual decision on his part, for one thing because, like his mom, he was already changed into pajamas. Another reason was that he wasn't one who typically gravitated to church unless forced. It didn't bother him in the least if his family skipped church on Sundays and he could instead take a nap or have an indulgent breakfast; he even preferred it.

He remembered being surprised at the number of people in attendance for a Saturday night service; the place was bustling. As he entered the sanctuary, his eyes immediately found Essie at the front, speaking with other members of the Worship Band. The first song, an upbeat melody, began and she took her place at one of the side microphones, providing only backup vocals. Meanwhile, Josh found a seat at the end of a pew with an unobstructed view, ignoring the glances he'd gotten from the people for his chosen attire, and the fact that he seemed to be in attendance alone.

Based upon the conversation at the house, he anticipated Essie would have more of a featured role singing so he found himself a bit disappointed, but he enjoyed watching/hearing her sing, regardless. The song ended and the band began to clear from the elevated stage. Announcements played and featured new life groups, prayer teams, outreach programs. The sanctuary fell silent and a pastor Josh had never met took the stage. He talked about how so often people focus on doing a year in review at the *end* of a year, but given all the impact that had taken place in just a few months, all the hearts who had turned to Jesus, the sheer growth Calvary had seen, the worship team had decided to do a special presentation slideshow. He then turned to his right and introduced Essie, saying that she would be providing the musical accompaniment, with assistance from someone on the piano. He said the name of the person, but Josh's mind was fixed on Essie.

She didn't look tremendously different than she had before she left the house, but there was something almost ethereal about her as she stepped up to the microphone in the focused spotlight to the side of the projection screen and began to sing, a slideshow of baptisms, of outreach, of food deliveries to at-need communities, of prayer teams, of worship played behind her. The song was about feeling lost in the world, how God hears prayers, how God will never stop trying to rescue His children.

As a teenage boy, Josh hadn't completely accepted what he'd been taught about living life with God's guidance. He'd felt a little lost, given his age, given the state of the world, given his perceptions of his place in his family. He'd appreciated and respected Essie's faith and he didn't dare question it; they seemed to find plenty of other things to talk about, but despite his best friend being deeply embedded within church activities and having a strong connection with God, he could never seem to find one for himself.

But in that church, in that Saturday night service, he watched Essie sing, he listened to the lyrics she sang with such effortless passion, and something invigorating and pure and hopeful awakened in him. He wanted to know Jesus. He needed to know Jesus.

"I felt like God was calling me close through the words you were singing. I'm not sure hearing the words through anyone else would have had the same effect. It had to be through you."

She shook her head, eyes very round.

"What?"

Essie leaned in next to his ear. "I kind of really, desperately want you to propose now."

He grinned. "You feel a lot more on-board with marriage than you did ten minutes ago?"

"Kind of warming to the idea, yeah. "

He lifted her hand and kissed her knuckles. "That's very good to know," he said, leading her toward the living room.

*   *   *

Just as Esther knew the feel of the air in the late afternoon, she knew the low murr of her dad's pickup truck. She knew her dad had a firm, but somehow muffled way of closing the driver's side door. He was home later than expected and yet she felt unprepared for his arrival. She had slept far longer than she intended; she thought she and Josh would have a chance to talk before he got back.

Essie could feel Josh twist his chin toward the screen door, probably verifying who had arrived, his muscles tensing.

Without opening her eyes, Essie turned her chin toward Josh's arm, essentially smothering her face in his armpit. She did this to shield her eyes, curious to hear how the conversation between Josh and her dad would unfold. It wasn't the first time they had snuggled on the couch together, but she was fairly certain she'd never strewn her arm across his chest like this before, her fingers tucked into his shirt sleeve, having fallen asleep gently stroking his arm. Definitely not in front of her dad anyway.

Her dad's footsteps on the porch were getting closer. One creak of the screen door later and she knew he was inside. He dropped his keys on the entry table, forced off his shoes, and cleared his throat as he turned toward the living room area.

The back of the tufted leather sectional couch faced the front door. From his vantage point, he'd have a clear view of the back of Josh's head since he was sitting upright, but he would have to take a step or two forward to see Essie lying across him.

"Hey, Teo," Josh whispered.

There wasn't a verbal response, but there was a click of both table lamps.

Josh looked down at her, his hand instinctively settling higher on her back, having previously been resting on her hip, his fingers delicately grazing the bare skin where her shirt had ridden up.

Deciding against leaving Josh to face the situation alone, Essie rotated her chin toward where she estimated her dad to be, standing at the far end of the couch. She settled her cheek into Josh's chest and opened her eyes, smiling lightly.

Her dad's cheeks tightened, eyes lifting momentarily to Josh, then back to her. "Hey there." He appeared to have picked up on something between them, but didn't seem to want to make mention of it in case he was wrong.

She gave a small smile. "How were life groups?"

"Good. How was your walk?"

"Good." Her cheeks tightened.

He gave a small *humph.* "Are you staying for dinner, Josh?" he asked, moving toward the kitchen. "Rocco? He has the pizza parlor? He's going to swing by and drop off a few pizzas."

"It's Italian food day, apparently."

"That's not *Italian* pizza, but it's delicious."

"People seem compelled to feed you, Daddy. That fridge is packed."

"Well, the food's for *you*, not me, since word got around that you've been 'under the weather.' There's been a meal train sign-up going around that I just found out about."

Essie rested her chin on Josh's shoulder. "That's a weird expression. Aren't we always under the weather?"

"Especially that storm earlier," Josh whispered.

Her eyes creased. "Yeah. So weird."

Matteo pursed his lips, too distracted in the kitchen to hear. "I haven't been offered so much food since when I started at Calvary. I had to make a new hole in my belt."

Essie twisted her expression, chuckling lightly.

"Not all of us have your metabolism, my dear."

She scrunched her nose, turned her chin and smiled at Josh fondly. "It *does* allow me to indulge. I probably don't appreciate it enough."

Matteo busied himself with preparing a pot of coffee, while Josh looked uneasy suddenly.

Essie leaned forward and gave Josh a light kiss on the lips, shielded by the back of the couch. "I love you, Josh West," she whispered beside his ear. Pleased to see his expression brighten, she quickly climbed off the couch. "What type of pizza is he bringing?" she asked, rounding to the kitchen, using various furniture items for brief balancing support until she could reach the kitchen island.

"One Chicago deep dish and two thin crusts. Your reputation for having a hearty appetite has apparently made the rounds." He began searching the fridge. "Maybe I'll ask him to bring a few sports drinks or sodas. We seem to be running low. Plenty of food. Very few beverage options."

Essie looked up as Josh stepped toward the kitchen, his hair tousled, his shirt a bit rumpled, and his eyes shadowed, as he too must have also fallen asleep at some point. Besides the beard, his cheerful exhaustion reminded her of him as a teenager. "Daddy, I'm afraid I'm going to tell you something about Josh that will forever tarnish your opinion of him."

Matteo perked up, turning from the fridge.

Josh seemed very uncertain again.

"Josh prefers deep dish."

Matteo nodded. "Don't feel bad, Josh. Nobody's perfect."

Essie approached Josh, grinning. "But you're *so* close," she said dotingly, placing a palm on his cheek. She gazed into his deep set, brown eyes. "You know what?" she whispered. "I don't think we could have you play Jesus, after all. You have too much natural smolder. It would confuse people."

Josh's cheeks tightened.

The air in the kitchen had turned extremely still. Neither of the men were taking full inhalations, while Essie grinned widely. She ran her thumb along Josh's bearded chin. "My dad wants *lots* of grand babies," she said, attempting severity. "Just so you *know* the kind of pressure you've signed up for." She lifted her eyebrows playfully.

Josh took a steadying breath, unable to shift his eyes off her. "Define 'a lot'," he said stiffly.

"Probably enough for a soccer team, *right*, Daddy? How many is that again?" Essie's smile broadened. She glanced over her shoulder at her dad, who stood in bewilderment.

His eyes shifted to Josh, who still appeared dazed, and back to her again.

"We're not engaged," she clarified. "Just to be clear. I begged and pleaded, but Josh very calmly and very rationally explained that it's not Biblical times."

"No one's asked," Josh said, with a lift of his brow, shoulders relaxing. "*Yet.*"

Essie's silver eyes widened, her cheeks turning a deep shade of pink.

Josh shuffled his feet, considering placement for his knee on the wood floor, then shook his head. "Nah, I can't ask you to marry me standing at a kitchen island," he said thoughtfully, glancing about the room as though searching for a more appropriate place to propose.

Matteo furrowed his brow. "The front porch is nice. Maybe wait for the stars to come out?" He gave a side wink to Josh.

Essie slumped her shoulders. "Well, if you two are going to team up, *I'm* not going to play anymore," she pouted, crossing her arms.

Teo cleared his throat, suppressing some emotion. "Well, I'm very happy for the two of you," he said quietly. "I don't want to intrude though. I think I'll go see what's happening over at the West House."

"No, you should stay. We need a buffer."

"What's a–" His eyes narrowed. "No, Essie, I will not be a *buffer*. You two are grown adults and you can make your own decisions and I just realized what we're talking about and I really don't want to be having this conversation, if you don't mind."

"What about *Eros*, Daddy?" she asked dramatically.

"I'm leaving."

She grinned widely. "No, now I feel bad."

"No, you don't."

"I *do* feel bad because now I'm *also* uncomfortable with the conversation."

"Should we maybe stop having it?"

"That would be great." She pursed her lips.

He nodded repeatedly. "*So.* You and the West Kid then?"

"Yep," she replied, grinning over at Josh.

Matteo looked back and forth between their faces, his smile broadening.

23
jonah

"My daughter pointed out to me that sometimes when I'm giving a sermon, I pace back and forth a lot," Matteo began. Reaching the end of the available space by the altar, he smiled. "And here we go," he said, veering in the opposite direction.

"I told her when I was a kid, my parents and I had gone to a few different churches before we found the one where we felt like we fit. One of the things that stood out to me, something I didn't personally like was that some of the pastors would stand behind a podium or up in a pulpit. To each their own, but to me, it was not an open dialogue. There was no interaction or connection. It was the pastor standing up there, sometimes arms in the air, directing all of us, big flowing sleeves on his pure white gown, like he's never committed a sin in his whole entire life.

"The problem I had with it was that even if the message was good—well, of course the message was *good*—but even if, as written, it had the makings of an effective sermon that could stir some hearts to action, there was a disconnect, right? A physical disconnect. Plus, as I mentioned, it makes the pastor, the minister, the preacher seem above everyone else, above sin. Not to smash any misconceptions, but no human is without sin. *I'm* not perfect, I'm not without sin. Not even close.

"So I didn't like the physical and perceived social disconnect by standing on high.

"I also didn't like the fact that they didn't move around. You know, a lot of communication is non-verbal and I felt the lack of movement, the rigidness of how they stood made the message sort of feel stiff, too. It can still feel stiff, I realize, even if I'm moving around. I've seen some very sleepy eyelids while I'm up here. I won't name names, Luke." Luke grunted, fixing his posture, the people around him chuckling.

"It's always been my natural impulse to move around, keep a natural rhythm going, make eye contact. Try not to make it *uncomfortable* eye contact, but keep it nice and–yeah, Josh is being a good sport right now, but I've known him a long time. His face is telling me to let his retinas *go*." He continued to widen his eyes, then finally broke into a smile, looking away.

"Now I can kind of get what she was saying. My daughter. You know, I'm not naturally an outgoing person. I tend to be pretty reserved. As a child, I was very introverted. My best friend, Luke, the extrovert, whoh I may have mentioned before, but certainly not today, also Josh's dad if you weren't aware–" he said, pointing out Josh briefly again, "-- would encourage me out of my shell. I use the word 'encourage,' but it was with the care of a young boy with ants–with physical force, a magnifying glass, and possibly matches. So to say it was out of my comfort zone to get up and preach would be an understatement. The first time I gave a sermon, I was dangerously dehydrated by the end of it.

"But I see what she was pointing out. She said I pace back and forth a lot, but she also said it tends to look like I'm doing stand-up comedy with my little stool, my bottle of water. I asked her if it's also because I'm a naturally very funny man to which she gave me the reluctant stare that really said all she needed to say and she simply said *no*. Her eyes got all big, she gave a little sympathetic smile, just there on the side of her mouth that told me she loved me, but also told me she was feeling the cringe real, real deep? Parents, you know the look. I used to think the look came about from social media, but I have learned that kids learn that look all on their own." He winced as he said this, stretching his back.

"Essie, sweet girl that she is, reassured me that it's challenging to bring humor to a lot of the topics, stories that I cover in sermons. The Bible is not a joke book, ladies and gentleman, but when she said that, I thought: Challenge accepted. So, *now* that expectations are set, today I will be discussing—*locusts*." He stepped behind one of the music stands and turned the page in the sheet music, as though he were about to read from prepared notes.

Silence filled the sanctuary.

His eyes lifted to the back of the church, and he bent forward over the stand, chuckling. "Of course Essie arrives at the exact moment that there's just this *long*, uncomfortable silence. She's looking at me like: '*What* did you *do?*'"

The congregation laughed, turning in unison to look toward the back of the church.

"Just doing my stand-up routine, kiddo. Come on in."

Essie furrowed her brow, smiling nervously, making her way up the side aisle, being careful not to spill the coffee cups she carried.

Matteo paced the altar, seemingly distracted. He nodded at her as she handed off one coffee to Josh and discreetly tried to take her seat. "Is one for me?"

She immediately stood and handed him the one in her hand, causing a few members of the congregation to 'aww.'

"Yes, so sweet. *Actually–*" He smiled tightly as Josh handed Essie his cup to replace hers. "Here, Josh. I was just giving her a hard time. You take that."

He frowned as Josh accepted the cup then traded coffees with Essie. "Was *that* one poisoned?"

"Josh doesn't use cream or sugar."

"Oh. I really caused some chaos there."

Essie shrugged, leaning into Josh's arm behind her.

"Shall I stop drawing unnecessary attention to you?"

She smiled, arched her eyebrows encouragingly.

Matteo indulged in one last look at the pair of them, then snapped to attention. "What were we talking about? *Yes!* My daughter doesn't think I'm funny."

Essie widened her eyes, whispered to Josh if that was really what he was talking about in his sermon.

He gave a slight nod and she buried her face in his shoulder. Several people laughed.

"That was not planned *at all*, but sometimes the timing just works."

The congregation chuckled.

"So in this conversation, she pointed out that sermons tend to be fairly serious. Hopefully some are inspiring. They can't all be diamonds, of course. Sometimes I leave after service when the words just didn't land where I hoped they would, and I just think to myself–" He took in a large gulp of air, gazing off into the distance, eyes narrowing. "*Yeah*, that could have been worse. I'm not sure how, but it could have *been worse*."

He began pacing again. "While humor in a sermon isn't always appropriate, it's nice to laugh, right? It feels good." He paused, grinning as he noticed Essie smiling over at Josh as she sipped her coffee. She relaxed into his arm again. Teo snapped his attention away. "So that got me thinking about coming up with a sermon that *was* humorous. I sat down to come up with some *material*. And I'm paging through, paging through, and I'm like, maybe I'll try a different version of the Bible. *Nope*.

"And then I remembered a reluctant prophet by the name of Jonah. Now, when you were in Sunday school and learned about Jonah, the big part of the story you probably learned was how he got swallowed by a whale. He spent three days and three nights inside the whale and then he was–*extracted*–at the beach. But there's a lot more to it.

"Jonah was a prophet that God called to warn the people of Nineveh that God's judgment was coming if they did not repent. Now, Nineveh was one of the most wicked societies imaginable. They were *enemies* of God's people. Honestly, Jonah hated them, so when God told him to go to issue the warning, he ran away. And when I say he 'ran away,' I mean he bolted out of there--he left a Jonah shaped *hole* in the side of his house, or wherever he was staying, and boarded a ship in the complete opposite direction.

And when I say he boarded a ship in the opposite direction, it wasn't some pleasure cruise to some neighboring place. It was a ship bound for Tarshish, which was twenty-five *hundred* miles in the opposite direction from Nineveh. So, I suppose it wasn't just a 'yeah, I don't want to do that,' Jonah made it unmistakably clear that he had no intention to set foot in Nineveh, even accidentally.

"And God *knew* this about Jonah, He knew he hated them, He knew he was selecting possibly the *worst*, most rebellious prophet for this mission. That's something you probably never had a Sunday School pastor say: Jonah was *the worst*." He grinned. "So what did God do when Jonah headed for Tarshish? Because He knew. He knows all. He knew what Jonah was going to do before Jonah did it. So what did God do? Well, He sent a great storm. And when I say, 'great storm,' you know God wasn't holding back either, right? When God makes it *rain*, he doesn't just send a little sprinkle, the clouds don't just do that little spitting rain.

So, the ship was being tossed about in this treacherous sea, there were lightning bolts, giant waves–and the sailors started to be suspicious of what was going on. This wasn't just any storm. So Jonah confessed that he had gone against God. They were nice guys. They offered to try to pull into land, but Jonah knew he wasn't going to outrun God, so he offered himself as a sacrifice. He told the other guys to throw him overboard. He would *literally rather die* than go to Nineveh.

"The sailors were like: Better you than us–So they threw Jonah overboard. Well, out of *nowhere* came this whale–most accounts say whale, or giant fish–something big enough to hold at least one very rebellious prophet. And that's where Jonah stayed for a few nights. That just sounds lovely, doesn't it? I mean, I spend a lot of time with farm animals, but can you imagine being in the belly of a whale?" He pinched his expression, cringing.

"So after a few nights, Jonah repented. God gave the whale a stomachache–again, really pleasant to picture–and the whale spit Jonah out on dry land.

"Any guesses where Jonah found himself?"

Thomas giggled from the second row.

"Nineveh! Could you *imagine* being Jonah right then?" Matteo shook his head, grinning. "So Jonah *finally* decides to do what God asked, but *literally* the bare minimum. He didn't offer some invitation to follow God to these people. He didn't go on about how gracious God is even to the worst sinner—no, no, no—it was a total fire-and-brimstone-burn-in-hell message. Jonah tells them they need to repent *or else*. That's it. A very inspiring call to action, right?

So Jonah walks himself up on a hill to watch the destruction happen. He wants to watch Nineveh *burn*." Matteo perked his brow. "But praise be, Nineveh repented! And God accepted their repentance.

"Anyone ever watch that show, The *Office*? I think of Jonah hearing this like Steve Carrell giving the camera a dead eye stare." He pointed to a few individuals who got his reference.

"But yes, the Ninevites *repented* and followed God for 100 more years.

"Now, Jonah's story doesn't end there. He could have been happy about his successful mission, but he wasn't, of course, and he showed it, in true Jonah fashion, by sulking like a child, which is kind of an insult to children. My apologies. Well, Jonah was sitting on his mountain where he'd hope to see an end of the world, apocalyptic end for Nineveh. There wasn't any shade up there and Jonah's getting cooked by the sun basically so God caused a plant to grow and provide shade for him, which helped a bit. Jonah liked his plant. *But* during the night, God sent a worm to eat the plant and cause it to shrivel up and die. This left Jonah baking in the sun again.

"Jonah—a full-grown man and a prophet for God—threw *another* tantrum, now saying he'd rather die than be without his plant. He was like: How can you *do that* to a poor plant? And God said: '*You have had pity on the plant for which you have not labored, nor made it grow, which came up in a night and perished in a night. And should I not pity Nineveh, that great city, in which are more than one hundred and twenty thousand persons who cannot discern between their right hand and their left, and much livestock?*'

314

"I'd like to tell you that Jonah learned a lesson, that he grew as a person, but we just don't know. We don't know what Jonah's response was.

"So, *what* is the lesson of Jonah? The worst prophet probably ever?

"Well, God was trying to show Jonah that he should care about lost souls, people Jonah hated, people who had done awful things. *God* cares about them. He wants to draw them close, have them repent, and turn to Him.

"Now, people enjoy saying that Jesus liked to hang out with tax collectors and prostitutes–the point they tend to miss is that it wasn't because he condoned their behavior. It was because he wanted to have them change their ways, he wanted to influence them, more specifically to compel them to put their faith in Him. It was a difficult concept for Jonah to grasp. To him, he didn't think the Ninevites were worthy of his help or his pity. Jonah ultimately obeyed, as we're called upon to do, but his heart wasn't, as we say, in the right place.

"God uses unexpected people to carry out His plans. It's something I've learned throughout my life. And He may want you to do something that you're reluctant about, that throws you off a bit, honestly. It may be something that you *really* don't want to do, or it could be something that feels intimidating or daunting--" Matteo lifted his eyes to Essie and smiled lightly. "--but He's calling on you for a reason. He's asking you to put your faith in Him. And when God calls on you?" He squinted one eye. "Try not to be like Jonah." He bowed his head. "Let's pray: Dear Father in Heaven, Thank you. Thank you for this life that You've blessed us with. Thank you for the people we get to share this life with. Thank you for the ultimate gift of eternal life through Your Son, Jesus Christ. I pray You open our hearts and open our minds to receive Him more and more in our lives. I pray we open up ourselves to live the life You call upon us to live and that we rise to whatever You call upon us to do to carry out Your work. I pray this in Jesus's name. Amen."

There was a collective breath of the congregation as everyone sat up and opened their eyes.

"Well, today's a special day indeed. You may have noticed that we have our baptismal jacuzzi out over here." He motioned to a couple ushers hovering in the side aisle along the wall of stained-glass windows, who immediately proceeded forward.

Essie and Josh stood, tucking their coffee cups together on the wooden pew and stepped to the side of the altar. Miles approached along the side aisle wearing a long pair of athletic shorts and one of the church's logo shirts.

"I love doing baptisms. It's one of the great joys I have in my role as pastor, having people commit their lives to Jesus, I get to make it official, and I get to dunk them in a tank; it's great." he said with a shrug.

"All baptisms are special to me, but this one in *particular* has significance for me personally–as you can tell by the individuals who are gathering around over here at the front. I'm sure my daughter Essie has inspired others in their faith in Jesus; I know she's done that for me, but she's actually the sponsor for the baptism we're having today. Today, she gets to become the Godmother essentially for this bouncing boy over here in the official baptism black t-shirt."

Miles grinned, putting his arm around Essie's shoulder.

"Joel Miles Kent is a young man I've actually known since he was probably 7 or 8, though I didn't know him very well back then. He was a friend of my best friend's son, Josh, but we lived 200 miles apart at the time, so we didn't see much of each other. More recently, he was reintroduced to me through my daughter.

"Now, Essie isn't one to speak negatively about anyone, *but* to be honest, it sort of surprised me when she introduced him to me late last year as her 'friend.' I specifically remember her talking about Josh's friend, Miles, when she was a little girl in as unkind of words as she used. Do you remember this?" he asked, turning to Essie, whose cheeks became very tight.

"Vaguely."

Matteo nodded. "So when she was maybe 6, Essie came stomping into my friend's farmhouse the way only 6-year-olds can, you know, in her overalls and muddy boots, looking very stern. Anyway, she came inside, and she was upset, kind of huffing about, and just struggling to get the words out. I had her take some deep breaths and once she was slightly calmer, I asked her what was wrong. She pointed very forcefully toward where the boys were playing outside and said, 'That Miles *person* just made me *very* angry.' And I said, well tell me what happened. And she said–and I'll try to quote verbatim: 'I let him take a ride on Thunder and afterwards he fed him ginger snaps, which he's *not supposed to have* because the sugar makes him too hyper and diabetes runs in his family, but he still *did*, and now Thunder likes him more than me.'

Essie briefly covered her eyes with her hand.

Matteo smiled. "I should *clarify* that Thunder was one of her imaginary horses. Her imaginary horse with a family history of diabetes."

The congregation chuckled.

"So I tried to console her. I'd taught her that if a problem comes up that just feels like way too much, the problem is too big, if she feels overwhelmed, she should pray, and she can hand the worry over to Jesus. If someone is being unkind, she doesn't need to accept the behavior, but she should pray for God to look in on them, to help them in whatever they're going through. So, as I'm starting to say something to this effect, her little hand came up and she said, 'I know what you're going to tell me to do.' And I said, okay, what's that? And she said: 'Pray about it.' There may have been a hint of annoyance with me. And I said absolutely, baby girl. You pray on it. And she scrunched up her face and scowled toward the window and said: '*Fine*. I'm going to pray that Thunder is happy and makes healthier *choices*.' I was about to praise her for that *effort* when she added: 'And I'm going to ask Jesus to wash that Miles boy's mouth out with soap.'

Matteo presented the baptism tub, perked his eyebrows. "And a short 14 years later, *here* we are."

The congregation erupted in laughter.

"Did he ever return the horse?" Matteo asked delicately once the sanctuary had quieted down.

Essie pursed her lips sadly, shaking her head.

Miles leaned in close and whispered something in her ear.

"Safe to say you've made amends now?" Matteo asked, smiling widely as Essie and Miles rested their heads against one another.

Essie nodded, her eyes brimmed with tears.

"Well, *Miles*, do you want to share anything about why you've chosen to be baptized today?"

Miles considered the question, moved forward toward the outstretched microphone, his face severe. "No."

"No," Matteo repeated, then turned to the congregation. "He said 'no.'"

Laughter echoed through the church again.

"I'm joking," Miles remarked, stepping forward and reaching for the microphone. He cleared his throat. "Well, Essie is here as my baptismal *sponsor*, but perhaps more importantly, she's here to be sure you hold me down long enough."

Matteo nodded toward Essie.

Essie grinned, silently counting out Mississippis on her fingers.

"How many Mississippis are you planning there, Girl? Sheesh." He moved back beside her, put his arm around her shoulder again and tugged her close. "In all seriousness though, this girl means so much more to me than she knows. She saved my life *literally* and I give her the bulk of the credit for saving my life *spiritually*." He cleared his throat. "People don't know this about me, but I was actually baptized as a baby. My parents were devoted Christians."

Essie gave him a gentle squeeze.

"I was six when they were killed. Car accident. My brother, who was eighteen, took myself and my two sisters in, but he was so busy working that it was really my oldest sister, Chloe, who took care of myself and my other sister, Kayla. She was only twelve at the time so that went about as well as you might expect, but she did the best she could. Our faith kind of fell by the wayside without our parents there. Over the years, I actually developed a dislike, a resentment for God, for religion.

"I remember giving Essie a hard time growing up–even after the imaginary horse situation."

"Thunder," Essie whispered.

Miles smiled widely. "Yes, *Thunder*," he said, leaning toward her, taking a steadying breath. "I liked to do things, say things that put her on edge. I think a lot of that came from me observing how strong she was in her faith. It gave her a confidence, a calm, to have a relationship with God that I had never known. Little did I know she was talking smack about me in her prayers. Kind of making me rethink some things," he murmured, looking across to her with an affectionate wink. "I didn't understand her faith or her relationship with God, and I naively assumed that she could only believe in God because she *hadn't* faced any challenges in life, any tragedy, any hardships. I convinced myself if she had experienced even a little of what *I* had, her faith would be broken, too." He lifted his brow. "I was *wrong*. But I didn't know it yet.

"When I got a little older, things had really fallen apart with my brother and sisters. My older sister Chloe died during her first month at Mandatory. We were never told what happened to her. I went to Mandatory when I was sixteen. When I came home for what they called 'respite' at eighteen, only my brother was left. Kayla had taken her own life." He nodded slowly, suppressing some emotion. "I crossed paths with Essie a couple of years later. This time, after initially falling back into my comfort zone, being my obnoxious self, I let myself get to know her. What I learned shook me up, in the *best possible way*." He nodded. "She's an amazing girl, who's endured *so* much, and is *so strong* and brave and giving of herself, and I was just absolutely mesmerized. I found myself wanting to be around her all the time because–*well*, she's feisty and fun and genuine and she filled a void in my life that I really needed." He took a deep breath. "She did more than that, but I didn't completely understand that yet.

"One day I asked her about her faith. I asked her about Jesus. And she didn't razz me for it, even after all I'd put her through. She got this very cute little smile on her face, and we went for a walk and she told me about her walk in the faith. And that was it. There was no going back to how I was living. *Well*, old habits die hard; I definitely have an obnoxious streak." He glanced across to her and smiled. "Yeah, I can see her struggling wanting to say, '*yeah* he can,' but then thinking this is his baptism, I should be nice, but then she can't say I don't have an obnoxious streak because that would be a lie."

Essie lifted an eyebrow.

He squeezed her shoulder. "One of the things Essie told me that really resonated with me, that really helped me open up my heart to Jesus was--" He paused, swallowing hard. "--was that we don't have to be perfect." He nodded. "*I* don't have to be perfect, that Jesus took that burden off us when He died on the cross. God knows who I am and loves me. He wants me to do better, be the best I can me, but he doesn't reject me if I don't. It's not for His benefit that He wants me to live better; it's because He wants a better life *for me.*" He took a deep breath.

"As I've started coming to church, gone to life groups, read the Bible, spent more time chatting with my sister from another mister over here, I continued to feel the presence and the love of Jesus in my life. And while God's love, God's gift of His Son, of eternal life is the greatest gift ever--Essie's a pretty close second–and without her, I wouldn't know Him." He gave a shrug and smiled.

Matteo nodded slowly, stepping forward to retrieve the microphone. He moved to speak and then stopped short. He put his hand on his side and took a steadying breath, his eyes brimming with tears. He opened his mouth to speak again, then lowered his chin, pressed his lips together.

Bill, one of the Associate Pastors, jogged up to the altar and grabbed the microphone. He turned toward the congregation with a pout and murmured: "I'm not crying, you're crying."

Essie released a breathy laugh and Bill nodded approvingly as she gave Miles a hug.

"Essie, I take it you're not feeling up to giving a speech right now?" Bill asked.

Essie shook her head, face buried in Miles's shoulder.

Matteo accepted the microphone back and released an exasperated breath, putting his hand to his chest. "I'm fine."

The congregation shared a collective sigh.

"Are we ready?" he asked.

Miles nodded.

Josh, Gunner, and two of the leaders for the Mens' Ministry filed up front as Miles climbed the steps into the baptism tub, remarking about the surprisingly tepid temperature of the water. Essie had once referred to the tub as the 'baptism coffin,' as it was encased in a wooden box and was made long enough for one to sit inside and still have room to be submerged backward. Though her word choice felt morbid, it was a fairly accurate description.

Matteo lowered his chin and gave his daughter a questioning look.

She nodded, smiling at the men who were circled around Miles as her dad talked about the purposes of baptism. She glanced over her shoulder, finding herself precariously close to the edge of the top step.

Josh placed his hand on her back. "I got you," he whispered, earning an appreciative glimmer of a smile.

Matteo stepped to the left side of the tub, lay his hand on Miles's shoulder. She started to reach for his right shoulder, as they traditionally prayed over the person being baptized, but Miles intercepted her hand, interlocked their fingers, and held their hands against his chest, lapping lightly at the water. His hand was trembling.

She heard her dad give the prompt for prayers, closed her eyes and said in a slightly wavering voice: "Heavenly Father, thank you for bringing Miles, my kind, thoughtful, *unexpected*, and much-loved friend into my life." She felt him squeeze her hand. "Thank you for guiding him into this congregation and into a lifelong relationship with You. I pray that You pour out Your goodness and Your blessings upon him. Please guide his path, protect him, shelter him in Your promises and fill his heart and his days with joy, hope and peace. I pray this in Your name."

Matteo nodded. "And all His people said?"

"*Amen.*"

Miles took a deep breath, adjusted his position in the tub, eyes closed, arms crossed over his chest, still holding Essie's hand.

"Miles, do you repent of your sins and acknowledge your need of a Lord and Savior?" Matteo asked.

"Yes, Sir."

"Have you put your faith in Jesus Christ as your Lord and Savior?"

"Yes, Sir."

"And is it your desire to turn from sin and know, trust and obey Jesus?"

"Yes, Sir."

Matteo gave a small smile. "Miles, because of your repentance of sin and faith in Jesus, today we acknowledge your old self is buried with Christ and you have been raised to a new life in Jesus. *Therefore*," Matteo said, slowly lowering Miles into the water, "I baptize you in the name of the Father, the Son, and of the Holy Spirit."

24

all is well

"Hey, Future Daughter-in-Law," Luke teased, kissing Essie's forehead as he stepped into the kitchen.

"Seriously, Luke?" Sara gasped. "You promised to behave."

"I didn't promise anything."

Essie shrugged, prowling the kitchen island where Sara had several cooling racks filled with cookies she'd baked throughout the early afternoon. She picked up a peanut butter one, smiling tightly as she took a bite. "What's the occasion?"

"The weekend," Sara said in a wispy voice.

"It's Thursday, Sara," she replied.

"Oh, *is it*? No, it can't be!"

Essie lifted her eyebrows.

"*You*. Her reason is you," Luke said. "When she's stressed, she cleans. When she's happy, she bakes. This is why our house is a disaster and I've gained 15 pounds in a matter of weeks. She's tickled pink to have not one, but *two* daughters."

"Luke, they're not engaged. They just became a couple a few weeks ago. Stop *pressuring* her." Then, under her breath, added: "You're going to scare her off."

Essie picked a chocolate chip cookie off a different cooling rack, casually took a bite.

"Does Essie look like she's going to get scared off?"

Esther stopped mid-chew. Covering her mouth with her hand, she managed to say: "Essie looks like she's enjoying this cookie a *lot*."

"Oh, to have a young metabolism again," Sara said with a sigh.

Luke chuckled. "And she thinks *I'm* being rude," he whispered, leaning over Essie's shoulder.

Sara stomped her foot. "What was that?"

"Would you like a glass of milk, dear?" Luke asked Essie with faux propriety, ignoring Sara's question. "Before you scarf down another cookie?"

Essie chuckled, nodding. "Actually, yes, please. Thank you."

He turned toward the fridge, chuckling to himself and shaking his head.

A hallway door clicked shut and Essie rotated herself in its direction. Gabe's face was filled with disbelief and wonder as he came around the corner. His expression remained even once he looked up.

"That's a happy face," Esther said with a knowing smile, pushing off the kitchen island. She sheepishly wiped her mouth as she moved toward him.

"So is that."

"Of course it is. She has a belly *full* of cookies," Luke remarked.

"Luke!"

Essie pushed through her toes and hugged Gabe. She allowed it to stretch for a few moments before taking a step back. "You give delightful hugs, Gabe. Have I told you that before?"

"You have. You do, too."

She smiled. "You were putting Hannah for a nap?"

"Um-hmm," he murmured, glancing up at his parents. "By the way, Hannah likes oldies."

"That's no way to talk about your mother."

"*Luke!*" Esther exclaimed, whirling on her heel.

"Too far?"

"It's okay, Essie. I have thick skin."

Essie snapped her chin in Luke's direction and intensified the glare of her eyes, her tight jaw threatening him to make any additional remarks.

"It wouldn't be true if I said it, but she teed it up perfectly."

Essie shook her head tightly.

"Fine, fine. I'm going to go muck stalls," Luke conceded, placing a glass of milk on the island. "There's your milk, Essie. Help yourself to as *many* cookies as you'd like. You'll get *no judgment* from *me*."

Essie laughed, meeting his eye.

"Who's judging?" Sara asked, perplexed.

"I wasn't the one giving her the envious 'you can't outrun an aging metabolism' look."

"I did *not* feel judged," Essie said firmly. "For the record."

Luke turned on his heel. "Well, aren't you sweet?" he said in a gentle southern accent. He glanced over his shoulder at Sara. "Darn it, Sara, she's an honest girl and you're forcing her to lie—I can't stand to be witness to this," he said in dramatic fashion, holding his hand to his chest.

Essie actively suppressed a laugh.

"You saw what I did there?" Luke asked her, giving a small wink. "That was spot on, wasn't it?"

Essie's cheeks reddened.

"Alright, off to muck stalls," he announced and threw open the front screen door. "Love you, all."

"Will you two keep an ear open if Hannah wakes up?" Sara asked, trailing behind him.

"You're mucking stalls, too?"

"Um," Sara said awkwardly. "*Yeah*. I have some chores—I need to take care of—in the barn. Horses. You know."

Essie had observed master's level parental meddling. This was not it. Sara West had never had a chore to tend to in the barn. Despite living on a farm for decades, Essie had few memories of Sara West actually setting foot in a barn. After giving up her counseling practice, she mainly focused on tending to the house, cooking meals, baking, homeschooling. Deciding against prolonging the awkwardness further, Essie said nothing and watched Sara debate a footwear choice before scurrying from the house.

"Was she wearing *sandals*?" Gabe asked.

"Yes. Yes, she was." Essie shook her head and turned back to face Gabe. "What'd you sing to Hannah?"

"It was one of the songs from the diner we stopped at on the way here? The Spaniels?"

"*Goodnight, Sweetheart.*"

"Yeah."

"That's a good one. Those low notes are tricky though," she said, clearing her throat. "I don't have the range for them."

He pressed his lips together, gently placed his fingers on her hip. "You're really okay?"

She nodded. "Yeah, I am. You'd *know* that if you weren't actively avoiding me."

He opened his mouth to put up a defense.

"I haven't seen you in weeks. You thankfully still go to church, but you started going to the 11am service. It's a more reasonable time, I get it. But then you *actually* ducked behind the hospitality counter to avoid running into me when I came back after service to rehearse with Worship Band the other day. *That* was hurtful." She took another bite of cookie, lifting her eyebrows.

He released his breath. "I'm sorry."

"*Hey,*" she said in a warning tone. She paused to swallow. "Don't you dare be weird with me."

"Is that an order?"

"Yes. You did nothing wrong. You would never ever hurt me. I know that. You know that."

He shook his head. "If not for–"

"*Stop.* I'm here in your parents' kitchen scarfing down cookies. I'm *fine.*"

He nodded, eyes panning over to the spread of baked goods and back to her. "*So,*" he began, dragging the word out to multiple syllables, "You and Josh?"

She smiled. "Yeah. Me and Josh."

"*Finally.*"

She squinted one eye.

"I'm happy for you. You deserve every happiness in the world, Essie."

She pursed her lips, searching his eyes. "Are you okay?"

"*Yeah.* Thanks to you."

"I meant–" she began, wincing.

"You meant because I made a really out of line move on you after you risked your life to save me?"

She shrugged casually. "Well, yeah. Kind of."

"I'm sorry about that. I'm not going to deny the motivation behind it or try to excuse why I did it. The more memories I get back, the more clear it is to me—it's always been you and Josh. Always. I've always known that."

She furrowed her brow and gave a small shrug. "You kissed me in the choir loft at church, I kissed you in the city when I was cosplaying as a proxy. It's fine. Things happen. It's been crazy, confusing times."

"So that *did* happen," he said, his eyes brightening. "I didn't--I couldn't be sure."

She twisted her expression. "Now granted, I kissed you because I thought one or both of us were going to die that day." She winced.

Gabe narrowed his eyes. "So you were *literally* kissing me goodbye."

"Yeah."

"That got dark and depressing real, *real* fast."

"Sorry. I do that," she said, dropping her chin to her chest. She swept the hair from her face, moving herself to the opposite side of the island. "I'm sorry I slapped you. That was an unexpected reaction on my part."

"The punishment fit the crime."

She furrowed her brow. "The *crime*? *Really*?"

He shrugged, taking a deep breath. "So, which are your favorites?" he asked, eyes scanning over the rows of cookies.

She twisted her expression, deciding to accept the change of topic. "Peanut butter. Your mom puts mini morsels inside so when they're warm, the whole thing becomes this melty, crumbly mess of baked deliciousness. I also have a nostalgic attachment to *these*."

Gabe inspected the colorful, speckled group of cookies. "What are they?"

"Sugar cookies coated in sprinkles. When I was little, your mom liked to take me grocery shopping with her. The bakery would hand out free cookies to kids and I'd always pick this kind." Her cheeks tightened. "They're so *pretty*," she said daintily.

He smiled.

"They're very sweet for my current taste buds though."

"I think I'll go with oatmeal raisin."

"Ah. Healthy."

"I can see chunks of brown sugar."

"It has oatmeal, it has some fruit," she said, counting the benefits on her fingers. "I actually enjoy oatmeal chocolate chip quite a bit, they strike a nice balance, but I'm not *seeing*— "

"Dough is chilling in the fridge."

Essie spun on her heel searching for the source of the voice.

Sara was sitting in a porch rocking chair, turned toward the opening in the front window.

"I thought you had chores to attend to *in the barn*."

"I'm supervising."

Essie took a breath, hoping she had spoken quiet enough so Sara hadn't heard the entirety of their conversation. "I don't think you have the sight lines from there to properly supervise, Sara," she teased.

"Sorry. Not listening, my ears just perked up when I heard you talking about cookies."

"Totally not listening," Gabe whispered.

Essie rolled her eyes, dropping her shoulders. "You're really okay?"

"Essie, how can I be anything but happy for you?"

She shrugged sheepishly.

"I mean, look at you. You couldn't stop smiling if you wanted to right now. You look like you slept with one of Hannah's clothing hangers in your mouth."

"That was oddly specific–*thank you*?"

"You're happy and it shows. That's a good thing."

Essie attempted to neutralize her expression.

"Yeah, you can't do it. And I don't want you to. You deserve to be happy. And no one brings a smile to your face quite like Josh." He took a deep breath, smiling distantly. "*Yeah*. Good for *Josh*."

She grinned.

"Actually, I *do* mean that. I'm very happy for him–and for you. And *I'll* be content to be the older and–well, not really *wiser*–but older brother. It appears to be my lot in life," he said melodramatically, gazing off into the distance again.

"I actually see potential if you're looking to be the funny brother."

"*Really*?"

She pursed her lips.

"Miles warned me that you can be mean. I didn't want to believe it."

*   *   *

Essie pulled into the ranch driveway, assessing the cloud cover, which was finally starting to dissipate, a beam of sunshine spotlighting the valley below the overlook. She slid out of the truck cab, being careful not to drop the plate and storage container filled with cookies and shuffled her boots toward the front steps.

"Do you have a new favorite human, Fenway?" she asked the German Shepherd affectionately, who sat like a statue beside Matteo, gently closing her eyes with each stroke of his hand across her head.

"She's just keeping me company for a while. Josh had to go help with an injured horse."

She stepped toward the pair, kissed her dad on the cheek and waved the plate of treats in front of his face. "The cookies on the plate are *community* cookies. This tupperware is mine. Hands *off*."

He smiled. "I'm more of a savory treats person anyway."

"Well, I'm an all the treats sort of person." She pursed her lips as the Shepherd stretched her neck toward her, desperate for a sniff and a pet. "*Helloo*, Miss Fenway."

The dog whimpered, her eyes widening, but she dared not move from her spot.

"Did you get to see Gabe while you were over there?"

"Yep."

"How's he doing?"

She finagled the screen door open with her boot, made her way to the kitchen. "He's good," she called back, tucking the cookie loot on the counter. "He's going to medical school, officially."

"Wow."

"Yeah. He's been working at the hospital, and he's had a lot of training, but now they've pulled together a decent faculty staff, a curriculum." Her voice was muffled as she munched on a cookie, stepping back onto the porch.

"That's great. Good for him. Whereabouts?"

"It's on the other side of the Northern Ark. Over by the Mississippi River?" She shoved the rest of the cookie in her mouth. Once she'd finished chewing, she stole a sip of her dad's drink, then continued: "Geography wasn't a focus in my homeschool's curriculum so I'm not totally clear, state name-wise where he'll be," she said with a grin. "They're still getting things figured out, so he'll go for a year initially for the classroom/lecture stuff. He's planning to come home when he can though." She peered toward the barn longingly.

"Going somewhere?"

"I was thinking of taking Bree out for a ride since the weather cleared out. Do you want to come along?"

He pressed his lips together. "Wish I could. I've got a private baptism and then Thursday groups."

She nodded.

"I can call in sick," he said facetiously.

She rolled her eyes. "Yeah, right. Whose baptism?"

He smiled lightly.

"You can't say?"

"Luther."

"Wait, *what*?"

Matteo nodded. "He was baptized as an infant, but he said he's been feeling a calling to reaffirm his faith and commitment to Jesus."

Her cheeks tightened. "That makes me really happy. He doesn't want anyone there?"

"He thought it would seem like a stunt to make it public since he's planning to take a more prominent stance in the Ark."

"What about me?"

"You know Luther; he wants to keep a separation between the two of you publicly."

"Yeah, I know. And this is about him, not me."

"He's protecting you. That's all."

"So who's witnessing?"

"Luke and Danny."

She nodded thoughtfully, holding the cross pendant on her necklace between her fingers. She took a breath, unclasped the chain from around her neck, cradling it delicately in her hand. "Will you give this to him for me?"

He took the necklace, examined it in his palm. "Are you sure? You've had this forever, Ess."

"Yeah."

"I don't even remember where you got it. It must have been someone at Calvary?"

"Luther's mom gave it to me."

"When you were two?"

She nodded.

He frowned. "I guess I didn't realize that you remember her?"

She smiled tightly, thinking of how she referred to her as '*Baby*' in the most doting, loving way, how her embraces were firm but tender. "Her name was Loretta, but she liked to be called Lola. She gave me my first bath, fed me my first dinner."

Her dad frowned. "I can't believe we've never talked about her."

"She gave me lasagna for my first meal. That just occurred to me," she said, furrowing her brow.

"Lasagna?"

"I guess it was something she made every Sunday. I'd never had real food before, and my first meal was a big plate of lasagna and a glass of milk." She twisted her expression. "It was a bold choice. I could have been lactose intolerant."

He exhaled deeply, lifted his free hand to her cheek. "You're sure about the necklace?"

"Yep." She pulled her hair up into a high, messy bun.

As she did this, Matteo's eyes focused on the elaborate design of her tattoo, which created a silhouette of the cross on her left forearm. There'd been a few members of the congregation who had been surprised when they saw her tattoo, associating it with some level of rebellion, or at least, a "different sort" than Essie, as most said she had a wholesome look about her. Which she did. But there was an assumption that being wholesome meant being naive, and that just wasn't a word he'd connect with his daughter. There were things that were new to her, things in the world with which she was unfamiliar, but over the past few weeks, he'd watched her step into her own. With confidence. With quiet grace. With a wisdom and patience that far surpassed her years.

Thankfully, still with her playful humor.

It seemed like it wasn't that long ago, weeks maybe, that they'd made the drive from Wallace, Colorado back to Calvary after Gabe West kissed her at the train station. Perhaps then 'naive' would have been a more appropriate word to describe her at that age, but certainly not anymore.

Bree whinnied impatiently, hip-checking the outer paddock fence with his haunches.

Essie laughed. There was something to how the sun, just peeking through the clouds illuminated her face, something in her smile. All of a sudden, he saw her clearly and he realized, with a bittersweet ache in his chest, that she had grown up.

"Essie, I'm so proud to call you my daughter."

Her chin turned abruptly in his direction. She furrowed her brow, cheeks pinched upward.

"Just thought you should know."

She had never been very comfortable receiving praise or flattery, usually turning silent, as she was now.

He nodded. "I don't want to keep you from your ride."

"Everyone says it kind of in a silly manner," she began, blinking slowly at him, "but I happen to *know*, for a *fact*, that I have the best dad in the world." She smiled tightly. "And I love you *so much*, Daddy. Times infinity squared."

He pulled in his breath, steadying himself on the rocking chair, remembering how she had used that phrase on a birthday card for him when she was a little girl.

She lifted her brow. "And I promise I won't make you wait too long for a grandkid," she added quickly.

An involuntary chuckle escaped his mouth. He cleared his throat. "No rush."

She smiled, meeting his eyes.

And then he pretended to check his watch.

"And *you* call *me* a 'turd.'"

"Yes. Yes, I do."

"Like father, like daughter."

His eye flinched. "I don't think so. Sara West seems to think you influenced *my* humor."

"And thank God I did," she said, her eyes widening. "One cannot survive comedically on bad dad puns alone." She walked into his arms, hugging him.

After a prolonged few moments, she sighed and kissed his cheek. "You better get going."

"Do you want Fenway to come with you?" he called as she started for the paddock.

"No, Bree doesn't like her. She's too mouthy." She twirled back around. "When's Josh supposed to be back?"

"An hour ago."

She nodded. "Well, she'd probably try to participate in the baptism if *you* take her. She should be fine if you leave her in the house. I'll probably just be a couple of hours."

*   *   *

Matteo turned on his heel at the steps as headlights from a newly arriving vehicle illuminated the porch. He waved, shielding his eyes with his opposite arm to confirm who it was. "Are you *just* getting back?" he called as Josh dropped out of the cab.

Josh's jeans were coated in dirt and what appeared to be dried blood, but he was wearing a fresh undershirt. "Yeah. We ended up needing to do surgery. I do *not* suggest being impaled by a longhorn cattle."

"Oww. How's the horse?"

"Things went well; she's just got a lot of healing to do." Josh ducked back into the truck cab and retrieved a book for Essie, as well as a cooler bag with dinner offerings from the ranch owner's wife. "Have you eaten yet?"

"I did. We had a barbecue potluck at family life groups." Matteo held open the door for Josh, glancing around the house on his way to rinse his mug at the sink. "She *cleaned*."

Josh took in the tidy setting, sliding off his boots by the entry. It was uncharacteristic of Essie to remain so quiet and not rush out to see them. He placed the book and the cooler bag on the kitchen island and made his way down the hallway where dim lighting poured out from her bedroom, along with a low growl. "Easy, Fenway."

The Shepherd was perched expectantly at the foot of the bed, debating about whether she should jump down to greet him or remain at Essie's side.

Essie was sitting upright, a pile of pillows behind her back. Her chin was angled toward her right shoulder, her eyes were closed, and her jaw was relaxed, lips slightly parted. She was wearing one of his old community little league shirts. He recognized the logo for the Mustang mascot on the left chest, kicking its back legs up in the air like a rodeo horse.

Fenway tracked him as he approached, resting her snout across Essie's legs, giving a small, nervous growl.

Josh gave the dog a quick scratch on the head then lifted the leather bound book flopped open in Essie's lap. He recognized the gold edging on the thin, crisp pages, her initials engraved into the cover. It appeared she had been working through the book of Psalms. He tucked the leather cord bookmark inside the pages, closed the Bible and placed it on the night table.

Josh applied pressure to get the pillow easement to deconstruct, then gently encouraged Essie to settle into the mattress. He tugged the blankets over her shoulder and made sure she was properly covered. He then switched off the bedside lamp, which caused her to stir and curl herself more determinedly on her side. Within moments, her breaths had deepened again. There wasn't a trace of tension in her brow.

He swept the hair from her eyes and kissed her cheek. "Sweet dreams," he whispered, moved silently out of the room and closed the door.

Matteo frowned as he re-emerged without her. "Is she asleep?"

"Yeah," Josh said in a similar disbelieving tone.

Teo suppressed a smile, lifted his brow. "Wow."

Josh glanced back down the hallway, both relieved she had at least for now overcome her affliction that kept her from sleeping at night, but admittedly a bit disappointed he wouldn't get to spend time with her. "I should get going. I need to take a shower and probably do what she's doing," he said with a lighthearted chuckle, the exhaustion of the day finally hitting him.

"Oh. Well, I was going to put on the 2016 World Series if you wanted to watch?"

Josh considered the suggestion. "I guess I didn't realize you were a Cubs fan."

Matteo shrugged, grabbing two beer bottles from the fridge. "I love a good underdog story."

25

hallelujah

"Well, don't you look domestic," Miles remarked, eyes lifting to the aisle where Essie had suddenly appeared, holding a sleeping Hannah in a baby carrier. "Is this a preview of things to come?"

"Ha ha *ha*," she chided, sliding into the pew, hand resting protectively on the back of Hannah's head. She silently directed Miles to move toward the end and squeezed herself into the pew between him and Josh.

"I love you dearly, Essie, but you really *can* be bossy."

She patted his leg. "Good morning, Miles. You're looking very debonair."

"Good morning, Essie Dear," he said, tipping his imaginary hat to her. "Always a pleasure."

"What are you two doing in here?" Josh whispered, smiling tightly.

"A little birdie told me my dad's going to sing in service this morning." Essie nodded toward the altar where the ushers were returning the baskets from Communion. She waved down the pew to Sara, who looked concerned about her sudden appearance, motioning questioningly toward Hannah.

Essie gave the signal for OK and settled in beside Josh. "You wore a *tie* today," she observed quietly, nudging Josh's shoulder, eyeing his multi-piece suit sans jacket. "Are you getting married or something?"

He grinned. "Not *today*."

She extended her fingers as though to shade Hannah's face from the lights. With her opposite hand, she grabbed the knot of Josh's tie and tugged him in for a kiss.

"You're in *church*, Esther," Miles whispered in a lecturing voice.

"Don't be such a stick in the mud, Miles," she replied, echoing his tone, cheeks tight. She leaned over to him and gave him a quick peck on the cheek.

Miles pursed his lips. "Okay, *now* God approves."

"Has he ever sang in church?" Josh asked.

"Only as a part of Worship Band. Not as a solo or duet. Usually he just plays the guitar, but Renee convinced him to sing somehow." She sat more upright. "I don't know how she does it, but people have a tendency to do what she says."

Josh frowned, raised his eyebrows pointedly toward the side aisle.

"Oh good, you took the bait," Renee whispered, leaning over Miles, who was looking very uneasy with this arrangement, her long blond ringlets falling in his face.

"What bait?"

"Come *on*, Essie. You're not going to leave your dad up there to sing by himself, are you?"

"*You're* singing with him, Renee. That's what you said."

"*Is* it?" Renee asked, scrunching her nose. "Must be a crazy misunderstanding."

"It was not a misunderstanding. You said you got my dad to agree to sing in church."

"To sing a duet."

"Yes.   With   *you.*"

She put her hand to her chest. "Did I say with me? I don't think I did."

"Renee Bethany Shaw."

"Middle name me all you want."

"Does he *think* I'm singing with him? Because he didn't say a word about it."

"No, he *does* think it's me. I felt bad lying to a pastor, but I really don't think he'll mind."

"So go sing, Renee. The two of you have practiced singing together, right?"

"Yeah, we have and I would, you know, I would, but I just don't think I can," she said, daintily clearing her throat. "Yeah, my voice is feeling scratchy. I must be coming down with something. Maybe it's whatever you had a few weeks ago." Renee smiled sweetly.

Essie narrowed her eyes. "*Renee.*"

"Be mad all you want, but you're getting up there."

"And singing *what?*"

"*The Prayer.*"

"Are you serious? You're talking about the English/Italian *The Prayer?*"

"Good,   you   remember   it."

"Oh, *The Prayer?* That's a beautiful song, Essie."

"Thank you, Miles. Very helpful."

He suppressed a smile.

"Now hand off the adorable baby," Renee said, raising her eyebrow directedly at Josh, who moved forward on the pew, moving with automation to unclip the carrier.

"Josh, did you know about this?" she whispered.

He shook his head, prying his sleeping baby sister from her arms, cheeks tight. "I did *not*, but I'd be lying if I said I wasn't very much looking forward to it."

"I can't just get up there and belt out *The Prayer* and do the song any sort of justice. That's not how vocal cords work."

Josh smiled.

Essie released a breath, eyes straining to look toward the front of the church without actually making eye contact with her dad.

Luke leaned forward, twisting his expression as he tried to make sense of what was going on down the pew.

"Essie, come *on*," Renee beckoned.

Essie turned her chin toward her. "For the record, I *hate you,*" she muttered tightly.

"That's very mature."

Miles smirked.

"I *hate* you, too," she said, tousling his hair, which he'd thankfully stopped over-gelling.

"No, you don't."

"No, I don't," she conceded, patting his cheek affectionately. "And I don't hate you either–" she said, indicating Renee, "--but–"

Josh ran his hand supportively on her arm as she stood. She whirled around, gave him a small smile, squeezed his hand and turned away, immediately grumbling something under her breath about Renee.

"Good luck," Miles whispered, then he laughed at whatever look she gave him in return.

Her eyes lifted to the altar as she reached the side aisle.

Her dad began strumming his guitar and leaned toward the microphone. "So *today* I have the honor of accompanying the very talented Renee Shaw in a song of hope. You've seen me up here playing the guitar, but tame your expectations for my singing ability–" He narrowed his eyes in confusion at the chaos in the fourth pew. "Sono stato selezionato per la parte solo perché parlo italiano." He turned to speak directly into the microphone, lowering his register. "I was only selected for the part because I speak Italian."

There were some chuckles throughout the congregation.

"Come *on,*" Renee said, grabbing onto Essie's left arm with both hands. "You sang this at Calvary. I remember."

"That was like 8 years ago, Renee."

Renee rolled her eyes and tugged Essie forcibly toward the altar, where she picked up the spare microphone. She handed it blindly to Esther, who was anxiously smoothing her dress where the baby carrier had wrinkled the fabric, so it walloped her in the chest.

Essie grabbed hold of the microphone and made eye contact with Josh. *Ow,* she mouthed.

Matteo paused strumming his guitar, covered his microphone and leaned toward Renee as she approached him. He nodded slowly in response to what she whispered in his ear.

As she stepped away, he peered over at Essie, whose eyes were very round. She lifted her microphone helplessly.

"Change of plans," he said, unable to hide the emotion in his voice. He stood, extended his hand to present his daughter. "Esther Natale, lead vocals."

Renee smiled victoriously as she brushed past Esther, who was taking up position beside her dad.

Essie shuffled her boots tensely across the stone floor. "Hai il testo della canzone, papà?" she whispered covertly. *Do you have the song lyrics, Daddy?*

Matteo furrowed his brow. "Aspetta, ti ha appena accecato con questo?" *Wait, did she just blindside you with this?*

"*Yes,*" she whimpered.

He shifted his music stand between them, reached for his bottle of water from behind the speaker and handed it to her. "Non devi cantare, Essie. Va bene." *You don't have to sing, Essie. It's okay.* "We'll just move on to the next song."

"Papà, ho sempre voluto cantare con te. Sono solo molto nervoso." *Daddy, I've always wanted to sing with you. I'm just really nervous.*

"Sei sicuro?" *Are you sure?*

She nodded, wrinkling her forehead, taking two long swigs of water.

He gave her a small smile, removed his guitar and placed it on its stand. He pried his microphone from the holder. "Full disclosure, this was just sprung on her without any sort of warm up or rehearsal." He took a deep breath. "And I'm about to be a blubbering mess so I'm going to forgo the guitar." He motioned to the pianist just taking her seat.

341

Josh gently bounced Hannah against his chest to soothe her after she'd woken to find she was no longer in Essie's arms. For the time being, she was distracted by his tie, twisting the material in her tiny fist and gnawing on the knot.

He watched Essie take a deep breath and move behind the music stand next to her dad.

As soon as the first notes played on the piano, he heard his mother gasp, recognizing the song.

While Essie had appeared jittery standing on the altar as the music began, all her nervous energy melted away the moment she started to sing. As he heard her rich, resonant voice fill the cavernous church, he felt his breath catch in his chest.

Renee had forced her to sing *Silent Night* with her the previous Christmas as a part of the candlelight procession, however, that felt different than her standing in the spotlight at the front of the church in front of a very full congregation. She hadn't done that since before the attack on Calvary.

He watched her gaze over at her dad, who was slowly lifting his microphone to his mouth. Before they were halfway through the first back and forth Italian/English duet portion, tears were streaming from both of their eyes. He could feel the collective inhalation of the congregation as the music swelled and their voices joined together in the Italian lyrics.

When their voices faded and the music slowed, cheers erupted in the church. Essie's nervousness had come rushing back. Josh could see her hands shaking as she held the microphone at her side.

"Damn," Miles said flatly, his voice nearly lost in the cheers.

Josh lifted his brow, nodding.

Essie laughed, wiping at her eyes as she turned to her dad, who embraced her snugly and kissed her several times on the cheek. She whispered something in his ear and he froze, seeming to be asking for clarification.

He smiled tightly at her, nodded toward Renee who was sheepishly stepping up to the altar.

"What's going on?" Miles asked as Essie spoke quietly to Renee.

Josh shook his head.

Renee nodded enthusiastically, scrambled to apparently pass a message onto the other Worship Band members, just coming up the side aisle.

Matteo picked up his guitar and began to strum casually, settling into a melody. He lifted his brow, getting confirmation from Essie that he had the right song.

She nodded.

The pianist joined in after the first instrumental verse.

Essie lifted her eyes to the congregation, her confidence faltering, as she watched people uncertain about whether they should continue to stand. But as her gaze found the fourth pew, she took a steadying breath.

Josh gave her an encouraging smile. *"Don't you get shy on me,"* he mouthed melodically.

His words had the intended effect; he could see her say the next lines to herself:

Lift up your song
'Cause you've got a lion inside of those lungs

She took a deep breath in, cheeks tight, and pulled back her shoulders.

"There you go," Josh whispered, nodding.

The band members had themselves situated at their stands and Renee was distributing the sheet music as Essie began to sing.

In the darkness we were waiting
Without hope, without light
Till from heaven You came running
There was mercy in Your eyes
To fulfill the law and prophets
To a virgin came the word
From a throne of endless glory
To a cradle in the dirt

Praise the Father, praise the Son
Praise the Spirit, three in one
God of glory, Majesty
Praise forever to the King of Kings

To reveal the kingdom coming
And to reconcile the lost
To redeem the whole creation
You did not despise the cross
For even in your suffering
You saw to the other side
Knowing this was our salvation
Jesus for our sake you died

Praise the Father, praise the Son
Praise the Spirit, three in one
God of glory, Majesty
Praise forever to the King of Kings

And the morning that You rose
All of heaven held its breath
Till that stone was moved for good
For the Lamb had conquered death
And the dead rose from their tombs
And the angels stood in awe
For the souls of all who'd come
To the Father are restored

There were cheers of anticipation for the next verse.

And the Church of Christ was born
Then the Spirit lit the flame
Now this gospel truth of old

Shall not kneel, shall not faint
By His blood and in His name
In His freedom I am free
For the love of Jesus Christ
Who has resurrected me

Praise the Father, praise the Son
Praise the Spirit, three in one
God of glory, Majesty
Praise forever to the King of Kings

Praise forever to the King of Kings

Josh glanced around the sanctuary to the hundreds of people with their hands held high, swaying gently, as the melody faded.

Essie slowly opened her eyes, her smile wide as she situated the microphone in its stand. She took a step back and encouraged Renee forward.

Renee took over position at the front microphone, but fanned out her arm and presented a reluctant Essie, which prompted thunderous applause.

Hannah released a cry and Essie's chin swiveled immediately in her direction. She gave a small curtsy then moved with purpose down the steps toward the side aisle, cheeks reddening with the continued attention, tucking her hair repeatedly behind her ears.

As she reached the fourth pew, she extended her arms, opened and closed her palms as a signal to Josh that she intended to now reclaim the adorable baby.

Josh scooted in front of Miles and agreeably handed off his baby sister. He leaned in next to Essie's ear. "You are *magnificent.*"

As he stood upright, Essie beamed at him, her eyes shimmering, cheeks tight. She appeared slightly unnerved by the amount of attention she was still receiving from the surrounding congregation, but she secured her arms around Hannah, pushed through her toes and gave him a brief kiss on the cheek.

The electric guitarist began to play the first notes of *My Jesus*.

With a flash of a smile, she had turned on the spot, moving quickly up the aisle. When Josh peered back over his shoulder, he saw she had paused at the back of the church to share a dance with Hannah as the melody picked up, shimmying in her fishhook pattern cowboy boots.

*   *   *

Josh didn't typically have a need to visit the Sunday School classrooms during pickup so the hallway came as a bit of a chaotic, sensory-rich surprise. He side-stepped around parents trying to corral distracted children holding crafts and small trinkets while chasing down jackets and diaper bags and lovies. He'd never seen so many, heard so many kids in one space before.

He made his way to the infant room, coming across three of them before finding the one where Essie was. Inside, two babies sat on the floor in posture positioners listening intently to a board book being read to them by a young woman with a whimsical looking braid, one baby slept in a high chair, and his own baby sister, with her wisps of blond curls giggled on the changing table.

Essie had her back turned to the doorway, which was secured with what he assessed to be an impenetrable baby gate. She seemed to be making a production out of the diaper changing process, walking her fingertips over Hannah's plump stomach, surprising her with spontaneous tickles.

"Okay, real talk, kiddo. Your mommy tells me that you don't spit up on anyone but me. Now, I *think* we have a pretty good thing going here, but I can't help but feel like it's something personal." She was lifting her voice in a playful manner, using wild gestures, and Josh presumed some animated facial expressions. "Don't you bat those eyelashes at me, young lady. Those stains don't always come *out*."

Hannah stretched her starfish hand and grabbed a chunk of Essie's hair.

Essie winced. "Oh no, is this some sort of baby interrogation tactic? I swear, I didn't do it. Whatever it is, I have an alibi."

Hannah twisted her hand.

"Alright, *alright*, as much as I'd love for you to chew on my hair, let's just release *that*," she said, prying Hannah's fist open gently. "Thank you very, very much. Oh dear, that hand is just coated in drool, isn't it?" She scrunched her nose as she used a wipe to clean Hannah's hand. "There we go. Now, down to business for *real* this time." She prepped the next cloth diaper, as well as a wipe with Sara's homemade 'butt cleaner.' "Alright, no surprises here, *right?*" She unclasped the diaper and gave an exaggerated *phew!,* which caused Hannah to release a low giggle, immediately followed by a fart.

Josh laughed.

"You really bring out the best in her, don't you Essie?" the young woman laughed.

"*Girl,* I swear it was too early for your momma to start you on solids. Wowee!" Based on the strained tone of her voice, she was plugging her nose. "Okay, *well,* I think we can safely say that was a warning shot. Not to treat you like a 'hot potato,' but let's get this diaper changed and have you handed off to your mommy as soon as humanly possible, shall we? *Yes,* that's a very wise idea, isn't it?" Essie wiped quickly, rolled the used diaper, tucked it to the side, and placed the new one. She gave a tight, staccato laugh as she buttoned up the new diaper. "Like. A. *Pro.*"

Hannah cooed, tossing all four limbs out at once.

"Oh, goodness gracious, you're *so cute*! I know, you hear that *all* the time, but you are. You have your daddy's hair, which isn't a terrible deal because he has an excellent hairline. You also have his chinny chin. Yes, you do. *And,* you have your mommy's eyes. Oh, my goodness, so pretty."

Hannah tilted her head, freezing her movements.

"What? You want me to continue doting on you and telling you just how beautiful you are? Fine. I can do that. Let's see–hair, chin, eyes–*ohhh*, well, you and your brothers all kind of have the same nose, but as far as noses go? It's a very cute one–and it's dainty, which is good because I read once that noses *never* stop growing. That is very weird, isn't it? Ears either. It makes sense I guess because they're both made of cartilage, which you don't care about, but yeah, super weird. Anyway, where were we? *Yes.* Can we take a second and talk about those dimples? *Oh*, that's your mommy again, but you know what? Your brother, Josh? He has them, too. You actually look a bit like him when he was little, especially when you giggle. He had a belly giggle, too. *Oh*, and then combine it with those dimples?" Essie clutched her hand to her chest. "*Adorable.*" She ran her fingers delicately across Hannah's stomach.

Hannah's face tensed up, her toothless smile broadening.

"Oh yes, that's a tickle spot. Are you trying to deny the giggle? The giggle cannot be *contained*!" Essie dropped her face to Hannah's belly and peppered her with kisses. "I shall hear my Hannah giggles!"

Hannah burst out laughing, squirming on the changing pad.

"Alright, girlie. Your mommy's going to be in here any second and she's gonna be all 'Essie, why is my baby half-*naked*?'"

Hannah chatted happily to herself as Essie pulled on her bloomers skirt.

"Logan's mommy is here!" The other nursery attendant announced, pushing herself off the floor. She retrieved one of the babies sitting on the floor, along with a diaper bag hung up on the cabinets. "Bye-bye, Logan. See you Wednesday." She turned her attention to Josh after handing the chubby, bald baby across to her mom. "Are you picking up?"

Essie peered over her shoulder, grinning. "Savi, that's Josh."

"Wait, *your* Josh?"

Essie carefully lifted Hannah and positioned her on her chest, turning toward the doorway. "Yes, *my* Josh."

Savi gave him a second, more thorough look over. "*Okaaay*," she said approvingly.

"Josh, Savi. Savi, Josh." She waited as they formally greeted one another.

The last two babies (other than Hannah), Dominique and Jaden, were picked up in close succession and then Savi quickly excused herself from the room, giving Essie a thumbs up behind Josh's shoulder...which he turned in time to see. She clenched her hand into a fist then dropped her arm to her side. "Really nice to meet you, Josh."

"You too, Savi," he replied, suppressing a smile.

"I don't think she likes you," Essie said with a sigh.

"Yeah, not very subtle about it either." He glanced down the hallway, which was still a chaotic mess. "There are *so* many babies."

"I know. We had six in here today–and there are *four* nurseries for the little littles."

"That's awesome."

She nodded, bouncing Hannah to keep her entertained. "What made you come all the way back here?"

"I wanted to talk to you."

She pursed her lips thoughtfully. She leaned in close to Hannah. "Your brother likes to spontaneously propose. *Be. Cool.*"

His cheeks tightened. "I have never proposed."

"While his claim is technically true, it's been implied," she clarified to Hannah directly.

Hannah became distracted by something outside the classroom window and began teething on Essie's shoulder.

Josh winced.

"I know. There's just *so* much drool."

"Does she have a pacifier?"

"No, no, your mom is trying to wean her off *those*."

"Well, this seems much better."

She pinched her face as a line of drool began dripping down her arm. "So, what did you want to talk about?"

"Well, I realized something." He pulled a handkerchief from his jacket, wiped the drool off, which Hannah found very funny, more bubbles accumulating on her lips. "I realized something," he started again.

She grinned. "Oh yeah? What did you realize?"

He furrowed his brow. "Well, for all this talk about marriage, I haven't properly wooed you."

"You haven't *wooed* me?"

"No."

"What is this wooing you speak of?"

"For one thing, taking you out on dates. Doing all the romantic things."

"We go out on rides together."

"*Yeah.*"

"We cook together."

"Yeah."

"We snuggle a lot."

He nodded.

"You bring me books," she offered, her voice lifting. "That's *very* romantic."

"Yeah, I can do better."

She considered what he'd said, grinning. "Alright, Josh West," she began, her eyes very round, her cheeks very tight. "My heart's all a flutter with all this talk of wooing."

"Is that right?"

She raised an eyebrow. "Kind of. When does this wooing begin?"

"What are you doing after this?"

26

nay

When Essie was about seven years old, she and Josh determined that the time after the afternoon, but before the evening needed a separate name. It was one of those silly conversations that emerged out of thin air, but had caused them an extraordinary amount of laughter and belly giggles, despite it being a sort of mundane topic. Their fun came from using the term without anyone's knowledge of what they were talking about. -"Josh, you need to clean up your room." Oh, I'll do that in the nay. "Essie, how about a shower?" I took that yester-nay.

The day they'd invented the concept of "nay," Luke West had called Josh away to go with him to pick up some supplies at the tractor supply store. Typically, he'd be happy to have Essie tag along, but he had ulterior motives for the outing. He had paid to have a vintage bicycle restored for Essie and he was meeting up with the guy at the store. She'd been making do with Gabe's hand-me-down bike and helmet, which were both black and neon green. She didn't seem to mind much, but her new one would be much more fitting for a little girl: all white with a wicker basket on the front (perfect for holding a toy or stuffed animal), white flowing streamers on the handles, and glow-in-the-dark noisemakers on the tire spokes. He'd bought her a new bike helmet featuring a horse pattern.

Luke was really excited to surprise her, but Essie had taken the rejection to heart; when Josh agreed she should stay back, she'd looked blindsided and ready to cry. But she didn't cry. Luke told her they'd be back

351

before she knew it and she pressed her lips together, nodded, and taken off running barefoot across the front yard toward the tree swing.

She'd been sitting idly on the tree swing for just a few moments when she felt the ropes pull back as someone prepared to push her on the swing. She peered over her shoulder and smiled at Josh. He pulled her back as far as he could manage.

"Ready?"

She nodded, eyes brightening with anticipation, and he released her, a calm sweeping through her chest.

"We're not ditching you, Essie," he said, after pushing her for a few minutes.

"I know."

"You do?"

She frowned. "I just don't understand why I can't go."

"Sometimes people do things that don't make any sense, but they're doing it because they care about you."

She planted her foot on the ground at her next opportunity, twisting herself around to face him. "You've never made less sense."

He smiled tightly. "There's a surprise."

"What surprise?"

"A surprise for you. I helped my dad pick it out. We're going to get it and bring it back here for you, but we don't want you to see it until it's here."

"Like a present?"

"Yeah."

She furrowed her brow. "But it's not my birthday."

"I know."

She twisted back around and sat patiently waiting for him to push her again, actively suppressing a smile.

While they were gone, Essie made it her mission to reach as high as she ever had on the tree swing. She loved the sensation of gliding speedily through the air, the wind in her hair. She loved the moment of near weightlessness. She loved the burst at the top of the curve before the momentum shifted backward.

It's better not to feel.
It's better not to think.
It's better not to remember.
Thoughts are the enemy.
Feelings are the enemy.
Memories are the enemy.
The nothingness is peaceful.
The nothingness is safe.

Her legs had started to ache so she stopped pumping them, allowing the momentum to naturally slow. She dragged her feet along the ground, the reason there was a patchiness to the grass beneath the swing. She glanced over her shoulder, checking the driveway for signs of Josh and his dad returning. Seeing none, she took a deep breath, considering what else she could do to occupy herself in the meantime.

It was as the stillness enveloped her that she felt someone seize hold of her arms, throw a sack over her head. She could feel the abrasive material brush the side of her face. It seemed to be some variation of burlap, like a potato sack, but much thicker. It smelled like it had been stored next to tires and tobacco. Tiny bits of dust and debris from the bag seeped through her eyelashes. She blinked rapidly, desperate to clear her eyes.

Her heart began to race.

She told herself to take slower breaths. There's air, just not as much as you're used to.

And then she was falling to the ground, an unforgiving concrete surface unlike the grassy lawn at the farm. Despite her struggle, her screams, she was being dragged by her broken, ragdoll arms.

The nothingness is peaceful.
The nothingness is safe.

27

plight

In the Loop w/ Christopher Loop: Sins of the Father?

"Let's review what we know about the so-called leader of this country. We know he went to school to study medicine, but had a keen interest in technology, specifically artificial intelligence. We know he built the company that was the big name in technology, specifically terrifying forms of artificial intelligence used to turn the county into a police state. His company developed the mind control programs utilized in Mandatory training, turning about a third of–well, they didn't actually enlist, did they?--let's call them what they are: 16, 17, 18 year old children. They'd accept as young as 15. A third were turned into mindless killers, peace officers who wouldn't recognize their own mother in a line-up. A third died. We've all seen the footage of the suicides? The children walking themselves off twenty-story buildings? I suppose we should be grateful for the third of these children who came home. Of course, most haven't been able to live normal lives, and it's probably a safe bet to say that many have taken their own lives at this point, never able to recover from their experiences.

"We know that Samuel Gowon was fraudulently handed the Presidency in an election where the voting numbers had to be so heavily inflated, the number of votes tallied exceeded the number of people estimated to be living in this country and of voting age, which as you might remember, was lowered to sixteen.

"We know that Samuel Gowon's 'presidency' could be better classified as a 'reign of terror.' Sure, our country is now familiar with genocide cloaked as a 'public health emergency.' We remember the bovine flu. We remember people dying, couples no longer being able to have children. We remember the government dismissing the idea that there was foul play at hand and called in conspiracy.

"Samuel Gowon had gotten involved in vaccine development many years ago. He got interested in funding research into the human genome. We know that in this 'research,' unborn babies were tested upon, they were grown, they were tortured. We've seen the footage of the little girl being gassed.

"Well, here's something we didn't know and it's staring us in the face of his newly-published autobiography: *Father of the Next Great Era in American History*. First of all, regardless of anything else, Samuel Gowon is not anyone's father in any sense of the word that means anything truly worthwhile. That said, it seems if there was going to be an 'upgrade' of the human species, Gowon wanted to be a part of it genetically."

Annette turned off the television, braced her hands over the computer keyboard as Samuel walked into the bedroom. He seemed to be in delightful spirits as he crossed the room, unfastening the top button of his dress shirt. He dropped into the armchair across from her, neatly crossed his right leg over his left, and drew his hands together in his lap, tapping them together rhythmically.

She furrowed her brow. "What has you so amused?"

His mouth turned upwards at the corners. Clearly, he had no intention to share his thoughts.

"Fine. Don't tell me," she said, in what she hoped he would take as a playful tone.

Mercifully, his smile broadened. "What are you working on over there?" His eyebrows lifted inquisitively.

"Some ridiculously daft proposal Botz sent over to include in the next spending package. He cornered me in the hall today, wanting to get my endorsement of it."

"He 'cornered' you?"

She shrugged, knowing better than to think Samuel actually felt protective of her. His tone felt more territorial than anything. "Happens a bit. People don't know how to be assertive without turning into a used car salesman."

"Would it make you feel better if you knew you wouldn't have to deal with him anymore?"

"Oh, I can handle Botz."

"But would it make you feel better?"

"I suppose so."

"Well, good. I've just had him murdered. Don't bother responding to his email; it'd be a waste of your time."

"That's a relief," she said facetiously.

"I'm being serious, Annie."

She pressed her lips together, nodding slowly.

He lifted an eyebrow. "Loop is wrong about you."

She frowned.

"It does bother you. I think you understand that people are expendable, that many exist only to stand in the way—but it still troubles you, knowing what has to be done."

"What's he saying now?"

"He's under the impression that *you're* pulling the strings of the Gowon Administration. That *you're* the mastermind. That you *revel* in the power, in bathing in the blood of the enemy, perhaps more than I do."

"That's a new angle for him." Annette glanced at the computer screen to be sure she hadn't inadvertently pulled something up that she shouldn't have.

"It's preposterous, of course. Look at you. You can't even cope with the thought of ridding the world of a prick like Botz."

She nodded. "I'm not without my usefulness," she remarked. "At least I'd like to think so."

"Agreed. I find you very useful."

Annette frowned, closing her laptop. "I can't get a read on you tonight, Samuel."

He pursed his lips. "My father took me on a business trip once to Las Vegas."

She rotated her task chair so she could face him, knowing it annoyed Samuel when he felt he was getting a split attention.

"We fit in a few shows–something with contortionist acrobats set to *Beatles* music, a boxing match, and we saw an illusionist. The illusionist was admittedly talented, but I didn't care for the show."

"Why?"

"Illusions aren't real. It's a slight of hand, misdirection. It's all fake. It's masquerading as magic, but it's far from it."

"You're saying you enjoyed the *Yellow Submarine* medley better."

He pressed his lips together. "I like to know what makes the noise in the rattle."

"I think I know that about you."

His eyes focused on the bruises on the underside of her thin arm. "I was very angry yesterday."

"I know."

"It wasn't with you, but I directed it at you–didn't I?"

She reached for her rocks glass, gingerly taking a sip. "Was the information useful?"

His lips tightened.

"Good."

"I wasn't actually angry with you yesterday--but I might be now."

She furrowed her brow, fixing her posture. "Why?"

"Maybe Loop is right, after all."

"I don't know why you watch that show."

357

Samuel allowed the silence to persist, gazing across at her reflectively. "Even if he's wrong, Christopher Loop is a clear indication of what the Insurgents think, what a significant portion of the people think."

She frowned.

He took a deep breath. When he spoke, it was in a silky voice: "What are we going to do about this, Annie?"

*   *   *

The Elusive Path to Redemption

"Annette Gibbons had tried to find redemption at every turn, but it seemed that fate conspired against her at every step. Her life had spiraled into a chaotic whirlwind, and every attempt she made to right her wrongs only pushed her further into the abyss.

"There was a glimmer of hope that remained for the Arks–and that was in Luther Graham, but Luther lacked conviction to act, to do what was necessary, as doing so would likely put those he cared for most in harm's way.

"Annette realized that a twist of circumstance could change everything. All that motivated him to remain passive could also compel him to act. It was a decision that tore at her heart, but a voice in the back of her mind assured her that it was the only way."

28

trace

"Thank you for being here today, Dr. Graham."

"I appreciate the politeness, but I don't suppose I had much of a choice, did I?"

Chip Elwes issued a polite smile, shook his head, eyeing his colleagues from beneath his mop of blonde hair.

Jonas Miller cleared his throat, ignoring the exchange. Instead, he narrowed his dark eyes upon Luther. "It's come to our attention that you ran something of–for lack of a better word–*adoption* agency at one point in your career?"

"I found homes for children, yes." He frowned. "*That's* what you brought me here to discuss?"

"You operated with no regulations, no licensing."

He took a deep breath. "The children were saved from government labs where they would have been used and likely killed in a research experiments. It would seem ironic to have to follow the regulations of that same government."

"So that's a 'yes.'"

Sadie Parker, the former Senator from Montana, straightened her posture. While the other members of the council favored muted colors, their dress code easing from their former government roles, Sadie wore a bold navy blue blouse with a delicate cross necklace. "Dr. Graham, the

Council *acknowledges* that extraordinary circumstances demand bold actions and no one is accusing you of foul play here–"

"How much money did you make off this business?"

She glared at Jonas around her curtains of long dark hair.

Luther furrowed his brow. "This wasn't a business."

"How much money did you make?" Jonas said slower.

"The goal was to save as many children as possible and get them situated in safe, supportive homes."

"So there were never any monetary transactions?"

"For much of the initial costs, which involved black web transactions, we utilized currency that had been funneled from other places."

"You stole it."

"From government funds hidden on the dark web to be used to bid on the lives of children that the government saw fit to torture and/or sell. Maybe it was a gray area, but I kind of felt like the result of saving children's lives justified the means."

"I agree," Sadie said solidly.

"So you didn't get money from anywhere else? Any*one* else?"

"People wanted to help. Several churches collected special offerings for what we were doing, but it all went into providing food, clothes, and shelter for the children."

"I see."

"Councilmember Miller, Dr. Graham was *commended* for his work. He's credited with saving the lives of hundreds of children. And that's only the beginning for what he's done for the people in the Arks."

Jonas pursed his lips and slowly bounced his chair, giving the impression he was nodding. "Do you think it's ethical to give away children without the knowledge of their parents?"

Luther cleared his throat. "I don't want to make assumptions about any of the so-called 'parents,' but it is my assessment that those who knew what they had signed their child up for, do not deserve the title, nor any decision-making authority. I thought it reasonable to assume that

360

anyone who *didn't* know what their children were going to be subjected to, would have given consent to get their child to safety."

"You said you don't want to assume and yet, that's a very big assumption."

"Well, you're entitled to your opinion."

"Did you try to reach out to the parents to check? Did you do blood tests? Research who the parents were?"

"Doing that would risk exposing what we were doing."

"Ah," Jonas said shortly. "*Well*, I think we've gotten a little off track here anyway. This was not intended to be an interrogation so much as an exchange of information session."

"So you'll be sharing information with me?" Luther challenged.

Jonas Miller narrowed his eyes, while Sadie Parker gave a small smile. "*Yes*. And you, in turn, you will share information with us."

"Regarding?"

"Were there any children who came from places *other* than government labs?"

He frowned. "There were a few situations where parents asked for my help to find an adoptive home for their child because they weren't able to properly care for them. People weren't very trusting of many of the traditional services since they were closely tied with the government. Information had started to come out about the government funneling children from the foster care system into research programs as well."

A few of the Councilmembers looked stunned to learn this information.

Jonas did not look stunned; he looked rabid. "But they trusted *you*?"

Luther shrugged. "I worked with churches. The children were all placed in Christian homes. That was tremendously comforting for these few instances I encountered. Obviously, if there were ways to get resources to these families so they could remain together, we chose that path."

"But you didn't check the legitimacy of their parental claim."

"I did."

"You *did*."

"Yes. I ran DNA tests to verify in those few instances. We're talking two or three children. The rest we were able to obtain resources for them so the families could stay together."

"You handled Esther Natale's 'adoption' proceedings?"

Luther felt a twist in his chest. He instinctively ran his palm over his pants pocket, which typically held his satellite phone, but realized with a sinking feeling that communication and recording devices were banned from council chambers so his phone was sitting in a security bin outside. He cleared his throat. "Yes."

"And was she one of these relocation instances?"

He frowned. "No."

"You're *sure*? You worked with hundreds of children. Is there a chance you have your information incorrect?"

"No."

"How can you be so certain?"

"Because she's the first child I ever helped *and* she's the daughter of a good friend of mine. I've known her since she was two."

"Adopted daughter," Jonas corrected.

"Excuse me?"

"She's the *adopted* daughter of a good friend of yours."

"No. She's his daughter."

"I'm just saying, there's a distinction."

"No, there isn't," Chip said in a solid voice. "I have three children through the blessing of adoption, Jonas. Do you want to look me in the eye and tell me there's a *distinction*?"

Jonas Miller winced, raking his fingers through his sticky looking black hair. "We've gotten off track again. *So*, Dr. Graham, if she wasn't a relocation case, where did she come from?"

Luther took a steadying breath. "She was the first child I removed from the government labs."

Jonas pursed his lips, nodding regretfully. "Here's where we hit our first impasse, Dr. Graham."

Luther furrowed his brow.

"You claim she came from one of these government research labs."

"Yes."

"At the age of 2."

"Yes."

"The trouble with that claim is that there were no children in any of the research labs older than a few months of age. At *any* time. Most were no older than a few days old, if not a few hours old." Jonas wore a small, satisfied smirk, as though getting enjoyment from this information.

"Other than the girl in the video," Sadie corrected.

Jonas resituated himself in his chair. "Yeah, *well*, that girl was killed, right? Burned in the furnace like 'any other evidence'? That's what the social media posts said? That's what *you* yourself said, correct?" he asked rhetorically, motioning to Luther.

Luther took a deep breath.

Sadie glared across at Jonas then fixed her posture. "Dr. Graham, there are members of this council who have been provided information that seems to contradict what you've shared. Do you have any proof to support your claim?"

"Claim that she was from a government lab?"

"Claim that she's who you say she is," Jonas Miller said forcibly, reaching for his microphone.

Sadie tensed her jaw, looking primed to backhand him across the face.

"Not that I'm willing to provide," Luther said tightly. "Without knowing what this is about. What 'information' has been provided to you?"

"You're refusing to cooperate?"

"If that's what you want to call it then, yes."

"I see," Jonas said, lifting his phone. He ran his finger along the screen, frowning.

"What *information* have you received?"

"Let's revisit your account of the government genetics labs."

Luther frowned. "Is *that* being questioned now, too?"

"Why don't you share how you met Ms. Natale?" Sadie suggested helpfully.

Jonas sat more upright. "Yes. I think that would be helpful."

"How I *met* her?"

"Yes," he said.

There was no way around telling them the truth. Luther took a steadying breath and began. He tried to be concise, which was made easier by the fact that he'd told the story many times and he'd re-lived that night countless times in his thoughts, in his dreams. He explained how he had just been put into the third trimester lab, that he went through the pressurized door thinking it was storage, as he'd run out of saline, and found Essie strapped to a metal table. He had just described the timer clock and associated it with the duration of her recovery time when he glanced up and watched a smile creep across Jonas Miller's face.

Jonas was peering at his phone, clearly not paying attention. Once the former congressman noticed the silence that filled the room, he turned the phone over on the tabletop. He cleared his throat, reset himself in his chair. Making direct eye contact with Luther, he nodded encouragingly as though he'd never stopped listening.

Sadie Parker furrowed her brow. "Dr. Graham?"

Jonas glanced across to an eager Declan Grainger and lifted his eyebrows affirmatively.

The former justice gave a satisfied nod and assumed a much more relaxed posture.

"This was the moment captured on the surveillance video—what you've just described," Sadie said, confused. "Are you saying the child in the video *is* Esther Natale?"

Luther cleared his throat. "Yes."

Jonas lifted his eyes, his face draining of color. He moved forward toward his microphone suddenly. "I'm sorry, I've missed a step."

"The child in the video was Esther Natale."

He went slack jawed. "*Well*, even if that's true, which we don't know for certain–this is the first you've told us of this–it shouldn't impact our handling of the situation at hand as we've discussed," he stammered, trying to sound confident.

Sadie did not appear convinced. "Our discussion was based upon Esther Natale being essentially *kidnapped* as a child and placed with an individual who happens to now reside in the Northern Ark. *That* was the discussion. *Now* we're talking about her being the one and only survivor from the government's genetics lab torture chamber. If that's the case, she survived Nazi gas, among God knows what else. And you think this changes *nothing*? This changes everything, Jonas."

Jonas had stopped blinking.

"It's neither here or there," Justice Grainger remarked generically, literally waving off the revelation.

"What an intelligent argument," Governor McNeary grumbled.

"It's a wonder you got passed up for the Supreme Court," Kyle Geoffreys added.

"Wow, some actual backup from my colleagues. How refreshing," Sadie said with a roll of her eyes. "Now, *Dr. Graham–*"

"Where did the information come from?" Luther pleaded.

Sadie glanced over at Jonas, over at Grainger, then down the row a bit. "Some of my colleagues have been in communication with individuals inside the Gowon Administration."

"Were they asking specifically *about* Esther?"

"No. They provided a DNA sample report and requested that we look for a match through our medical database," Gayle Mayes offered, her face solemn, her eyes lifting to Jonas.

"The sample was matched to a blood sample taken at Emergency six weeks ago," Sadie clarified.

"Did you notify Gowon's people about this?"

"No, of course not," Gayle replied. "We received this information from Gowon's people, we found the match, and then we brought it back to the council for discussion. We needed further clarification on the situation before we could take any other steps, which is why we called you here."

Luther took a steadying breath, but caught something in Jonas Miller's expression that made him very uneasy.

Sadie leaned forward onto her elbows, drawing her hands together and intertwining her fingers. "Their claim is that Esther Natale was not only kidnapped as a child, but they also claimed–" She shook her head. "That she is the biological child of–"

Luther felt his heart rise into his throat. Danny had assured him the changes he made to Annette's medical file, her DNA sequencing, were untraceable. He'd modified every backup file. The renderings, the analysis, they were all modified. She shouldn't have come up in any database.

"--that she is the *daughter* of Samuel Gowon."

He exhaled deeply. "*No.* She's not."

Sadie's shoulders eased.

"It sort of makes sense, if she's the child from the video," Jonas said, now striking a collaborative tone. "Christopher Loop did a whole expose about how Gowon had fathered hundreds or thousands of embryos, babies, used in the genetic experiments."

"I *know* about the expose. I knew about him fathering all those children–though let's be clear. A stir in a petri dish does not make a man a father. They created several hundred babies sharing his genetics, but that didn't start until more than a year after she was born. She is *not* his daughter."

"You know this for a fact?" Jonas asked.

"With 100% certainty. She was turned over to the research facility directly just after she was born. Her birth mother had enrolled in the STRONG program for the financial incentives. They used donated sperm. Gowon is *not* her father."

"Dr. Graham," Sadie began, her approach delicate.

Luther shook himself from his rigid stance. "They compared her bloodwork from the hospital with *what* DNA? *With* Gowon, allegedly?"

"Her own sample. They provided a report of *her* DNA sequencing."

"Who did? Who in Gowon's Administration?"

"A Gowon representative. Millie something. She made the claim about Gowon's daughter being kidnapped–she referenced news articles about her disappearance," Jonas said, matter-of-factly.

Sadie narrowed her dark eyes. "They could have faked all that about a kidnapping. There was never anything about that when he was 'campaigning' and they definitely would have used it. Maybe they had her DNA sequencing from the lab when she was a baby?" She looked up at Luther questioningly.

He shook his head. "They pulled it from the antidote. They must have secured a dose from somewhere." His chest tightened.

Annette.

Annette had a syringe of the antidote, at his insistence.

He cleared his throat. The antidote could have come from somewhere else. They distributed them last year–it wasn't beyond the realm of possibility that one got left behind, despite their advanced tracking/inventory system.

"She was involved in the development of the antidote?" Jonas asked, turning pale again, his eyes wide and beady. He'd been given both the antidote and the full-spectrum vaccine at his own insistence, along with his wife, despite advocating for a "pause" on it to "establish efficacy" for some unbeknownst reason.

"*Yes.*"

"There had to have been dozens of donors though, right? Wouldn't that be a mixed bag of DNA? How would they even isolate *hers*–" Jonas said dismissively.

"*Unless*–" Sadie said, frowning.

"She was the only donor."

Sadie blinked slowly.

"This was called the Phoenix Initiative, correct?" McNeary asked.

"Yes."

"Esther, she participated willingly?"

Luther took a deep breath. "Yes. *Against* my advice."

Sadie brow creased. "You told her not to?"

He nodded.

"From what we've discussed previously about the antidote development, this must have been difficult for you to see her go through all that."

"Yes. It was."

"You're very attached to her," Sadie observed, giving a friendly smile.

He nodded shortly, suppressing some emotion, thinking of Essie saying goodbye before heading out for a date with Josh. He was standing with Matteo along the paddock fence watching the horses have breakfast and discussing Annette's assessment that he should step into leadership when the screen door slammed and Essie came floating down the front steps. She was wearing a long, belted white lace dress, boots, and what he figured was probably one of Josh's cowboy hats.

Matteo laughed. "Aren't you two going fishing?"

She smiled tightly. "*Yep.*"

"Not your most practical outfit."

"I'm messing with Josh. It's silly, don't worry about it," she said, giving her dad a hug.

"You're not eloping and just not telling me?"

She grinned at Luther over her dad's shoulder. "Nope."

"Well, you look beautiful," Luther said.

She stepped out of her dad's arms and gave a small curtsy, tilting her head to the side. "Thank you, Luther."

He noticed she was once again wearing the cross necklace that his mom had given her and nodded approvingly. "Your knight in rusted pickup truck is arriving," he said, lifting his eyebrow toward the driveway.

Essie giggled under her breath, moved quickly toward Luther, and hugged him. "Love you, Luther," she whispered. When she heard the brakes squeal as the truck parked, she broke free and jogged toward the truck, stopping short when Josh started to look in her direction. She assumed a casual pose, crossing her boots, waiting for him.

Josh chuckled upon seeing her as he opened his door, shaking his head. He waved to Luther and Matteo, then focused his attention on Essie, smiling tightly. He dropped out of the truck, holding a bouquet of wildflowers.

Essie had to uncross her feet to keep her balance, but then began bouncing up and down on her toes a little as he approached her.

Just as Josh presented her with the flowers, he did a quick fake-out, as though he was about to drop to one knee.

Essie burst out laughing, waving him off, and he immediately scooped her into a hug.

"Luther?" Sadie said, clearly not for the first time.

Luther shook himself to awareness, frowning.

"Why haven't you *told us this*?" Jonas demanded.

Sadie tightened her jaw. "He was protecting her, Jonas–and honestly, I *don't blame him*."

Jonas shifted to lean on the arm rest furthest from her.

She slowly rotated her chin back to face Luther. "*That's* why Gowon wants to track her down. There's something significant about her–that's why she survived the lab, that's why she was able to generate the antibodies–"

Luther nodded.

Sadie sat forward in her chair. "*Well*, we can't let that happen."

29

trespass

"What are you working on?" Essie asked, rounding the kitchen table where her dad sat typing on an old laptop.

"The next sermon series."

She nodded, moving to the refrigerator. She filled a short glass with lemonade and shuffled her feet in his direction. She furrowed her brow as she took a sip. "You seem to be the lead pastor, Daddy. I'm old enough to remember when you said you were the *backup*."

"Pastor Caleb started another church on the other side of the Ark."

"He couldn't take the pressure," she said, pursing her lips. "Those pews have been *full*."

"It's not a competition."

Her eyebrows jumped playfully. "This *is* what I'm saying."

"Caleb is a great pastor."

"Ain't no pastor like the Daddy I've got."

He shook his head, his cheeks tightening. "You're in a good mood."

She smiled broadly, her eyes dancing to the front windows and back. "Josh is taking me on a date."

"You've been going on a lot of those."

"He decided a few weeks ago that there's a 'wooing' process that needs to take place."

"'Wooing'?"

"Yes. It's a weird word. Is 'courted' better? I thought it sounded too medieval."

"Well, whatever the word, it sounds like a good idea. Where are you going today?"

"He said something about a miniature golf establishment being renovated? Are you familiar with the concept?"

"Vaguely familiar. Take it easy on him."

"Take it *easy*? I've never played."

"Yeah, but your competitive drive tends to cancel out any learning curve."

"I'll refrain from victory dances," she said with a shrug, taking another sip of lemonade. "But I can't promise I won't partake in friendly wagers or smack talk."

"Well, can't say Josh didn't know what he was signing up for."

"I was just going to check on the animals, get things tidy. He should be here soon."

"Want some help?"

"Nah, you work on your victory sermon." She placed the glass down on the table, moved to give him a side hug, but he stood abruptly, wrapped his arms around her. "I'm so happy that you're happy."

"Me, too," she said in a small voice, her smile audible.

"Oh, my beautiful girl. Have a wonderful time. Ti amo, ti amo, ti amo." He kissed her repeatedly on the top of her head.

Essie tightened her arms. "Ti amo, ti amo, ti amo."

Matteo kissed her once more on the head before releasing her. "Are you sure you don't want help with the animals before you go?"

She nodded. "If we're not back before sunset, will you feed the animals dinner? I'll set everything up."

"I'll feed them. Go have fun."

Esther squinted into the midday sun as she jogged down the porch steps, pushing her sunglasses onto her face. Hwin whinnied when she saw

371

her approach and Bree tossed his head high in the air, trotting enthusiastically toward the fence. He lined up his back longways along the paddock.

"Hey, Narnian. We'll go on a long ride tomorrow, okay? I promise."

Bree neighed, bumped the fence with his haunches.

"Hey, *you're* the one who doesn't let other people ride you. I'm sure Teo would be happy to, but you'd have to be as sweet to him as you are to me." She climbed up on the first post, patted the Percheron's thick neck.

"Have you been playing in your water, Hwin? It's all *muddy*," Esther said with a pout. She hopped down, moved to the gate, noticing Bree's wobbly gait as he followed along beside her. "You've got a mud pie in your hoof, don't you?"

The horse snorted.

She reached for the hoof pick dangling on a key ring on the outside wall of the barn and slipped into the paddock.

"Alright, Buddy. You know the routine."

Bree readjusted his weight and tenderly lifted his front hoof, like a dog begging for a treat.

Essie dug the pick firmly but carefully into the compacted mud speckled with hay, prying it from the horseshoe. "Ow, there was a rock in the middle of all the nasty mud. That didn't feel good, did it?"

He dropped his muzzle beside her, nudged her cheek.

"Yeah, you're welcome. Is that better?" She stood, patting his side. She was about to affectionately scold Hwin when a sudden breeze sweeping dust into the air caused the hair on the back of her neck to stand on end. She rotated her chin toward the driveway.

*   *   *

There were three traffic lights between Josh's cabin and the Natale ranch and he had managed to hit each and every one on red. He checked

372

his reflection in the rear view, ran his fingers over his smooth cheeks, having shaved off all the stubble that had managed to grow since that morning. He could just imagine her running her palm delicately across his cheek, remarking indulgently about the softness of his skin.

He eyed the bag sitting on the passenger side of the bench seat, which contained a book box set he'd found at a base rummage sale, a favorite that had been left behind in Essie's bedroom at Calvary Church. He smiled lightly as he anticipated her excitement to once again be able to slip into the fictional world of Narnia.

Esther had been suggesting to her dad that the ranch needed an official name added to the rather plain curved sign that framed the dirt drive and had been campaigning the idea of "Narnia Ranch" as the name for the property, suggesting a bold lion carving as part of the logo.

Since then, she had started naming all the new animals after characters in the C.S. Lewis books. There were Bree and Hwin already, of course. In the next paddock were four horses she'd named after the Pevensie children, Edmund being her favorite of the group. The goats were led by Mr. Tumnus and included Reepicheep, Mr. and Mrs. Beaver, and Trumpkin, a group she said were the most endearing of characters, though she admitted there was a discrepancy between timelines so not all of them would have known each other in the books. A pair of wild Mustangs brought to the ranch after a predator attack were named Caspian and Lilliandil, Lil having given birth to a colt named Rilian. There was also a beautiful, shimmering white Arabian with a moody streak named Jadis as well as some side character horses, like Trufflehunter and Digory. To her delight, a bushy tabby cat had taken up residence in the barn and had naturally been named Aslan.

He made the last main turn, following Chesapeake as it weaved around the protected lands to the ranch.

It occurred to Josh as the truck finally trudged up the long dirt drive that one of his MET teammates he'd recently ran into in town had developed a hobby in metalworking. Perhaps he could create something for the ranch.

It was as this idea gained traction in his mind and he felt excitement building about suggesting it to Esther that Hwin appeared out of nowhere, rearing back in front of the truck.

He slammed on the brakes. When he expected she might gallop away in panic, she returned to four legs, whinnied frantically and began pounding at the ground. Her muzzle was coated in blood.

Josh put the truck in park, pried off his seat belt, and dropped out of the driver's side. "Hey Hwin, did you hurt yourself?" he asked calmly, offering his hand for her to sniff. Hwin borrowed a lot of her bravery from Bree, following him around, trusting his read on situations and people so it was rare to see her without him unless he was out for a ride with Essie. Her eyes were wide and panicked as Josh approached. She broke left suddenly, taking off for the main paddock at full speed, releasing an ear-splitting cry unlike anything he'd ever heard as she reached the outer fence.

The first thing he saw was the open paddock swing gate next to the barn. Then, under the barn awning, he saw Bree. The body of the large gray Percheron was sprawled across the dirt, unmoving.

Josh took off for the gate at full speed, calling out for Essie. When he reached the paddock, his breath caught in his chest.

There was no question that Bree was dead. As he took in the scene, he was having trouble processing anything else. There were several bullet wounds in the horse's chest, neck, and head. He must have been rearing back when he was shot as the angle of the fall had snapped his back leg.

Josh avoided looking at any of the wounds, at the flies drawn to the exposed flesh. He instead looked at the displacement of dirt and mud under the horse's back, which had clearly occurred after he had fallen.

He had fallen *on* someone and they had been dragged from the paddock toward the driveway. As he turned toward the drive, his eyes fell upon a body collapsed at the bottom of the porch steps, a shotgun loose on the ground, just beyond his grasp.

Teo had never gone near guns, not since his wife shot herself. He didn't like the idea of having one in the house, but Luke had convinced him to have the shotgun for safety, just in case.

There would only be one reason Matteo would be holding that gun:

If he was trying to protect his daughter.

THE DAY *TRILOGY*:

THE RAIN FALLS
THE EARTH SHAKES
THE SUN RISES

www.ingramcontent.com/pod-product-compliance
Lightning Source LLC
Chambersburg PA
CBHW070838260626
47170CB00007B/2416